The Dutchman's Gold

Larry Weill

BOOKS
NORTH COUNTRY BOOKS
Essex, Connecticut

BOOKS
NORTH COUNTRY BOOKS

An imprint of The Globe Pequot Publishing Group, Inc.
64 South Main Street
Essex, CT 06426
www.globepequot.com

Distributed by NATIONAL BOOK NETWORK

Copyright © 2025 by Larry Weill

All rights reserved. No part of this book may be reproduced in any form or by any electronic or mechanical means, including information storage and retrieval systems, without written permission from the publisher, except by a reviewer who may quote passages in a review.

British Library Cataloguing in Publication Information Available

Library of Congress Cataloging-in-Publication Data

Names: Weill, Larry, author.
Title: The dutchman's gold / Larry Weill.
Description: Essex, CT : North Country Books, 2025.
Identifiers: LCCN 2025006029 (print) | LCCN 2025006030 (ebook) | ISBN 9781493085545 (paperback) | ISBN 9781493092703 (epub)
Subjects: LCGFT: Novels.
Classification: LCC PS3623.E43225 D88 2025 (print) | LCC PS3623.E43225 (ebook) | DDC 813/.6—dc23/eng/20250211
LC record available at https://lccn.loc.gov/2025006029
LC ebook record available at https://lccn.loc.gov/2025006030

∞™ The paper used in this publication meets the minimum requirements of American National Standard for Information Sciences—Permanence of Paper for Printed Library Materials, ANSI/NISO Z39.48-1992.

CONTENTS

In Gratitude v
Foreword vii

CHAPTER 1: Birth of the Legend 1
CHAPTER 2: Blood in the Mountains 10
CHAPTER 3: Abandoning the Mine 15
CHAPTER 4: Too Little Wilderness 20
CHAPTER 5: Helping Out a Grandson 31
CHAPTER 6: The Great Train Wreck of 1913 34
CHAPTER 7: The Call from Dallas 39
CHAPTER 8: Billionaire Boss. 47
CHAPTER 9: Everything's Bigger in Texas 55
CHAPTER 10: Final Buy-in .76
CHAPTER 11: Getting Started 82
CHAPTER 12: Sammy 92
CHAPTER 13: Threading the Needle 99
CHAPTER 14: Wrong Kind of Bug 108
CHAPTER 15: The Legend of Ghost Hawk 120
CHAPTER 16: No Place Like Home 135
CHAPTER 17: Chasing a Ghost 154
CHAPTER 18: Catching a Train 168
CHAPTER 19: Alvah's Gift 188
CHAPTER 20: Busted 206

CONTENTS

CHAPTER 21: Return to the Hellhole 217
CHAPTER 22: Which JW? 225
CHAPTER 23: Starting Over 238
CHAPTER 24: Do You Believe in Ghosts? 255
CHAPTER 25: Party at the Ranch 275
CHAPTER 26: The Final Week 286
CHAPTER 27: Coming Home 293

About the Author 309

In Gratitude

This was a very different kind of book for me, especially since part of it takes place outside of the Adirondack Park. Because of this geographic shift, I had to rely on other people and references for those subjects that were outside of my realm of expertise.

I'd like to first thank the entire staff of the Lost Dutchman Museum in Apache Junction, Arizona. Their expertise in guiding me through the maps, references, and exhibits at their facility provided me with a superb background to commence my research of this topic. They were comprehensive and patient as I asked the obvious questions that they have probably answered for thousands of other visitors.

Much of my background material on the personalities of the Superstition Mountains and the theories of the gold mine came from a few references, which are not listed in any bibliography in this book. These include Michael Chabak's *The Lost Dutchman Mine Legacy* and Jack San Felice's *Lore of the Superstitions*. There are hundreds upon hundreds of other references on this same subject, including many that are longer and adorned with glossy covers and bookstore appeal, but these two notebook-style publications were invaluable in my initiation to the subject.

I'd also like to thank Chris Anderson, who at the time of my visit to the Superstition Mountains was a guide for Arizona Outback Tours. Chris led me on a one-day visit from the Peralta Trail parking lot to the top of Fremont Saddle overlooking Weaver's Needle. He explained not only the theories of the origin of the Lost Dutchman Gold Mine but also the entire natural (and human) history of the region, including that of the Native American tribes who resided therein. His patience in encouraging me to keep moving onward and upward toward our destination that day was laudable and highly appreciated.

In Gratitude

Peg Masters, the historian for the Town of Webb, was instrumental in locating some key references on the Great Train Wreck of 1913. She conducted the research and provided me with a baseline of information, including the names of some local residents who could serve as subject matter experts on the topic.

Several references of Adirondack literature were key aids in pulling together the names and dates linked to the Great Train Wreck of 1913. Michal Kudish's book titled *Where Did the Tracks Go in the Central Adirondacks* contained detailed information of the train routes, including the location of tracks and stations. Other information has been selectively harvested from articles appearing in the *Adirondack Almanac* and *Adirondack Life Magazine*. Specific details on the train's route on the day of the wreck came from Henry A. Harter's book *Fairy Tale Railroad*.

The staff of North Country Books themselves were a wonderful resource on the topic of the Great Train Wreck, providing the names of reference books from their catalogs that contained additional information.

I also want to thank Bruno Petrauskas, my dear friend and voluntary proofreader/editor, for his time spent noting all my inept typos and grammatical errors. I am so happy to have a "detail person" as a friend, who makes this work so much easier.

Finally, to my family, who put up with a great many nights of "1:00 AM typing" and the uttering of the occasional expletive. Their patience with my chase of these pursuits is always reassuring and permits me to follow my literary passions.

Foreword

THIS IS THE THIRD IN A SERIES OF HISTORICAL NOVELS, WHICH INCLUDES *Adirondack Trail of Gold* and *In Marcy's Shadow*. Both of these other books have had their initial roots grounded in historical truth before at some point leaving the tracks of reality and veering off onto the side rails of fiction. In fact, one of my favorite pastimes in the pursuit of a storyline is to identify a series of favorite American events and folk heroes, and then tie them together in a common thread.

This book deals with a number of such heroes and happenings, both in the Adirondacks as well as the desert mountains of Arizona. One of the most famous hermit-guides of the Adirondack Mountains, Alvah Dunning, has been re-created and woven into the fabric of this story that includes his travels to the expanses of the great American West. Although the account of his travels and contacts with Native Americans in this book is entirely fictional, it does embrace an aspect of this legendary guide's life that is otherwise unknown and unreported.

Also addressed in this story is the fictional relationship between Dunning and the Great Train Wreck of 1913. Tens of thousands of visitors to the Adirondacks stop each year to read the historic sign post on Route 28, a few miles outside of Inlet, New York. Yet very few know much of the real story behind this tragedy, which took the lives of three employees of the Raquette Lake Railroad. The final ride of this engine and crew form an integral part of this story, along with the reasons of why it became so important over one hundred years after the crash.

Finally, this story splits its time between the stories of Alvah Dunning and the Great Train Wreck with the Lost Dutchman Gold Mine of the Superstition Mountains of Arizona. Unlike the former subjects, the latter is one that is less familiar to the citizens of New York State. "The

FOREWORD

Dutchman" was a prospector of German descent who sometimes lived in Phoenix, Arizona, but was better known for discovering a massive gold mine in the Superstition Mountains west of the city.

The origins of the gold mine story vary so wildly between three or four different major themes that many people doubt that the mine really exists. Between "the Dutchman" (Jacob Waltz) theory and contrasting themes that include early American soldiers or Spanish gold from Mexico, the actual number of plots and clues has ballooned to the point of absurdity. Many of these clues, such as the "Peralta Stones" that supposedly detail the mine's location in coded symbols, have appeared seemingly out of nowhere, yet are considered sacrosanct by those who still actively search for the treasure.

Additionally, the retelling of these stories over the past century has generated hundreds of new and evolving clues that are impossible to piece together. This includes descriptions of ridges, ledges and tunnels, arrows in the rock, and faces that appear when struck by just the right angle of sunlight. It's no wonder that a Google search on "Superstition Mountains gold" generates a list of almost two million websites. Because of this massive stockpile of references on the topic, I made a conscious decision to bypass any attempt at complete adherence to the "factual" record. Accordingly, some of the geological features and directions in this book may differ from those provided in the piles of books and guides on this subject. That is to be expected and should not detract from this story.

The lore of the Superstition Mountains and the gold supposedly contained therein continues to spark interest to this day. Dozens of treasure hunters resolutely attempt to crack the code every year, including several of prominent background. They follow in the footsteps of those who have gone before them for the past hundred years, several of whom have lost their lives in the pursuit of this venture.

Before I started my research for this book, I made a personal trip into this territory to see it for myself. I hired a guide to lead me up to the Fremont Saddle overlooking Weaver's Needle, and I was awestruck by the rugged beauty of the area. It is a massive, desolate country with incredible expanses of open air, rock formations, and towering Saguaro cacti. On the day of our climb to the Saddle, the temperature reached

FOREWORD

108 degrees Fahrenheit. My guide deserved a medal for tolerating my frequent stops, and for carrying most of the eight canteens of water that I consumed during our hike. The adventure provided me with the insight to understand just how difficult it was in those early days to survive and toil in that environment. I wouldn't have lasted a single week, of that I am certain.

One other advantage to my visit to this beautiful country was the exposure to the stories and history of Arizona's indigenous tribes of Native Americans. Although I discuss only two of these tribes in this book, the Apaches and the Pimas, several others do (or did) reside in the areas in and around these mountains, and my guide discussed all of these at length during our time together. I have always been fascinated by the culture of our country's first Americans, and I freely admit that this was one of the more enjoyable parts of my trip to the Superstition Mountains.

The last two-thirds of this story then moves ahead at light speed to the modern day, when the same cast of contemporary characters (Chris, Sean, Kristi, et al.) tackle the mystery head-on and bring it to its fast-paced conclusion. For those who are expecting this book to end similarly to the previous two in this series, I will only say that you will be surprised (but hopefully not disappointed) at the conclusion. My main goal has always been to provide an entertaining story with plenty of twists and turns. To this end, I hope I have succeeded.

One last point that I would like to make here is that, similar to my last two novels, this book discusses a well-known historical site in New York State and then places a made-up treasure within its boundaries. I urge all readers to recognize and understand that this is purely fictional. There is no gold buried at the site of the Great Train Wreck of 1913, and searching for such a treasure is not only a waste of time but also against the law. Please enjoy this part of the story as an artifact of the author's imagination and nothing more.

With this all said, I would now like to flip the pages of the calendar back to July of 1880, and transport you westward into the central part of southern Arizona. You are about to meet "the gold bug" face-to-face. Please try not to get bitten. It is a disease that is easy to contract but nearly impossible to cure.

CHAPTER ONE

Birth of the Legend

July 1880

THERE WAS NOTHING OUT OF THE ORDINARY ABOUT THE DISHEVELED, dust-covered stranger as he plodded up the dirt-packed avenue in Phoenix. He was of average height and girth, with thick hair and a full beard that were both well speckled with gray. He appeared to be a typical prospector of the day, as were so many of the men in that era who hoped to strike it rich with little more than a pickax and shovel. He was simply clad in well-worn tan work pants and a long-sleeve checked shirt, both of which had seen better days. His battered leather hat had a wide brim that served to protect his brow from the brunt of the intense Southwest sun. The man appeared to be in his early to mid-seventies, and his somewhat painful gait provided a hint of a lifetime filled with strenuous physical labor.

Behind the weary traveler trod a pair of pack mules that were tethered and led by a simple hemp rope. The nomad could have ridden on the back of either one of these sturdy animals, and yet he had apparently decided to walk ahead of them as he moved along Adams Street. The mules were unhindered by riders but appeared to be heavily burdened, each with a number of satchels laid across their backs. The leather packs were accompanied by canteens, rolled blankets, and sacks containing clothing and other personal effects. It was as though the old-timer was prepared to spend several weeks on the trail passing from one territory to another. In truth, he had only traveled for five days to reach his destination.

Before entering the busiest part of the burgeoning community, the prospector turned off the avenue and stopped in front of a recently established business that appeared to be half bank and half assay office. The Wells Fargo sign above the door confirmed that he was at the right location, and he tied his mule team to the hitching post by the front door. He removed a canteen from one of the loaded animals and took a long swallow as he squinted up at the blazing sun overhead. Although there were no thermometers present by which to measure the heat, the air temperature was a steady 106 degrees.

Without further pause, the elderly man lifted one of the leather satchels off the first mule, grunting and struggling beneath its weight. Time had drained him of his youthful vigor and strength, making such efforts painful and more arduous than he cared to admit. Inside the shop, a number of employees jumped up to offer their assistance, which he gladly accepted. He appeared as though he wanted to keep an eye on the remaining cargo as he unloaded the balance of his bags.

The employee in charge of the assay office directed his men to offload the freight directly into his office, where he lined the bags on a series of sturdy tables in back of the room. He motioned for the prospector to take a seat across from him at a heavy wooden desk.

"Benjamin Carter's my name, Mr. . . . ?" he asked, seeking the newcomer's name.

"Jacob Waltz," the stranger replied, his eyes not meeting the gaze of the bank employee. He did not appear open to conversation, only to conducting his business and departing on his way. But even in his short, terse reply, Carter could detect a foreign accent—perhaps German or another European dialect.

"I assume you're here to have your ore assayed and valued?" asked the banker.

"That's right," said the older gentleman. "Then I'd like to sell what I can and deposit the proceeds into your bank before I head back home."

"Home," repeated Carter. "Then I assume you live somewhere in the area?"

"No, not really. I traveled several days to get here, and I've got to make the return trip as soon as our business is done."

BIRTH OF THE LEGEND

The banker sighed and leaned back in his chair, looking at the old-timer with an expression of regret. "I'm sorry to tell you this, but this is not a transaction that we can do in an hour. We've got to crush your ore and put it through a rather lengthy process called a fire assay. It's really a three-step process that will take overnight, so we can't rightly appraise your load until sometime tomorrow."

"Whatever it takes," said Waltz, his face remaining as constant and staid as any poker player. "I'll find a place to put up overnight and we can finish our business in the morning."

Carter got up and walked over to the table holding the traveler's leather satchels. Selecting one at random, he strained to lift its bulk from the surface and carry it back to his desk.

"Heavy bag!" he commented, surprised at the mass of the container. Waltz only nodded back in reply, his eyes glued to the employee.

The banker placed a tray on top of his desk to catch any of the small-grain particulate matter that might otherwise fall on the floor. "OK, let's just get a feel for what you've got in here," he said, untying the leather drawstring from around the top and pulling the bag open.

Benjamin Carter had been in the business of assaying and valuing gold for over thirty years. He had lived and worked in California through the 1850s boom years of the Gold Rush, and had seen the complete range of gold ore, from highest grade to lowest. He was savvy enough to detect "fool's gold" from the real thing in an instant and possessed enough working experience to judge the value of gold-bearing ore per ton in almost any sample of rock. But nothing could prepare him for what he was about to witness.

Instead of dirt and sand-covered quartz, Carter's first fistful of material exposed about a cupful of clean, glittering golden nodules that sparkled even under the reduced lighting of the office lamps. Impossible as it seemed, they appeared to be pure gold with few (if any) impurities.

Carter's initial glimpse of the precious metal made him involuntarily catch his breath, his eyes wide in an awe-inspired stare. As though unable to believe his own senses, he reached into the bag to extract another handful of the heavy contents, and then another. Difficult as it was to comprehend, the more he extracted, the larger the nuggets became, all of the same gleaming color and purity. His hands trembling, he examined one of the same up close with the use of a magnifying lens, turning it over and over again looking for impurities.

There were none.

After repeating his examination of an additional four chunks, Carter put down the samples on the desk and then placed his hands flat on the wooden surface. He noticed he was sweating through his palms, which was not due to the warmth of the room.

"Mr. Waltz, where did you get this material? Did you mine this yourself?"

"I got a place in the hills," replied Waltz, his eyes still averting the banker's gaze.

Carter remained silent for a period of time, his eyes fixed on the man seated across from him. Finally, he gave up waiting for additional details. "Can I ask you which hills you're talking about?"

"I got a place in the hills," repeated Waltz. It was clear that he didn't want to say any more.

"Well, then," started Carter as he launched himself up from his seat, "we'll get these bags weighed out and get you a receipt for the entire load. I won't be able to get you a dollar figure until after we've assayed samples from all four bags, in case there is a significant difference between the contents. But I've got to say that based on the stuff we just looked at, there won't be much to separate; this stuff appears to be almost pure gold. In my entire lifetime in this business, I've never seen anything like it."

Carter stepped into another office and summoned three of the employees who had helped to originally transport the satchels into the building. Straining under the weight, the workers moved the collective load into the assaying lab where they would be weighed one by one. Another banker with a writing pad kept track of the individual weights as they were called out, while Carter ensured that the scales were operating properly as the parcels were weighed. His eyes still appeared to bulge from the front of his face as he noted the figures on the instrument. It was seemingly beyond belief.

"Well, Mr. Waltz, the total of the four loads comes in at about 312 pounds. If we subtract eight pounds for the leather bags and straps and all, that still leaves us with about 304 pounds of ore. But as you know, most of this is not 'ore.' Most of this is pure gold, assuming that all four bags have similar content."

"They're the same," said Waltz, still remaining stone-faced.

Carter shook his head again in disbelief as he walked with the prospector out to the front office. "Well, that's going to be some payday for you tomorrow. I can't imagine what the final take will be, but I'm sure you know that you're already a very rich man."

Waltz looked back at Carter again and simply nodded. He didn't seem happy or even impressed, which left the banker somewhat puzzled. In that day, some of the best lots in Phoenix could be purchased for the price of forty dollars, and this gentleman had just handed over what would surely assay out to tens of thousands of dollars. But Carter's job was not to judge his clients, only to take care of their needs and ensure the profitability of the bank.

As they stepped from the front door of the business and prepared to part ways, Carter handed Waltz a piece of paper with the recorded weights of each bag and an official certification that would serve as a receipt until the following day. Then, he put his hand on the prospector's arm and fixed him with a stolid expression.

"Mr. Waltz, there's one other thing that I think you probably already know."

"What's that?" replied Waltz, untying his mules from the hitching post.

"This is a rough part of the country, and there are a lot of hooligans out there who would shoot you dead if they had any idea you were carrying even a small fraction of what you had."

Waltz motioned to the butt of a lever-action Winchester, which protruded through the top of a leather scabbard on one of the mules. "Thank ye, but I can handle myself just fine."

Carter nodded back at Waltz and simply said, "OK, until we meet again tomorrow."

THE DUTCHMAN'S GOLD

* * * * * *

The bank closed at 5:00 PM on most business days. Yet on this day, while the front room with teller service shuttered its doors, the back office remained open. The sheer size of this transaction required as much attention and care as the bank could muster, and the local manager remained on the premises to supervise the proceedings. The ovens used for the fire assay process blazed throughout the evening into the early hours of the morning. Sample after sample were mechanically crushed and then pumped through the heat and chemical processes, all returning the same results.

Meanwhile, the manager, an aging financier by the name of Eugene Tillman, kept transferring the completed samples and other portions of the gold into the bank's substantial vaults, which were locked immediately after the completion of each phase. He had also hired two of his associates from the local Sheriff's Department to stand watch over the proceedings, in case word had leaked out about the massive cache. News like that would travel quickly, and might attract the attention of some of the region's less savory characters.

It was almost 4:00 AM when the last of the samples had been assayed and the ovens cooled. The three bank employees with financial experience and computing skills all worked the same figures, independently arriving at the same tallies. Their figures concluded that the net sum of gold in the total lode worked out to almost 196 pounds, or 3,136 ounces of pure gold. The figure was staggering.

The last vestiges of nighttime were fading from the sky as Carter said goodnight to the other employees. His boss, Eugene, shook his hand and thanked him for his efforts. Then, all the other bank workers headed out the door to catch a few hours of sleep before returning to work in the morning. Only Carter and a single sheriff, who they'd decided to pay to remain on duty until morning, stayed behind. For Carter, it made no sense to walk back to his house on the edge of town for a single hour or two of sleep. He collapsed on a couch in the corner of his office while the deputy took up a seated position in the room holding the vault. It had been a most exceptional day.

Birth of the Legend

* * * * * *

It was almost noon by the time Jacob Waltz made his way back to the bank, this time riding on one of the mules that had previously carried the bullion. If anything, he appeared more tired than on the previous day, with deep creases in the skin on his sunburnt face.

"Mr. Waltz, a pleasure to see you again this morning," said Carter, smiling and bowing slightly as the elder stepped into the bank.

Waltz, for his part, simply gave one of his characteristic nods and strolled across the lobby to approach the banker. "Is it all done?" he asked in a monotone voice.

"If it's the assaying and valuation of your metals, then the answer is yes. Please follow me into my office to discuss the particulars of our offer."

Waltz followed Carter into his office and they took their positions of the previous day. Waltz noticed that none of the gold was present; only the empty leather satchels that had served to transport the ore to the bank. These Carter handed to Waltz, who waited patiently for the results of the assay.

"I hope we've cleaned out your bags to your satisfaction," began Carter. "They were a bit stained from the ore, so one of our employees had them dressed by a local shop that specializes in laundering. It was the least we could do for you for selecting our bank for your transaction."

"Thank you, but I haven't agreed to anything yet," answered Waltz, still emotionless. "I brought the gold here to be assayed and valued, and that's all so far. But I am interested in hearing your results and offer."

Carter assumed a judicious pose, placing his elbows on the desk and bringing his hands together beneath his chin while smiling benevolently. "Our bank had completed the assay and evaluation of your parcel of gold and has arrived at the figure of 3,136 ounces of bullion. The value of gold today, as you probably know, remains fixed at 20.67 dollars per ounce, which we are prepared to honor. If we multiply the weight by the price, and subtract the 1.5 percent fee for the bank's transaction, processing, and transportation costs, we arrive at a dollar figure of 64,043.27 dollars. I hope you find that to your satisfaction."

THE DUTCHMAN'S GOLD

"I accept your offer," said Waltz, his face registering a small trace of a smile for the first time in two days. "However, I want to leave most of that amount on deposit with your bank, and take only a small amount of that in cash."

"Very well," beamed the banker, pleased at his ability to close a deal of such major proportions without haggling or delay. "I will lead you to one of my associates who will help you to fill out the appropriate forms to establish your account. I'll also get you the cash balance of your transaction so you can take that away with you today. And how much did you wish to take in cash?"

"Two thousand dollars," replied Waltz, reverting to his stone-faced expression. "I have some debts to settle and some provisions to purchase. Then I'd better head back into the hills to oversee my associates. I sometimes suspect them of helping themselves to part of my claim."

"I could understand that," agreed Carter as he gathered up the last of their paperwork. "If the rest of your claim even approaches what you've shown us here, they could become very rich within a matter of hours. You must be very careful and watch every move."

"That I must," said Waltz.

It took but another twenty minutes for Waltz to set up his accounts, which were then credited with over $62,000 in funds. Meanwhile, Waltz himself received a cash payment of $2,000, which was provided in a pile of currency notes with some gold coins stacked on top. Waltz filed the currency into a well-worn leather billfold, which he placed in his rear pocket. The coins were dropped into a small leather pouch with a drawstring, which he then placed in a side pocket of his trousers. It was the same pants and shirt he'd worn the previous day (and which Carter guessed he'd worn the entire week).

"Please keep us in mind the next time you come to town with your next load, whenever that might be," called Carter, eager for more of the lucrative business.

Waltz simply nodded as he climbed on the back of his trusty mule, ready to ride back off into "the hills," wherever that might be.

As Waltz disappeared back down Adams Street, one of Carter's associates came outside and stood next to him, watching Waltz blend in with the other traffic. The heat of the sun overhead caused a mirage over the expanse of desert visible outside of town. The visual effect of the heat waves seemed to swallow the stranger as he headed westward, back into the hills.

"Odd kind of a fellow," the associate commented. "Sounded somewhat like a Dutchman by his accent."

"Yes," said Carter, still staring down the road. "A Dutchman he was."

Chapter Two

Blood in the Mountains

July 1880

THE BUSINESS OF EXTRACTING GOLD AND OTHER PRECIOUS METALS from the ground by hand is a backbreaking job. Countless hours a day with the pickax, hammered into the solid earth under a scorching sun, was enough to do in almost any man, regardless of age or conditioning. Food was sometimes short and water even scarcer. Many strong-willed individuals had died trying to find the mother lode, and the job was fraught with other perils as well. The land was populated by hostile Indians, rattlesnakes, man-eating cougars, and overly protective prospectors who would shoot first and ask questions later.

The land containing the mine of Jacob Waltz was on just such a parcel of ground, perched on the edge of a cliff in the middle of an arid region that God had forsaken. The land was parched, and full of cacti and sharp brush that would cut you like a thousand knives if you attempted to traverse the wrong place. Spires of cathedral rock soared hundreds of feet straight up into the cloudless blue sky, as though stacked by unseen hands at an earlier time. The beauty was incredible, yet the dangers were immense. It was as though some divine force had attempted to combine heaven and hell in a single location.

Toiling inside a deep pit high up on a ridge, obscured from view below, was a single man who was actively engaged in working the earth. He had several tools at his disposal, including a variety of shovels, a crow bar, and a heavily weighted pickax. Also situated nearby was his rifle, a Springfield Model 1873 that was always loaded and always ready. Although accurate in its performance, it was still a "single-shot" weapon that offered him close-in protection in the event of a wild animal but not much else.

He was Jacob Waltz's hired hand, and by coincidence was also named Jacob, although his last name was Weiser. For reasons unknown to Weiser, his boss always called him "Jaco," but with an accented "J" so that it sounded like "Yaco." Weiser was over twenty years younger than Waltz and blessed with a strong back and a mentality to succeed. He was industrious and intelligent, and he did not require continuous supervision to move forward with a task. Unfortunately, though, he was not always forthcoming with his finds on the land claim and found it easy to justify "sharing the profits" when his boss was away from the site. This time, Waltz would be away for at least eight days, maybe longer.

Over the past several days, Weiser had developed a pattern of theft and deception that would have gotten him shot on any other gold claim. Working throughout the long, intense days, he would use the pickax to pull up more and more of the precious vein, cleaning and stacking the nearly pure pieces of gold as they came from the ground. He and his boss had been overjoyed at the initial discovery of this vein and had celebrated every day at their good fortunes. But throughout each session of digging and picking, Weiser secretly deposited a few nuggets at a time into a cavity beneath a large boulder on the other side of an outcropping near their site. Their find was so amazing that he knew his small bits would never be missed.

Several weeks later, when Waltz announced that he was heading into Phoenix alone to sell some of their gold to trade for provisions and to pay Weiser, the assistant formed some plans for getting rich on his own. After all, why should he suffer the backbreaking manual labor to make money for someone else? Why shouldn't he share much more than the 5 percent of the profits promised by his employer? It sounded so right to him, so justified that he immediately confirmed these plans in his mind. He would do what he needed to do to make himself wealthy while still allowing his boss to keep the lion's share of the proceeds.

Once Weiser had made up his mind, there was no stopping him. Waltz departed camp with their two pack mules the following Wednesday, and the younger associate went into immediate action. Retrieving the stash he'd hidden beneath the boulder, he formed a small pile of gold nuggets the size of an apple. It was an impressive start, but he knew that the mine could provide him with much greater wealth.

Working throughout the day and into the evening, Weiser struggled on by himself, picking, digging, cleaning, and stacking. All the while he placed about 75 percent of his finds in the "camp pile" while holding back 25 percent for himself. At the end of the day, he would place his own pile into the various pockets of his pants and shirt and then start down the mountain. In a separate location, about a quarter mile away and up another incline, was another small cave-like indentation in the rock. It wasn't nearly as big or as deep as the one holding Waltz's claim, but it was deep enough to hide a man or protect him from a sudden storm. This is where Weiser kept a tightly locked metal trunk, known only to him. This container had originally served to transport his belongings from his home in Arkansas to his new abode in Arizona. It was large enough to carry a significant bulk of clothing or other material, and it could be secured with a padlock through a hasp on the top surface. Weiser trusted this trunk as a way to safeguard his part of the gold. He was also confident that no one would wander that way and discover his hiding place. Not even Waltz knew of its existence.

Weiser's week of solitude went on day after day in a joyous progression of finds. Working at the bottom of the pit inside the mine, he pulled out chunk after chunk of the shiny precious metal, some as large as a man's clenched fist. He wondered whether anyone had ever located a site such as this, and he continued to build his own stockpile as he increased the size of the camp pile. It was completely win-win.

After six days had passed since his boss's departure, Weiser's accumulation had already exceeded his wildest dreams. The locked case in the nearby cave felt like it weighed over fifteen pounds, and he could still stash away more if he did it carefully. If he bided his time until he'd socked away another ten pounds, he could live like a king for years without working a stitch. His daily trips to his hiding spot now took longer, as he stopped to linger over the glittering pile of nuggets lining the bottom of the case. He just couldn't resist staring in admiration of that which would make him rich. And soon!

It was on the seventh day when Weiser left the hiding cave and started back to the site when he heard it. The noise from behind him sounded like a quiet footstep. A single footstep. But when he turned around to investigate, there was nothing but the rock and the sky. The sun was beginning to dip lower on the rock spires, and the shadows were becoming longer and more pronounced.

Another step and another sound. Another footstep, like an echo, following like one of the many shadows cast by the surrounding mountains.

Weiser began to feel his pulse race, and he quickened his pace heading across the expanse between the upright walls of rock. He tightened his grip on his weapon, looking to ensure that it was fully loaded.

Another footstep. But nothing in sight.

By the time the mine cave was in sight, Weiser was in full sprint. He knew he wasn't capable of running up an incline in that manner, but yet his legs and his lungs seemed to know no limits. He was hearing more footsteps around him, and turning his head he saw a form that was indeed following. Or was it two? Or three? Perhaps if he made it to the cave and could use it for protection, a single blast from his rifle would serve to scare them off. They were human, from what tribe he was not certain. But they were certainly after him.

Weiser crested the final bluff leading up to the cave, his heart pounding itself out of his chest. Ahead of him was the front lip of the protective enclosure, and he prepared to dive headfirst into the darkness.

But someone else had arrived first.

As he closed the final few yards to the rock, a head appeared out of nowhere and raised a tightly strung bow into the air. He was totally unprepared for the sight and his remaining breath was sucked from his lungs. As though time had ceased to exist, he heard the high-pitched "ziiiip" of the arrow as it flew from the bow, straight and true into the middle of his chest. He was moving too rapidly to halt his forward progress and fell forward onto the arrow, which penetrated even deeper into his heart. It was quickly joined by another arrow from behind, which found the hollow between his two shoulder blades. Both entry points were quickly flooded with blood, which spilled from his rapidly pumping heart.

Additional arrows and ax heads were sunk into the dying miner who would soon be a corpse. These were not the actions of individuals looking to profit from removing gold or any possessions from their victim. They did not even attempt to look for anything of value in his pockets or about the site, although they did take with them his trusty Springfield rifle. Instead, this was the retribution of a people who felt invaded, their territory taken and their resources plundered without so much as being asked. The scene was bloody and the violent killing completed in near silence, until the very end. With the remains of the miner now lifeless and completely bathed in blood, they erupted in an ear-shattering whoop before quickly disappearing into the background. Within a matter of minutes, it would have been impossible to know that anyone had been near the site. Except for the still-warm body and the neatly sliced entry holes in the miner's clothing. Even the arrows had been removed.

Then there was silence.

CHAPTER THREE

Abandoning the Mine

July 1880

JACOB WALTZ CARED FOR HIS PACK MULES AND TREATED THEM WELL, which is why he chose to walk alongside them most of the way from the mine to the assay bank in Phoenix. With almost four hundred pounds of gold and ore divided between the two animals, plus the weight of water and his other supplies, he didn't care to further tax their strength and stamina by adding his own weight to the cargo. However, since they were now both relieved of their loads, he saw no reason why he shouldn't ride "muleback" on the return trek.

Taking advantage of the mules' walking speed, Waltz made much better time on his trip back to his gold mine. Averaging close to five miles per hour, he could have made the trip in a couple of days, although he took an indirect route in order to visit some acquaintances and repay some debts. He also stopped whenever water was available to allow his animals time to rest and quench their thirst. Still, the route back into the mountains would take no more than three days, even at the leisurely pace.

After leaving Phoenix and crossing the Salt River, Waltz headed east, toward the Superstition Mountains. Crossing the flatter areas that held minor population centers that would become Tempe, Mesa, and Apache Junction, he could usually maintain a steady heading by keeping the mountains in view. Early on the third day, he arrived at the outer abutments of rock that signaled the start of the ascent into the Superstitions. From there, his trail turned slightly southward as he headed down the

THE DUTCHMAN'S GOLD

canyon and over Parker Pass. The sun blazed relentlessly and he had to keep his skin covered in order to avoid a blistering burn.

Although it was getting on in the day, Waltz decided that he would not stop until he reached his camp for the night. Pushing through O'Grady Canyon and over the last few climbs, he continued moving onward and upward, the Saguaro cacti poking their fleshy bulk over forty feet in the air. The air temperature had already dropped significantly and the birds were in full song as he approached the final steep inclinations of rock leading to the hidden cave.

Then, Waltz stopped involuntarily, cautiously assessing the scene. Normally, his employee would be somewhere around the site, either moving rock or performing some other bit of manual labor. Unless he was already inside the cave and asleep, which would have been unusual given the time, Waltz was usually able to hear his associate somewhere in the vicinity. This evening there was only quiet, punctuated by the whisper of the wind.

"Yaco!" called Waltz, moving closer to the entrance. "Yaco, can you hear me?" Still silence.

So intent was Waltz's gaze into the darkened entrance of the cave that he completely missed seeing the darkened remains of his deceased assistant. It was a sight that stopped his breathing and his heart for what seemed like an interminable amount of time. Weiser's corpse had been exposed for two full days and had been ravaged by vultures since the hour of his death. This, when added to the desecration of the Apache attack, resulted in an unforgettably gruesome scene. Blood stained the rocky soil across much of the small clearing, and the now-bloated appearance of the corpse only added to the macabre sight.

Waltz turned his head away from the body and gagged, and then he vomited on the ground. He felt dizzy and on the verge of blacking out, all the while continuing to feel his stomach muscles retching in horror and disgust. And yet, even in his physical and emotional distress, he knew that he had to protect himself in order to survive from whatever or whoever had killed Yaco.

Forcing himself to stand and approach the body, Waltz could easily see the dried blood stains that had congealed around the holes in his shirt. They weren't bullet holes, but obviously arrowheads that had provided the killing shots. He also noticed that Weiser's rifle was nowhere to be seen, and Weiser was never without his firearm. Especially when left alone in camp as he'd been for the past week.

The story was now obvious.

Waltz rapidly spun around, scanning the area for hostile intruders while he simultaneously lunged for the rifle from the scabbard on his mule. Although not seeing anything in his area, he quickly raised the weapon and prepared to fire at the first sign of movement. There was none, so he retreated in a backward crouch toward the entrance of the mine.

A rapid inspection of the shallow excavation area revealed nothing. Whoever had perpetrated this crime had probably left immediately after the killing. It made Waltz feel no better, and he felt his heart racing as he lowered himself to a prone position. He knew that he wanted to leave the place immediately, but sundown was rapidly approaching and he couldn't make it down the incline before dark. He would have to remain in the mine for one more night before leaving for civilization one last time.

It was a very long night, and Waltz did not want to call attention to himself by lighting a fire. Instead, he lay on a bed of multiple blankets, his Remington by his side and pointed out the front of the cave. He tried not to doze off as the last colors of dusk vanished from the sky, but he sometimes felt himself slipping away as the hours passed. It wasn't a very dark night, the moon being more full than new. And all the while he pondered just what his future would hold. He had money in the bank, and he could probably manage to grab a few more of the larger nuggets that still lay buried in the bottom of the mine pit. But would he return? Would he try to recruit another assistant? Would he tell anyone what had happened to Weiser up on the mountain? Would he even bother to retrieve the body, now in very bad condition, and return it to a nearby town for burial?

Waltz opted for the quickest route away from the scene. When the first light of dawn crept into his rocky abode, he slipped two small nuggets into his pocket and then loaded the mules with only those items he felt necessary to make town. He barely waited long enough to consume a few pieces of stale brown bread and mouthfuls of water before heading his mules back down the canyon.

THE DUTCHMAN'S GOLD

It was still very early when he reached lower ground, and he saw no one else as he retraced his steps of the previous day. The farther he made it alive, the more determined he was to never return to the mine. Let others who were more determined, or more brave, or less intelligent, move to claim the vast riches that still lay in the soil. As far as Waltz was concerned, he now had all he could use, and he was still alive. That was enough.

Waltz did not stop until he reached the town of Phoenix, where he had once owned a partial interest in a farm near the Salt River. He used some of his funds to purchase a small holding, where he raised some crops and kept a few head of cattle and sheep. Age was beginning to creep up on his weathered body, and he was finding it harder to keep up with the chores of running a farm.

By the time a flood wiped out much of his fields and buildings, he was beyond the point of caring. When he fell ill for a period of time, he paid a local acquaintance named Julia Thomas a weekly fee to look after him and his few remaining belongings. Thomas owned a bakery in Phoenix and converted a storeroom in the back into a comfortable bedroom where Waltz could rest in quiet. He had expected to make out a will in order to leave his substantial savings to Thomas, but he never got the chance. His health continued to fail him until he barely had the strength to raise himself from his bed.

In Waltz's final days, he attempted to tell Thomas about his bank deposits, but she dismissed it as the ravings of dementia in the dying man. Try as he might, he wanted to leave her with something of significance, something that would see her through to a comfortable retirement. Finally, on a dark night about a week before he died, he drew her a map of the route to his gold mine along with some oral instructions on how to find the cave. Once again, she refused to believe the story. Waltz then instructed her to search inside a box he kept in a wooden chest in the back of the storeroom. When she opened the box, she immediately saw the two nuggets, small but impressively pure.

Waltz died a few days later, alone in the back of a bakery, his memories gone forever. Thomas made a single attempt to use the map and his descriptions to find the mine before giving up on the idea. Her son, bitten by the gold bug, ventured into the same wilderness, only to lose his life under mysterious circumstances. Since that time, the legend of the Lost Dutchman Gold Mine has grown and become more complicated with each passing decade.

Although Jacob Waltz could not have imagined, his legacy has served as a catalyst for one of the greatest treasure-hunting frenzies in American history. Hundreds of searchers have headed off into the rugged wilderness that is the Superstition Mountains every year, only to return empty-handed.

Or not return at all.

CHAPTER FOUR

Too Little Wilderness
June 1899

THE HISTORY OF THE ADIRONDACK MOUNTAINS IS FULL OF STORIES OF hunters and trappers, hermits and guides, each famous for their exploits in their own particular regions. Some were undoubtedly better and more authentic than others, more knowledgeable of their own woods and with greater refinements in woodcraft. But perhaps none of these proclaimed "mountain men" were more authentic than Alvah Dunning, the Hermit of Raquette Lake.

Dunning was born in Lake Pleasant, of Hamilton County, in June of 1816. He was the son of Shadrack Dunning, another primitive woodsman who was also a self-sufficient hunter and trapper, although his earlier years had been spent engaged in warfare with the Indian population of the area. A coarse man of few words, he had young Alvah along with him in the woods on hunting trips from a very young age. Observing his father on these early hunting excursions, Alvah quickly learned the art of the kill, and took his first moose when he was little more than a child.

As much woods savvy as he possessed, he was equally as deficient in social and domestic skills. He did marry, although he later learned that his wife had been unfaithful during one of his extended trips into the woods. His retribution against her for her adultery was so violent and abusive that he soon found himself an outcast from the settlement as well as an outlaw from the local deputies. He had to leave his home, and quickly.

Dunning migrated north to Raquette Lake, where he lived for a number of years in total solitude. He made a living off the land and was perfectly content in doing so. He also picked up some money serving as a guide to those "sports" who sought to engage his services, although he did so reluctantly, and considered many of his clients to be complete fools. Many of the stories of his exploits describe a fiercely independent soul who would rather live a life in complete solitude than tolerate contact with those who paid him as their guide. It was part of his nature and he could not be changed.

Dunning was forced to move from one location to another over the decades he spent in the Adirondacks. Sometimes he was forced off the land because the actual owner wanted to build a house or other structure, and sometimes he just became disgusted with the mass influx of "city folks" who appeared out of nowhere, infiltrating his wilderness and rendering it uninhabitable for his taste. He never actually owned the properties where he homesteaded. Instead, he simply arrived at a location and erected a crude shack, which became home. That he didn't hold title to that plot made little difference; he was still willing to defend the place with his life and his rifle, and he was a very keen shot.

Dunning's perambulations led him to reside in a number of Adirondack locations and townships, including Raquette Lake, Eighth Lake, Blue Mountain Lake, and back again. Finally, in 1899, he was forced away from a shanty on Raquette Lake for a second time. It was then that he decided enough was enough. There was simply too little wilderness left in the East to meet his needs. He had listened to stories of the great American West, with majestic mountains and endless forests, where the fish and game were bountiful and the solitude impenetrable.

And so, in 1899 at the tender young age of eighty-three, he boarded a train heading west, into the territories known as the Dakotas. There he would find himself again and submerge himself in the larger wilderness where no one would bother him and no one would find him. Alone at last in the environment that best suited this true man of the woods.

The fact that Alvah Dunning never made it to his original destination was of little consequence to him, nor was he even aware of his misdirection. He had cashed in those belongings that would bring him any significant funds, and used them to purchase his ticket on any train headed west. The journey would take many days, and he wasn't particularly aware of his desired terminus. As long as it was wild country and "in the West," it would suffice. While it was true that he had intended to make it to the Dakotas, he was vague in his instructions while purchasing his tickets, and his lack of literary skills limited his ability to interpret his travel documents.

"Dem mountains out west" was about all he asked of the ticket seller in St. Louis, who had himself been a resident of central Arizona earlier in his life. And so it was that Dunning found himself passing through Kansas City and then on to a branch of the Texas & Pacific Railroad heading south instead of another line that would have turned north and toward the Canadian territories. He eventually found himself at a railway station in Phoenix, where he was told by the conductor that he "had arrived" at his destination.

It was late in the day, so Dunning paid for a room at a local boarding house before heading out of town the following morning. He bargained with a nearby rancher to purchase an eight-year-old horse, which would serve to take him and his belongings into the mountains where he would start life anew. Then he headed east, into the hills.

These Arizona mountains did not appear as he'd imagined them. Instead of being heavily wooded, they were more barren except for the thick scrub bushes that made "cross country" travel difficult. Meanwhile, he was amazed at the massive bulks of the Saguaro cacti, some as tall as the spruce and hemlock trees of the Adirondacks, but very different and covered in sharp spines. He had heard about these things called cacti but had never seen one for himself. One quick touch of a needle was enough to convince him that they were better seen than felt.

Dunning's legendary survival instincts were enough to permit him to set up residence in the mountains. He selected a location situated on a ridge, up from the bottom of a canyon, where there was a natural rock overhang that would provide protection from the elements. The shelter had two natural walls that met in a "V" shape, which he utilized as the rear walls of his abode. Rather than attempt to complete the structure using wood, which was in very short supply, he simply constructed rock walls from the endless supply that littered the canyon floor. He then collected a supply of smaller branches and sticks, which he weaved into a thatched roof for any exposed portions of the structure. It certainly wasn't an attractive residence by any measure. But then again, neither were any of his Adirondack habitations. As long as they would keep the elements and wildlife at bay, it was enough.

Obtaining food was a much different proposition in the Superstition Mountains than it was back home. The animals available to hunt were very different and the terrain offered little cover for stalking. That Dunning became proficient within a matter of weeks spoke volumes of his natural senses in the great outdoors. He quickly became versed in the habits of the desert antelope and the big-horned sheep, which were among the more common big game species he encountered. These animals and the less common black bear presented a dilemma for the hermit, as they were very large and he hated to waste any part of his kill. For that reason, he was much more in favor of taking one or more of the many rabbits and hares that populated the shrub-covered canyon. They were easy to find and easy to kill, all without wasting a majority of the carcass.

Dunning also became familiar with many of the desert plants and fruits that grew across the arid region. He knew where to find the canyon grapes and the prickly pear "apples," watercress plants and dandelions, Arizona walnut trees, tubers, and a couple varieties of sunflowers.

What Dunning did not find comfort with were the desert Indians, who appeared from time to time with stunning silence. Some of these native people appeared to be friendly while others behaved in an extremely hostile manner, although none actually initiated an attack against Dunning himself. He did not present a threat to any of them, and did not appear to have any interest in pursuing the gold or other natural resources in their territory.

Over time, Dunning discovered that the native peoples he encountered were divided between at least two tribes, and these two did not coexist peacefully with each other. A storekeeper in the settlement of Tempe had explained that the Apaches were much more violent and prone to attack even a solitary recluse such as himself. The Pima Indians, however, were much more peaceful and could be made into friends, which would be useful for trading as well as serving as an ally. Dunning had no reason to make enemies, although he had that reputation while residing in the Adirondack Mountains. But here, potentially facing a large band of arrow-shooting natives, a shooting war was the last thing he desired.

One reason why Dunning was able to survive in the midst of the Apache warriors was that they feared him, both in appearance and ability. His appearance, tall and narrow with an eagle-like beak of a nose, was profoundly imposing. He could move silently about the mountains without making a sound, and he appeared out of nowhere when there was nothing to provide cover. Once, he was descending a trail to approach one of the few springs that provided water following a rain. Without warning, he rounded a column of rock and found himself face-to-face with two Apache warriors. Both the warriors were preparing to collect some of the water themselves when they caught sight of Dunning, rifle in hand.

The reaction was immediate; the Indians both raised their bows and reached over their shoulders for their quivers, ready to load their weapons for a close-range shot. It would have been deadly, as the hermit had no place to hide. However, Dunning already had his rifle in the raised position, and could have quickly killed both of them without even aiming. The hesitation in his movement took but a split second. Then, in a flash, he raised his sights up into the sky and fired a single shot. A red-tailed hawk, which had been flying high overhead, gave a single screech before tumbling from the skies, landing with a thud about fifty feet from the spring. Dunning then brought the gun back down and held it across his chest, staring at the two Apaches with an expression that required little explanation.

To the Apaches, it was as though they'd encountered a god. They both froze in place, hands over their heads as they reached for their quivers, not daring to move a muscle. They both realized the ghostly apparition of a man that stood before them could end their lives at any moment. Had there been more of them, they would have attacked. But with only two of them they wouldn't stand a chance.

The staredown lasted another thirty seconds before Dunning, with a slight nod of his head, raised his right hand to his side and displayed an open palm, and said but a single word: "Go."

The Apaches did not understand the command, but they did interpret the movement as a sign that Dunning did not wish to fight. After the display of marksmanship, they also wanted to avoid a confrontation, one that most likely would end their lives as it had ended the hawk's. They both turned around and immediately took off in a dead run, ascending a step-like set of boulders on the other side of the stream before disappearing over a rocky bluff.

On a different occasion, Dunning was approaching the same spring hole (there weren't many in the area) when he came upon a pair of Indian children who were filling some empty gourds from the spring. Nearby was a pair of Indian men and a woman, although Dunning could not tell who were the parents of the children in this group. He had met these natives before, and he knew they were friendly. One of the men previously had shown him how to remove prickly pear fruit from the cactus and had attempted to communicate with him, although Dunning was not able to understand his words.

As Dunning approached the group, they hesitated, warily watching the rifle in his right hand. Was he still friendly? Did he remember them from their previous encounter? The two males suddenly froze in horror as Dunning raised his rifle and, in a flash, fired a shot at the two children by the water hole. The adult woman screamed, and the children leaped straight up from their position by the water, apparently not hit. The only other movement was the now-headless body of the rattlesnake that fell off the rock ledge next to where the youngsters had been squatting.

The two Pima warriors were still standing, eyes agape, as Dunning strode the few remaining steps to the water, where he lifted the remains of the poisonous reptile, its tail still rattling in the arid afternoon air. He had put a bullet through its small head from a distance of thirty feet without even stopping to aim. One of the warriors approached Dunning and embraced him, speaking more words that he did not understand. The other warrior waited until the clinch was over and then took Dunning's arm into his own grasp while reaching into a small leather pouch by his side. From the sack he extracted a turquoise-jeweled band of silver, which he placed around Dunning's wrist. Speaking in his native tongue, the Indian stared into his eyes with an expression that could only be

THE DUTCHMAN'S GOLD

described as intense admiration and gratitude. Dunning couldn't keep his own emotions in check as he immediately teared up and wept.

From that day on, the Indians of the Pima tribe and Dunning got along famously. They would bring him samples of their crops, as they practiced agriculture and even performed minor irrigation in places where it could be constructed. Dunning would provide them with some larger game when he could obtain it, including several big-horned sheep, which they highly favored.

Meanwhile, the Apaches stayed their distance, respecting not only Dunning's accuracy with the rifle but also his humane decision to spare the lives of their two warriors when given the chance. It was a bit of a stand-off, and the Apaches realized that he was doing no harm and would not hurt their people.

Dunning never did learn how to speak the language of his Pima friends, although they attempted to gain a rudimentary grasp of English. They gave him the Indian name of "Ghost Hawk," which was derived from his stealth and his hawk-like appearance. He tried to teach them his first name, "Alvah," but the closest rendition they could make from it was "Ah Hah," which always moved him to laughter. He quickly gave up on the language lessons.

One evening, after Dunning had given the Pimas a fine big-horned sheep that would feed their families for many days, a member of their tribe showed up outside his shelter and called out to him. When the nomad stepped out of his hut, he found one of his Indian friends, hand extended, offering him a piece of parchment with a drawing on one side. When Dunning examined the artwork, he saw that it was a fine sketching of himself, standing tall with a serious expression as he gazed at the horizon. It was a magnificent piece of work that must have been completed by an accomplished artist who was very familiar with Dunning's facial features. This became a treasured possession and remained with him until he left the region the following year.

The old guide was very set in his ways, and although he could no longer stalk the forests and lakeshores of the Adirondacks, he still craved an intimate knowledge of the land that surrounded him. For that reason, he spent a great amount of time walking the peaks and canyons of the

Superstition Mountains. His favorite area included the magnificent rock abutments that swept around the steep rocky spire known as Weaver's Needle. He had often thought of leaving his horse behind and trying to ascend part of that peak just to say that he had done it, although he never got around to actually starting it. Still it fascinated him as he had listened to some of the locals out in the settlements when they spoke of a lost gold mine that was buried somewhere within a shadow's length of that particular formation.

Dunning had been in the Arizona mountains for over nine months now, and the hotter months of summer were approaching once again. He had been out hunting rabbit throughout the early afternoon when the clouds began to thicken, darkening the skies. He was a true outdoorsman, not one to let the weather bother him. However, as the clouds grew darker and darker, his keen ears detected the rumble of thunder from far to the west. The claps grew louder over the next twenty minutes, the staccato bass sounds reverberating about the canyon walls.

He had already been elevated somewhat from the bottom of the ravine, his route dictated by the path of the game he was hunting. But now, as he sought a place to take shelter from the impending downpour, his eyes detected a rock overhang about one hundred feet above his current location. It looked like a sufficient place to ride out the storm, and he quickly began the ascent to reach the spot. The going was steep, but Dunning's long legs and sure feet had him inside the shallow cave-like refuge within a matter of minutes.

There was not a minute to spare. As soon as Dunning's head passed beneath the overhead rock shelf, the downpour commenced. It didn't rain often in this part of the country, but when it did, it came hard. Sheets of windswept water were whipped past the cave's opening, not more than six feet in front of the old guide's eyes. He was glad to be up off the canyon floor as he was aware that flash flooding was a very real possibility in such weather. He hoped that his horse had remained on the bluff where he'd left him, as it should offer sufficient height to protect him from such a flood.

As the storm raged, Dunning looked around the cave to take stock of his surroundings. His eyes were becoming accustomed to the relative darkness of the recess, and he began to pick out features marking the sides and rear of the enclosed area. Then, he spotted something that did not fit in.

It appeared to be a piece of metal, darkened by the elements but not old. He moved closer to make a more detailed inspection. The item had been intentionally covered with small rocks and then tucked away in a corner of the cave. It was also covered by a thick layer of grayish dust, indicating that it had been left intact for a number of years. Dunning bent over and pulled the rock off the surface, uncovering a small metal suitcase, its dimensions no more than twelve by eighteen inches. He also noticed that when he tried to lift it, the parcel was surprisingly heavy.

The suitcase was locked shut with a small padlock, and there was no key in sight. As he turned the case over in his arms, the contents tumbled about inside, obviously rock and significant in quantity. Dunning returned to the indentation in the ground where he had originally spotted the suitcase. On his hands and knees, his eyes close to the ground, he carefully examined the earth to see if there was anything else that he had missed. As his eyes further adjusted to the dim light, he detected specs of gold flakes that sparkled as they reflected the ambient light. He also picked up a couple of small, crumb-sized nodules that appeared to be the precious metal in its purest form. These he studied carefully, a deep scowl creasing his face. He was now fairly convinced of the contents of the suitcase, although it did not appear to better his temperament.

Alvah Dunning was a very simple man with simple needs. He did not desire to be burdened down with material possessions or extensive holdings. His earthly desires consisted of nothing more than having sufficient food and drink, a roof over his head, and the means for obtaining these commodities. All else was superfluous and could be left to others. He did transport the locked suitcase from the shallow cave back down to his horse once the storm abated, and from there to his shelter. On a later trip into Phoenix, he would eventually remove the lock and visually inspect the contents, which consisted of several dozen medium-to-large nuggets of pure gold with a combined weight of at least ten to fifteen pounds.

Dunning was enthusiastic about the amount of wealth in his possession, although not on a personal level. He had no plans to use any of this for his own needs, nor did he even seek to locate a bank that would assess the value and provide him with cash. In his mind, the fewer people who knew of this cache, the better. With this in mind, he toted the suitcase to the Phoenix railway cargo station and arranged to have the case shipped back east, to his sister's house in Syracuse, New York. Her husband had been ill for several years and they had fallen on some hard times. She was also one of the only relatives with whom Dunning had maintained contact. He was certain that she could find a good use for the value of this gold.

Before shipping the crate, he paid one of the freight company employees to write a brief letter to his sister, which he mailed separately from the bullion. It explained the source of the gold along with his intention for her to do with it as she chose. No restrictions. He then locked the case with a bulky new padlock and sent it on its way. He knew his sister would be pleased.

The following months were long and tiring for the aging hermit, who had never really acclimated to the hot climate of the Arizona desert. It puzzled him that these mountains didn't bear any semblance to the rough-and-tumble badlands of the Dakotas, his intended destination. The heat, the bare rock, the scarcity of water, and the presence of hostile native tribes all wore on him and had him thinking more of the woods back home.

In his earlier years, Dunning had not shirked away from confrontations, with some of his skirmishes bordering on developing into actual feuds. It was always said that he was accomplished in making enemies, and that statement was certainly true. But never did he kill a man or come close to being killed himself. In this country, the Indian tribes (primarily the Apache and the Pimas) made it a regular practice, and the hatred was so ingrained and inbred that it would never subside. Dunning had actually witnessed some of these deadly engagements from a distance, without being personally involved.

The violence and the killing sickened him and further contributed to his desire to return to the Adirondacks of his youth. The fact that he might no longer be able to fend for himself was no longer critical. Time had softened him and even lessened his need for absolute solitude. It just wasn't as important as it used to be, and indeed he found himself seeking company from time to time.

THE DUTCHMAN'S GOLD

It was another hot day in early June 1900 when the steam locomotive pulled out of Phoenix, bound for Kansas City. Behind it were six passenger coach cars, one of which carried the old, weary hermit back to the wilderness of an earlier day. He had packed all of his belongings into a single case, leaving behind a great many possessions that he didn't deem necessary in his new life. Some of these were both valuable and sentimental, including some paper records and the sketched portrait presented to him by the Pima artist. But Dunning was a rolling stone that gathered little moss. He took what he needed and left the rest behind.

After returning to New York, Dunning once again took up residence around Raquette Lake, although without nearly the same vigor or zest for life. He did still hunt and fish some, but his desire for solitude appeared to have vanished, and he actually sought to be around other people. He also ceased spending winters by himself, instead keeping company with his sister in the city of Syracuse, New York, and others in the area.

In a final irony, Dunning passed away in a hotel room in 1902, the victim of a leaking gas line. He who had spent so little time in civilization in the dwellings of others lost his life in just such a place.

In those final two years of his life, he never once asked his sister about the metal trunk loaded with gold that he had sent her from the "great Rocky Mountains." Little did he know that it would be almost 120 years before the contents of that container would once again see the light of day.

CHAPTER FIVE

Helping Out a Grandson

October 31, 1913

MARTHA DUNNING WAS ALVAH'S SISTER, AND THE BABY OF THE FAMILY. Born like her brother in the town of Lake Pleasant, New York, she arrived early in the spring of 1824, the youngest of six children. Her life was rather ordinary by most standards, the wife of a carpenter named Luther Sykes, who moved the family away from the Hamilton County community in search of greater employment opportunities in 1850. They settled in the city of Syracuse, where they earned a modest living between his carpentry and her part-time work in a laundry and cleaning business. They had two children, both of whom lived within ten miles of their parents' home in the city.

The older of their two children, Michael Sykes, ended up moving back to Raquette Lake, where he helped to manage a small store where the local residents purchased their food and other necessities. It wasn't a lucrative existence, but they got by and managed to raise a family on their modest means. They had three children of their own, living in a small two-bedroom house within a stone's throw of the lake. At a later time, one of their three children, Michael Jr., reached out to his parents and grandparents when he needed funds to purchase a house just south of the Raquette Lake community. Money was not plentiful in the early days of the 1900s, and he did not earn enough of a salary to qualify for a mortgage to cover the monthly expenses.

31

Michael's parents were able to contribute very little to his plea for financial assistance, having led an austere lifestyle on one small income. However, his grandmother, Martha Sykes, was able to make her grandson a very unusual offer. She wrote a letter to Michael in which she described a locked case that she had received from her deceased brother a decade earlier. In her letter, she referred to the case as though it was filled with gold, and of immense value. However, she also issued a warning that the metal container was probably cursed and could bring nothing but harm to whoever looked on its contents. She stated that, for that reason, she had never opened the case herself and was very worried about allowing her beloved grandson to do the same.

When Michael wrote back asking his grandmother to describe the curse, she relayed the following story:

Michael,

When my brother Alvah was living in the mountains of the Dakotas, he came across this chest that contained a large amount of gold. The owner of the chest had apparently died soon after sealing it and hiding it in the mountains for whatever reason he did. Alvah found this chest and shipped it back east, where he hoped to sell it to help Luther and me to retire comfortably at an early age. The case was never opened until Alvah arrived the next winter, when he removed the lock and showed us the collection of beautiful gold nuggets. He was going to help us to have the gold valued and sold, but he passed away under the most unusual circumstances while returning home from a sporting show that same month.

A few months later, Luther opened the case to inventory the bullion and obtain the combined weight of the nuggets. He did this, and was overjoyed with what he found. He announced that the two of us were going to immediately retire and live a life of leisure from that day on. Unfortunately, he died in his sleep two nights later. I am not a superstitious person by nature, but I cannot help but reason that three men have now met their demise after handling this "treasure." I want no part of it.

If you wish to use this gold to purchase your new house, you are more than welcome to it. I will have the case shipped to your parents' house in Raquette Lake, where you can use it however you desire. However, I do recommend that you dispose of it as quickly as possible, as I still believe that the gold brings the holder nothing but bad luck. I know it has done this for me, and I do not wish the same consequences for you.

May God bless,
Grandma

It took Grandma Sykes almost a week to have a young man from her church move the chest to the railway shipping office. At eighty-seven years of age, she could not lift the twenty-pound container off the ground much less move it to the train station. Together they replaced the bulky padlock that Alvah had originally used to secure the case and then lifted it into the man's carriage. The date was now November 6, 1913.

At the station, Martha filled out the appropriate form with the shipping officer and paid the required fee from her cloth purse. She took the small yellow receipt for the payment and placed it into the same purse along with her paper money and coins. Her intention was to retain the receipt until the locked case was picked up by her grandson in Old Forge. Unfortunately, she was never afforded the opportunity. The next morning, while singing with her church choir, she suffered a massive stroke and passed away within an hour.

CHAPTER SIX

The Great Train Wreck of 1913

November 9, 1913

THE EARLY DAYS OF THE ADIRONDACK MOUNTAINS ARE REPLETE WITH dozens of small railways that crisscrossed the periphery of the park. Most of these were small operations that were confined to a regional area, shuttling passengers and cargo alike from town to town inside the Blue Line. They connected to other railways at bigger cities in towns like North Creek that served as hubs for the Adirondack traffic.

One such company was the Raquette Lake Railway, which operated a small set of tracks leading northeast to Raquette Lake, passing through towns like Old Forge and Eagle Bay along the way. These trains made only one or two trips a day between their terminus towns, and operated with just a handful of employees to staff both the trains and the boarding stations. Many of these trains had only a few cars, depending on the number of passengers or freight being shipped.

In addition to the train conductors, engineers, and other office workers, the railways of olden times hired "rail walkers" who would walk on foot over predetermined lengths of track every day. These foot patrols looked for obvious problems, such as fallen trees, rocks, and other debris on the tracks as well as other conditions that might deem passage dangerous to the train and its passengers.

The Raquette Lake Railway was no different than any other in its desire to maintain safe travel conditions. Its rail walkers collectively hiked the entire distance of track every day from Clearwater Station to

Raquette Lake, making sure that the tracks were clear of any obstructions. They walked many miles every day in this pursuit, and were keen observers of their assigned tracks. Very little went unobserved and unreported by these diligent guardians of the rails. However, the railroad only hired these people to work between the months of May and October, the rest of the year being too weather-averse (between snow and cold temperatures) to permit year-round coverage.

It probably wouldn't have mattered anyway. Chances are that little could have been done to prevent the disastrous meteorological conditions that were presented to the entire Northeast from November 7–10, 1913. A life-threatening scenario called an "extratropical cyclone," caused by the convergence of two massive storms, struck in a wide swath from the Great Lakes through much of Ontario, Canada. The storm went by several names: the "Great Lakes Storm of 1913," the "White Hurricane," and "Freshwater Fury" were three of the appellations given to the monumental weather event.

The devastation on the Great Lakes was enormous. Winds up to ninety miles per hour piled up waves in excess of thirty-five feet in height. Such was the strength of the blow that it destroyed nineteen ships and did lesser damage to many others. The storm peaked on Sunday, November 9, dumping several feet of snow or rain throughout much of the northeast. In the Adirondacks, the effects were significantly reduced, although the precipitation and winds were still severe enough to wreak havoc throughout the region.

Sometime during the morning of Sunday, November 9, the howling winds wrapped their fury around the central Adirondacks, knocking down thousands upon thousands of trees and flinging precipitation down in buckets. Unfortunately, one of the multitudes of trees felled in the storm came down squarely across the tracks of the Raquette Lake Railway. It was large, heavy, and deadly.

On this particular morning, the Raquette Lake Railway train was making its way northeast into the teeth of the storm, en route from Carter Station* to Raquette Lake, a distance of less than thirty-five miles.

---

*Carter Station was formerly known as Clearwater until 1912.

The train was carrying some freight packages and the daily parcel of mail to the station in Raquette Lake. The small crew was actively engaged in the chores required to run the train, with the engineer, conductor, brakeman, and fireman each performing their respective duties.

As the train came out of a slight curve, the engineer, Benjamin Hall, looked behind him to observe a series of gauges indicating the engine status. When he turned his eyes back toward the tracks, his eyes flew wide open, his facial expression registering extreme distress. Staring through the front windshield in disbelief, Hall caught sight of the downed tree laying across the tracks.

There were two things that Hall knew he could not do in the short interval before impact. The first was that he could not stop the train in time to avoid a collision. The second was that he knew the trunk of the tree was too wide for the engine to simply push it aside. At the engine's current speed, it would have taken approximately 450 yards to come to a complete stop. The tree was now less than one hundred yards away.

This would be an impact with violent force, and he noted that the track ahead was bordered on the right by a steep embankment. Even worse.

The final two hundred feet of forward progress was made as in slow motion. The brakeman, Albert Lashaway, pulled the brake lever that set the brake blocks, which began screeching in full volume as the wheels skidded down the track. The initial slam of the engine into the waterlogged tree trunk was felt throughout the train, along with the immediate reduction in velocity. The entire engine rocked initially to the left and then even more to the right. It rapidly passed the "tipping point" where its left-side wheels rose too far off the tracks to recover. The center of gravity now hopelessly off-centered, the entire engine rolled off the tracks, pulling the following coupled cars behind it as they rolled down the steep cliff-like embankment. At this point there was nothing that could be done.

The noise and vibration from the massively weighted engine filled the air with demonic sounds that guests of the North Woods Inn could hear almost a quarter mile away. Each roll of the engine provided its own punctuation to the cacophony, with cargo, equipment, and train parts being flung far and wide. Some of the cargo had simply rolled out of an open freight door and was then mashed into the soft, wet ground by the weight of the engine. The earth at the bottom of the incline was snow-covered but not yet frozen solid, so a portion of the cargo was immediately incorporated into the mud beneath the train.

The collision and the carnage seemed to go on forever. And then there was an eerie near-silence. The only sounds were the creaks and groans from the settling cars accompanied by the residual hissing from the engine.

That several train cars and a locomotive engine were lost that day was secondary in importance to the loss of life, as three members of the crew were killed in the incident. Benjamin Hall, Albert Lashaway, and fireman John Case were all killed instantly as the massive locomotive threw their bodies amongst the wreckage like so many rag dolls. Only one engineer survived the collision and ensuing tumble down the cliff.

Later came the recovery and salvage of what remained of the rolling stock, which was a mammoth task. It took weeks to completely clear the scene and to remove the cars from the embankment. Railway employees and dozens of laborers struggled to move the wreckage and retrieve any cargo that could be rescued. Most of the goods being transported had remained inside the freight cars, as had the bins containing the U.S. mail bound for Raquette Lake. However, some of the freight that was thrown from the open doors was concealed in the mud beneath the weight of the cars, which now rested on their sides.

To those who awaited shipments via the Raquette Lake Railway that stormy week, most were able to find and claim their parcels. Some were destroyed in the collision, and others were quite damaged. But for the most part, the railroad company did a superb job of matching the cargo to their intended recipients.

One such claimant was not so lucky. Michael Sykes Jr. waited patiently for the suitcase that would never arrive. For decades he wondered what had happened to the shipment of gold described by his grandmother.

He never learned of its disposition, nor could he ask his deceased grandmother whether she had indeed shipped it before her death. Over time he adopted a philosophical view that perhaps it was for the better. Perhaps it had been cursed from the very beginning.

There were no survivors left to answer the question.

CHAPTER SEVEN

The Call from Dallas

May 1, 2020

IT WAS A COLD DAY FOR LATE APRIL, EVEN FOR THE COOLER CLIMES OF upstate New York. The parking lot of the small restaurant in Westmoreland was still surrounded by snowbanks that reached over twelve feet in height, the result of a long winter with very few warm spells. Patrons entering the eatery were still dressed in winter coats, although the temperatures had finally broken through the freezing point.

Slightly before noon, a forest-green Jeep Liberty pulled into the parking lot and directly into a spot between two other SUVs. The driver never touched the brake until he was halfway into the tight parking space and yet stopped on a dime at the front of the spot, perfectly centered between the white lines. The door immediately opened, and an energetic young man leaped from the driver's seat as though on springs. He was a rugged-looking individual, standing a touch over six feet two inches tall and possessing a thick head of bushy black hair. He was athletically built and had a bounce to his step indicative of someone who maintained an active training regimen. Although twenty-seven years of age, he looked youthful enough to still be attending college.

Christopher Carey had spent much of his young life in the areas around Syracuse and Utica, New York, having attended college and graduate school in the Mohawk Valley before starting his career in the same region. An aggressively "Type A" individual, he had succeeded in everything he'd ever undertaken, which was a trademark of his entire family.

He had excelled in high school and college academics while also being a standout lacrosse player at Syracuse. His father was a prominent lawyer in Washington, D.C., where he still spent the majority of his time. His mother, meanwhile, held down the family residence in a rambling hilltop mansion outside of Utica.

Within a few short minutes, another vehicle pulled into the same lot and parked in a spot three spaces away from the Jeep. The second auto attracted a lot of attention, being a 1966 Mercedes-Benz 250S that was in mint condition. The original tan paint was unmarred by the passage of over a half century of time, its highly waxed finish reflecting the midday sun. The antique vehicle's owner was used to the stares of admiration and enjoyed the attention.

The driver of the old Mercedes stepped out of his car and strode over to Chris, his lifelong friend, greeting him with a fist bump. Sean Riggins had grown up with Chris, and the two had been inseparable since their earliest years in grade school. Sean was a full head shorter than his friend, with closely cropped hair that tiptoed the line between light-brown and blond. Together they had shared many facets of their lives together, and their careers paralleled each other's, although in different subjects. Chris had always been a numbers person, and had gravitated into accounting during college, which he followed up with an MBA in the same field. Sean, meanwhile, was a self-described "technogeek," and had chosen to enter the lucrative business of computer and online security.

By coincidence, both had decided to establish their own consulting firms rather than work for someone else. Sean made this decision because he felt that he had a better business model on his own, whereas Chris just never wanted to work for someone else. Both men originally had plans of climbing the corporate ladder. However, their independent practices had granted them both time to take off on various adventures and trips into the wilderness whenever they desired, which is a tradeoff they both gladly accepted.

Their exploits had led them to the discovery of two massive, historic treasures within the past four years. One of these was a huge stockpile of gold that had been hidden by a British sympathizer prior to the Revolutionary War, while the other involved the discovery of a cache of rare early American silver dollars worth hundreds of millions of dollars. These two landmark finds earned them a level of fame in the treasure-hunting world that neither of them desired, but it came with the territory. They were both asked to appear on television and radio shows to discuss their uncanny abilities to track down items of monetary and historic value that had been lost for centuries.

Their purpose for meeting in Westmoreland on this particular day was more than just for lunch and conversation. The diner, known affectionately as Wendy's International Café, represented a convenient halfway point between Chris's residence in North Syracuse and Sean's house in Little Falls. They could each reach this spot within an easy thirty-minute drive, and had adopted it as a rendezvous point when there was something important to discuss that could not wait. Today was no different.

The two headed inside the small, red brick restaurant without saying much until they were shown their seats.

"Well, hello again!" called out Wendy Culligan, the owner and sous chef of the bistro. "It's been a while since I've seen either of you. To what do I owe the pleasure?"

"I haven't had a good grease burger in months now," replied Chris, smiling back at the proprietor. Although tossing the feigned insult at their host, Wendy knew that it was entirely in jest. She had trained at one of the best culinary institutes in the country, and was constantly being recognized for her creativity with designing new delicacies on the menu.

"Just for that, I'm not going to allow you to order the Lobster Benedict with Brie," she countered. "So there!"

"Just ignore my fickle-minded partner in crime," said Sean, not bothering to look up from the menu. "He's been locked up with tax returns for the past three months and his brain has gone soft."

"Tough life," murmured Wendy, shaking her head as she walked back toward the kitchen.

Sean watched her retreat through the swinging doors of the scullery before turning his eyes back to Chris, who was still perusing the list of daily specials.

"What do you know about the Lost Dutchman Gold Mine?" asked Sean, bypassing any small talk.

"The Lost Dutchman Gold Mine," repeated Chris, his eyebrows furrowed in thought. "That's a historic dig located somewhere out west, isn't it?"

"Not a bad guess," said Sean. "Most people have never heard of the place."

"I think I read about it once in a book about mines and ghost towns," added Chris. "If I'm not mistaken, the mine had been lost for decades, and there were supposedly a bunch of people who lost their lives looking for it."

"Pretty good summary," agreed Sean, who was always amazed at his friend's ability to recall details from the past. "Actually, if you go by the references, it's been lost for at least a hundred and thirty to a hundred and forty years, maybe longer. And that's assuming that it ever existed in the first place, which is questionable. So many prospectors have searched for so many years that some say it's more myth than reality."

"Is that why you asked me to come here today? To help you look for a possibly non-existent gold mine that might get us killed?" asked Chris skeptically. "No thanks. I've got better things to do with my time right now."

"Whoa, slow down there, partner!" intoned Sean, not used to experiencing such resistance from his friend. "There is a lot I'm not telling you yet. I'm not talking about going out on a wild goose chase here. But I've been contacted by someone offering us a lot of cash if we 'volunteer' to help out a group that is going in whole-hog on a search."

"Hmm, sounds a little more promising, but I'd need to hear a lot more before committing to anything. Especially this close to the end of tax season, which is barely over. I'm up to my eyeballs in extension forms right now. It's just bad timing."

"Just to fill you in on a few of the minor details, we're not committing to anything," said Sean as he took a sip from his water glass. "Like I said, we've been offered to serve as 'hired hands' on a project that will pay us a lot of cash up front, whether we find anything or not."

"How much?" asked Chris, suddenly looking weary.

"A quarter of a million, split between the two of us for two months' work."

Chris's eyes suddenly brightened, his eyebrows hiked higher on his forehead. "Say what?" he asked in obvious surprise. "OK, now you've got my interest."

They took a pause in the conversation as an attractive young waitress stopped by to take their order. Sean selected an Asian chicken noodle soup with shiitake mushrooms while Chris ordered the cheddar-stuffed burger with pickled slaw and shallots.

"It sure beats Burger King, doesn't it," said Chris as the waitress stepped away from the table.

"Yeah, Wendy's pretty darn good when it comes to inventing new dishes," agreed Sean. "I can't think of another place along the Thruway that even comes close."

"So anyway, 'a quarter of a million dollars.' Let's start there," said Chris. "That sounds like a nice round number. Who is offering that kind of bucks and what do they want from us?"

Sean lifted a tan envelope off the seat next to him as he began to speak. "I received a phone call from a wealthy businessman . . . no, change that, a *very* wealthy businessman out in Dallas yesterday."

"'Very wealthy'—I like the sound of that."

"Yes, I sort of thought you would," replied Sean as he sorted through some papers. "His name is L. Thomas Durham, and he owns the skyscraper that houses his office. He's big into Texas oil, oil pipelines, shipping, real estate, and almost anything else that makes a lot of money."

"And this guy just called you out of the blue? How does he even know you?"

"Beats me," replied Sean, still shuffling through the pages. "For that matter, I don't know how he got hold of my cell number. But people like that have ways of getting whatever they want."

"So give me the CliffsNotes condensed version of the conversation," requested Chris.

"It didn't last long, not more than about three minutes," replied Sean, focusing once again on the conversation at hand. "He said that he'd followed the news of our hunt for the 1804 silver dollars, and he was impressed with our ability to track down clues and put them together.

Oh, and by the way, he also bought one of those dollars; paid over 1.2 million dollars for it!"

"Well, it's nice to know that *someone* is profiting over our find," said Chris, still somewhat resentful that they hadn't received more than a few thousand dollars as a finder's fee for their role in discovering the long-lost coins.

"Anyway, this Durham guy wanted to know if we'd agree to travel out to meet him to discuss his offer in person," continued Sean. "He promised that it would be an 'out-and-back' visit lasting only a day, and he'd put up all expenses for everything: plane, hotel, meals, the works."

"Why do we have to spend the time to fly out to discuss this in person? Why can't we just set up a phone conference with the three of us and hash it out in a half hour conversation?"

"Thomas Durham sounds like the kind of guy who wants to talk eyeball to eyeball," explained Sean, shrugging his shoulders as he spoke. "He never even provided me with an email address. He just seems like he does everything over a handshake. Maybe that's the Texas way."

"What else did he have to say?" asked Chris.

"If we decided to take him up on his offer, we'd be working as part of a team that had two other search parties out on the same project. I think we'd be working by ourselves most of the time, but we'd be part of a total team of six or eight people sharing information and dividing up the search area. It sounds to me as though he's got some new information on where this mine is located."

"Uh huh," said Chris, looking skeptical once again. "Him and every other treasure hunter with a metal detector. I'm just not sure I'm buying into this one."

"Look, what do we have to lose, unless this guy is just lying to us? And what would he have to gain by doing that? He's basically paying us a salary for working for him for two months, whether we find anything or not. *And*, he hinted that we'd share in the profits if we did discover the mine, which could really turn into something if we're successful."

"When do you want to head out there?" asked Chris as he absent-mindedly stirred the ice cubes in his glass.

"Well, I think we both need to wrap up any loose ends in the office," replied Sean. "How long before you think you'd be ready to jump on a flight?"

"Maybe a week or two."

"Mr. Durham asked if we could meet with him before the end of this week," said Sean, looking apologetic.

"Wow. He doesn't mess around, does he?"

As Sean replaced the papers into the envelope, the waitress reappeared with a pair of plates that she positioned in front of the two men. The aromas wafting off the dishes immediately distracted the conversation away from business as the men dug into their food.

"I always find it amazing how Wendy can take a simple piece of comfort food like a cheeseburger and convert it into a gourmet treat," remarked Chris as he prepared to take the first bite.

Sean meanwhile was wrapping the Chinese noodles around his fork and spoon in his chicken noodle soup. "I know. It's amazing what she does with a simple dish and a little expertise with the spice rack. She should write a cookbook."

"I heard that, and I love you boys," chimed Wendy, calling over a partition near the back of the room.

"See that?" said Chris, grinning back at the concealed voice. "No compliment goes unpunished around here."

"You've really got to stop by more often," Wendy replied. "I've got a lot of specials that aren't on the menu. I'd like to try some of them out on you."

Sean looked up and smiled back in her direction. "Chris is good for that. He's the proverbial guinea pig; he'll try anything once."

Chris's face returned to a serious expression as he mentally reviewed his upcoming schedule. "What do you think about this coming Friday? If Durham wants to get us tickets and set up the trip, I suppose I could spare the time to make a one-day visit, especially since it would be going into a weekend."

"That sounds like a plan," said Sean. "I could be onboard with that, too. I've got some network software upgrades to do for a customer in

Albany, but I should be able to wrap that up by Thursday morning. I'll call Mr. Durham's office and have them make the arrangements."

"Cool, we'll do this," said Chris as he pushed the remains of his dish away from him.

Sean had a rather cunning smile on his face as he looked across the table at his friend. "So, did you think we'd ever be back at this kind of thing so soon, especially after hitting the jackpot on our last two ventures?" he asked.

"No, I've got to admit that it never crossed my mind," admitted Chris. "Personally, I think we're both a bit crazy even considering this hunt. It sounds practically hopeless."

"I know," replied Sean. "That's what makes it so much fun."

Chapter Eight

Billionaire Boss
May 5, 2020

Chris was shocked with the rapid efficiency of Mr. Durham's staff. The afternoon after his lunch with Sean, he received an email that outlined the itinerary for the short trip. Airline ticket reservations, hotel rooms, even a rental car booked in their name at the Dallas/Fort Worth International Airport. It was all very quick and very organized. In the back of his mind, Chris wondered how Mr. Durham could have made his reservations without "the details," including information such as his address and Social Security number. He made a conscious decision to avoid thinking about that part, and instead decided to reserve judgement until after they had met later that week.

Chris was halfway through preparing a set of invoices later that afternoon when his phone issued the three-tone chime indicating a text message. He pulled the device from his pocket and looked at the screen, smiling as he did. The text was from Kristi, his girlfriend of the past four years.

Rock_gurl: I heard through the grapevine that you're going on a road trip soon.

chriscarey1986: That's a fact. Leaving on Friday morning.

Rock_gurl: Dallas?

The Dutchman's Gold

chriscarey1986: I see you've been talking to Maggie* again.

Rock_gurl: That's the only way I can get information since you're so secretive.

chriscarey1986: Sorry. Been a little busy this week finishing up the tax extension season for my biggest customers. Want to do dinner tonight?

Rock_gurl: Not sure. Are you certain you can spare the time to take me out?

chriscarey1986: Stop it. Pick you up at seven?

Rock_gurl: Sure.

chriscarey1986: Great. See you then.

Chris smiled to himself as he pressed the button to return his cell phone to standby mode. "Rock_gurl" was the name Kristi used because she was a geologist who had met Chris when she was a graduate student at Cornell. A self-avowed individualist with a will as strong as Chris's, the two had found an immediate attraction to one another and had remained a couple since she graduated from school. She had also used her knowledge of geological formations and interpretation to help Chris and Sean solve some of their most baffling problems.

In addition to working his clients' tax files and getting himself prepared for the one-day excursion to Dallas, Chris logged onto an online book store and did a search on "Lost Dutchman Gold Mine." Not expecting to find much there, he was astonished to see that the online search engine returned almost a million results. Everything from the descriptions of historical searches to modern-day ventures to geological analysis of the Superstition Mountains and the resulting mineral deposits of the area. It was way more than he wanted to see, but he did use the express shipping service to have a topographic map and a couple of the more prominent volumes sent overnight.

---

*Maggie was Sean's girlfriend.

Sean spent his next few days wrapping up business and reading as much as he could on the history of the Lost Dutchman Gold Mine. Although not ordering any books online, he conducted a number of database searches and pulled up all he wanted to read on the history of searches over the past one hundred years. He was fascinated by the stories of the many men who had lost their lives in the rugged Superstition Mountains. It wasn't something he cared to think about, and he hoped that the days of attacks by hostile Indians were a thing of the extremely long-lost past.

On Thursday evening, Chris completed his own packing and took advantage of some spare time to complete a five-mile run. He always enjoyed his time alone on these extended jogs and found that he could think more clearly while striding down the shoulder of a back road.

After returning to his small, A-frame house, he quickly showered and prepared to meet Kristi. Because of their early flight the following day, she had volunteered to drive the ninety minutes to pick him up instead of having him make the trip. Their flight departed at 6:00 AM on Friday, which meant a 3:30 AM alarm. It would have to be an early night, Chris thought to himself. Earlier than he would have liked.

Chris was just pulling on a gray and blue polo shirt when he heard the front door close. He had given Kristi a key to the house long ago, and she always entered without knocking. Looking down from the loft, he observed his attractive partner moving through the living room in front to the kitchen on the right side of the house, where she opened the refrigerator and helped herself to a bottle of water.

"Hey, why don't you help yourself to my refrigerator," he called out in jest. "Better yet, take a beer and maybe some of my food for next week. Go ahead!"

Kristi looked up and smiled, responding to his dry sense of humor. "Don't worry, I'll leave the bottle of Dom Pérignon alone for now." Even in her brief glance, Chris could not help but notice her naturally radiant smile. It seemed to light up the entire room and make everything around her appear brighter. She was wearing a cream-colored one-piece outfit, her long shiny black hair flowing down the middle of her back.

THE DUTCHMAN'S GOLD

"Well, since you've driven all the way up here tonight, I guess I can't complain about a bottle of water. Where do you feel like going tonight anyway?"

"You know, for some reason I'm really in the mood for something like fondue," she replied, flopping herself into one of the couches in the living room. "Have you ever tried that place in the Destiny Center Mall?"

"You mean The Melting Pot?" Chris asked as he skipped down the stairs. "Yes, I had lunch there once, but I've never had their whole four-course dinner spread. You want to try it tonight?"

"Yeah, if you'd be up for it," Kristi replied. I know it's not the cheapest place in town, but I won't see you this weekend anyway, so let's do it."

"I'll only be gone until Saturday," countered Chris, as he leaned forward and gave his girlfriend a kiss.

"I know, but aren't I worth it?"

Chris just rolled his eyes and made a soft whistling sound. "OK, young lady, let's go."

The drive to the massive shopping mall containing the restaurant took about twenty minutes, which they used to discuss Chris and Sean's upcoming meeting with the Texas businessman. Kristi provided a short synopsis of the potential for finding any significant amounts of gold in the Superstition Mountains. It was not a very positive report.

"So you think we're on a wild goose chase here?" asked Chris, his lips turned down at the corners on hearing of the low odds in the search.

"Well, I wouldn't get too discouraged quite yet," Kristi replied, her voice with an uplifting tone. "There are several possibilities. I've been doing some reading on the area, and I've found there were a couple of very successful mines in the Superstition Mountains, so it is possible. And there has been some hydrothermal activity in that region, which is usually required to reduce any gold into a solution that would eventually form your gold-bearing quartz. But I haven't read about many quartz veins in the rock out there, at least not in the references I've reviewed."

"So once again, your assessment is that we're probably on a no-win venture to nowhere," stated Chris gloomily.

50

"I never said that," said Kristi, staying with her original opinion. "I'm just saying that my research doesn't indicate a high probability, even though gold has been found there in the past."

"Thanks."

"Anyway, aren't you getting paid for this trip no matter what? Sean told Maggie that you're both going to make a lot of money whether you find anything or not."

"Yes, that's true," agreed Chris as he turned his Jeep into the parking lot and found a nearby space. "We are getting paid a nice amount even if we don't come up with a single grain of the stuff. But it's much more fun being successful."

The couple both avoided talking about geology as they were seated inside and ordered their meals. The restaurant presented a very intimate setting, with low lights and private booths. Kristi thought it would be nice to enjoy the entire meal without ever returning to the topic of prospecting.

"Wow, everything is so good," said Kristi, trying a few experimental bites of bread and vegetables with the savory fondue. "And it's really kind of fun watching them make it right on our table."

"I know, I enjoyed it when I came here for lunch about a year ago," agreed Chris. "I liked it so much that I tried doing it at home in an old double-boiler pot I took from my mom's kitchen. Except my version didn't come out so well."

"Didn't taste too good?" Kristi asked, feigning innocence.

"No, somehow I managed to burn the thing completely black on the bottom of the pot. I wouldn't have thought it possible, because I had a good amount of water in the outer pot. But somehow I completely toasted the stuff. The cheese on the bottom resembled charcoal, and I never could get it out of the pot. As a matter of fact, since you're the geologist, I can honestly relate it to you by saying that it looked and tasted like anthracite."

Kristi was giggling uncontrollably as she listened to the story. "And how would you know what anthracite tastes like?" she asked through her laughter.

"It tastes exactly like the burned cheese in that pot."

"One of these days I'm going to have to teach you how to cook," she said. "And I *don't* mean fried Spam with onions."

"What's the matter with fried Spam and onions?"

"Forget I ever mentioned it," replied Kristi, rolling her eyes as she coated another chunk of bread in the fondue pot.

They were halfway through their chocolate fondue dessert when Chris returned to the topic of the upcoming trip. "This guy Durham, he seems like the real Texas oil millionaire," he remarked. "I wonder if he wears a ten-gallon hat in his office."

"If you're talking about Mr. L. Thomas Durham, he's actually a billionaire," said Kristi. "I looked him up online, and he's incredibly wealthy. He owns about half of Dallas, and controls most of the rest."

"I wonder why he's even interested in taking such a long-shot risk in finding something as elusive as a gold mine that's been lost for over a hundred years," pondered Chris, talking more to himself than to Kristi. "It seems to me that those are pretty long odds for someone who is used to being on the winning side most of the time."

"If I were to take a guess, I'd say it was for the prestige of being the one who finds it, *if* he is able to pull it off. I mean, just think this through for a minute. If he fails, no one is going to make a big deal out of it because he's probably not telling anyone that he's even searching for the place. And if one of you does end up finding even a small amount of gold, enough to make a profit and announce the discovery of the mine, he gets his picture on the front of *Time Magazine* and wins the free trip to Disneyworld."

"Yeah, that's possible," said Chris, considering the statement. "But it does seem odd that no one has found anything in all these years, considering how many people have been out looking. I mean, with all the clues that have been recorded over the years, you'd think someone would have solved the riddle by now."

"Well, I must say, I am a little worried about you, with everything I've read about the strange deaths and disappearances in those mountains," Kristi said, looking across the table with appealing eyes. She reached over and took his hands in hers and intertwined her fingers with his. "There are lots of stories of people who went searching for that mine over the years who never made it out alive. People have been found shot to death, killed by mountain lions, or just died of reasons unknown. It worries me a lot."

"Oh, it'll be fine," Chris reassured her. "I mean, first of all we don't even know if we're doing this. Remember, we're only going out to talk to this guy Durham to see if we want to join him and see if he wants us."

"I know you're going to accept this offer, honey. I know you, and I know you can't turn this down. Or you *won't* turn this down."

"Time will tell," agreed Chris, shrugging his shoulders as he spoke. "It depends on what he wants us to do and if it fits in with our capabilities. We won't accept any offer if we can't do what he wants."

"I believe you can do anything you set your mind out to accomplish."

"Thank you, baby," Chris said, squeezing her hand back over the table. "That means a lot to me."

* * * * * *

It was 4:15 AM when Sean's Mercedes pulled into the gravel driveway that bordered the right side of Chris's A-frame house. The sky was still completely dark, and the high-pitched songs of the crickets and spring peepers filled the air. Chris had been completely ready the night before, so all he had to do was dress and throw his small leather overnight bag into the back of the sedan.

"You travel pretty light, don't you?" said Sean, commenting on the size of Chris's luggage.

"One night, not a lot to bring along," answered Chris. "One spare pair of underwear and a shirt don't take up much space. But I am wondering how much time we'll spend out there if we do end up joining this project. I hope Durham doesn't expect us to stay out there for the entire two months."

"I don't think that's part of the plan," commented Sean. "We'll find out a lot more this afternoon, but I think he wants us to be doing the research for the team in addition to helping out in the field."

"What happens if we can't find the references to research anyplace but in Arizona?" asked Chris. "It's not like we're going to find original documents on the Lost Dutchman Gold Mine in the library in Albany."

"No, probably not," countered Sean, his mind wandering ahead several steps.

As they drove, Chris used a small pen light to check their travel documents and airline tickets. Spotting one detail he'd overlooked the night before, he muttered a simple "Wow!"

"Wow what?" asked Sean. "Anything wrong?"

"No, nothing's wrong at all. I just see that Mr. Durham booked us on first-class tickets the entire way from Syracuse to Dallas."

"Direct flight?"

"No," replied Chris, a rueful expression on his face. "I doubt there's a direct flight from Syracuse to anywhere. We go through Dulles in D.C., but both legs are first class. Looks like the same on the flights home tomorrow."

"Anything wrong with that?" asked Sean, navigating the car around some darkened curves in the road.

"No, nothing's wrong at all. It's just that I'm not used to flying first class. The tickets cost three times the coach fare I buy for myself."

"Thank you, Mr. Durham!" chimed Sean, appreciative of their boss's apparent free spending style.

"I agree," added Chris. "I think I could get used to working for a billionaire."

Chapter Nine

Everything's Bigger in Texas

May 8, 2020

The 6:00 AM flight from Syracuse to Washington, D.C., was precisely on time, landing at exactly 7:25 AM. Chris slept the entire flight, unlike Sean who was awake and reading up on the Superstition Mountains.

"Wake up, sleepy head," Sean chided his friend. "You slept right through the free booze they passed out to everyone seated in first class."

"Ugh," Chris grunted as he rubbed the sleep from his eyes. "Don't tell me people were really drinking the hard stuff for breakfast."

"No, but the guy across from me did order a mimosa, and the flight attendant didn't even bat an eyelash. He had his drink within a minute."

"Personally, I could go with some caffeine right now," Chris remarked. "Think we have time to find a Starbucks in the terminal?"

"No worries," replied Sean. "We have almost an hour before our connecting flight, and we leave from the same terminal."

The two friends got their coffees, both with extra shots of caffeine poured in for good measure, and then found their way to the next gate.

"Our flight is due to arrive at Dallas–Fort Worth at 10:55 AM," noted Chris as he perused his boarding pass. "Did Mr. Durham's secretary tell you how we're supposed to get from the airport to his office downtown? Do we have a rental car reserved at the airport?"

"I'm not sure what he's got in mind, except that I've been told that they 'got it covered,'" answered Sean.

"They've got it covered," repeated Chris. "And how exactly are we supposed to know what *that* means and how we're supposed to find it?"

"I don't know, but something tells me that we'll know when we see it," said Sean with a smile. "And if our airline reservations are any indication, my guess is that our ground transportation will be long and shiny and come with a driver."

"A limo?" asked Chris incredulously.

"That's my guess," said Sean as he plugged his cell phone into a charging station. "Nothing about our host appears to be second class."

The flight into Dallas–Fort Worth International Airport also went as scheduled, the flight taking about two hours and forty-five minutes from the Capital. The first-class cabin flight attendant came through with sandwiches and yet more rounds of drinks, both alcoholic and soft.

"You know, if we'd wanted to arrive completely inebriated from all the cocktails they've been pouring, it would have been pretty easy," observed Chris.

"Yeah, I'm sure that would have gone over well," agreed Sean, passing up yet another offering.

They both gazed out the window at the size of the airport visible from the right side. Far below they could see planes both taking off and landing. It lived up to its billing as one of the busiest airports in the country.

"Oh my God, this place is enormous," remarked Sean, looking at the endless maze of runways spread out over the terrain. "It looks like a city unto itself."

"You're actually not far off the truth," said Chris, also looking out the small pane at the scene below. "I read that this is the second largest airport in the country by size, and it's bigger than the island of Manhattan. It also has its own zip code, and its own fire and police departments, so try that one on for size!"

"Maybe it's true what they say; everything really is bigger in Texas."

"Let's hope the same is true about the paychecks," added Chris.

The plane pulled up to the gate and the two friends walked out the ramp and into the terminal. They had both brought light carry-ons rather than checked baggage, so they were able to bypass the luggage pick-up carousel and head straight out toward the "Arrivals" area.

"We'll know when we see it," said Chris again, in a slight mocking tone as they walked along the "arriving passengers" area containing the baggage claim belts and the rental car stands.

"And I think I see it," replied Sean in a confident tone as he nodded at an impeccably dressed gentleman in a black chauffeur's outfit. He was holding a neatly printed sign card that simply read, "Riggins/Carey."

"I believe we're the ones you're waiting for," said Sean as he stepped up to the driver.

"Mr. Sean Riggins and Mr. Chris Carey?" he intoned from beneath his black-visored cap.

"That's us," replied Chris, smiling at the Durham employee. The smile was not returned, nor did his expression change in the least. Chris wondered if he was required to maintain his stone-faced appearance or if he was just having a bad day.

"This way, please," signaled the driver as he led the way through the front glass doors and along the pick-up lanes of the taxi area. He then opened the door of a sleek black limousine and motioned them inside. "May I put your bags in the trunk?"

"No need to bother," answered Sean as he climbed into the back seat. "They're small; we can bring them in the back with us."

"As you wish, sir."

Once they got settled in the soft leather rear seat, Sean took a moment and scanned the luxurious interior of the vehicle appreciatively. It looked and smelled new, and had every conceivable feature available to the wealthy individual who could afford such a set of wheels.

"Kind of reminds me of your Jeep," he said, smiling at the thought of Chris's SUV, which was usually half-covered in off-road mud.

"Uh huh," agreed Chris in return. "Or your seventy-five-year-old clunker jalopy."

"It's not a clunker and it's not a jalopy," stated Sean, defending his old Mercedes. "But seriously, this thing is amazing. I know it's also a Mercedes, but I'm not familiar with their line of limousines. Any idea just what model we're riding?"

"If I'm not mistaken, this is a Mercedes Maybach S-600 Pullman, which is their top-of-the-line limo," explained Chris. "I looked inside one at an auto show in the Meadowlands last year, although I don't think it was as amped up as the one we're in. I think it started at about five hundred and fifty thousand dollars per copy, so figure this one is probably a lot more."

"I think I could get used to living this lifestyle," said Sean as the limo pulled out of the airport and onto the express lanes of Route 114, southbound for the city.

Little else was said as the limo glided down the highway en route to the north side of Dallas, where the vehicle turned off the highway and navigated onto McKinney Avenue. The road was busy with commerce and lined with tall, elegantly designed office buildings and chic storefront businesses. Chris randomly wondered how much the average worker must get paid just to park their car in this area. It screamed of affluence.

It was still a few minutes before noon when the chauffer opened the rear door and let the two men out onto the sidewalk in front of a thirty-floor tower with mirrored windows and a creatively peaked roof. The building was unadorned on the outside, with the only name appearing above the entrance: *Southern Corp United*.

"Looks like we've got almost an hour before our appointment with Mr. Durham," observed Sean.

"That's fine with me. I could use some time to decompress from the traveling," replied Chris, noting the presence of a coffee shop directly across the street from the corporate building.

The pair crossed the busy exchange and entered an average-looking coffee brewing café expecting to find an operation similar to those in Syracuse. They were shocked to find that the large front area was only the area used to peruse the electronic menu and place orders. Connected to that area were room after room of chic, artistically decorated dining areas where customers could either sit and converse or conduct business using complimentary tablets and free Wi-Fi service. A variety of wide-screen televisions in each room displayed the latest business and news updates of the hour, while free on-demand viewing stations dialed in to any sporting event in the world.

"Unbelievable," said Sean, shaking his head as he viewed the futuristic scene before him.

"Yeah, this will make it to upstate New York . . . sometime before the start of the next century," agreed Chris.

The two sat down in one of the back rooms and reviewed their thoughts on the initial verbal proposal that Mr. Durham had discussed with Sean, making sure that they were both in agreement on the terms.

"Two months, that's all we're agreeing to give him," noted Chris. "And you're sure that he's OK with that?"

"Of course," said Sean. "That's all he offered to give us. I don't know if he plans on extending us beyond that time, but he never mentioned it to me."

"I probably couldn't do that," said Chris, stirring some half-and-half into his coffee. "I'm putting myself in a hole already by taking this much time off. But I must admit that the timing is pretty good, with the major part of the tax season already behind me."

"You have to admit, the money is good," added Sean. "A quarter of a million split between us, that's over sixty thousand dollars a month for each of us. We're making fifteen thousand dollars per week, plus whatever incentive this guy is giving us if we actually find something worthwhile. And we're getting to spend the time outdoors, out of our offices."

"True, but that's assuming we don't run into any of the problems that killed off some of the prospectors who've looked for the same pot of gold."

"I read some of the same stories about people disappearing back in the Superstitions," said Sean. "My guess is that most of the undesirables who were responsible for those killings are long gone. It's a much more civilized world than it was a hundred years ago."

"I hope so," said Chris. "Kristi told me that if I get killed, she'll never speak to me again."

Chris and Sean entered the lobby of the office building to discover a foyer with a thirty-foot ceiling and adorned with impressive marble sculptures depicting different aspects of American industry. They passed through a security checkpoint where they each received electronic badges to affix to their shirts.

"Mr. Durham's office is on the thirtieth floor," said a uniformed guard at the desk. "Go down to the second bank of elevators and take the one on the right. That's Mr. Durham's private elevator that will take you directly up to his penthouse office."

"Do we need a pass code or special card to get into that elevator?" queried Chris.

"The security cards you're wearing will do that for you. It will also unlock and open any of the doors to areas you're authorized to visit this afternoon. Do you have any other questions?"

"No thanks," replied Chris. "We'll see you on the way out."

The elevator to the top floor ascended with astounding speed, and in no time the two stepped out into an outer office with receptionists and other office personnel. An array of computers, phones, and communications devices filled the desks in the space, which was illuminated by natural sunlight streaming down through a series of angled skylights.

"Good afternoon, Mr. Riggins and Mr. Carey," said an attractive secretary as she approached from behind a desk. "I hope your flight from New York was pleasant." She was dressed in a purple floral-pattern dress, which roughly matched the color theme of several other workers in the large room. Chris wondered whether there was a mandated dress code that specified a color of the day.

"Good guess," replied Sean, looking at his watch. "Although we're probably the only ones arriving for a 1:00 PM meeting with Mr. Durham."

"There's no guessing involved," smiled the receptionist. "I can also tell you your home addresses, your flight number, and the number of your hotel rooms for tonight. It's all coded into the strip on your security badges, which follow you as you move throughout the building."

"Yikes! Sounds a little like 'Big Brother' to me," remarked Sean as he looked down at the card clipped to his shirt pocket.

"Mr. Durham just likes keeping track of details," replied the employee. "Speaking of which, it's about time for your appointment, so I'll walk you back to Mr. Durham's office if you're ready."

Chris and Sean followed the woman through a series of doors that opened automatically as they approached them. They entered a long, walnut-paneled hallway with plush blue carpeting and lined with paintings of various seascapes and woodland scenes. Chris recognized some of the paintings as works of art by Winslow Homer. He didn't need to guess that they were originals, rather than re-creations or prints.

"I believe that Mr. Durham has you scheduled from 1:00 PM until 2:00 PM," said the secretary as they approached a door at the end of the passageway. "After that, one of Mr. Durham's drivers will take you to your hotel room. Do you have any other questions before I leave you?"

"No, nothing I can think of, thanks," replied Sean.

"I'll see you on the way out," she said, holding the door for the two before retracing her steps to the front office.

Chris and Sean entered the outer offices of Durham's spacious roof-top complex. It was far from being austere, although it did not match the extravagance of the building's ground floor lobby. A main reception desk was positioned along the rear wall of the rectangular office, which served as the work space for Mr. Durham's private secretary. To the right were three small cubicles, which were occupied by assistants to the principal administrator. The office was lit by fluorescent lamps and augmented by skylights overhead.

The woman in charge of the office sat behind a name plate that read "Angela Spitalny." She looked up at the two men from behind a pair of pearl-framed glasses. "You're here to see Mr. Durham?"

"That's correct," said Sean.

The aide pushed a button on her headset and spoke through a minia-ture microphone. "The two men from New York are here to see you, sir." She then nodded at the inaudible response in her headset.

Motioning toward a pair of large, wooden double doors in the back of the office, she added, "You can head in whenever you're ready. Mr. Durham is waiting for you."

Sean led the way, pulling open the weighty door and stepping inside Durham's inner sanctum, followed by Chris. They both caught their breath and did involuntary double takes as they quickly scanned the enormous office, which looked more like a corporate headquarters setting for a major sports team or merchandising company. The space was at least fifty feet by seventy-five, with one entire wall lined with huge glass win-dows overlooking the city of Dallas. The desk was centered near the back of the room with the large leather chair facing away from the windows. To the left side of the room was a long, elegant mahogany conference table with twenty upholstered wooden chairs that matched the color and grain of the table.

Another area of the office contained a pair of comfortable beige-colored couches that were positioned in an "L" shape around a thick glass table. The other side of the office held a series of long glass display cases with numerous shelves and bright internal lighting. The cabinets were at least eight feet tall and loaded from top to bottom with various pieces of memorabilia from Durham's life, from early days to current. A wooden railing wrapped around an internal stairway that led to a higher floor, although both Sean and Chris knew that the only level above them was the roof.

Behind the desk sat Mr. Thomas Durham, who rose to greet the two visitors. At a later time, Chris would describe the moment in a comical manner by saying, "He began to stand up, and he kept on standing up. And just when we thought he'd stood up all the way, he stood up some more." Although in his mid-sixties and "on the decline," as he described himself, Durham still stood a full six feet six inches tall. The businessman was dressed in dark charcoal slacks and a Texas-style shirt with embroidered shoulders. A Western bolo tie with a patterned silver inset with turquoise stones hung from around his neck. He was a very imposing figure as he emerged from behind his desk and took his first strides toward the couple.

"Well, by Gawd, you must be Sean and Chris from New York," he called out, his voice booming inside the office like a bullhorn turned up to full volume. "I can't say what a pleasure it is to meet you! Come on over and have a seat so we can get acquainted."

Chris, at six foot two, was not used to meeting people who stood a full head taller than him, and he was even more surprised when he shook his hand. Durham had hands the size of a professional basketball player, and his fingers seemed to extend past Chris's wrist and halfway up his arm.

"I'm Tom Durham, but all my friends just call me 'Tex.'"

"It's a pleasure to meet you too," offered Sean, who was likewise impressed by the man's sheer size. "And in case you didn't know, I'm Sean and this is Chris."

"Of course I know," bellowed the business magnate, flashing a wide smile at the two. "First of all, you're wearing badges! But more important than that, I've read all about your adventures and discoveries over the past few years. Which, in case you didn't know it, is why I contacted you in the first place."

"I'm impressed that you've taken an interest in our little adventures halfway across the country," said Chris, who felt a little embarrassed at the effusive compliments.

"I'd hardly call them 'little adventures,'" countered Durham as he directed the two toward the couches in the back corner of the office. "Finding a treasure of gold bullion that's been lost since the Revolutionary War and then discovering the existence *and* the location of three thousand silver dollars that weren't ever supposed to exist? I'd say that puts you into the category of 'wizards.'"

"Thank you," murmured Sean, also overcome by the billionaire's praise. "I heard that you bought one of those 1804 dollars," said Sean.

"That's true, I picked one up at auction not more than six months ago," confirmed Durham, looking across the office at the chain of display cases. "Before you leave here this afternoon, take a look inside that case on the right side, one of the top shelves. It's in there on display, along with a couple of ancient Roman coins I found on a dig over in northern Italy. It looks pretty good if I must say so myself."

"You've got a coin on display in an unlocked cabinet that you paid over a million dollars for?" gasped Sean. "Aren't you afraid it will get stolen by someone when you're not here?"

"Oh, it's locked. It's also alarmed," noted Durham. "Anyway, my director of security has hired half the guards in the state of Texas to keep an eye on things around here, so I don't have much to worry about."

"So Sean tells me that you want us to help you try to find the legendary Lost Dutchman Gold Mine," said Chris, trying to move the conversation onto the topic of their trip. "Is that true?"

"Yes, some parts of that are certainly true," replied Durham, gazing back at the two men. He had an intense stare that seemed to penetrate right through anyone he engaged in conversation.

"I'm starting a search that will take advantage of some previously unknown information. I already have two teams hired and ready to start Monday of next week. These are hard-core prize-hunters who are chomping at the bit to get started. They've got strong backs and a nose for anyplace outdoors with mountains. But they're lacking in one skill that you two have in spades."

"And that is . . ." prompted Chris.

"The ability to do the research and use their brains to solve the riddles and pull the pieces of a puzzle together. What the two of you did to discover the hiding place in that blast furnace up in the Adirondack Mountains," said Durham, shaking his head in amazement. "It was just amazing. Just incredible intuition and dogged persistence. *That's* what I want you to bring to my team. Smarts, brains, persistence, and the ability to solve problems."

As the billionaire spoke, he banged the table with his clenched first for emphasis. Although using very little of his available force, the entire tabletop vibrated halfway off its mirrored silver base.

"We'll do our best," promised Sean. "But could you provide a little more detail about what you'd like us to do?"

"I'd be glad to," said Durham. "The other two teams both have three men, and we're starting them out on opposite sides of what I call the 'Prime Search Area.' We have about eight primary targets we want to see first, just based on topography and descriptions of prior searches. Then, each of those primary targets has several 'items of interest' to investigate. But first we're going to systematically run transect lines over the more promising ground until we cover all of the ledges and formations that could possibly hold the entrance to what once was Jacob Waltz's gold mine."

"I'm curious, and I just have to ask you," began Chris, "this mine has attracted treasure hunters since the last decade of the 1800s. Since then, thousands of people have searched the mountains of the Superstitions, some using very modern methods and equipment. What makes you think we're going to be able to find something that none of those others could find?"

The Texas businessman smiled back and adjusted his necktie as he began to speak. "Let's just say that we've come across that new source of information, as I was telling you, that will set us up like no one's ever been set up before. Plus, we'll have three search teams out there *and* your bloodhound research efforts. I've also engaged a couple of hired hands whose sole job will be to bring water and supplies to the crews in the field, which will reduce or eliminate the need to constantly return to town for provisions."

"In other words, we won't stop until we find this mine," stated Durham, his face turning into a mask of granite. "I'm not used to losing. Ever. And I'm not about to start now. I know we can do this if we look hard and we look smart."

"And our part is the looking smart?" asked Sean.

"That's what I'll be paying you for: a combination of field work and research, which can be done wherever you feel would be most productive. There is a great library and museum right nearby the trails leading into the Superstition Mountains, in a place called Apache Junction. I don't know what you'll find that hasn't been found before, but you two seem to have a knack for getting to the bottom of things."

"So it's OK if we conduct our research in other locations that may not be in the area around the Superstition Mountains, or even in the state of Arizona?" asked Chris, confirming what Sean had initially stated in their first discussion on the topic.

"I want you to do your detective work wherever you think it would best serve to help us find the mine, whether it's in Arizona, New York, or Timbuktu. From everything I've read about your methods, they've led to astounding results and I don't want to get in the way of that kind of performance."

"And the term of this agreement will be for two months' work?" asked Sean.

"That's right. It will be two hundred and fifty thousand dollars for two months of work from the time you accept the offer and report to the search area. That will be your base pay. I'll also throw in an incentive for you two if you make the discovery that uncovers the Lost Dutchman Gold Mine."

"And that is . . ." prompted Chris, looking for the bottom line.

THE DUTCHMAN'S GOLD

"Two percent of anything that exceeds five million dollars in bullion," replied the businessman. "You know I have to make something for myself to fund this little job," he added.

"Of course," Chris agreed.

"You can divide the money however you care to split it; makes no difference to me. And as far as the percent of your time spent onsite versus away, I'll leave that up to you, but I'd prefer that you spend at least fifty to seventy-five percent of your time in the field. If you need more time chasing down clues to refine our search, we can allow that as well, but please keep Max informed."

"Max?" repeated Chris, hearing the name for the first time.

"Maxwell Kinney. He's the person who is overseeing the overall team of the eight of you," replied Durham. "The group is comprised of Team One, which is Shane, Jake, and Hoss. Team Two has Max, Big Jim, and Carter. Then there's you boys. I've also got the two men I've hired to resupply you in the field, although they alternate trips in and don't both work the same days. They're also not part of the search team—they just carry in the food and water."

"This all sounds really interesting," said Sean, "but Chris and I were talking earlier and we both agreed we wanted time to consider the offer before saying yes or no. Is that OK with you, and when do you need a definite answer?"

"That's fine with me," said the businessman, looking back and forth between the two men. "Today is Friday, and I'll give you until Tuesday of next week to say yes or no. If you decide to join us, I'd like to have you fly out to Phoenix by one week from today. That'll give you a chance to get yourselves outfitted for the mountains and acclimated to the weather. I'll expect you to be on the job for an orientation meeting by the following Monday. Those are my terms."

"Do you have a contract ready for us to take back and sign?" asked Sean, used to a formal agreement with his clients.

"Son, around these parts we conduct business face-to-face, and cement our agreements with a handshake. I've given you my conditions, and they're not going to change whether we put it in writing or not. Are you OK with that?" Durham's face had returned to the stone-cold expression that Sean and Chris had seen earlier in their conversation.

"Yes, sir, I'm fine with that," replied Chris. "We both know you're a man of your word, and we like the offer."

Durham stood up, the smile returning to his face. "Tex, Tex, I told you already! And I do hope you decide to join us, because I like your ability to make big discoveries that everyone else misses."

Mr. Durham then looked at his watch again and exclaimed, "My Gawd, our time has gone by so quickly! We have more to discuss, but I'm due on the other side of town in less than ten minutes. So I've arranged for Max to come to town to give you boys an orientation of sorts." Then, as he hustled across the office and onto the flight of stairs leading upward, he gave his final parting message.

"Anyway, Max should be here in about fifteen minutes. Feel free to look around until he gets here. I'll expect to hear from you between now and next Tuesday."

Even as Durham was speaking his last words, Chris and Sean could detect a low, bass thumping noise that started out low and quickly grew in volume. *Thump, thump, thump, thump* as the clamor seemed to pass directly overhead and settle on the rooftop.

"Helicopter," said Sean, looking up through the skylight.

"Yup," agreed Chris. "Taxicab of the wealthy. How else could you get across town from your office in midday traffic in less than ten minutes?"

As Durham disappeared up the carpeted stairs to the rooftop launch pad, the front door to the office opened and the aide who had walked them to his office reappeared.

"Hello again," she called out to the pair, who were still standing by the couches. "I just got a call from Max, the onsite project manager who will give you more on the search operations. His flight from Phoenix came in a little late, but he should still be here in about twenty minutes."

"No worries," replied Chris. "Mr. Durham told us we could look around at his trophy cases, and there appears to be a lot to see."

"Oh my God, yes," smiled the secretary, following Chris's nod across the room at the heavily laden glass shelves. "I suppose you'll be able to find memorabilia and other goodies all the way back to when he was hatched."

"Thanks," said Chris. "It will help to know a little more about our employer if we do accept his offer, Ms. . . . ." Chris left the ending of his sentence hanging so that the aide could fill in the blank with her name.

"Just call me Annie. We don't operate on formalities around here."

"Annie it is," answered Chris. "We'll be here whenever Max arrives."

"Great. And if you need anything before then, you can either come back down the hall to our outer office or press the blue button next to Mr. Durham's phone." She then disappeared from sight and closed the door behind her.

Chris looked at Sean and motioned across the room at the backlit cabinets. "Care to do a little light reading?"

"Age before beauty," quipped Sean, gesturing for his friend to lead the way across the huge office.

The two approached the vast display of photographs, articles, trophies, sports items, and other artifacts as one would advance on a museum exhibit. The cases seemed to display huge segments of the billionaire's world, from high school and college varsity sports to business ventures to various hobbies, pursuits, and archaeological excavations. It was all there, neatly labeled and arranged as a testament to his storied life.

Sean started at one end of the displays and took note of Durham's previous gold prospecting adventures. He had evidently taken a team into the area around Coloma, California, on the American River in the Sierra Nevadas, panning some of the goldfields that had started the Gold Rush in the late 1840s. Among the exhibits behind the glass were a much-dented antique gold pan and a vial containing a significant accumulation of gold dust.

"I wonder if this is how Mr. Durham made some of his early money," wondered Sean.

"That wouldn't do it," replied Chris, looking at the vial from the other side of the cases. "That probably took weeks to pan out of a creek, and wouldn't pay for much more than one person's provisions."

"Spoilsport," said Sean, moving on to the next objects of interest.

Meanwhile, Chris was scanning item after item in the cases on the left side of the collection, moving casually between the shelves until his

EVERYTHING'S BIGGER IN TEXAS

eye caught something of interest. His trained eye focused on an enlarged photograph of a high school football team, with about forty to fifty boys in uniform arranged in two rows in front of a goal post. The photo was labeled "Ryan High School, Championship Team of 2003." The bottom margin of the photograph was labeled with the names of the players in small black font. It was propped up in back by an old and slightly deflated football that had been autographed with a wide black marker.

Chris remained silent, but Sean could tell from his subtle change of expression that he'd found something worthy of investigating.

"Whatcha got?" Sean called out, curious about the find.

"Oh, probably nothing," answered Chris, who had extracted his cell phone from his pocket and was zooming in for a photograph. "But you know me, I'm always curious." He then snapped several photos of the picture before moving on to the next frame.

"There's some nice stuff over here," announced Sean, who was examining a couple of chunky gold nuggets in back of another photograph. He also admired some old silver jewelry and a pair of leather moccasins that looked to be of Native American origin. "I bet he could tell you exactly where everything came from," he guessed.

Chris stopped once again and silently examined a photograph, his face squinting as he peered deeply into the case. He paused to take another close-up photo with his cell phone before backing off and returning to the shot of the football team. He repeated this systematic scrutiny several times as he compared the two pictures.

"Well, that's kind of curious," he murmured, more to himself than to Sean. "Quite curious."

"What's curious?" asked Sean, still on the other side of the displays.

"I'll let you know later," said Chris as he returned to his shelf scanning.

"Oh, sure," said Sean with mocked indignity. "I wouldn't keep any secrets from you."

Chris was about to reply, but his comment was interrupted by the office door opening once again. This time it was a man who entered: large, tall, and "Texas" in appearance and stature. He looked at the two men in his boss's office before immediately launching into an introduction.

"Well, howdy, y'all," came the exaggerated drawl from the big man bearing down on them. "My name's Max Kinney, and you must be Sean and Chris, although I couldn't guess who is who."

For the second time in a half hour, Chris had to reach up to an enormous hand to exchange greetings. "That's right, Max. I'm Chris, and my partner here is Sean."

"Well, I'm damn glad to meet y'all. Mr. Durham said we'd probably all be working together by the middle of next week." Max's hand closed on Chris's like a vise grip, and Chris could feel his bones and ligaments being compressed as they shook hands. He involuntarily massaged his sore fingers while he conversed with the large Texan.

"That's a good possibility," he said. "But I just have to ask a question. Are all you guys from Texas over six foot four?"

Max got a good laugh out of the question and had to dab the corners of his eyes before responding.

"Well, now, that's a funny one, but y'know I gotta admit, the guys on this team are pretty beefy, so you'd better get used to it," he replied.

"Bigger than you and Mr. Durham?" asked Sean incredulously.

"You gotta be kidding," answered Max, his eyes staring in disbelief. "Why, I'm just about the baby in this group."

"They're all bigger than you?" Sean asked again.

"Now that's something we really need to talk about," replied Max, seemingly worried about the outcome of the conversation. "Yes, they're all very big men; some friendlier than others."

"Give us the lowdown," requested Chris. "It sounds like there's one or two folks on the team that we might want to avoid."

"I wouldn't use the word 'avoid,' but you wouldn't want to cross 'em either," began the leader. "First you've got my group, which is me, Carter, and Big Jim."

"Big Jim," repeated Sean to Chris. "Sounds kind of like 'Bubba' on steroids."

"Big Jim is about six foot seven, and he's not a bad feller. Likes reading and playing his harmonica, but he can handle himself in a fight. He's a pretty good shot with a pistol too, and he can also move more dirt with a shovel than anyone I've ever seen."

"And Carter?" asked Sean.

"Carter can go either way, too. Sometimes he's quiet, and you don't know what he's thinkin'. But other times he's about the loudest cuss around, and he'll get you into a fight before y'know what hit ye. But he's another good worker who has a knack for knowing the shortest route between any two points, which helps a lot out in them mountains. Oh, and he's also an amateur rodeo champion. He can ride out some of the meanest bulls I've ever seen mounted."

"How about your other search crew?" asked Chris.

"Now that's where you can get yourself into some hot water," replied Max. "That'd be Shane, Jake, and Hoss. They was made for each other."

Rather than say anything to correct the Texan's barroom grammar, Chris felt his own desire to start slinging the rustic lingo back and forth with the modern-day rustler.

"Rough bunch, are they?"

"Well, Shane's actually OK. He's a little hard-headed, but buy him a beer and he'll be fine with you. But the other two . . ."

"Jake and Hoss?" continued Chris.

"Yeah, the two of them kind of feeds off one another," said Max. "Jake is the leader of that trio, and they're all good men. They're good at their jobs, and they usually find what they're lookin' for, one way or another. But you've really gotta watch yourself around Jake. Both him and Hoss are fighters, but Jake has a bit of a mean streak in him, and Hoss usually follows him."

"Also big guys, huh?" asked Sean.

"Uh huh. You'll be impressed when you see Hoss. He's not quite as much a fighter as Jake, but he's about as big as they come. You'll know him when you see him."

"As long as we can all work together, we'll be fine with everyone," said Sean.

Max had a solemn expression on his face as he looked down at his shoes." "I'd recommend taking it kind of slow with them guys," he said, looking up with a frown. "I've heard Jake talking about Mr. Durham hiring the two of you, and he keeps callin' you 'college boys' and 'Yankee creampuffs.' Just take it slow with them and give them all the help you can, at least until they get used to you."

Chris turned to Sean and gave him an alarmed look. "Well, I guess that puts my mind at ease."

"I'm just tryin' to tell you the way it is," explained Max. "They're good at what they're doing, but it's a rough group."

"Thanks for the heads-up," said Chris, smiling while he patted Max's shoulder with gratitude.

"Is there anything else we should know, before we head back home tomorrow?" asked Sean.

"As a matter of fact, there's a couple of things we gotta talk about," Max said. "The first two is about gettin' you boys outfitted with what you'll be needin' in the mountains, assuming you're joinin' us. That's guns and a pair of horses."

Chris shot Sean a quick expression of amusement before replying. "Guns and horses?"

"That's right. You wouldn't be going into them hills without either one, not that I'd recommend. You ain't got a problem with that, do ye?"

"Well, both of us have fired weapons," replied Sean, "but hardly on a regular basis. "What kind of firearm are we talking about?"

"You could probably ask Mr. Durham for just about anything you wanted," said Max, "but he's got a supply closet with a bunch of Glock 19s that he gives out to most the folks who don't already have their own piece with them."

"Glock 19, I've never fired one," commented Chris.

"It's a good, reliable piece," said Max. "It's fairly compact and light-weight with a ten-round magazine, so you can carry everything you'd ever need in one place. It uses nine-millimeter shells and has good stopping power. It's a nice handgun; I think you'll like it."

"It's almost irrelevant," said Chris, looking at the date on his wrist-watch. "Even if we do accept Mr. Durham's offer and start work in the next week or two, it will still take us up to seventy-five days to get our pistol permits in the state of Arizona. So we wouldn't be legal to carry yet anyway."

"Texas."

"Huh?" asked Chris. "We're not talking about Texas. We'd need permits for the state of Arizona, which is where we'll be working. And Arizona's law says seventy-five days."

"Now you boys don't worry about the small stuff like that, OK?" smiled Max, looking back and forth between the two. "Mr. Durham's staff is pretty good on taking care of details, and you can trust me when I say that he's already got you covered."

"But we haven't even signed anything or even filled out any paperwork!" gasped Chris in disbelief.

"Or asked for any personal references or taken any tests or anything," added Sean.

"Are you boys done yet?" asked Max, clearly amused at the two men's objections. "When I tell you that you don't have to worry about it, ye don't have to worry about it. You'll be wearing a fully loaded holster when you hit the field in a couple weeks. An' as far as having an Arizona permit, you'll be gettin' one from Texas instead, which is respected in Arizona as well."

"Must be nice to have connections," muttered Chris, shaking his head.

"Now, let's talk about puttin' you on a set of legs that can take you where you need to go," continued Max. "Mr. Durham works with a dealer who can have a pair of reliable horses or just about anything else at the trailhead whenever you're ready to go. The two of you have any special requests? Quarter horses? Appaloosas? Or maybe a mule or donkey?"

Chris just smiled back before speaking, not wanting to pretend that he possessed even the most rudimentary riding skills.

"To tell you the truth, the only kind of horse I'm comfortable riding is one that's got a pole through the middle from top to bottom, and goes around in a circle with music playing in the background."

"That good, huh?" asked Max.

"Actually, we're both what you'd called novices," admitted Sean.

"Or pedestrians," added Chris.

"Is there any reason why the two of us can't just go on our own two feet?" asked Sean. "We both hike a lot, and can carry some pretty serious packs and tents. Seems like we should be able to cover almost as much distance without the animals."

"I think you're wrong there, boys," countered Max, his expression returning to a stern countenance. "But if you wanted to give it a try, I'd support you. At least until you'd shown that you weren't keeping up. After that, Mr. Durham would probably insist that you upgrade to 'hoof power.'"

"I suppose we could give it a try for a week or two," conceded Sean, "assuming that the horses are tolerant of riders without much experience."

"Fair enough," agreed Max. "Either that or you could walk but maybe have one mule along to carry your water and supplies. It sure would make things easier on you."

Chris and Sean looked at one another before agreeing on the concept of the pack mule.

"That might work pretty well," said Chris, making the comment for both of them. "We'll take along one mule to carry all our supplies and gear, as long as it can tote its own water and grub."

"I'll make the arrangements," said Max, "as soon as I hear from the boss that you're joining the team."

"You'll know as soon as we know," replied Sean, shaking hands with Max one more time.

"Which should be by early next week," added Chris.

"If the answer is yes, I'll be seein' the two of you at Mr. Durham's office in Phoenix," said Max. "He's hoping you'll be out there, and I know he wants to introduce you to the other boys on the team before you get started in the field. He also wants to make some area assignments too, just so we're not all steppin' on one another's toes."

"Sounds like a good idea," said Chris before moving on to one other topic of conversation.

"By the way, Sean and I were just looking at all the photos and things here in Mr. Durham's trophy cabinets. Do you know if he was involved in any of the earlier searches in the Superstition Mountains? It looks like some of the photos were taken in that area."

"I can't say for sure," replied Max as he began retreating toward the door. "But I think I heard that he was related to some of the earlier prospectors who roamed the territory in the early days. You might want to ask him about that next time you see him."

"Maybe," agreed Chris, who also shook Max's hand again in parting.

EVERYTHING'S BIGGER IN TEXAS

* * * * * *

It was Saturday afternoon by the time their Syracuse-bound flight lifted off from Dallas International, en route for a quick layover in Chicago. The two friends had already discussed the proposal for hours, including all the legends and curses of the historic gold mine and the quirks of their potential coworkers. The generous financial compensation provided them with additional incentive to consider the offer.

After continuing the conversation for the first twenty minutes of the flight, they decided to postpone making a final decision until discussing the matter further with their families back home. That being resolved, they focused their attention on the bottle of Ron Zacapa rum, which sat in the middle of the flight attendant's serving tray. Their seats were once again situated in the first-class section, and they didn't want to sleep through yet another flight without sampling the complimentary goods.

"Here's to Tex Durham and his first-class seating," declared Chris as he raised his complimentary drink to toast the Texas tycoon.

"Actually, I think I know why he buys all first-class seats," said Sean.

"Why's that?" asked Chris.

"All of his people are too big to fly in coach," replied Sean.

"And from what Max said, none of them like us," lamented Chris.

Sean returned his gaze to the clouds outside the window. "I hate when that happens."

CHAPTER TEN

Final Buy-in

May 10, 2020

IT WAS ALMOST NOON ON SUNDAY BY THE TIME CHRIS STEERED HIS Jeep through the slate stone entry posts of the hilltop driveway outside of Utica, New York. He pulled his vehicle alongside the two-car garage rather than park in back of the other cars, vans, and SUVs that were already stationed on the old pavement. He recognized all of the vehicles present as belonging to friends or members of his extended family.

Hopping from the Jeep, Chris strode up the walkway and then bounded up the front steps to the old mansion belonging to his parents. Although his father, Christopher Sr., maintained a separate residence to run his law firm in Washington, D.C., he had found his way back for the weekend party. His mother, Theresa, was in the kitchen with Chris Sr. when Chris came through from the entranceway.

"Hey, honey, nice of you to join us!" said his mother in a sarcastic tone. "Staying for lunch?"

"Hi, Mom; hi, Dad," he chirped back as he kissed his mom on the cheek. "I'm only about ten minutes late, so 'excuuuuuse meeeee!'" he said, performing his best Steve Martin impersonation.

Chris Sr. shook his hand and offered to provide some answers to a text his son had sent him earlier. "We can talk later, once you've said hello to your entourage," he said. "In the meantime, Sean is out back getting the grill started. And I think your young lady friend is receiving the full attention of your grandfather, so you might want to go rescue her sometime soon."

Chris smiled at the thought of his grandfather, Denny, cornering Kristi and talking her ear off. He decided to proceed through to the back gardens posthaste, where he saw his silver-haired grandfather sitting in his wheelchair being tended by Emma, his private caregiver of many years. He was actively engaged in conversation with Kristi, who was smiling back at the elderly Carey as he spoke. Chris approached from the side and put his arm around Kristi's shoulders.

"Hello there, young man," said the ninety-six-year-old patriarch. "It's a good thing you showed up. I was about to steal your girl from you."

"Ha. I bet you would, too!" said Chris, returning the humor. "How are you doing, Gramps?"

"I'm doing fine, thanks for asking. And if you don't think I'd do it, you'd better think again!"

Chris gave his girlfriend a light squeeze and a kiss. "Am I missing something here?" he asked her jokingly. "Are you and Grandpa moving in together?"

"I don't think Emma here would allow that," said Denny, looking up at the elderly aide who accompanied him everywhere. Although she was still a hired assistant, she had lived in the house with him for over fifteen years and was considered part of the family by the entire Carey clan.

Kristi nodded over at an office file folder sitting on a nearby table. "I did some research yesterday and brought you some material to browse. I don't think it's anything you haven't seen already, but it might make for interesting reading if you can't sleep."

"Thanks, honey," he said as he watched Sean breaking open packages of hot dogs and hamburgers for the grill.

"I didn't know we'd hired a chef for this event," said Chris, greeting his friend.

"I don't work cheap," said Sean, arranging the meats on the grill. "Your mom promised me a couple dozen of her famous chocolate chip cookies for pulling the grill duties today."

"Step aside, buddy. I got this," Chris replied as he picked up the bar-b-que utensils from the side of the grill. "But I do want to hear what you've been thinking overnight, and maybe we can compare notes on what to tell Durham."

"Well, I think the offer is fine, assuming that we can both really spare the time away to put in two full months of following a wild goose chase."

"Same," replied Sean, as he continued to place another row of hamburgers on the grill. "I have only one client that I'll need to deal with after we're gone, and I think I can hire a friend to install a new network security package for me. So I'm thinking of asking Mr. Durham if he'd be willing to pay for the assistance in addition to the money he's already offered."

"I've got the same concerns with two or three clients who need some business tax extensions," said Chris. "I think I could wrap up all three in about six business days, so I'll make the same request for the additional funds. I doubt he'd have a problem with that."

"Sounds like between the two of us, we're probably talking only three or four thousand dollars added to the bottom line," figured Sean. "Considering that he looked us up and asked us to work for him, that's pretty small potatoes."

"The rest of the deal sounds like fun," said Chris. "Although I'd like to know what's really going on behind the scenes with Mr. Durham. He seems to be just a little too efficient in getting things done. Including getting us pistol permits in less than a week."

"That is a bit odd, but guys like that are usually pretty well connected," added Chris Sr., who had walked up behind the pair to join in the conversation. Kristi had followed along behind the father, so the foursome could discuss the potential deal.

"Do you know anything about this Durham guy, Dad?" asked Chris. "Is he on the up and up, or has he been involved in anything really shady that we should know about?"

The Washington lawyer got a good laugh out of the question. "Well, first of all, you should know that *no one* starts with next to nothing and becomes a billionaire without at least some hocus pocus," he said. "In Thomas Durham's case, he's used some strong-arm tactics to gain control over a number of profitable oil wells that were owned and operated by competing firms. He's also used his influence with a number of ranking Texas politicians to gain mineral rights to sizable tracts of land that had already been claimed by national oil companies. Somehow, he's always come out on top."

"Smart businessman?" ventured Sean.

"Strong-armed businessman," replied Chris Sr. "And smart. But don't get in his way, because he will find a way to take you out."

"Have you been able to find out anything since I called you last night?" Chris asked Kristi, who had been listening attentively.

"Nothing much more than what I already told you," she said, shaking her head for emphasis. "The prospect of finding gold in the Superstition Mountains seems like a long shot, given the geography of the area. But on the plus side, some nice veins have been discovered, and a few mines with significant placer gold have yielded surprising paydays."

"If the Lost Dutchman Gold Mine ever did exist, it sounds exactly like one of those concentrations," Chris noted. "But I'd be amazed if it's anything more than a myth, given all the amateur prospectors who have searched for it every year and failed to turn up a thing."

"That's just the thing," Kristi agreed. "There are so many stories of buried treasure in those mountains, all of which have been recorded multiple times, and they all seem to contradict each other on every level. By now, it would seem impossible to figure out the truth even if it was buried in the volumes of folklore on the topic."

"But the fact remains, you're still getting paid three thousand dollars a day, regardless if you find a thing," said Chris's father. "That's not bad for a hired hand, and you really have nothing to lose for walking in circles around Weaver's Needle for a couple months."

"Except possibly their lives," countered Kristi. "I assume you've read the tales of all the treasure hunters who have turned up missing or dead since 1890," she said while directing her gaze at the senior Carey.

"Yes, honey, and I share the same concerns as you. He is my son, you know," said Chris Sr. "But the days of the rogue Native American tribe are long gone. Plus, there will be two other groups working together with the two boys. I think the risk of human intervention is pretty small."

"How about crazy old territorial men panning for gold and not wanting anyone near their little patch of ground?" Kristi asked. "Some of those renegades can be pretty trigger-happy. I've read about unprovoked shootings for little more than unintentional encroachment; someone got a little too close and they shot before asking questions."

"I think we're OK with that risk," said Chris, taking his girlfriend's hand. "We should know if someone else is in the area, and we're really not 'prospecting' per se. We're just looking for signs of an old mine. Once we find something that looks really promising, we can turn around and then come back later with the whole cavalry."

"I agree," said Sean, who had been leafing through the maps in Kristi's folder. "I think I've heard all I need to hear. I vote that we go for it."

"I think my vote makes it unanimous," agreed Chris. "I can't see anything that would drive me away from playing, at least for a couple months."

"Do I get a vote?" asked Kristi.

"My guess is it wouldn't be a 'yes,'" ventured Chris Senior.

"I can't help it," replied Kristi, a frown creasing her face. "There just seem to be so many risks and almost no chance of finding anything."

"Two months, that's all," promised Chris as he kissed her on the forehead. "And you can come out as often as you want. Heck, we'll be back several times ourselves doing research, so it won't even seem that long."

"We have until Tuesday to call Durham with our answer, but I think we should be ready to give him a shout tomorrow," suggested Sean.

"Nothing like diving in headfirst," said Chris Sr.

"To tell you the truth, I would have expected nothing else," added Kristi, "even if I don't agree with the decision. I think you're both nuts."

"Yeah, that pretty much sums it up," said Chris.

"And you know what?" asked Chris Sr. "I honestly believe that if anyone on this planet could walk into that mountain inferno and come out with gold from the Lost Dutchman Gold Mine, it would be you. You've already shown that you can put the pieces of the puzzle together and solve the riddle when no one else can. This would simply be a continuation of the trend."

"Thanks, Dad," said Chris. "I appreciate the confidence, but we have no assurance that it even exists."

"No one ever thought that the 1804 silver dollars existed, but you found them," said his father, referring to the crate of coins that his son had tracked down in the ghost town of Adirondac.

"Pure luck," said Chris.

"Now that's the biggest crock of bull I've ever heard," said Chris Sr. "Maybe once, I'd believe it. But finding *two* landmark American treasures, no. That is *not* an accident."

"Let's just hope that lightning can strike three times in a row," said Sean.

The two friends then concluded their conversation with a fist bump. The decision had been made.

CHAPTER ELEVEN

Getting Started
May 11, 2020

BOTH CHRIS AND SEAN WERE AMAZED AT THE SPEED AND SIMPLICITY of their call with Tex Durham the following day. The call went through a single secretary before being transferred into the billionaire's office, who showed no interest in haggling or negotiating down their requests for business expenses.

"I'm glad to hear you're both interested in joining us, and we can't wait to get you down here and on the job," his voice boomed over the phone. "Don't you worry about hiring people to keep your offices going. Just give me an itemized invoice of your expenses and I'll see that it's covered."

"That's very generous of you, Mr. Durham," said Chris, talking through the speakerphone on his desk. Sean, who was sitting by his side, nodded his concurrence. "It's actually more than we'd asked for, but it certainly will help out with our businesses at home."

"I believe in getting the best people I can get and then keeping them happy," said Durham. "The way I look at it is this: if you want top-grade oats, they're kind of expensive. But if you're willing to settle for the ones that have been passed through the horse already, well, they come a little bit cheaper."

"I hope you're not comparing us to a pile of horse manure," said Sean, chuckling at the analogy.

"No, and you're not going to get me to dive into that rabbit hole," replied Durham. "As a matter of fact, I think we've pretty much wrapped

GETTING STARTED

up the details here. My secretary sent you an email with all the notes about your trip down here tomorrow. Your flight info, hotel, and everything should have been in there. I assume you both got that?"

"We did," confirmed Chris. "We're good to go as far as I can see."

"I agree," added Sean. "We're all in."

"Good. Then I'll see you in Phoenix next Monday," said Durham. "You'll get to meet the other members of Teams 1 and 2, and we'll get you outfitted with everything you need to go out into the field. We'll also have a guide ready to lead you out into your area on Tuesday just to show you the lay of the land. By Wednesday morning, you'll be on your own."

"Roger that," said Chris, acknowledging the instructions. "We'll see you on Monday."

The phone conference ended on an up note as the two friends bid their new employer farewell. They then parted ways to pack and make final arrangements for their excursion.

Team 3 was about to become operational.

* * * * * *

The flight touched down in Phoenix at 4:35 PM on Sunday afternoon. Although it was still late in May, the temperature on the thermometer outside the airport read 97 degrees.

"Hardly the same as northern New York, is it?" asked Sean.

"Just wait until July," replied Chris as he released the brake on the luggage carrier that held his and Sean's baggage. "It often hits 108 degrees Fahrenheit, although it doesn't feel it because the humidity is so low."

"Lovely," quipped Sean. "I know that makes me feel a lot better."

The two walked along the airport concourse with their baggage cart until they located the driver hired by Mr. Durham to shuttle them to their hotel. Similar to the driver in Dallas, this individual was dressed in a dark blue chauffeur's uniform and held up a sign with the two men's names neatly printed in large black letters. The driver loaded their bags into the trunk of the limo and then began the drive into downtown Phoenix.

Unlike the previous week, they covered the distance from the Phoenix airport to the downtown hotel in less than fifteen minutes. The luxury

83

hotel was located off West Van Buren Street, in the vicinity of a number of modern office buildings. The two checked into their hotel rooms and then quickly turned around to find some good food and drink in Phoenix's prime downtown restaurant scene.

Deciding to take advantage of possibly their last night of genuine civilization for a while, they walked to the Blue Hound Kitchen, where they settled into a comfortable table and reviewed the trendsetting menu. They decided to split the artisan meat and cheese board appetizer, which featured various spiced dried meats and sausages, pickled vegetables, apple butter, and noble bread. For the main course, Sean selected the trout with golden raisins, capers, green beans, and brown butter, while Chris ordered the flat iron steak with roasted potatoes, watercress, and garlic cherry glaze.

"You know, I could get accustomed to this lifestyle pretty easily," said Sean, sampling his first mouthful of trout.

"Don't get too used to it," advised Chris. "By the end of next week you'll probably think that Marine Corps MREs* qualify as gourmet food."

"Don't make fun," protested Sean as he looked over the contents of Chris's plate. "You're the one who's got the watercress in his entrée."

"OK, point taken," agreed Chris. "I've got to admit, I've never had the stuff and I don't have a clue what it is. But actually, it doesn't taste half bad."

"You're not going vegan on me, are you?"

"Surely you jest," replied Chris. "I'm the one who always wants part of a dead cow, bird, or fish on my plate."

After the meal, the two headed back to their rooms in order to get an early start in the morning. Their meeting was scheduled for 9:00 AM, although they both benefitted from picking up two extra hours with the change in time zones.

* * * * * *

Unlike the corporate office building owned by Tex Durham in Dallas, the billionaire had simply rented office space in a modern building located near the hotel in downtown Phoenix. Chris and Sean arrived fifteen

---

*MRE is an acronym for Meals Ready-to-Eat.

GETTING STARTED

minutes early for the meeting and were provided with security badges at the guard post in the main floor lobby.

A line on the corporate directory read *Southern Corp United—12th floor.* The two men took the elevator to the appropriate level, which opened into a posh lobby with thick red carpeting and dark wood furniture. A secretary sitting at a desk greeted the two and motioned them through a door in the right corner of the office.

"You two can just go on in," she said in a friendly Southern drawl. "Mr. Durham is back there with the rest of the boys, and you can get coffee inside as well."

Chris nodded at the woman behind the desk, adding a friendly "Thank you, ma'am," as he went by. The two then proceeded single-file into the conference room.

As Chris passed through the doors, his face immediately took on a stunned appearance. Sean's did the same a moment later. The presence of so many huge men in one place and time was shocking. All Chris could think about was the time he walked past an NBA basketball team at the Newark airport. The visual effect was the same.

Tex was already on his way to the entranceway to say hello.

"Well, hello, boys. I hope you had a nice flight out here yesterday," he greeted them in a commanding voice.

"Yes, sir, we did," replied Sean, the first to shake hands with the tall businessman.

"Well, that's just great. We're all glad to have you join us, so welcome to the team. Let's go ahead and make some introductions here."

As he spoke, the other mammoth-sized men gathered around the end of the room to meet the two. Chris, at six foot two, was not used to looking up to an entire assemblage, while Sean (at five foot ten) was left staring up at men standing over a full head taller than himself.

"These three gentlemen here are part of Team 1," began Tex as he gestured to the individuals. "You've already met Max, so that leaves Carter and Big Jim."

They all lived up to their billing, as "Big Jim" measured in at six feet seven inches tall, while Carter stood just two inches shorter at six five. Max himself split the difference at six foot six.

85

"Now these characters standing in back are Team 2," Tex intoned, calling the other group forward. Shane, at six foot six, was perhaps the least-hostile looking of the group. Jake, at six foot seven, looked like he was ready to take on an entire bar of brawlers by himself. Finally, there was Hoss, at six foot ten, who looked more complacent but was intimidating in his sheer size and width. Both Chris and Sean, standing side by side, wouldn't have matched the big man's shoulder width. He seemed to single-handedly block out the sun that streamed through the conference room windows.

Chris and Sean shook hands with each of the men during the introduction, offering a polite "nice to meet you" to each. Carter and Jim both responded to the salutations while Shane and Jake said absolutely nothing. Chris noticed that Jake wouldn't even make eye contact with either of them. Hoss merely nodded while shaking hands, his huge paw wrapped entirely around Chris's hand. It was as though they had planned an intentional show of force through a combination of size, body language, and complete lack of verbal communication. *Not a good start*, thought Chris to himself.

The nine men took seats around the large wooden conference table according to their team affiliation. Max stood at the back of the room, his hand palming a remote that controlled a portable projector. Shane, Jake, and Hoss sat in the three seats to Tex's left, while Carter and Jim sat to Sean's left. Chris and Sean were closest to the projection screen at the front of the room.

Without any additional conversation, Max turned on the projection system, which cast an image of Weaver's Needle* onto the white screen. The rest of the men looked on impassively, including Mr. Durham, who scrolled through some emails on his cell phone.

"I'm sure this looks familiar to those of us who have been in the field this past week," began Max. "It will serve as our reference point for almost everything we do for these next few months."

"Goddamn ugly chunk of rock," spat Jake with distaste. "I hate the damned thing already."

---

*Geographic prominence in the Superstition Mountains that is commonly believed to be within sight of the Lost Dutchman Gold Mine.

Max ignored the comment and proceeded with his presentation. His next slide displayed a zoomed-in topographic map of the area around Weaver's Needle, including topographic lines of altitude, trails, and water sources. It also included an overlay with labeled sectors correlating to each of the teams' search areas.

"This map shows the starting assignments for each of the three teams," he continued. "Jake, you know where you're going. You're going to continue the routes along the southwest and western canyon walls, including everything up to height of ground and beyond if you see anything promising."

"Yeah, we got it," said Jake, his face registering a mixture of boredom and disdain.

"My team has the section west and north of Jake's; roughly from nine o'clock to twelve o'clock of the circular canyon surrounding the Needle," Max stated. Max's teammates, Carter and Jim, both nodded as they looked at the map on the screen. "We've already covered about ten percent of our sector and noted a couple spots that need to be revisited."

Chris had counted on listening more than talking, but he had to ask the question. "Just out of curiosity, it seems as though all this ground has been combed over pretty carefully by other hunters over the years. Do you have anything that indicates there ever was a source of gold in this specific area?"

Max nodded his head as though he'd anticipated the question and was ready with the response.

"First of all, yes, we do believe the story of Jacob Waltz's final testament on the gold mine. We are accepting that as a given."

"Why?" asked Chris, ending his query with an abrupt silence.

"That's a question I'm not about to answer for you right now," said Tex, interrupting from the back of the room. "Let's just say that we have an inside source on this one, and we're going to play it for all it's worth."

Chris's raised eyebrows indicated his surprise at the response, but he remained silent as the presentation continued.

"Chris and Sean, you are Team 3, and your search area will start with the southeastern walls around the Needle, and will then work your way north to meet our team," explained Max.

THE DUTCHMAN'S GOLD

"Why is their search area so much smaller than everyone else's?" asked Shane, pointing to the confined area of the Team 3 box on the map.

"First of all, there's only two of them. Our other two teams have three people each," replied Max. "Also, these two are going to be spending a lot of time in the libraries finding more clues that should make our searches easier. Research."

"Bullshit," said Jake, his face again registering open disdain for the new teammates. "If we're sharing any gold we find in equal shares, we should be working in equal shares."

"It isn't bullshit," said Tex in a stern tone. "If you knew about their track record, you wouldn't even consider saying that. But that's not why we're here, so just drop it. OK?"

Jake looked the other way, still muttering under his breath, but said nothing further for the group to hear. Meanwhile, Max returned to the presentation.

"Chris, you asked about the search area, and the fact that it's already been picked over by others," said Max. "But we have some new ideas based on some special imaging techniques that focus on the earth's movement in this area following the earthquake of 1887."

Max flashed a new slide on the screen showing the seismic activity in and around the local region both during and following the powerful quake. "We believe that our imaging techniques can pinpoint at least twenty-four to thirty locations where mining activity had taken place that have been shaken or covered by rock and debris. We're hoping that one of those locations translates to the location of the original mine."

The next slide showed the areas of interest highlighted in yellow shading and outlined in gold.

"Some of these areas have been prospected inside the past forty years, and a few even have claims filed on them."

"What happens if we find a significant vein of gold in one of the areas covered under an existing claim?" asked Sean.

"Then we go in at night and grab everything we can get before the next sunrise," snickered Jake. Shane and Hoss laughed along with the comment, obviously agreeing with the strategy to steal whatever they could get without being caught.

GETTING STARTED

"Seriously," repeated Chris, "what do we do if we locate a really good vein on someone else's claim?"

"We'll be giving you a satellite phone to take on the trail with you," said Tex, stepping into the middle of the conversation once again. "You just use that to give us a call, and we'll take care of it for you."

More laughter erupted from around the table.

The next hour was used to further describe the survey lines between the search sectors, discuss search techniques, and establish communications between the groups for routine and emergency situations. Members of Tex's staff who had served in the military forces devised a simple code that would permit the three teams to communicate without disclosing their locations and findings. Each of the many search areas was numbered, and patterns of letters and numbers were assigned to represent actions, movement, meetings, and other activity. Each group received laminated pages that served as translation guides for the coded phrases.

By early afternoon, Sean and Chris had everything they needed to start their orientation tour into their search areas. The conference room had cleared with the exception of Tex, Max, and the two of them. Max provided them with some last-minute instructions on where to meet their first-day guide the following morning. He also instructed them on the identity of their "supply guy," a Mexican fellow named Alejandro.

"You can just call him 'Alex,'" said Max. "He'll actually answer to almost anything, as long as you leave him a couple bucks' tip."

"How will he know where to find us?" asked Chris.

"Don't worry, he'll find you," replied Max. "He knows the territory like the back of this hand. He knows where almost everything is out there."

"Except the gold mine?" quipped Chris.

"Yeah, except the gold mine," agreed Max. "Anyway, I've got to catch up to my men. We're going to head back into the hills tonight. Remember, you've got a satellite phone, so call me if you need anything."

Once Max departed, Tex turned back toward Chris and Sean and motioned for them to once again have a seat at the conference table.

"So, what did you boys think?" asked the billionaire once they had settled back into their seats.

Chris and Sean exchanged glances before answering.

89

"I hope it went well, although I think we both have a couple concerns," said Chris, voicing his concerns. "First of all, I get the distinct impression that Jake and Shane don't care for us one bit."

Tex leaned back in his chair and laughed for a minute before responding.

"Jake doesn't like anyone who isn't from Texas and doesn't ride a horse, so don't worry too much about that."

"I guess I could understand that," said Chris gloomily. "Still, I'd rather get along with everyone on the team."

"You'll get along with everyone if you can come up with the keys to the riddle to solve this thing," said Tex. "You have to understand, you two are different from the other guys, and I'm paying you for a different kind of work. I want you out in the field the last three days of this week, but then I want you to start hunting the references next week. You can start with the museum library in Apache Junction and then expand out from there. Whatever it takes. And if Jake and those dudes are jealous that you're not out in the heat, then that's just too damned bad."

"OK, we'll do as you ask, and just sort of step around Jake and Shane, if that's what it takes."

"Don't worry about Shane," said Tex. "He's actually a really good kid. He's just got to warm up to you. But he does tend to follow Jake's lead, and Jake can be a bit ornery. You've got to watch out for him sometimes."

"Thanks for the warning," said Chris.

"There is one other thing I wanted to bring up with you," said Tex. The tone of his voice changed, indicating that he wasn't as comfortable with the new topic of discussion.

"You asked about what to do if you found gold on someone else's claim. Or if you find something that may be less 'available,' for whatever the reason." He then paused to look for a reaction from the two friends.

"Yes?" asked Sean, which was followed by an awkward moment of silence.

"Well, I've learned a few things in my life that have helped me to get where I am today. One of those things is this: if you wait long enough to get permission, or to ask if someone else objects, there is *always* someone willing to get in your way. So I've learned to not ask. If you find something, it's yours. Don't ask permission. And if anyone tries stopping you or gets in your way, you've got a lot of help out there in the other two teams. Call them anytime you can't handle something on your own. Do you understand me?"

"Yes, sir, we do," replied Chris.

"Good, then I think we're all set," said Tex. "I'll just leave you with some material here to help you get started tomorrow." As he spoke, he slid a yellow envelope across the table. It contained a rental car reservation and instructions on where to meet their guide the following day.

"Thanks. We'll keep you posted on when we're out of the search area doing research, OK?" asked Chris.

"I'm due back in Dallas tonight," answered Tex. "Just keep Max informed on everything. He briefs me every day, so I'll get the details from him."

The three parted after shaking hands, after which Tex boarded his limo for the ride to his private jet at the airport. Chris and Sean were left alone in the conference room, where they sat in silence for a moment before speaking.

"Still glad we signed up for this rodeo?" asked Sean, looking at Chris with a wistful smile.

"Yeah, I think so," replied Chris. "Except I think it's going to be tougher to pull the rabbit out of the hat on this one. How about you?"

"There's only one thing I know for sure," confessed Sean. "And that is, after meeting this bunch, I've never felt so short in my entire life."

Chapter Twelve

Sammy

May 19, 2020

The drive to the parking lot of the Peralta Canyon Trail was hot, even at 8:00 AM. The oversized tires on the SUV kicked up clouds of dust from the dirt road, which turned the air hazy in the rear view mirror. The thermometer on the dashboard instrument panel read 90 degrees.

Sean and Chris arrived at the lot and instantly spotted their contact. The guide was sitting in a large black Ford pickup truck with a trailer in tow that was designed for transporting horses. They approached the truck and stepped up to the driver's-side window.

"Alejandro?" asked Sean, looking up at the dark-complexioned man beneath the San Diego Padres ball cap.

"At your service," the guide replied as he turned off his engine and opened the truck door.

"Mr. Durham said you're giving us the grand tour this morning."

"He's the boss man," replied Alex, smiling back at the two. "He's the man who signs the checks, so whatever he says, goes."

"I think he just wants you to take us in to see the area on the southwest side of Weaver's Needle," said Chris. "We're not staying in there tonight, but he wants us to know how to get there and back out again."

"No problem," said Alex as he stepped in back of the towed trailer. "But first, I want to introduce you to someone."

"I think I know who this is . . ." said Sean, allowing his words to taper off as Alex opened the latch on the trailer and pulled a ramp out from beneath the bed of the vehicle.

The guide led an animal down the steel ramp and over to the two men, who watched in fascination. It looked like a smaller version of a donkey, standing little more than four feet tall at the withers, with a grayish-colored coat speckled with white throughout.

"This is going to be our companion, huh," said Chris, extending a hand to the animal's muzzle.

"Guys, meet Sammy," said Alex, leading the animal over to the two men. It followed peacefully as the guide held onto a worn leather halter.

"Hey, Sammy," said Sean, stepping closer to say hello. "Sammy the donkey! You going to carry our supplies for us, Sammy?"

"No, no no," said Alex, holding up his hand to object. "Sammy is not a donkey or a mule. He's a burro."

"What's the difference?" asked Sean.

"A burro isn't much different than a donkey, but usually smaller," explained Alex. "Sammy here is a little bigger than most, because his withers are a little over four feet up, which is kind of unusual. But he's been raised right, with good nutrition and good care. And he's a good boy, aren't you?"

As he spoke, he put his face in front of the burro's nose, and the animal responded by nuzzling the side of his face against the Mexican's cheek.

"Gee, he acts just like a big dog," observed Chris.

"He's a real gentle animal," replied Alex, continuing the affection. "But I wouldn't try to get too cozy with him too fast. He and I have worked together for almost three years now, so we're pretty close and he knows what to expect from me. But burros can get a bit upset if you try to force them to do something they don't want to do."

Alex then showed the two men how to take care of the animal, how to give it food and water, where to let it roam, and how to load it with their gear.

"Sammy here weighs almost four hundred pounds, so you don't want to make him carry more than about one hundred pounds, including his own food and water," explained Alex.

Chris quickly performed some mental math on their load of cargo.

"The way I see it, if water weighs in at about eight and a third pounds per gallon, Sammy here can carry about six gallons of water and still tote another fifty pounds of gear and food," he said.

"That sounds about right," said Alex. "And there are a few spots where Sammy can drink from some pools that are usually filled, at least for the next several weeks. You should be OK for a couple days at a time, even if you don't get resupplied back there."

The three men were able to hit the trail within the hour, with Alex leading the way and explaining items of interest about the Superstition Mountains at each turn in the trail. Chris and Sean were impressed by the way that Sammy followed along passively without being led by the tether. The trail, which had started out relatively flat, began to climb at a steeper grade as they made their way up the Peralta Canyon Trail.

As they drew closer to Fremont Saddle,* the trail grew steeper and more rocky, and both Sean and Chris asked to stop for a water break.

"That's good, boys, you've got to get used to doing that more," remarked Alex. He too was taking some large swigs from a canteen while he also filled a small metal bowl for the burro. "It can get so hot out here, but the humidity is so low that you'll never notice it. People can get dehydrated in this sun without even feeling it. So keep drinking whenever you stop."

Sammy backed up the guide's words by noisily draining the entire bowl of water that had been placed on the ground. It didn't take long.

As they stood there enjoying the view for a spell, Sean made a comment about the presence of the tall, spear-like Saguaro cacti. Sometimes it appeared with side arms, and other times it just boasted a single, missile-like spear. The huge cacti dominated the rest of the vegetation like emperors of the desert.

"They're so common around here that most people think they grow all over," explained Alex. "But really, they only grow in these parts of the Southwest. We're lucky to have them."

---

*Fremont Saddle is the pass through which the Peralta Canyon Trail passes to reach Weaver's Needle. The view from the top of the Saddle provides excellent views in either direction.

SAMMY

The three men, accompanied by the burro, continued their trek up over the Saddle, where they gained their first sight of Weaver's Needle. It was an awe-inspiring sight that took their breath away.

"Just think, this is exactly the same thing that Jacob Waltz would have seen in the 1800s as he made his way to his mine," observed Sean.

"Yes, but he might have also seen a few things that he didn't want to see," added Alex.

"Like what?"

"Like maybe a couple dozen Indians and a few hundred arrows being shot at him from all angles," said Alex. "No thanks, I'm glad we're here now instead of a hundred years ago. I don't want no arrows flying at me, thank you."

Having crested the Saddle, they began their descent into the ravine that encircled the massive Needle, which jutted hundreds of feet into the air above the canyon floor. At this point, they parted ways with the trail and began cutting across rougher ground en route to their search area. Alex led the way and seemed familiar with the best routes to avoid the steep ledges and impassable rock.

"How worried should we be about rattlesnakes in this area?" asked Sean, peering at the rocky terrain that lay in their path.

"Not too worried," replied Alex with a toothy grin. "We only lose one or two people a month to the rattlesnakes around here."

Sean stopped dead in his tracks and fixed the guide with a serious stare. "Really?"

Alex bent forward in laughter, amused with his own humor. "No, no, I'm kidding you, my friend. You do need to look out, but I've never known anyone who's actually been bitten. They will get out of your way if you let them. They'll only bite if they feel cornered and have no way to get out."

"That's good to know," said Sean. "I've heard stories of rattlers coming after people."

"Why would a snake do that?" asked Alex, returning to a serious expression. "They know you're too big for them to eat, and if they waste their venom on you, they know they won't be able to eat for another two or three days."

95

"That makes sense."

"Just don't do anything stupid," said the guide. "Look where you step, keep your ears open for their rattle, and don't place your hands between any rocks without looking carefully first. You'll be fine."

The next hour was spent losing altitude as they dropped into the lower reaches of the canyon, which was surrounded by the outer walls on one side and Weaver's Needle on the other. Alex continued to shepherd the group ahead toward their destination while he simultaneously navigated up and down the walls in order to check out some promising formations. This restricted their progress somewhat, but it also served to show the two men what to look for in their search.

At one point, Alex stopped and kicked at some soil with the toe of his boot. "Do you see this wash that looks like a dried stream going down this way?" he asked in his accented voice. "If I was panning for gold and I had a source of water, I'd try right here."

"What makes you think there's anything here?" asked Chris.

Alex didn't say much, but just placed his index finger to his nose and tapped it a few times.

"Alex knows," he replied. "Alex lived here a long time, and he knows when he sees a place where there's gold in the dirt. I'd pan here."

It was almost 2:00 PM by the time Alex had walked the two men through the outer reaches of their search quadrant, and the group decided to take a short break before starting the trek back. He reached into one of the bags on Sammy's back and retrieved both the water bowl as well as a feed bag, which immediately attracted the burro's attention. He then extracted another sack from one of the pack bags and offered brown bags to both Chris and Sean.

"Tuna or turkey?" he asked, his arm extended with the meals.

As they ate, Sean remarked that "this food tastes good, but it's turning into cement in my mouth."[*]

---

[*]This actually happened to the author when completing this same hike with a registered guide, despite drinking ten canteens of water during the course of the morning.

"That's because you haven't been drinking enough water," advised Alex. "I told you before, you've got to drink more than you think you need or you're going to get in trouble back here."

The three continued to down their lunches while Alex pulled yet another case out of the saddle bag.

"I assume you know what this is," he said as he opened a small black case and grabbed a device that looked like a modified cell phone.

"Yes, that's an Iridium satellite phone," said Chris. "I have a similar model back in our hotel room."

"This one will be yours," said Alex. "You can save your personal phone and use this one while you're out here. Your regular cell phone will be worthless to you down here behind these canyon walls."

Alex then tapped in a series of numbers and listened to the phone ringing on the other end of the line. After three rings, Max's voice came through loud and clear on the other end.

"Hey, Boss, it's me. Just testing the phone," said Alex.

"You're coming in loud and clear over here," replied Max.

"Good. I'm giving this one to these two boys over here," said Alex. "We're about to clear out of here and head back to the parking lot."

"Great," said Max. "Are they ready for their start tomorrow?"

"I think so," answered Alex, with Chris nodding his approval at the question.

"That's good, too," Max intoned over the phone. "You let them know that their side arms are waiting back in Chris's room for them, locked inside his room safe. I set the combination to his birthday."

Chris leaned over and spoke into the phone mouthpiece. "Thanks, Max. I should be able to remember that."

"Well, no worries," replied the Texan. "Just make sure you don't shoot anything that don't need being shot."

"Thanks."

"Oh, and by the way, I also left you something that you probably didn't bring with you," added Max.

"What's that?" asked Chris.

"A snake bite kit."

Sean's eyes opened wide as he turned to the guide and asked in a surprised voice, "I thought you said no one ever gets bitten by rattlesnakes out here," he said in a shaky voice.

"Eh, there's a first for everything," answered Alex, his hands upturned in appeal. "Maybe they think boys from New York taste better."

CHAPTER THIRTEEN

Threading the Needle
May 20, 2020

CHRIS AND SEAN HAD ALREADY DECIDED THAT THEY WOULD SPEND the rest of the week in the field getting used to their search area. Their package of information from the Monday briefing contained a series of maps with close-in views of "areas of interest" that had been flagged by either former searches or satellite imagery following earth movements in previous tremors. Close-in views, coupled with topographic line overlays, afforded them a well-defined series of locations to start their first explorations.

They had arranged to meet Alex in the parking lot at 8:00 AM on Wednesday morning. He would pass along their supplies that would last for their first three days in the mountains. He had also agreed to help them load the burro for the first time, and to ensure they had all the provisions needed to keep them safe in the wilderness.

What did feel out of place for the two men was the presence of the Glock 19 pistols, which were packed away in a corner of their respective backpacks.

"One of you might want to consider putting that in a holster on your hip," suggested Alex, as he watched the two leave the weapons in their packs.

"We might do that once we get inside the area," replied Chris, not really bothering to check whether the guide believed him. He knew that neither he nor Sean had bothered loading any of the 9mm shells into the weapon, neither believing there was a need to carry a piece in the first place.

"I'll meet you here at 5:00 PM on Friday," said Alex, confirming the pickup time when he would take custody of the pack burro.

"We'll be here," answered Chris, extending his hand to shake with Alex. "And I also want to say, on behalf of both of us, thanks for the tour yesterday and all the support you've given us. It's really gotten us off on the right foot."

"My pleasure," said Alex, bowing slightly at the compliment. "And remember, if you two need anything, or get yourselves into a hole, use your satellite phone to call me. And remember to drink enough water every day, and to take care of Sammy. He'll be depending on you to take care of him."

"Of course," said Sean, his hand scratching the back of the animal's neck. "He's already part of our team. We'll look after him just fine."

The pair said their farewells to the guide and began the trek into their area. They both wore light packs that weighed in around fifteen to twenty pounds in order to keep the load on the burro down to one hundred pounds. It was a very workable arrangement, and each of the two carried a pair of canteens so they wouldn't have to unpack the animal more than once on the way up to Fremont Saddle. They were both surprised at Sammy's surefootedness as he plodded ahead over the uneven rocky ground.

Once they were about two hundred yards up the trail, Chris turned his head toward Sean with an expression that combined both concern and amusement.

"I think next week, we should get a start on some research focusing on some non-gold-related matters," he said.

"Well, that sounds mysterious as all hell," replied Sean. "Mind telling me what you've got in mind?"

"Sure. Most of it has to do with some of the souvenirs I saw in Tex Durham's office," he said. "Some of the photographs he had in there just didn't add up and got my mind thinking about our own boss. I'd just like to check out some of my suspicions before we go too far on this."

Sean stopped in his tracks and looked at his friend. "I noticed you took some pictures on your cell phone back in Dallas. What was it that you saw back there?"

"I'm not one hundred percent sure," Chris said thoughtfully. "But I have a sneaking suspicion that not everyone on this extended search party is who they say they are."

"Now you're getting even more cryptic."

Chris took his personal cell phone out of his pocket and tapped the screen a couple times; then he scrolled through the screen with his recent photographs. When he found the one he wanted, he enlarged it and passed the phone to Sean.

"This is a photograph of a championship football team from a place called Ryan High School. It's in a city called Denton, Texas, which is about forty miles northwest of Dallas," explained Chris.

"OK, what am I looking for?" asked Sean as he took the phone.

"Take a good look at the guys in the photo and then compare them to the names written on the bottom. You'll probably have to zoom in a bit, but it'll hit you when you see it."

Sean used his thumb and index finger to enlarge the photo on the screen and then began panning from left to right across the top row of faces. He worked his way down the rows, and then viewed the names on the bottom, which had been written in black ink on the white border of the photo. His examination lasted several minutes, and Sammy began grazing on a patch of grassy vegetation by the side of the trail.

After a few minutes of examining the images and the corresponding names on the lower margin, Sean looked back up at Chris with an expression of admiration.

"Top row, fifth boy from the right?"

"Yup, you got it," confirmed Chris.

"Yeah, except you saw it on the first pass, back in Durham's office. I never would have noticed that during a casual stroll past all those cabinets," confessed Sean.

"Look at that kid's face and then compare it to Tex Durham's face. They're almost one and the same," remarked Chris. "Then, if you look at him standing next to the other players in the back row, my guess is that he's probably around six foot five or six foot six, the same as Tex."

"Considering that his name is listed as Shane Durham, my guess is that he's Tex's son," ventured Sean.

"I'd bet money that he is as well," agreed Chris. "There's another photo in the same display case that isn't labeled, but shows the entire Durham family at a graduation ceremony sometime in 2005. He's definitely the same person, so I'm sure he is Tex's son. But what I don't understand is why Tex wouldn't have mentioned the relationship when he introduced us in Phoenix on Monday."

"Well, if you recall, he did stand up for him and call him a 'good kid' when we were talking about the group members," recalled Sean.

"I guess there's nothing illegal about hiring your son to work on a gold hunt," mused Chris. "But still, I can't help but shake the thought that there's something that doesn't add up there. Nothing we can do about it right now, but we'll check it out when we get into the libraries next week."

* * * * * *

The two men made good time walking up to the height of land that was Fremont Saddle and down into the canyon beyond. The sun was beating down from an almost cloudless sky, and the temperatures were climbing into the low 90s. They had already agreed on a strategy of letting the burro drink its fill whenever they came upon a source of ground water, in order to preserve their own supplies.

"The way I see it, we shouldn't need Alex to come out very often, if at all," said Chris. "Maybe we'll go through more water a month from now, but Sammy here can drink his fill a couple times a day from pools that are still filling the gullies."

"Who is the second man, anyway?" asked Sean.

"Second man?" repeated Chris. "What are you talking about?"

"Mr. Durham told us that there would be two men resupplying all the teams in the field. So if Alex is one, who is the other?"

"Alex's son," replied Chris. "That would be Alex II."

"Sounds like the name of some foreign king," chuckled Sean.

By 1:30 PM, the men were on station and looking at the series of annotated maps. They decided to work in a counterclockwise pattern, searching from low-to-high on the various slopes of the terrain. Sometimes they found that some of the search targets were located in areas that were inaccessible without technical climbing gear.

"I know that some of the clues left behind said that the mine was on a ledge, high above the base ground," remarked Sean. "But Waltz was not a young man, and he didn't sound like much of a climber. Why are we being asked to check out spots that would require an above-average climber to reach? It doesn't make sense to me."

"Same here," replied Chris. "Unless he arrived there by descending from the other side of the canyon wall."

"That's right," said Sean, out of breath from ascending to yet another pit on the hillside. "From what I read, they're still not sure whether the mine was located on the inner side of the canyon around the Needle or the outside."

"What's the difference?" asked Chris. "If there is anything to be found, almost every account points to the other side of the circle, where the other two teams are looking."

"Gee, what a coincidence, huh?" muttered Sean.

Following the end of the day, which they decided would be 5:00 PM, the two men found a conveniently flat patch of ground with few rocks and decided to set up camp for the night. Their tent was set up quickly and they commenced preparations for their dehydrated meals. Sean then set out in search of combustible material to start a fire for later in the evening.

Within a short period of time, he returned with a hefty armload of long, straight pieces of wood. "Saguaro ribs," he announced, letting them fall heavily to the ground.

"Now there's something we don't have in the Adirondacks, huh?" remarked Chris, looking at the stack of smooth wood. "I hope it'll burn."

The two were able to use the dried-out cactus ribs to get a decent blaze going, which they then used to heat their water for dinner.

The Dutchman's Gold

"Looks like we have a choice between beef stew, chicken with rice, or chili con carne," noted Chris as he pulled the dehydrated packages out of the saddle bag.

"Yum! I know that sets my taste buds on fire," quipped Sean.

"And to think, we have the same choices every night this week."

"I can't wait until Friday," sighed Sean.

The two consumed their meals as they sat on the edge of a boulder near the fire. Meanwhile, Sammy had finished the bag of grain and water bowl set out for him, and had started rummaging for edible plants around the outside of the campsite. He seemed quite content in his grazing so the two men left him to browse at will.

"Just what exactly did you have in mind for next week?" asked Sean as he soaked up some of the stew with a biscuit.

"I thought the best place to start would be at the Lost Dutchman Gold Mine Museum right here in Apache Junction," said Chris. "It's got quite a collection of old artifacts and documents that were originally owned or written by the early prospectors. It's also got a lot of material that's been donated to the museum that hasn't been fully cataloged, so we'll be able to get a glimpse of some items that may provide unknown clues."

"Do you really think that's true?" asked Sean, his face creased in doubt.

"Not for a second," smiled Chris. "I'm just trying to maintain an optimistic outlook."

As the two lay back on the rock outcropping, the colors of the sunset darkened overhead and the flames of the fire retreated into the ring of rocks constructed by the pair, leaving only a bed of glowing embers. They were amazed by the vast array of stars that appeared overhead, seemingly endless in the open void of the Arizona sky.

"You know, if the entire day was as beautiful and relaxing as this," noted Sean, "I wouldn't mind spending our entire two months out here."

"That's OK," said Chris. "I think I can smell myself already, and we've barely begun to work. Give me a hot shower and a cold beer anytime."

The following two days were carbon copies of their first day on the job. They found themselves constantly referring to their maps and the handheld GPS device from Sean's backpack and then trudging up and down the rocky slopes as they checked out site after site. In some of the locations noted on their maps, they came across promising signs of previous activity, some more modern than others. Items discovered included old cans, a length of rusted chain, and in one spot an old pair of boots, abandoned after wearing completely through the toes. Some of the litter was obviously from later eras. Sean uncovered a plastic bowl from a single-serving cereal package.

"I wonder if Jacob Waltz had Pop-Tarts out here, too," Sean joked as he moved the disposable dish aside.

"As a matter of fact, he did," returned Chris. "He heated them up in his microwave."

"He wouldn't need a microwave," grumbled Sean. "It's so hot out here that he'd just have to leave the damned things on a flat rock for about five minutes."

"And just think, it's still only late May. Just wait until July if you want to see some serious heat."

"Thank God we'll be done by then," said Sean. "I have no desire to be anywhere outside when it's 108 degrees."

It was almost noon on Friday when Sean and Chris came upon a spot high on the canyon wall containing a vein of light-colored quartz material. The mineral deposit looked strangely out of place with the surrounding red rock, and they both kneeled down to make a closer inspection for flecks of gold. There were none that they could see. Still, they decided to check in with Max to see if he wanted them to retrieve a sample for assaying.

The screen on the satellite phone lit up as Chris punched in the numbers for the foreman's line. He answered on the second ring.

"Kinney," came the short, terse response on the other end of the line.

"Max, hey, it's Chris here on the side of this giant soup bowl. How are things going?"

"They're going OK. We haven't found much, but we've covered a lot of ground for the time we've spent here. You got anything?"

"I don't think so, but I did want to ask you about a vein of nice quartz we found on the southern rim down here. It doesn't appear to have any trace of gold in the ore, but I wanted to find out if we're bringing out samples to test."

THE DUTCHMAN'S GOLD

"If you can't see anything in there, not even a flake, it's probably not worth the effort," replied Max. "But you can toss a couple chips into your bag just in case. And make sure you make a note on the map where you found the stuff."

"Will do," replied Chris. "And one more thing. I think we're going to spend the first couple days of next week in the local museum libraries, just trying to see if we can pick up on anything that the other hunters and researchers might have missed."

"Sounds like a plan," said Max. "I'll pass that along to Tex tonight. Just keep us updated on anything you find, and also keep your regular cell phone up and handy in case we need to reach you in town for anything."

"Understood. Thanks, and we'll talk to you next week," said Chris as he signed out.

The trek back to the parking lot took them until almost 5:00 PM. There, they recognized the animal trailer belonging to their trusty guide. Only this time it was accompanied by a much younger version of the man they'd met earlier in the week.

"Hey, Sammy old boy," greeted the young fellow as he approached the two. "You ready to come home for the weekend?"

Chris and Sean both introduced themselves to Alex's son, who was the spitting image of his father.

"And you must be Alex," said Chris as he extended his arm to shake hands.

"No, Alex is my old man. I'm just Al," he grinned.

"Ah, I see," replied Chris. "My dad and I both share the same name as well, but I still just go by Chris."

"Actually, I'll go by anything as long as it isn't 'Junior.'"

"Ha! I can't blame you there," exclaimed Chris. "OK, I'll never call you 'Junior.'"

"How did Sammy do for you this week?" asked Al. "My dad said you didn't ride horses and you'd never worked with a burro before."

"He was just great," said Chris. "He carried everything we gave him and he never seemed to mind going anywhere, whether on the trail or off. Will we get the same animal next time we go into the area?"

"You want him back again?" asked Al.

"Yes, by all means," replied Chris, stroking the burro's forehead. "We got along famously. I think he likes us, too." The burro gave a sudden bray, as if signaling his approval.

"Well, then, I think that seals it," chuckled Al. "I'll make sure my dad knows to bring him for you next time you go in."

The trio shook hands on the arrangement, and then Chris and Sean piled their belongings into the rented SUV for the drive to the hotel. Less than an hour later, they arrived at their lodging, ready to enjoy a comfortable room bathed in air-conditioned comfort. Little did they realize just how uncomfortable that room was about to become.

CHAPTER FOURTEEN

Wrong Kind of Bug
May 22, 2020

THE TWO MEN TOOK THE ELEVATOR FROM THE UNDERGROUND PARKING garage of their hotel up to the main floor lobby in order to check back in for the next five nights. The rooms were held on the expense account of Tex Durham, who used the hotel for all his business guests when staying in the Phoenix area. It was a luxury accommodation that neither Chris nor Sean could normally afford.

"I notice we both have the same rooms we were in last weekend," Chris said to the reception desk worker. "Is that just a coincidence?"

"Somewhat," replied the clerk, whose name badge had the name "Jason" printed across the bottom. "You're both in rooms held permanently by Mr. Durham, who has people staying here quite often. He's got about a quarter of the rooms on the sixth floor under permanent reservation. So it's not as much of a coincidence as you'd think. Were the rooms comfortable for you during your last stay?"

"Absolutely," replied Sean, who also enjoyed the extra amenities in their oversized accommodations. "I wish I could have a shower back home like the one in my room here. I could literally fall asleep in there!"

The staffer smiled and said, "I probably wouldn't recommend doing that, but I'm glad to hear that you enjoyed it."

After completing the check-in process, the two took the elevator up to the sixth floor. Their rooms were not adjoining but were separated by less than fifty feet of hallway. On entering their rooms, they found that they both had large yellow envelopes left on the surfaces of their desks.

Chris immediately put down his baggage and opened the envelope, extracting a series of large maps that had been marked with updated notes on the portions of the search areas that had already been covered by the three teams. He was impressed that the maps already included those areas they'd called in only a few hours earlier.

He then indulged in another luxury he wouldn't have used when staying on his own dime. He removed a bottle of cold lager beer from the refrigerator "convenience bar" and poured the contents into a tall clear glass. He had always thought the term "convenience bar" came from the fact that the hotel had conveniently forgotten to announce the inflated price for the drinks. But that would be Mr. Durham's concern this week, not his.

Drink in hand, Chris headed into the huge bathroom and turned on the hot water in the shower. It boasted one of the oversized showerheads that dumps literally gallons of water over the bather, which felt wonderful following the three days in the baking sun. He felt as though he could have spent hours under the torrent as it relaxed him from head to foot.

After his shower, Chris dried off and removed the complimentary terrycloth bathrobe from the shelf in the closet. He wasn't meeting Sean for dinner for another half hour yet, so he had time to relax and watch part of the news. Picking up the remote, he hit the "On" button to activate the power on the oversized flat screen. Next, he lifted the listing of television stations from the credenza next to the base of the television. However, his hands were still wet, and the plastic holder of the directory card slipped clumsily from between his fingers and fell behind the credenza.

Chris silently cursed himself as he bent forward to peer between the credenza and the wall. He leaned forward until his forehead was touching the wall in order to try and determine the location of the plastic holder. However, what he saw made him freeze in his tracks.

Barely moving a muscle except his left arm, he activated the mini-flashlight on his cell phone to better view the backside of the credenza. Affixed to the dark wooden surface was a device, cylindrical in shape with a wire and a small antenna attached to the top. A small, flat lithium battery was connected to the lower surface of the cylinder, and the entire assembly had been connected beneath the upper lip of the surface, in order to partially hide it from view.

A bug.

Chris slowly pulled away from the wall and returned to a standing position. He recognized competing emotions inside himself, including confusion, anger, and anxiety. He harbored no doubts of who had ordered the listening device placed in his room. He just didn't understand why. Hadn't Durham been the one to call *them* to work for him? Why would he do so if he felt the need to secretly listen in on their conversations? Were there other spying devices in the same room? Was Sean's room bugged as well? Chris had no doubt that it was.

Chris pulled out a notepad and quickly scribbled some words on the top sheet of paper. He then hastily pulled on a T-shirt and some shorts and left the room, walking down the corridor to Sean's room. Sean answered the knock immediately, surprised to find his friend there so much earlier than they had agreed.

"I thought we said 7:00 PM," said Sean in a puzzled tone. "It's barely 6:30. I'm not close to being ready."

"I'm famished," replied Chris, winking at his friend. "I'm going downstairs go get something from the lobby."

"You're what?" asked Sean.

"I'll meet you down there," said Chris as he repeated the wink. He then handed him the note and walked away before Sean had a chance to say another word.

Sean unraveled the crumpled note in his hand and read the scrawled words.

Listening device in my room. Probably yours, too. Do not say a word. Meet me in lobby.

Sean crunched the note back into a tight ball and shoved it into the bottom of his front pocket. He quickly got himself dressed and took what he needed from the room. Then he, too, departed.

The hotel lobby was busy with overflow from the adjoining bar room, which was surprisingly packed for this early in the evening. Sean crossed the lobby searching for Chris, who wasn't visible at first glance amongst the crowd. Then he saw him, perched on a chair beneath a large television screen watching a baseball game. He approached without Chris looking up from his seat.

"Red Sox game?" he asked, being familiar with his friend's favorite team.

"Is there any other team worth watching?" Chris replied, still engaged in the action on the screen.

"So what the heck did you find up there?" asked Sean, intentionally stepping into his friend's line of view. "A listening bug?"

"Yup," said Chris, "attached to the credenza right next to the hotel room phone."

"Think there are any other devices up there to listen or look?"

"I don't know for sure," Chris speculated. "I'm not good at that kind of thing. But I do know that you can buy equipment that will find stuff like that in a room. Listening devices, hidden cameras, voice recorders, the works."

"They cost much?" asked Sean.

"They run the gamut, from under thirty bucks to over five hundred. I guess it depends on how sensitive you want it to work."

"I hate to ask this question, so I'll just come right out and say it," said Sean. "We've got to assume that it's Durham who had it bugged, right?"

"I don't know anyone else out here, do you?" asked Chris as he shrugged his shoulders. "The only thing I can't figure out is why? Why does he feel like he can't trust us without spying on conversations inside our hotel room?"

"Think it has anything to do with wanting to find the mine first?" ventured Sean.

"Hmm . . . you mean maybe he wants to pick up on our discoveries before we announce anything and then claim it was their find? All that would do would be to avoid paying us the two percent incentive, which hardly seems worth it."

"I agree," added Sean.

"Anyway, whatever the reason, let's head out and find some chow," suggested Chris. "I feel like I could eat a horse."

"Would you mind if I went back up to my room and checked on something first?" asked Sean.

"Let me guess; you want to see if you have your very own bug, right?"

"I'd be offended if they took the trouble of miking your room and neglected mine," quipped Sean.

"Sure, I'll even go up there with you," offered Chris. "But let's not say a word once we're inside the room, whether we see anything or not. Don't even motion toward it if you see it."

The two headed back up to the sixth floor and reentered the room. Sean made a beeline for the credenza, pretending to look closely in the tall mirror positioned against the wall. He visually scanned the rear surface of the furniture until he spotted a miniature antenna protruding from beneath a control box for the cable television.

Sean then turned around and faced Chris, simply nodding with an imperceptible movement of his head.

"OK, I'm set to go now," he announced. "Let's go find some pizza."

The two decided to stretch out their legs by walking a number of blocks to a restaurant that staked its reputation on having the "best New York–style pizza."

"Who ever imagined we'd fly over two thousand miles from New York to Phoenix so we could go out and get some New York–style pizza?" asked Sean, grinning at the irony.

"It seems fitting," returned Chris, "as long as we can go home sometime soon and get some Phoenix-style pizza."

"Is there such a thing?"

"Sure, it's got prickly pear cactus and microphones on top," replied Chris.

The two men settled into their seats in the modern, brick-and-glass restaurant that was adorned with photographs of New York City. They ordered their pizza and a pitcher of draft beer to quench their thirsts.

"Assuming there are no listening devices inside the pizzeria," began Sean, "what should we do about the bugs in our rooms?"

Chris considered the question while he turned the candle on the table around in his hands. "Well, the first thing I want to do tomorrow morning is to take a ride out to Scottsdale. Tomorrow's Saturday, so it shouldn't take more than about twenty-five minutes."

"Scottsdale? What's in Scottsdale?"

"They have a store that sells spy equipment. It's got a pretty good rating, so I want to go check it out."

"Ahh, yes," exclaimed Sean. "We need our spy equipment to find their spy equipment."

"Precisely."

"Do you plan on getting rid of the bugs that are already in our rooms?" asked Sean.

"No, I have something a little more devious in mind than that," smiled Chris. "As long as Durham doesn't know that *we* know, we can use this against him."

"Now it sounds like we're plotting against an enemy instead of working for the guy as an employer," observed Sean. "I mean, he is signing our paychecks."

"And spying on us at the same time," remarked Chris. "Don't get me wrong. I still want to do the job and give him value for our work. But I hadn't counted on a complete lack of trust, which is what I'm feeling right now."

"How much do you think it will cost to buy something that will do a good job and possibly locate any other devices?"

"The model I was looking at online was about eighty dollars, but I'm going to ask the folks in the store for a recommendation."

"And I take it that will be a 'non-reimbursable expense,' correct?" asked Sean, mostly in jest.

"Ha, correct. I don't think it would be a good idea to list a bug-finder device on our expense report spreadsheet," agreed Chris.

"Hey, I have a great idea!" exclaimed Sean, his eyes brightening noticeably. "Why don't we report finding the bug to Mr. Durham and then ask him what we should do with it?"

"No, let's just leave it alone," said Chris. "Assuming that his people are the ones who planted them, which is already a ninety-nine percent certainty, they can't really do us any harm as long as we don't say anything in the rooms."

"True."

"And we'll be one hundred percent sure about their origin very shortly," said Chris with a sly grin on his face.

"You mean the bug detector will also tell who planted them?" asked Sean.

"No," replied Chris. "We're just going to use some of that deviousness I was just talking about. I'm thinking of a great way of using those listening devices against them . . . at least enough to expose their duplicity."

"I'm interested already," said Sean. "Deal me in!"

* * * * * *

The following morning was Saturday, the start of the weekend for the two men. They had agreed to get together for a casual run through some of the outlying park areas of the city, although Sean peeled off at the three-mile mark, whereas Chris continued on for an additional two miles. They were both showered and ready in time to get them to the door of the Underground Spy Shop in Scottsdale by 10:00 AM. The doors were just opening for business as they arrived.

The two men stepped inside the shop and were immediately greeted by a gentleman who seemed to run the place. He identified himself as "Ron," and offered his advice and expertise in anything covert.

"Wow, I had no idea there were so many products in the spy world," said Sean, looking around at the heavily laden shelves and display cabinets. "This is really impressive."

"Oh, yes," replied Ron as he followed Sean's gaze around the store. "We have voice recorders, hidden cameras, security systems, phone bugs, you name it. We also have devices that look like almost anything in the world, from ballpoint pens and USB memory sticks to wall outlets and houseplants. If you want to catch someone doing something, we can help."

"Actually, we're on the other end of the cat-and-mouse game," said Chris. "We're the ones who are being spied on, and we'd like to find a way to put an end to it."

"Of course," said the shop owner, nodding in understanding. "I take it your office is being bugged?"

"Not our office, but our hotel rooms," responded Chris.

Ron's eyebrows immediately shot up on his forehead. "Your hotel room? Now that's a new one," he exclaimed. "Would you mind sharing the details with me?"

"It's really not important, and I don't want to divulge too much about the people or places involved," explained Chris. "But suffice it to say that the people who paid for our hotel rooms in Phoenix felt the need to listen in on our conversations."

"So if you know about the bug already, which I believe you already found, how can I help you further?"

"I think what both of us want to know is whether there are any other devices in our rooms, including maybe a video recorder or transmitter, or even any other hidden microphones. We'd like to have something that we could use to scan the place on a daily basis, as we'll be working here for another seven weeks."

"Of course, I can help you with that," offered Ron, who led them to a display case on the back wall of the shop.

They were even further surprised by the diversity of items for sale in other areas of the store. They passed shelves displaying night vision devices, motion alarms, and listening headsets. Yet another section contained a variety of stun guns plus a set of well-polished "throwing stars."

"Yikes," exclaimed Sean, looking at the Ninja stars. "Remind me not to try to break into this place on a dark night."

The store owner smiled at his comment and replied, "I've never tried becoming proficient at throwing those Ninja things. I don't think it's hard, but I can't seem to hit the broad side of a barn with them."

Ron then opened a case and retrieved a box from one of the upper shelves.

"Here you go, gentlemen. This is one of my better sellers, as long as you don't mind spending a couple hundred dollars."

"What are the advantages over the model I was reviewing online? It was about eighty dollars, and I think you also carry that model," said Chris, pointing to the cheaper detector.

"The key is that you said you're suspicious of other devices, ones that may be recording video or other forms of surveillance," explained Ron. "This detector is really a professional piece of gear that will do anything you need, but at a reasonable price. It can pick up not only hidden microphones and cameras but also things like GPS bugs, whether they are using encoded signals or not. It can also pick up a host of sophisticated signal types including Bluetooth, GSM, 4G and 5G cell phone transmissions, and more. Plus, you can adjust the antennae to increase or decrease the sensitivity as needed."

"So you're saying that if we have a recording device in our rooms, this baby will find it?" asked Sean, holding the box while reading the outside labeling.

"No, not entirely," replied Ron. "It will detect anything that is transmitting in the range between fifty megahertz and six gigahertz But if it is simply a recorder that is hidden somewhere and doesn't transmit, this device won't find it. Also, if it is more than a certain distance from the transmitter, which is determined by the device and its signal strength, you may miss it. But generally it will pick up anything within fifteen to twenty feet."

"Thanks, we'll go with this one," said Chris, agreeing to purchase the detector.

"I'm sure you'll be satisfied with its performance," stated the owner. "And don't forget to use it on other locations where you might be working or traveling. For example, if you have a rental car, you might want to run a scan on that as well."

Chris and Sean both stopped dead in their tracks at the suggestion. If there was a bug in their room, why couldn't there be a similar device in their rented SUV? It was a possibility that had never crossed their minds, and since they would have the same rental vehicle for the next two months they decided to try it out on that as well.

"Just don't forget to turn your own cell phone off, and then move away from other cars while running the scan," advised Ron. "Otherwise you'll find yourself picking up their cell phones and portable devices."

"Got it, thanks," said Chris. "We'll give you a shout if we have any more questions."

As they were getting set to pay for the bug detector, Sean silently picked up another box from the shelf and placed it on the counter. It contained a compact sound-activated voice recorder that looked like a fancy ballpoint pen.

"You want that, too?" asked Ron.

"Yeah, I do," replied Sean. "I'm not even sure what I'm going to do with it, but I really like it."

Ron grinned once again and commented, "See—the spy bug is pretty contagious, isn't it?"

They paid for both devices at the same time and then departed the store and commenced the drive back to Phoenix. Although they both doubted that the SUV was bugged, they agreed to avoid conversations about the project until after they had completed a scan with the bug detector.

Deciding to take the long way back to their hotel, Chris pulled the vehicle into the parking lot of the Desert Botanical Garden, off East McDowell Road on the outskirts of Phoenix.

"Want to learn about cacti and butterflies?" inquired Sean, puzzled at the stop.

"Not butterflies, but maybe just bugs."

"Oh, of the electronic kind, I assume?"

"Correct," confirmed Chris. "It's early enough in the day that their parking lot should be pretty empty. We'll be able to do a scan without any outside interference."

They pulled the car into one of the outer parking lots, which was completely devoid of cars. They both exited the vehicle while Sean pulled the detector from the box, checked the battery, and completed the setup steps. They then opened the remaining doors and prepared to commence their scan.

"I'm going to start it on its lowest sensitivity and then walk it up," announced Sean.

"Let's do it," replied Chris.

Sean activated the detector and held it inside the passenger-side front seat. It immediately displayed a yellow LED light and an audio signal, detecting that it was picking up something in its search criteria.

"Oh, lovely!" exclaimed Sean, following the signal inside the vehicle until finding himself in the back seat. "Our car is bugged, too."

"Can you get a read on it?" asked Chris, looking to localize the source of the signal.

"If I'm reading this thing correctly, it appears to be coming from your backpack."

Sean then opened up the top drawstrings on Chris's pack and looked inside.

"Well, no wonder, Einstein," he said. You've got both your tablet and your portable GPS running in here. I'm surprised the detector isn't giving you a special error message calling you an idiot!"

"Sorry," replied Chris sheepishly. "I forgot to turn everything off before you got started. Here, let me shut these down for you and we'll test it again."

Chris then turned off the handheld devices in his backpack and then checked to ensure that both his personal cell phone and the satellite phone were powered down. Sean did the same with his own cell phone before reactivating the detector from the spy store.

The device once again displayed a yellow LED and the audio tone chirped in the background.

Sean scowled and looked at Chris, standing outside the vehicle. "You got anything else turned on that you're not telling me about? Anything at all?"

"Nope."

"Neither do I, so something's wrong here," said Sean, poking his way between the seats, consoles, and other nooks inside the SUV. He then removed the AutoPass toll device from the Velcro holder on the front windshield and tossed it to Chris.

"Try putting that on the ground about fifty feet away and see if we're still getting a signal."

Chris walked across the lot and deposited the transponder beneath a tree on the other side of the parking row, and then he returned to the vehicle.

"We're still getting something here," said Sean, scowling at the area beneath the front seats.

Chris bent low and looked between the driver's-side seat and the center console, feeling beneath the seat with his hands. It was when the fingers of his left hand were examining the seat adjustment rails that he came upon the antenna of the concealed device. He removed it from its position long enough to show Sean before replacing it under the seat. He then put his index finger to his lips, signaling that he wanted Sean to remain silent while he followed Chris away from the SUV.

When they were a good hundred feet from their ride, Chris turned to Sean and confided in a low voice, "Well, we were talking the whole time we were looking for the thing. If Durham has any way of picking up those transmissions, then he knows that *we* know we're on to him."

"Not necessarily," replied Sean. "Remember that we're nowhere near any Wi-Fi signal, wireless router, or anything else that could decode the signal and forward it on. I'd say it's a pretty safe bet that our conversation since we pulled into this lot is still private."

Chris considered the explanation before nodding in agreement. "It's possible that we did just luck out here. So let's still avoid talking business in the car until we can get this sorted out."

"In the meantime," said Sean, "I think the safe thing would be to either leave the bug here or destroy it and then leave the remains inside the car. As long as it no longer works."

"I can do that," said Chris, placing the device on the blacktop of the parking lot and then mashing it with the heel of his boot.

"Problem solved," he announced. "I think I'll put it back under the seat, just to make it look like it was smashed when I adjusted the seat forward."

"It's getting so it's hard to talk almost any place," noted Sean.

"Very true," agreed Chris as they strolled slowly back to their vehicle. "I knew I should have taken up sign language."

CHAPTER FIFTEEN

The Legend of Ghost Hawk

May 25, 2020

THE SUPERSTITION MOUNTAIN MUSEUM, KNOWN BY OTHERS AS THE Lost Dutchman Museum, sits on a lonely stretch of U.S. Route 60 outside of the town of Apache Junction, Arizona. The street address lists it on North Apache Trail, which aptly describes the dusty, largely underutilized road.

The museum opened its doors in 1990 with a limited number of members and then moved to its current location in 2003. Since that time it has rapidly expanded in size and scope, and today attracts a fair-sized body of people who are touring the area to experience the culture and beauty that are the Superstition Mountains.

Chris and Sean entered the main building through the front door on the left corner of the structure. They had made previous arrangements with the assistant director to make use of the facility's library, and also to look through the museum's exhibit storage and receiving rooms. The entire museum, including its outlying buildings and displays, looked rather small, so they weren't sure how much benefit the visit would provide.

"Excuse me, but we're looking for a Ms. Dorothy Redding," said Sean to the woman behind the gift store counter.

"That would be me," came a disembodied voice from a doorway leading into the office spaces. It was followed up by the appearance of a short, middle-aged woman with a dark complexion and tight curly black hair. "And what can I do for you boys?"

"I'm Sean Riggins, and this is my partner Chris Carey. We spoke to you last week about coming in and doing some research in your library and collections."

"Yes, yes, I remember," recalled Dorothy and she came around the counter to shake hands. "You two were interested in going through some of the older accounts of the region, 1870s through 1920s, correct?"

"Yes, that's correct," confirmed Sean.

"Just like the rest of them," sighed the woman as she pulled some registration papers from a file.

"Do you get a lot of people in here doing research on the Lost Dutchman material?" asked Chris.

"More than you can possibly guess," replied Dorothy. "And they all think they have a new angle on where to find the mine. As if it would still be hidden if it was really that easy."

"As we mentioned last week, we'd also like to browse through your collections, especially anything you have in storage that is both old as well as uncataloged," continued Chris.

"That might be a little harder to do," said Dorothy, looking up from her work. "I can't leave you in our warehouse room by yourselves. Please understand when I say that I'd like to, but we'd lose half our collections to every half-sober treasure hunter with a hunch who came through here."

"I do understand," said Chris apologetically.

"Let me see what I can do," said Dorothy. "Maybe I can get one of the volunteers to stay back there with you for an hour or two."

"Is there anything we can do to help make that happen?" asked Sean.

"Yes. Make out a donation check for over ten thousand dollars and I'll go back there myself!" cackled the manager, amused at her own humor. Chris and Sean continued to wait for an answer with a steady gaze.

"I'll see what I can do," she said. "In the meantime, I need you both to fill out these forms and sign them before I can let you into the library." She handed the forms to the two and then walked out the back of the shop into the exhibit rooms to try to find help.

Using two pens "borrowed" from the hotel rooms, Chris and Sean both filled out the short forms that promised they would abide by the museum's rules and would not use any of the documents viewed in the

The Dutchman's Gold

library for purposes outside those specified on the list. By the time they finished signing the forms, Dorothy had returned with an elderly gentleman who had volunteered to remain in the storage room while Chris poked through the assortment of boxes and cabinets. The name on his volunteer badge read "Benjamin," and he looked almost as old as the mountains themselves.

"Sir, it's nice to meet you," Chris said, bowing slightly as he shook the senior citizen's hand. "My name is Chris, and I think Dorothy said we're going to work together for a little while." He made sure not to exert force with his handshake for fear of doing damage to the senior's bony old hand.

"Well, it's nice to meet *you*," repeated the gentleman. "My name is Ben, and I'll be keeping an eye on you because the boss here doesn't trust you." He said this in a joking tone of voice as he turned his eyes toward Dorothy.

"Oh, go on, you two," she scoffed at the men. "Get started back there before I change my mind and charge both of you for the cost of admission!"

At this point, Chris and Sean split up to work separately. Sean headed into the library room to commence a search of the early documentation, while Chris marched into the rear corner of the building that housed the receiving and storage room. He was accompanied by Ben, who promptly sat down in an overstuffed chair to observe.

As Sean began his search of the document filing system, he quickly came to the realization that he had drawn the tougher of the two assignments. The library consisted of thousands, or possibly even tens of thousands of books, pamphlets, manuscripts, transcribed accountings of expeditions, and more. Almost everything in the files had been checked out on multiple occasions, with many of them also having been reproduced by prior researchers. Finding something that had been overlooked in the past appeared to be a hopeless proposition.

Chris, however, found that his task was both fun and interesting from the very start. Most of the boxes in the storage room contained items of historical note that had never made it out on display and had never been examined carefully before. Many of these artifacts were quite mundane in nature, including old pieces of prospecting and mining gear, clothing, and personal effects of those doing the prospecting. But each told a story, and Chris's nimble mind seemed to hasten to complete the story for those items that contained less than a full explanation.

"Do you know what it is that you're holding?" asked Ben from his easy chair.

Chris carefully examined the device that looked like a modified surgical instrument that had been conjured together like a Rube Goldberg device. "No, sir, not really," he replied.

"That's something they used to use to pick the gold flakes from the final panning of the sediment," he explained. "That little lens on top flips up and serves as a magnifying glass so you don't miss any. And you don't have to hold it either, which wouldn't work. Because if you had one hand holding the pan, and one hand holding the magnifying glass, and one hand holding the tweezers, well . . . I presume that you see what I'm saying."

"Yes, sir, I do," replied Chris. "That's fascinating. Thank you for the explanation. Does it have a name?"

"How about you can call it the 'pair of tweezers with magnifying glass attached'?" replied Ben.

"Sounds good. That's what we'll call it."

Chris proceeded to move through the boxes in the back row of shelving and was amazed at the diversity of materials he uncovered. First was a section filled with mining equipment, mainly smaller, handheld pieces. By the time he turned the corner and started the next row of shelves, the focus had turned to the personal belongings of some of the prospectors who had lived and searched in the Superstition Mountains over the past hundred years. There was plenty of this material because the number of prospectors had skyrocketed since the early days of the 1900s.

Working slowly and methodically, Chris progressed from the later days of the 1950s and 1940s back toward the end of the last century. Many of the boxes were labeled with the names of the owner as well as the donor, but some contained less information than others. As he worked, the comments from Ben became more infrequent until all he could hear emanating from the overstuffed cushion chair was the rhythmic sound of heavy breathing and the occasional muffled snore. Ben was sound asleep.

In the library, Sean was finding some interesting documents, but most were less than helpful. In some cases, they were in direct conflict with other accounts of the early explorations. Sean found himself shaking his head in amazement that anyone would be trying to make sense of it all. It appeared to be a nightmare.

Almost two hours into his search, Chris pulled out a plastic container that held a number of personal possessions of a short-term resident of the area. There weren't many items in the box, and there were pitifully few details written on the labeling on the outside surface. A simple white tag with an inner border of blue was annotated with two simple words.

Ghost Hawk.

Nothing more, nothing less. Also found inside the box was a broken knife handle, a box of matches, a small cookpot, a few papers, and an empty cartridge from an early rifle.

Chris was leafing through the papers, which contained a few maps, a crude drawing that indicated the location of game, and a shipping receipt with a name listed in the city of Syracuse, New York. Chris smiled when he saw the home of record of the recipient, recognizing the connection with his own home.

It was only when he turned the last page and viewed the final document that he caught his breath, shocked at the sight in front of him. There, staring face-to-face with him was a charcoal etching of an old man, hunched forward with white hair, wrinkled skin, and a prominent, beak-like nose. He knew he'd seen the face before. He was sure of it.

The bottom of the sketching was labeled in two places: the bottom middle and the far-right lower corner. Both of the legends were in English and recorded in the same handwriting. The inscription in the middle, which appeared to identify the subject, was "Ghost Hawk." The writing in the lower-right corner was a signature. It read, "Soaring Spirit." No year was recorded on the artwork.

Chris dropped everything else and just gazed at the charcoal sketching for a very long time. As he sat, contemplating the image before him, a great number of names flashed across his mind as he tried to recall the identity of the man in the drawing. The old-timer who had been assigned to monitor Chris's activity in the store room slept passively through the period of inactivity, softly snoring in the background. Suddenly, a mental bolt of lightning struck as a flash of inspiration shattered the tranquility of the room.

Alvah Dunning.

Chris knew that Dunning had been one of the great hermit guides of the southern Adirondack Mountains of New York in the 1800s. His woodcraft and skills in surviving alone through the coldest Adirondack winters were legendary. He had tramped the woods from Lake Pleasant to Raquette Lake to Blue Mountain Lake, building rudimentary huts wherever he ended up and then homesteading those residences until forced to move. Chris also knew that he had traveled across the country at one point in time. But not to the Superstition Mountains. He was baffled.

After inspecting the charcoal piece for an extended period of time, Chris moved on to the shipping receipt from the train freight office. It was dated May 5, 1900, and it had Alvah Dunning's name listed as the sender. The receiver was someone named Martha Sykes in the city of Syracuse, New York, which was starting to become a common theme this afternoon. He wondered who this woman was and what the relationship was between the two.

As he continued to scan the lines of the yellowed receipt, he became more and more engrossed with the details. He found himself perspiring slightly at the implications of his find. This was a major discovery, especially since it concerned a shipment of *something* of great value from Phoenix to Syracuse in May 1900. He noted that the shipment had been heavily insured to the amount of $5,000.

So many questions flooded into Chris's mind that he had a hard time putting them in order. He had no doubt that Alvah Dunning was the subject of the sketching, because it was found in the same box as the receipt with his name on it. What the heck was he doing in this part of the country? Was he the same person as the "Ghost Hawk" labeled at the bottom of the artwork? Who was "Soaring Spirit," and why did he sketch this transported hermit from the Adirondacks? What was the connection? And finally, what was inside the suitcase that he shipped back to a residence in Syracuse, New York? It must have been very valuable,

THE DUTCHMAN'S GOLD

because it was insured for $5,000, which was a vast sum of money in those days. None of it made sense.

Chris wanted to consult with Sean in the library, but yet he didn't want to get Ben in trouble for falling asleep on the job. Even as a volunteer, he was expected to perform his duties to a certain level of proficiency, and falling into a profoundly deep slumber did not meet those expectations. So, with great tact and consideration, he carefully awakened the old-timer from his nap. He turned his head toward the easy chair and asked for help.

"I don't know, Ben, what do you think about this?"

Nothing but snores.

"I don't know, Ben, what do you think about this?"

Still just the sounds of silence.

"BEN, I'VE GOT TO GO INTO THE NEXT ROOM TO ASK MY FRIEND ABOUT THIS!"

The volume of Chris's voice had risen at least thirty decibels, and he hoped that Dorothy could not overhear his callings in the front office.

"Wh . . . wh . . . what, young man?" said Ben as he sat bolt upright, his speech punctuated by a loud snort.

"I've got to run up to the library to show Sean something," he said, holding the drawing up for the old man to see. "I'll be back in a couple minutes, OK?"

"OK, son. I think I may have fallen asleep anyway."

"Oh, did you really? I didn't notice if you did," replied Chris. He felt entitled to one little white lie that day, especially if it was intended to make Ben feel better. "Why don't you just rest in your chair while I consult with my friend."

Chris almost floated from the storeroom into the library, where he literally ran into his friend standing behind the entryway. In the process, he knocked a stack of maps and other documents from Sean's hands onto the floor.

"Oh, sorry," he said apologetically as he helped pick up the pages from the floor tiles and set them back on the large reading table.

"What's up with you?" asked Sean, looking at Chris's excited expression. "You look like you've just seen Santa Claus."

126

"More like Agatha Christie," referring to the famous mystery writer of the previous century. "We've got to talk."

"Find something good?" asked Sean as he put the rest of his documents on the table. "I hope so, because all I'm finding in here is a ton of useless references that point in a thousand different directions."

"Well, we expected that, didn't we?" suggested Chris. "Even from what Kristi was reading online, no one can even make a definitive guess as to what 'the mine' really was or who first discovered it."

"It's actually a lot worse than that," confirmed Sean. "But let's leave all that for later. Show me what you've found."

"Look familiar?" Chris then slid the drawing onto the tabletop for Sean to view.

Sean bent over the sketching for a second or two and then stood up and looked at Chris with a smile. "Sure. That's Ghost Hawk. I'd recognize him in a heartbeat," after reading the caption on the bottom of the page.

"Seriously, do you recognize this person?"

"I can't say for sure, no," admitted Sean. "I mean, his face does look vaguely familiar, but I wouldn't have a clue as to his real identity."

"You're looking at a sketching of Alvah Dunning, the Hermit of Raquette Lake, except drawn by a local Native American artist of the 1800s. At least I *think* he was local, which is what makes it so much more puzzling."

"Explain," said Sean, looking for the connection to their search for references to the Lost Dutchman Gold Mine.

"Here's my line of thinking, and you can tell me if you think I'm crazy," said Chris. First of all, no one ever suspected Alvah Dunning to be in the Superstition Mountains. All the Adirondack history books I've ever read stated that he went out to the territory of the Dakotas when he felt too cramped in the Adirondacks. Yet here he is, sketched by a local artist, which hopefully fixes his position here, in Arizona, not in those northern territories."

"OK, but I still don't see the connection to the gold mine," countered Sean.

"In May 1900, Dunning shipped a locked case of something back east. It weighed over twenty pounds, and he insured it for five thousand dollars."

"Whoa! OK, now you've got my attention," exclaimed Sean. "A heavy suitcase, locked, that was insured for five thousand dollars. I see where you're going with this. You think that the hermit somehow stumbled onto the remains of Jacob Waltz's mine?"

"I think we have to consider it a distinct possibility," said Chris. "I still want to see if we can find any references to the artist, 'Soaring Spirit,' just to see if he did anything else depicting Dunning. There's always the chance that he sketched something with some background in it. You know, landmarks we could use to localize his whereabouts while he was living out here. If we could find that out, it might put us within shooting range of the mine."

"You sound like you're starting to believe that this place exists, too," said Sean, smiling at his friend's enthusiasm.

"I don't know one way or the other, but you have to admit this sounds promising," replied Chris. "A locked suitcase that weighed in at over twenty pounds, and he insured for five thousand dollars. I doubt it was filled with his dirty laundry."

"OK, so what's the plan?" asked Sean. "You want to keep looking here?"

"For today, yes," replied Chris. "Keep on doing what you're doing, going through the obvious references in search of things that others might have missed; people and places that might seem overlooked, misinterpretations or directions, alternate ways of interpreting maps . . . you know, that kind of stuff."

"Uh huh. I still think I should have brought along my Ouija board."

"Seriously," stated Chris earnestly. "You never know, especially since we're coming at this from a different angle from everyone else in the past."

"If you want to hear an idea from the peanut gallery," said Sean, "I'd take a few good photos of the Peralta* Stones and send them to that girlfriend of yours. She's done wonders with that kind of thing in the past, especially on things we haven't been able to figure out."

"That's a great idea," agreed Chris. "I'll snap some shots of the re-created stones they have here and text them to her. In the meantime, I'd

---

*The Peralta Stones were a series of carved rocks that supposedly provide an encrypted map to the Lost Dutchman Gold Mine. The origin of these stones is a much-debated subject, and many researchers consider them a fraud.

also like you to search the library here for anything else done by the artist 'Soaring Spirit.' Meanwhile, I'm going to head back into the storeroom and do a little more poking around."

"OK. Maybe I'll head in there with you after I'm done in here. It sounds like you've got the more interesting stuff in your room."

"Alright," said Chris. "But be careful of Ben, the volunteer, if you do decide to join me."

"'Be careful of Ben?'" repeated Sean. "Why do I need to be careful of Ben? He looks like he's ninety years old. Is he going to beat me up?"

"No, but just be quiet. We don't want to wake him up."

Sean returned to the library search, this time with a focus on finding other works of art by Soaring Spirit. He did succeed in locating a small portfolio with some other drawings and paintings, some of which were done in color using pigments of an undetermined source. But none of the pieces depicted the Adirondack hermit as the one found in the storeroom. Sean did notice that there was a printed sheet in the front of the portfolio that stated that "some of the works of this artist are on permanent loan to the Heard Museum, Phoenix, AZ." He wrote this into his notepad before closing the portfolio and carrying it into the storeroom.

Chris was standing on top of a step ladder going through some higher shelves when Sean entered the room. By this time, Ben was awake and standing with one foot on the bottom of the ladder to stabilize it.

"You said you were interested in other things done by 'Soaring Spirit,'" said Sean. "I've found a whole folder of his stuff, but I think we've struck out on finding anything more on our Adirondack hermit."

"That's OK," said Chris as he backed off the ladder. "Let's take a look anyway."

Sean placed the portfolio on a short filing cabinet and opened the front cover. They flipped through piece after piece of artwork, most of which depicted people of the tribe engaged in various activities. However, some of them focused on nature or the landscapes surrounding them, and these were the ones that drew Chris's attention.

"This is still good news," said Chris, looking up with a hopeful expression. "I think you'll agree that almost all of these showing any landmarks at all reflect the mountains of the Superstitions range. That means that this artist lived, or at least spent most of his time, in this area."

"Which is just one more proof that Alvah Dunning spent a year here instead of in the Dakotas, right?"

"Exactly," replied Chris. "Now if we could just find anything in his paintings that indicated exactly where he was, or pinpointed Dunning's presence during that time, we'd be golden."

"Literally!" chuckled Sean.

* * * * * *

A stop at the Heard Museum of Native American Art confirmed their guess that the artist Soaring Spirit was a member of the Pima tribe who painted almost entirely within the region around the Superstition Mountains. Some of the other works appeared to have come from the flats surrounding the Salt River up north, where the Pima tribe had many of its ancestral roots.

Their luck did not extend to finding anything else of Alvah Dunning. The one piece from the Lost Dutchman Museum was the only rendition they found of his likeness.

Sticking to their plan about avoiding conversations in their bugged hotel rooms, the two decided to share a couple drinks in the hotel bar before heading out to dinner. The lounge area was much quieter this visit, being a Monday night, so they were able to find a small table in a quiet corner of the room.

Chris was about to make a remark about the price of the drinks when his cell phone issued a signal signifying a text message. He quickly pulled the phone off his belt clip and glanced at the screen. It was Kristi, responding to his text showing the Peralta Stone carvings.

Rock_gurl: I printed out the pictures you texted earlier. I hope those aren't the only clues you have to go on, are they?

chriscarey1986: I take it that means they didn't make much sense to you.

Rock_gurl: They look like they were carved out by a sixth grader playing a practical joke on a teacher. And they DON'T look old.

chriscarey1986: Even with the date 1847 carved into the heart?

Rock_gurl: Even with the date. The type of red sandstone they used just wouldn't hold up like that for 170 years without a lot more wear.

chriscarey1986: How about the inscriptions? Do any of them make sense regarding the location of a mine?

Rock_gurl: I'd feel more comfortable reading tea leaves. Some of the carvings show only a series of squiggles.

chriscarey1986: So no hunches and no educated guesses, huh?

Rock_gurl: Sorry, sweetheart, not this time. I think they are a hoax created much later in time, IMHO.

chriscarey1986: Thanks for looking. Could I call you later this week just to chat?

Rock_gurl: You'd better!

chriscarey1986: OK, honey, goodnight for now.

Rock_gurl: Nite. XOXO

"Well, so much for a quick solution," said Chris as he poured a bottle of ale into his glass. "She can't make any logical guesses from the inscriptions, and doesn't even think they are authentic."

"Neither do at least half of the people searching for the mine," replied Sean. "The fact that no one knows where the things came from tends to make that argument all the more plausible."

"What do you think Tracey is doing these days?" asked Chris, rather absentmindedly.

Sean shot a surprised look at his friend, his head swiveling rapidly back in his direction.

THE DUTCHMAN'S GOLD

"Tracey? Our Tracey from the University of Pennsylvania?"

"One and the same," Chris confirmed.

Tracey Lee had been a college student they had encountered two years earlier while tracking down some leads on a case involving the Philadelphia Mint. She was present at the house of her aged aunt when Sean had visited while checking out the case. She was a sophomore at the time, possessing a high level of intelligence and a knack for scouting out the critical details of a story without getting stuck by obstacles. She was also drop-dead beautiful, with looks that got her in many doors that would have been shut to other investigators. Sean and Chris had paid her handsomely for her researching abilities that helped them solve the case of the missing 1804 silver dollars, and she had appreciated the opportunity.

"I don't know," replied Sean. "We kept in touch for a little while, but I haven't heard from her in quite some time. I guess she'd be a senior now, getting ready to graduate."

"You think she'd like to work for us again, maybe make a few spare dollars for her summer vacation?"

"Sure, I bet she would," said Sean. "What do you have in mind for her to investigate?"

"We have a number of things I'd like to learn, and we really don't have the time to run it all to ground right now. Plus, some of the things I want to chase down involve our employer, and I don't want him to know it's us doing the looking."

"I know what you mean there," agreed Sean. "So pray tell . . . assuming that she is available to work, what is she trying to find?" As he spoke, Sean pulled out a pen and small notepad from his pocket and started jotting notes.

"First of all, I'd like her to look into whether Tex is Shane's father. I'm pretty sure that will be an easy one to find, but I still want it confirmed. She can find him in the records of the Ryan High School of Denton, Texas."

"OK, next," murmured Sean as he scrawled in his pad.

"Number two will be to look into the address in Syracuse, where Alvah Dunning shipped that locked case. We want to find out who this Martha Sykes woman was and what her relationship was to Dunning. Ideally, we'd like to be able to track down a living descendant of Sykes, but that might be asking too much. But someone in the family tree must remember that story, especially if it was filled with gold and what happened to it."

"Got it," said Sean, trying to keep pace with Chris's dictation. "Anything else?"

"Something that might be impossible to determine was how the heck Alvah Dunning ended up in the Superstition Mountains when everyone in the world, including the historians and his biographers, thought he was in the Dakotas."

"I agree, I don't think that's going to be possible to find," agreed Sean, still scribbling furiously. "Especially since I don't believe Dunning could read or write. I know he made some crudely drawn maps that he made marks on, but he certainly took no notes."

Sean noticed that Chris appeared lost in his own thoughts, even as he was still trying to convey his ideas for Chris to record. His internal struggle was interfering with his ability to communicate, as though he was fighting an internal battle with some unseen force. Finally he turned to Sean with a concerned expression and voiced his thoughts.

"There are a few other things I'd like Tracey to check out, but here's something I want her to look into quickly," he said. "I want her to go into the databases of family lineages and check out Tex's ancestors, at least two or three generations back. If she doesn't know how to do that, perhaps you can give her some coaching just to get her started. It may come in handy for later searches we'll need her to do."

Sean's eyes lit up at the suggestion of getting together with Tracey to work on the investigation. "When do you want me to fly down there?" he asked without hesitation.

"Ha! Yes, I thought you'd like that idea," he said, grinning over his friend's eagerness. "And I'll make sure that Tex puts up the extra funds for a plane ticket for Maggie* to keep you company."

"Spoilsport," retorted Sean.

"Anyway, now that we've got this whole piece about Alvah Dunning and a possible connection with the gold mine, I think we need to return to New York to check out those angles. I'm going to call Max to ask him

---

*Maggie was Sean's girlfriend.

about us spending the better part of a week back home to investigate all these matters."

"Do you think Tex will be upset that we're spending less than seventy-five percent of our time in the field, which was part of his original plan for us?" asked Sean.

"I think we could be working on Mars for all he cares, as long as we find his gold mine," replied Chris.

"Agreed," said Sean.

"As a matter of fact, I think we should make the call requesting our trip from a phone in our hotel rooms," suggested Chris. "Let's let Tex's microphone pick up our thoughts about Dunning having found a large amount of gold in the search area. Maybe he'll be reassured that we don't know about his listening devices."

"I like the way you think," said Sean. "You're right, you do have a devious mind."

"And I know how to use it," added Chris.

CHAPTER SIXTEEN

No Place Like Home

May 31, 2020

CHRIS HAD BEEN RIGHT IN HIS PROGNOSTICATION ABOUT THEIR DIS-
coveries. Max relayed word of their find involving Alvah Dunning to Tex,
who instantly agreed that the trip to New York may pay big dividends.
Max asked them to make a little more progress in their search areas
before departing, so the two men spent the next three days covering more
ground inside the canyon surrounding Weaver's Needle.

Prior to their Sunday flight back to Syracuse, Sean was able to contact Tracey via cell phone, who instantly accepted the offer of employment by the two.

"Are you serious," she replied with obvious glee in her voice. "Working for you is still the best paying job I ever had. By, like, double! Of
course I'll do it! My final exams are over and all I have to do is go through
a graduation ceremony!"

"That's great. We'll be flying into Syracuse tonight and working in
several different locations next week," continued Sean. "One of your first
assignments will be to look into some ancestry issues with a guy from
Texas. It may take you some time, but I figure we could get together on
Monday or Tuesday and I could show you how to use the collection of
services and databases I've found over the years."

"That's great," replied Tracey. "I'll reserve one of the conference
rooms in the library so we can work in quiet and get things done."

"That'll work," agreed Sean. "There are a number of other things we'd like you to check out, but I'll explain them all to you when we get together. I'll text you after we land to arrange our meeting."

"I'm looking forward to it," she said before signing off the call.

* * * * * *

The flight to Syracuse was uneventful, and the two friends used the time to plot out their strategies for the week. They decided that step one would have them splitting up to tackle their two main tasks simultaneously. Sean would drive to Philadelphia where he would meet and brief Tracey on their research needs, as well as provide her with the resources she'd need to conduct the database searches. Chris, meanwhile, would head to the Adirondack Museum to search their libraries for anything related to Alvah Dunning and his time in the Superstition Mountains. After completing those tasks, they would arrange to meet in Syracuse and jointly track down anything they could find about Martha Sykes or her descendants.

It was an aggressive agenda for a one-week excursion, although Chris had been able to coax Max into talking to Tex about open-ended flights. They would return to Phoenix and the search area the following Sunday, but could extend their stay if they found materials that looked promising to fixing the location of the mine.

As soon as they landed, Chris placed a call to the Adirondack Museum in Blue Mountain Lake to leave a message with the Curator, Debbie Santori. He was amused to hear the new title of the institution, which was now called the "Adirondack Experience: Museum on Blue Mountain Lake." *Nothing remains the same for long*, he thought to himself as he listened to Santori's voice message.

"Hello Debbie, this is Chris Carey calling from Syracuse. Sean and I just returned from a project we're working out in Arizona, and I'd like to know whether I could stop in tomorrow and conduct research in your place for the day. I'm looking for anything on the hermit Alvah Dunning, especially the years of 1899 and 1900. Please give me a shout early tomorrow morning if you have a problem with me stopping by. Otherwise, I'm hoping to be there by 9:00 AM. I look forward to seeing you again."

Chris looked forward to working with Debbie once again, as she had provided the two with pivotal support in their previous two historic finds. Chris always chided her about "keeping her in the dark," because in both searches she wasn't aware of her role in the discoveries until after it was completed. For her part, Debbie was a wonderful partner to Chris and Sean, and always provided them with everything she had at her disposal.

Sean, meanwhile, agreed to meet with Tracey in the university library at 1:00 PM on Monday. He figured that the drive, which would normally take five and a half hours without traffic, would hit several snags along the way. He left seven hours for the trip to account for any delays.

They parted ways at the Syracuse airport "Arrivals" concourse, both intending to stay at their own homes for the night. For both men, it felt good to be back in the comfort of their own houses rather than sleeping in a hotel room or outside in the rough terrain of the Superstition Mountains.

* * * * * *

Sean's 1966 tan Mercedes attracted quite a few double takes as it cruised across the East Philadelphia campus of the University of Pennsylvania. It maintained a steady speed as it glided between the ivy-covered buildings until finally decelerating into a guest parking space nearby the Van Pelt–Dietrich Library. From there, Sean strolled along the sidewalk in front of the Blanche P. Levy Park until he was directly in front of the library door.

"May I help you?" asked the staff librarian in a voice that Sean thought was louder than appropriate for the location.

"Yes, I'm a guest of a Penn student," replied Sean. "I'm here to work with her in the Tech Center Conference Room for a few hours. I believe she left the form for my visitor's pass here."

"Name, please."

"Sean Riggins."

The librarian rifled through a file cabinet drawer and pulled out a printed page with an attached card, which she slipped inside a clear plastic badge holder.

"Please wear this in plain view at all times," intoned the library lady mechanically. "It's good only for today and must be turned in before you leave. Do you need any directions to get to the Tech Center?"

"No, I'm good. Thanks for the help."

Sean used the library map to navigate his way back through the Goldstein Undergraduate Study Center and directly into the small Tech Center in the middle of the wing. Tracey was standing in the middle of the outer room talking with another woman who was seated at the office desk.

Sean caught his breath once again on catching his first glimpse of her; she was even more beautiful than he remembered. Almost the exact same height as himself at five foot ten, she had perfect facial features framed by hair that was somewhere between light brown and dirty blond. Her highlighted tresses flowed over her shoulders and down her back in wavy golden swaths. Her azure blue eyes nearly danced out of her face, combining perfectly with her gleaming white smile, which she wore often. She also boasted a figure that was shaped by good genetics paired with hundreds of hours on the volleyball court. It went without saying that many of the university's male students had spent time following her around the campus.

"Sean!" she squealed in delight as he came through the door. "I can't believe you're here already!" as she threw her arms around him in an all-embracing hug.

"Good news and old men both travel fast," he quipped as he returned the clinch. Stepping back a pace, he regarded her fondly and complimented her on her appearance. "You've aged well, young lady. You must be driving half the male population of the school crazy."

"Stop," giggled Tracey. "It's a good thing Chris isn't with you or we'd never get anything done."

"Please excuse us," said Sean to the woman at the desk. "We graduated from the same insane asylum together and this is our class reunion."

Tracey was able to control herself long enough to make the introductions. "Cindy, this is my friend Sean, from near Syracuse. He and his friend have hired me to do some work for them, so Sean here will be in the Tech Center with us this afternoon."

"Nice to meet you," said Cindy.

"I've got us set up in the conference room here," said Tracey, gesturing the way back into the small enclosed space. I've got my laptop set up with full connectivity online."

"Great," replied Sean. "We've got a lot for you to work on, and it spans a bunch of different topics that all tie in to our current project out in Arizona."

"Oh, wow," remarked Tracey. "So you've got to head back out there again soon? Will I see you again after today?"

"Possibly. But I've got to meet up with Chris again in about twenty-four to forty-eight hours. We've got to run some things down that hopefully you'll get an early lead on."

"I'll do my best," promised the college student.

Sean printed out a listing of the topics they wanted her to work on, with the primary focus on the relationships between Tex, Shane, and any ancestors from the previous two or three generations. He then spent about thirty minutes reviewing a list of family tree databases and ancestry lookup services for which he already had membership logins. He also gave her his username and login for an online service that looks up background information on anyone in the country.

"This is really cool stuff," said Tracey as she tested one of the systems on her own family tree. "I'm seeing a few relatives from my grandmother's generation that I never knew existed."

Sean then walked her through the rest of the list, including the information about Martha Sykes in Syracuse in the years starting with 1900, when Dunning shipped her the suitcase.

"We want to find out whether there is anyone from that Sykes family anywhere in the area who we could talk to. Ideally, we'd like to find out about the suitcase, what was inside it, and what happened to it," said Sean.

"I'll see what I can do," said Tracey. "And I'll keep you posted if I do find anything."

By 4:30 PM, Sean had finished giving Tracey all the help he could to get her set up on the job. He called Chris to report his progress on the task at hand before volunteering to treat Tracey to a quick meal before

THE DUTCHMAN'S GOLD

starting the ride home. They decided to walk a short distance over to Sansom Street, where they ducked into the White Dog Café, which was a favorite of hers for vegetarian food.

"They have an udon noodle salad to die for," she promised Sean with a smile. "I just don't get to eat there very often, living off my student dining plan."

"Well, young lady, if you score some big hits and find us what we need to know, we'll give you a bonus that will pay for a number of visits for anything you want," promised Sean.

"Oh . . . really?" asked Tracey, a gleam in her blue eyes.

"Count on it," said Sean.

* * * * * *

Chris left his A-frame house in North Syracuse at 6:45 AM in order to make it to Blue Mountain Lake by 10:00 AM with time to spare. With little chance of ever finding a Starbucks in the central Adirondacks, he figured he'd stop for a few filling station coffee breaks along the way and still make it to the museum in time for opening.

Debbie Santori welcomed him with open arms as he came through the doors and into the main foyer.

"I knew you'd be the first one in the door," she said, giving him a big hug and pulling him toward the reception desk. Three museum associates were standing at the desk discussing other matters when Debbie interrupted them to introduce the visitor.

"Jim, Ed, and Tina, this is Chris Carey, the man responsible for both the Robert Gordon Treasure Exhibit and the 1804 Silver Dollar Exhibit," she said excitedly. "Chris is back to do some more research on a case he's working on in Arizona."

"It's nice to meet you," said Ed, the membership director, as he offered Chris a handshake. "Our exhibits on the 1804 silver dollar and the ghost village of Adirondac* are two of our more popular attractions. We're all grateful to you for making those discoveries."

---

*The ghost village of Adirondac, spelled without the final "k," was home to the historic blast furnace of the McIntyre Iron Works.

Chris blushed slightly at the recognition and immediately deflected credit for the find to his friends and others.

"Thanks, but so many other people were involved with that discovery," he said. "Still, it was exciting to learn of the Adirondack's part in solving one of the greatest mysteries in American numismatics. It was amazing to think that those coins had been sitting in that massive blast furnace for over one hundred and sixty years."

"If you don't mind me asking, what brings you to the Adirondack Experience museum for a case you're working in Arizona?" asked Ed. "I can't think of a single line that connects those two dots."

"We've uncovered some pretty convincing evidence that Alvah Dunning spent a full year living in the Superstition Mountains, just east of Phoenix," explained Chris. "We're just trying to establish this as fact in order to correct the biographies of his life and his part in the history of the Adirondacks."

As Chris spoke, he felt slightly guilty about omitting any reference to the Lost Dutchman Gold Mine and the shipment that Dunning had sent back east. The last thing he wanted to do was to touch off a wild goose chase amongst the public to find a large cache of gold, presuming that's what the case contained.

"I think you may be a little confused on the destination of Alvah Dunning's pilgrimage to the American West," said Debbie. "I don't know a lot about the man, but I am certain that I read about him traveling out to the Dakotas during those years, not the Southwest. I've seen it in at least two books on the subject."

"Stand by for history to be rewritten," said Chris, winking at the curator. "We have uncovered some pretty indisputable evidence that Dunning was in the Superstition Mountains of Arizona. Now I'm *not* saying that he wasn't also in the northern regions of the Dakotas at some time during 1899 to 1900. But it's my theory that he wasn't. Heck, he couldn't read or write . . . he might not have known himself where he was."

"Hmm . . . interesting theory," said Debbie. "Anyway, we have quite a few documents on Dunning in our reference library. I got here an hour early this morning and pulled a lot of those out for you."

"Thank you so much," acknowledged Chris. "I owe you one."

THE DUTCHMAN'S GOLD

"We also have a number of boxes of Dunning's personal belongings that have been donated to us over the years. You are welcome to go through those as well."

"OK, I owe you two," said Chris, grinning at the curator. "Thanks again for all the assistance. We couldn't have had all our past successes without your cooperation."

"That's OK," replied Debbie. "Just don't walk out of here with any of our stuff again!"*

Debbie walked Chris back to the reading room of the archives building, where he sat down in front of a pile of books, articles, photographs, and maps all connected to Alvah Dunning. Chris was impressed that so much existed on the topic, and he quickly began organizing the material into the phases of the hermit's life.

"Whenever you'd like, I can show you the location in the storage building where Dunning's personal effects are stored," Debbie offered. "There isn't much, outside of a few large pieces like guns, traps, and stuff like that. All the rest of his belongings fit into a handful of small boxes. You can probably sort through all of it in under an hour."

"Thanks, Deb—I'll come get you when I'm ready."

Chris began with those documents from the later part of Dunning's life. None of these were in Dunning's hand, as he did not write. However, some were correspondences that were sent to him, including a letter from the wife of Thomas Durant inviting him to their camp for tea. There were also a number of his crudely drawn maps with annotations regarding the placement of traps and other paraphernalia throughout the woods.

After looking through a number of these maps, most of which appeared to reflect areas of local interest, Chris's attention was suddenly drawn to a map of an unknown location. It didn't seem to fit in with anything he'd seen in the museum's collection. This one resembled a wide-brimmed Mexican hat, with some wavering lines and smaller circles in the middle. What was even more fascinating to Chris was the presence of an "X" at one point on the far right side of the drawing, almost out of

---

*This comment refers to Chris's previously "borrowing" two coins from a storage bin to solve the Robert Gordon treasure mystery.

142

the circle completely. A line had been drawn straight across the bottom edge of the page, as though the sketcher had wanted to denote that as the base of the drawing. Also, a plain arrow appeared on the bottom of the page that pointed straight up at a smaller circle in the middle of the map. The shape of the circle strongly resembled that of Weaver's Needle.

Chris looked at the map for a long time, trying to figure out the intended subject of the drawing. There were no bodies of water drawn on the page, and he couldn't be sure which side represented north. But his intuition and interpretation of the map presented the possibility that this may have been Dunning's attempt to sketch the area around Weaver's Needle. The likenesses were compelling. So what was the arrow? Could that have been the side of the canyon from which Dunning made his approach? Would that mean that it represented the Fremont Saddle? Or did the early explorers even approach the Needle from that direction?

With a myriad of questions floating through his mind, Chris decided to put the map aside and ask Debbie to make a copy for him. He then proceeded on with the rest of the papers and booklets, stopping to read through a couple of extracts with information about his time immediately after returning from out west.

Another item that attracted his attention was a folder containing both a copy of his portrait, as taken by the famous photographer Seneca Ray Stoddard, and the etching drawn by Dr. Arpad Gerster from that photo. Chris had carried a photocopy of the sketching made by Soaring Spirit in Arizona, and he compared the two drawings side by side. The Indian's version was taken more "face on" rather than from the side, and the difference in styles was also well defined. But the subjects of both works of art were obviously the same, with Dunning's fierce air of independence burning in both.

It was almost 1:00 PM by the time Chris finished with the documents in the reading room. He immediately made his way to the curator's office. He found Debbie at her desk, peering through a large magnifying lens at a small shard of pottery. She looked up at him as he stood in the doorway.

"Ready to move on to the storage building?" she asked.

"Sure. I think I've found just about all I'm going to find in the library," he replied. "Thanks for the copy of that map. Hopefully, it turns out to be something we can use in our current project."

"You really think old Alvah would have brought back something like that from out West?" asked Debbie.

"Who knows? He may have even drawn it on a piece of paper after he returned from Arizona," speculated Chris. "I can't even be sure that it isn't something he remembered from the Adirondacks. There may be no way of telling."

Debbie then rose from her desk and walked Chris across the museum campus to an unmarked storage facility. She removed a very large key ring from her purse and quickly unlocked the door.

"I'm glad I don't have that many keys," observed Chris. "I'd never find my way into my own house."

"I can't ever find the key to my house, either," noted Debbie with a smile. "It's only the museum keys I'm good with."

After turning on the lights, the curator led Chris through an unlocked door to a storage room with a series of metal shelves and cabinets. There were four boxes already sitting on a long metal table, and other objects lined up nearby. These included a toboggan, three rifles, some metal traps, and other personal items.

"You probably remember the rules," said Debbie as she cast an appraising eye on Chris. "Not that you've paid any attention to them in the past."

"I've tried, Boy Scouts honor," Chris replied, holding his three middle fingers in the air to represent the official Scouts sign.

"Well, you'd better, because I'm putting you on the honor system today. I don't have any volunteers to spare, so I'm going to have to trust you."

"I appreciate that, Deb," Chris stated earnestly. "You know I won't let you down."

As soon as Debbie left the room, Chris positioned the four boxes in a row and used all of his six-foot-two stature to peer down for a bird's-eye view across the collection. At first glance, there was nothing out of the ordinary. The first box contained some folded shirts and socks, one pair of extremely worn-out trousers, and an outer vest garment. It also contained

No Place Like Home

his famous wide brim hat along with two other covers of lesser fame. Some coiled rope and a leather belt rounded out the collection in Box #1.

The second box contained two pairs of shoes, several more pairs of socks, a few folded handkerchiefs, and some undergarments in various states of disrepair. *None of these items would have brought ten cents at a white elephant sale*, thought Chris to himself.

The third box contained a number of items that surprised Chris, including some old china plates, a few pieces of silverware, two drinking cups, and a canteen. One of the drinking vessels appeared to be made from an unidentified metal alloy, which Chris guessed to be either tin or pewter. On the bottom appeared two insignias, probably stamped by the manufacturer. One of them looked like a small crest, and he couldn't identify the other. The cup was different than the other utensils in the box, and Chris studied it for a time before setting it down.

The parcel also contained a small black box that closed with a non-locking hinge. Finally, there was a small, topless box in the corner of the larger container that held materials for cleaning his guns.

The fourth box held a collection of knives and other blades that appeared to be used for cleaning skins from his trapping collections, along with a wide assortment of fishing lures and line, two pairs of leather gloves, several boxes of wooden matches, a small cloth pouch containing some old pennies, another small wooden box with more fishing tackle along with a few folded papers, and finally an old ax head that had been detached from its handle.

The other items on the floor were all easy to identify as they were larger in size and well defined. Chris spent some time examining the construction of the toboggan, wondering whether Dunning had built it himself or acquired it in trade. He also marveled at the outer garments and coats that were folded separately in the room, wondering how this legendary guide had kept himself warm through the frigid Adirondack winters.

Chris then commenced a slow, methodical examination of every item in the boxes, starting with the first box and then moving from right to left. A lot of the material was in rough shape, worn out from decades of use in the Adirondack wilderness. He spent some time going through the small wooden box, unfolding each of the papers and reviewing its

The Dutchman's Gold

contents. Nothing in the packet provided any clues as to where Dunning spent his time in the Great American West from 1899 through 1900, so he quickly moved on to the next box.

The small black pouch contained an interesting collection of coins, including about a dozen "Indian head" pennies that ranged in date from 1877 through 1893. Two Liberty nickels from 1890 and 1894 were also nestled in the sack along with one ten-cent piece, a "Barber"-style dime from 1894. Chris recognized these all as common dates, and within the range of denominations that a man of Dunning's means would carry.

After completing his inspection of the coins, he was preparing to replace them into the sack when his fingers felt something hard in the bottom of the fabric. His thumb and forefinger closed around the hard lump, feeling for its size and shape. It was slightly larger than a pea and irregular in mass, making it impossible to identify without removing it from the bag.

Chris opened the top drawstring to its widest possible dimension and reached into the bottom seam of the material. His fingers lifted the mass out of the bag and into plain view.

Stunning.

Chris found himself eyeballing a small chunk of what appeared to be 24 karat gold. It wasn't anything that would have come from anywhere in the state of New York, and certainly would have been considered "a find" on any gold panning trip. Chris guessed its weight at about ten grams, or roughly a third of an ounce. It wasn't enough to make anyone rich, although his mind quickly ran through the list of possibilities regarding its source. Could it possibly have had its origins in the Superstition Mountains? There was no way of knowing, although it was a distinct possibility. Chris used his cell phone to take a picture, and then set it aside for later examining.

As if to prove his honesty, Chris immediately texted a photo of the nugget to Debbie before continuing on with the next box. The caption of his text was, "See how honest I am?"

Chris next moved on to the box with the plates and silverware, which provided nothing of interest in their search. He was just turning over one

146

No Place Like Home

of the plates to examine the back side when the door to the room flew open and Debbie entered, followed by an assistant curator.

"Wow!" Debbie exclaimed without preamble as she approached the table. "Where is it?"

Chris reached into the previous box and pulled out the black pouch for her to inspect. She dumped the contents into the palm of her hand and fished out the chunk of gold.

"I don't know why we didn't see this when we went through his belongings the first time," remarked Debbie. "I think I went through this stuff myself, but I know I never saw this with the other coins. Was it hidden somehow?"

"You probably didn't reach all the way to the bottom," suggested Chris. "Its irregular shape might have caused it to stick in the fabric and not fall out with the other stuff."

"I'm going to start calling you 'Midas,'" joked Debbie. "Everything you touch turns to gold."

Then, turning to the assistant, she commented, "Anne, please see that this is added to the inventory list of contents in Alvah Dunning's possessions. We'll weigh it later and assign a value, but for now I just want it documented."

The aide took the nugget and left the room with her assignment in hand.

"Have you found anything else of interest?"

"No, but I'm not finished yet," replied Chris. "I'm getting there, but I still have two boxes and then the loose stuff to check out. I should be done in another half hour or so."

Once Debbie departed, Chris continued on with his search, which included going into every pocket of every piece of clothing, leaving nothing to chance. He knew that this would be his only opportunity to examine these materials, and he desperately wanted to catch every detail.

It was when he moved into the next box, which contained the small black hinged box, that Chris discovered an unexpected prize. Inside the box, there were two items, neither of which made immediate sense. One was a long feather from a bird, obviously good sized, with unusual markings along its length. There were striated colors in banded patterns—mostly a light brown, but punctuated with white stripes that ran perpendicular to the shaft of the feather. It was extremely attractive, but he could not identify the species of bird from which it came.

The other item inside the box was of far greater interest and worth. Extending the length of the base was a silver-and-turquoise bracelet, with fine polished stones inlaid into the silver base. A hook-like clasp was attached to one end to secure the piece onto the wearer. Chris was fascinated by the patterns engraved in the silver surrounding the stones. It was, he guessed, produced in the Southwest, perhaps by an early artist of the day, possibly Native American.

For the second time in as many hours, Chris sent a text with a photograph to his curator sponsor. It showed the bracelet displayed on the metal table, its turquoise stones reflecting the overhead light. He captioned this text with the words, "Do you know the origins of this piece?" He then went back to his examinations of the other contents.

Once again, Debbie made a speedy appearance, only this time she was alone.

"Nine and a half grams," she announced.

"Pardon me?" replied Chris, still looking at the markings stamped onto the back of an old silver spoon.

"The nugget you found," Debbie explained. "It weighed in at nine and a half grams. Not bad for a morning's work."

"Enough to make a nice engagement ring for someone," chided Chris.

"And yes, we did know of the bracelet you photographed," said Debbie. "That came inside a larger package with a lot of Alvah's personal stuff. We only wish we could identify its source, because we have no idea of its origin or how he acquired it. It looks Native American, and those stones certainly didn't come from inside New York State."

"No, I agree, they didn't," concurred Chris. "If it's OK with you, I'd like to take this to a friend of mine in the State Museum in Albany. He's an expert on Native American artifacts, which I suspect is the origin of this piece."

Debbie frowned slightly but appeared to be giving the offer its due consideration.

No Place Like Home

"I'll allow that, but I need you to fill out some additional forms, and also get you to agree to return the item *with the documented evaluation* as soon as it is looked at in Albany."

"I'll agree to that," Chris said.

"You look as though you've gone through almost everything we have here on Dunning. Is there anything else that I could do for you?"

"As a matter of fact, there is," said Chris. He picked up the large feather from the desk and held it up for the curator to see. "Do you have a naturalist on your staff who might know what this is?"

"We do," said Debbie, "but you don't need an ornithologist to identify that. What you are holding is a feather from a Red-Tailed Hawk. I'd bet my paycheck on it."

"You sound pretty certain of yourself, and I'm no bird watcher, so I'll take your word on it."

"My husband and I both enjoy birding, and this is an easy one," said Debbie.

"You wouldn't happen to know if the Red-Tailed Hawk also lives in the Southwest, as in Arizona?" asked Chris.

"The Red-Tailed Hawk lives just about everywhere in this country," replied Debbie. "For a birder, it's one of those species that you'll see no matter where you travel."

"Great," said Chris. "It was in the box with the turquoise bracelet. I suspect that both of these came from Arizona, while Dunning was out there in 1899 into 1900."

"Possibly," replied Debbie. "Now remember to stop by my office to sign those forms on the way out, and make sure to return the bracelet via Certified Mail with the expert's appraisal."

"Yes, ma'am," said Chris, snapping her a mock salute. "At your service!" The curator then left once again, allowing Chris to finish his work.

Chris completed the task of studying the remaining contents of the four boxes, along with the other items left out of the containers. He also used his cell phone to take photographs of each of the boxes, with additional focus on some of the smaller objects. He already had a picture of the gold nugget, but he added a shot of the Indian-head pennies and other coins, which he lined up in two rows to show the dates on each.

Feeling satisfied with his work, he replaced all the boxes in their original positions and gathered his notes and photocopies, placing them into a single notebook. Absentmindedly, he wondered how Sean had done with Tracey in Philadelphia. Hopefully, they would be able to get together the following morning to start tracking down the Sykes family in Syracuse.

Chris stopped in Debbie's office on the way out of the facility and took care of the required paperwork. After signing the forms, she gave him a secure box to hold the bracelet and protect it from damage.

"Now you take care, and make sure you come back and see us again soon," she said as she hugged Chris goodbye.

It had been a productive visit, Chris thought to himself, and it was barely 2:00 PM. He had found several items that potentially linked Alvah Dunning to the American Southwest, and found a valuable gold nugget that the museum didn't know existed. This was yet another possible artifact that may have had its origins in the Lost Dutchman Gold Mine.

* * * * * *

Chris had been home for close to two hours when his cell phone began to chime. He put down the meatball sub he'd been devouring and looked at the screen, noticing that it was Sean's number calling. He immediately pressed the button to accept the call.

"Hey buddy, you home yet?" he asked, knowing that Sean would have a much longer commute to get back to his residence in Little Falls, New York.

"No, only about halfway back right now," replied Sean, calling from the hands-free phone in his car. "I probably won't make it back until a little before midnight."

"Midnight! How long did you stay down there?"

"We worked until about 4:30 PM, and then I took her out for a bite to eat before leaving the campus," reported Sean. "Surely you didn't expect me to drive home on an empty stomach."

"No, just the same as I wouldn't have expected you to leave the state without taking a beautiful girl out to dinner. I'm surprised you didn't try to get her to go out dancing after that."

"You know me, I don't dance," retorted Sean with fake indignation in his voice.

"So give me a recap. What did you guys cover today, and what will she be able to give us by tomorrow morning?"

"We discussed everything on our list, especially the two things at the top, which were the ancestors and family tree of the Durham family, as well as any living descendants of the Sykes family in Syracuse," Sean said. "She said she was going to work until late tonight since we want to get started in Syracuse tomorrow morning."

"Will she call us with anything she finds?" asked Chris.

"I told her to give me a shout any time, day or night, if she finds anything major."

"That's great," said Chris. "Hopefully she'll have some good information to get us started in the morning. But just to let you know, I might be in Albany for the first couple hours tomorrow, so you may start the hunt by yourself until I can join you."

"What are you doing in Albany?"

"Stopping in to see Dr. Turner in the Native American section of the State Museum. I have a piece of jewelry I found with Alvah Dunning's stuff that I want him to identify."

"Why don't you just send him a photo of the piece?" suggested Sean. "It would save us a lot of time, and he'd probably see all he needed to see from the picture."

"Good idea," Chris said. "I'll take a few more shots of it tonight and see what he can do with it. I think I can get his email address from the museum's website."

"Cool. I'll come by your house tomorrow morning, probably around 9:00. I need some time to sleep after all this driving. We can call Tracey together and then head into the city, assuming that she has something for us to go on."

"Sounds good. I'll see you then."

151

Chris then hung up the phone and turned on the television set for some mindless entertainment. Noticing that the Red Sox were playing the Yankees on national television, he tuned in to the game and watched a few innings. With Boston up by seven runs in the eighth inning, he turned the set back off and prepared for an early evening.

As he was preparing to power down his laptop for the night, he took one last look in his email inbox. Seeing there was an email from traceylee7@yahoo.com, which was Tracey's personal email account, he double-clicked the line to read the correspondence. It read as follows:

Sean & Chris,

I used all of the genealogy databases you showed me today, although I don't know whether I found anything you needed. But I did try my best, I promise. First, I was able to confirm that Shane Durham is Thomas Durham's son. I can prove that with 100% certainty. Thomas Durham is otherwise known as Tex Durham, which you already know. He is a self-made billionaire with real estate and corporate interests all throughout Texas and the Southwest. He's known for being a somewhat ruthless operator who gets whatever he wants, often by buying information on his enemies and using it against them.

His son, Shane Durham, does work for him most of the time, although the two have not always gotten along. Shane moved out of the family house when he was 18 years old, and didn't speak to either of his parents for over five years. They reconciled when Shane was arrested for Assault and Battery outside a bar in a small town about thirty miles outside of Dallas in 2010. His father worked a deal with the sheriffs and the charges were dropped. The subject who filed the charges suddenly moved out of town. (Draw your own conclusions.)

Finally, I was able to use one of the ancestry databases to track Tex Durham's ancestry back, but only two generations. After that, it appears to have come from overseas, in central Europe. I can continue that search, but it would take extra time and use of additional databases.

No Place Like Home

Anyway, Tex's father was another Texan, first name was Jonathan, mother's name was Anne. There was nothing special that I noticed in either one of them. They lived a modest lifestyle, always in Texas, nothing extraordinary there.

Things really start to get fuzzy in the previous generation. Looks like the grandfather came over from Europe as a young man. Not much I can find on him; appeared to be a bit of a drifter. He spent some time as a prospector. Reports placed him in the southeast, then Texas and Arizona. Nothing else on him besides his name, which was also odd. It was Jacob Weiser.

Nothing else here yet. I'll try more tomorrow.

Toodles,
Tracey

Chapter Seventeen

Chasing a Ghost

June 2, 2020

TRUE TO HIS WORD, SEAN'S MERCEDES PULLED INTO CHRIS'S DRIVEWAY at 8:57 AM. Chris was still slipping on his Docksider shoes when the doorbell rang, and then it rang again two more times in quick succession.

"Where's the fire?" asked Chris as he opened the door. A wide-eyed Sean pushed his way into the house and then turned and stared at Chris with an open mouth. He was ready to say something but didn't know where to start. So Chris preempted him.

"Yeah, I know," said Chris. "I read Tracey's email, too. Pretty bizarre, huh?"

"Oh my God," was all Sean could say.

"So, not only is Shane Tex's son but all of them are direct descendants from Jacob Weiser," Chris stated, shaking his head in wonder. "Who on earth would have guessed that?"

"Well, we already know that Shane doesn't care much for Native Americans, and the same is probably true of his father," stated Sean. "At least now we have a theory why. Their grandfather was slaughtered by the Apaches. At least that's what most of the references say."

"Yeah, and we know how accurate 'the references' are," added Chris sarcastically. "They don't even agree with each other."

"I know. I've read a bunch of them and I'm now more confused about the story than when we first started on this thing," said Sean.

"I also think we can safely assume that the Durhams will protect anything they find using force and won't hesitate to break out their full arsenal should anyone of Native American descent show up trying to claim mineral rights on the land," stated Chris.

"Agreed," said Sean.

"Before we call Tracey this morning to find out if she has any leads, we've got a few other matters to take care of," said Chris.

"Such as . . . ?" asked Sean.

"How about we'll 'divide and conquer' here for a short while," suggested Chris. "You take a few photographs of the turquoise necklace I got from Alvah Dunning's stuff in Blue Mountain Lake. Then go onto the State Museum's website and look up the email address for Dr. Stanton Turner. Email him a copy of the photos along with a note saying that we'd like to know if he could identify the source of the jewelry. Even what part of the country it comes from would be helpful, but more specifically we'd like to know if he could take a guess at the tribe of the artist. And do me a favor, and give him my email address and phone number, while you're at it."

"OK," agreed Sean.

"Meanwhile, I'm going to send an email to Max, copying in Tex, telling them what we've discovered so far and that we're going to spend the next day or two trying to track down any living descendants of the Sykes family."

"I take it you're going to leave out the part about investigating the Durham family tree, right?" asked Sean with a smirk. "We probably want to leave that bit out."

It was after 9:15 AM by the time the two men completed sending their respective emails. They then dialed Tracey's number in Philadelphia and waited for her to pick up.

"Hey, Sean," the pleasant voice called out over the speakerphone. Chris and Sean were seated at the kitchen table with a notepad at the ready.

"Hi, Tracey," replied Sean. "I'm here with Chris, we've got you on speaker."

"Well, hi to both of you!" pealed Tracey. "I wish we had a video connection here. Chris, I haven't seen you in a couple years. How is everything?"

"I haven't changed much, just as ornery as ever," quipped Chris. "And Sean wanted to see you kind of badly, so he left me to do the boring work yesterday while the two of you were gallivanting in some gourmet restaurant down there."

"Hey, I don't normally get to go out like that, so maybe you can take me somewhere good next time, OK?"

"Sounds good," said Chris, trying to steer the conversation to the topic at hand. "Were you able to find anything about this Martha Sykes person in Syracuse?"

"Believe it or not, I've had a very good morning here," reported Tracey. "And I have a lot for you to do and places to go."

"Sounds promising already," said Sean.

"I started with the historical lineage databases and found that Martha Sykes started out life as Martha Dunning, and she was none other than Alvah's younger sister."

"Believe it or not, I was kind of suspecting that from the beginning," said Chris. "Alvah really didn't have many friends, and a blood relative was the most logical person for him to send a trunk full of valuables to."

"Anyway, she was born eight years after Alvah, and she became a Sykes through marriage. They moved to Syracuse in 1850. Their home of record was at 422 Baldwin Street, which is near Onondaga Creek in the city."

"I don't suppose anyone from the family still lives at that residence?" asked Chris.

"No, the property actually fell into default more than once, and the name on the deed was not anyone related to the family by that time," reported Tracey.

"OK, you said that you had good news," said Sean hopefully. "So far, this family in Syracuse sounds like a dead end. What else do you have?"

"I was able to trace the family down to find a living descendent of the Sykes family, and they still live in New York State," said Tracey triumphantly. "Score one for me!"

"Great news," agreed Chris. "Do you have any information on him or her?"

"Yes, and the family name changed from Sykes to Simms in the third generation after Martha Sykes. It was her granddaughter who married a Simms, and their daughter, who was born in 1942, is still alive."

"Were you able to get any information on where she is and how to contact her?" asked Chris.

"You can find the lovely Barbara Simms at 111 Chapel Street in the town of Canastota, New York. She's been at that address for over thirty years."

"Phone number?" asked Chris as he jotted down the details.

"It's (315) 426-0886. I didn't try calling it to confirm, but that's the last number that appears in the database you guys gave me. By the way, I can't believe everything you can find about people in there. I took the liberty of looking up her criminal record, too."

"Does she have one?" asked Sean, sounding incredulous.

"No, but it would have been in there if she had," replied Tracey. "That thing gives you a report on *everything*."

"Thanks again, Tracey," added Chris. "We'll get back to you later on today. In the meantime, keep on working your way down that list and call us if you find anything really interesting. OK?"

"OK, talk later," said Tracey, signing off.

* * * * * *

The town of Canastota is a sleepy little hamlet about twenty-five miles east of Syracuse. Incorporated in 1835, it lived and died with the commerce along the Erie Canal, which provided much of its early character. A number of the town's original homes are still standing.

Chris and Sean had called the number provided by Tracey with little hope of actually reaching someone. Phone numbers change and people move, so it's unusual to find a number that's stayed the same for long. Yet they remained hopeful as they heard a ringing on the other end.

"Hello," sounded the aged female voice through Sean's speakerphone.

"Hello, I'm trying to reach Barbara Simms," said Chris in his most calming voice.

"Well, you've reached her," replied the elderly woman. "Who is this, please?"

"Miss Simms, my name is Chris, and my partner and I have been trying to find you for some time now. We're doing some research on a famous Adirondack person by the name of Alvah Dunning, and we have reason to believe that you are a direct descendent."

"As a matter of fact, that is correct," said Barbara in a spritely voice. "He was the older brother of my grandfather's grandfather, so I'm not sure how much blood we have in common."

"Wow, that's quite a family history," said Chris. "Alvah is one of the most famous characters in Adirondack history. You must be very proud."

"Actually, he didn't have a very good reputation out in town," said Barbara, contesting Chris's statement. "But I suppose he was who he was. Those were different times."

"Miss Simms, we are very interested in talking to you about Alvah, and even more interested in his sister Martha, who lived in Syracuse in the mid-1900s. Would it be OK if we stopped by to chat with you? We promise it wouldn't take long."

There was a long pause on the other side of the phone as Barbara weighed the request.

"I wouldn't mind, but I wouldn't want to waste your time, either. I don't think there's much that I could tell you. I certainly never knew Martha, and I couldn't even tell you where she lived."

"Believe it or not, we already have that information," said Chris. "We're just interested in anything else you might know or remember, or any old family records you might still have."

Chris's last statement evoked a burst of laughter from the elderly woman.

"Now that's something I could probably give you," she said. "This house is filled with old stuff, including papers. My parents never threw away anything, and a lot of their stuff is still stored up in the attic. The only problem is, I'm almost eighty years old and it's hard for me to get up there anymore."

"Please don't worry about that," Chris said. "We'd be grateful for any assistance you could give us."

CHASING A GHOST

"Well ... OK," she said. "What time would you boys want to stop by?"

"What time would be best for you?"

"How about right after lunch, if you're coming from nearby. Around 1:00 PM?"

"That works for us," said Chris. "And thank you so much. You have no idea how much we appreciate it."

The ride from North Syracuse to Canastota takes only about forty minutes, but Chris insisted on leaving over an hour ahead.

"We need to make one stop along the way," said Chris as he pulled his Jeep from his driveway.

"Why?"

"Never mind. Just come along for the ride."

A few miles down the road, Chris pulled his Jeep off the highway and turned down a few roads before pulling in to a Wegmans supermarket.

"What's the deal?" asked Sean. "I already had breakfast."

"Banana bread," replied Chris without explanation.

"Banana bread?" repeated Sean.

"Yes, banana bread," said Chris again. "Let me explain something to you about senior citizens. First of all, every one I've ever met is always tickled pink if you bring them a gift, especially if it's edible. Secondly, I've never met a senior who doesn't like banana bread."

"So now we're resorting to bribery. Good!" remarked Sean.

"Whatever works."

It was two minutes before 1:00 PM when Chris's forest-green Jeep pulled into the driveway alongside the old house on Chapel Street. The house was white, with pale blue shutters and a wide front porch. An elderly woman accompanied by an even older-looking man were sitting at a table on the porch with a pitcher of iced tea between them.

The two men stepped out of the Jeep and approached the house with Chris in the lead.

"Miss Simms?" Chris called out, the loaf of bread beneath his arm.

"That's me," replied the woman, smiling from beneath a pink-brimmed hat. "You've come to the right place."

"Hi, I'm Chris, and this is my friend Sean. It's so nice to meet you."

"Likewise," replied Barbara. "And this is my friend Mike."

159

THE DUTCHMAN'S GOLD

Chris guessed that Mike was really there to protect Barbara in case they were there for duplicitous purposes, although Mike appeared to be too aged to offer anything but token resistance in the event of any real trouble. The fact that he was wearing a "World War II Veteran" ball cap lent further credence to Chris's assumption.

"Very nice to meet you, Mike," said Sean, shaking the old-timer's bony hand. "Did you actually serve in World War II?"

"Yes, young man, I was there, first in the Atlantic and then in the Pacific," he replied.

"Where did you serve?" asked Chris.

"I was in the Navy, serving on cans* the entire time. I mainly did escort duty in the Atlantic before Germany fell, and then ended up in Tokyo Bay on September 2, 1945, when Japan surrendered. So you might say I saw the full show."

"Wow, that's really impressive," gasped Chris. "There's not many of you left."

"No, there aren't, that's for sure. Most of my Navy buddies have been gone for many years."

Barbara was delighted with the banana bread presented by Chris.

"Oh, my favorite! How did you know?"

"Just a hunch," ventured Chris with a wink.

"I'm going in to get a knife and cut into this right now. I hope you'll join me for a slice."

When Barbara returned, Chris and Sean brought up the topic of their visit, which was to find out what, if anything, she knew about the shipment sent from Alvah Dunning to his sister over 120 years earlier.

"Not much," she admitted. "That was such a long time ago, and they both lived four generations back. All I've heard were some old stories, passed down, and I can't even vouch that those are true anymore. Are you two writing a book about Alvah Dunning?"

"No, not really," replied Chris. "Actually, we're interested in the period of time from 1899 to 1900, when Alvah moved out west for a year. There's a theory that he accidently learned the location of an old gold mine out

---

*"Can" is the nickname given to any small destroyer, frigate, or escort vessel in the old navy.

160

there, and we've been paid to try to find out anything that might still be connected to that rumor."

"Oh," exclaimed Barbara, spinning the word out for an extended period of time. "Now the story about the gold, that's something that *has* been passed down between generations, but not in a good way."

"What do you mean?" asked Chris.

"Many people in our family believe that there was a trunk full of gold sent by Alvah to his sister, who lived in Syracuse. But the trunk came with a curse, and everyone who touched it ended up dying. Everyone."

"Really?" asked Chris with a surprised expression on his face.

"Yes. The story goes that Alvah shipped the case to his sister in Syracuse, and he died within a year of sending it to her. Plus, Alvah had told her that the person who originally owned the chest had died as the result of an Indian attack. Martha's husband, Luther, died the day after he opened the chest to weigh the contents. So Martha was always afraid of the thing and never opened it, even though she knew it was probably filled with gold or other valuables."

"What ever happened to the chest?" asked Chris.

"Our family folklore says that Martha arranged to ship it to her grandson, who was my grandfather. Supposedly, he wanted to use the contents to buy a house up near Raquette Lake. But two things happened that presented this from ever coming to fruition."

"And those were . . . ?" prompted Sean.

"Well, first, Martha died of a sudden stroke, supposedly the day after she put the chest on a train bound for Raquette Lake."

"Oh my gosh, I've got to admit, that is kind of spooky, even if you don't believe in curses," admitted Chris.

"Yes, it is," said Barbara. "And secondly, the chest must have been stolen, because it never arrived in Raquette Lake. "

"You mean it just vanished into thin air?" asked Sean.

"Yup. No trace of it was ever discovered. I heard it discussed once by my grandfather around forty or fifty years ago. Some of the family elders figured it just got stolen by someone who worked for the railroad."

"But if it was secured by a heavy lock, how would anyone even know what was inside, assuming that it was gold?"

"I don't know, I don't know . . ." said the old woman, her voice trailing off.

Barbara disappeared into the house and returned with a plate and knife, which she used to cut into the banana bread. She offered slices to everyone.

"You mentioned that you had family records stored in your house. Is there any way that Sean and I could look through those papers, especially anything you still have from Martha or her children?"

"Goodness gracious, I wouldn't know where to start," answered Barbara. "I do know where the original family Bible is, and there are a lot of other papers in the same box. That's probably the best place to look. I just don't know if I can still make it up there anymore. The stairs leading up to the attic are steep and kind of rickety."

"Would it be OK if Sean or I climb those stairs and bring the box down for you? I assure you that you can keep an eye on us as we look through the papers. We'd even be willing to pay you for your time and effort."

"That's OK, boys, I understand it's all in the interest of history," she replied.

"And a little gold," added Mike, who had remained quiet until now.

Barbara escorted the two up to the second floor of the house, where they pulled down a small door in the ceiling exposing a pull-down ladder. Sean climbed up the steps slowly, taking directions from Barbara down below. She directed him to follow the wall on the right side of the attic until reaching a bright blue chest of drawers.

"Now just on the other side of that chest, do you see a really big wicker basket, with two handles on the upper edges? It should be filled with an old Bible and a lot of papers."

"Yes, I've got it," replied Sean from above.

"That's the one you want. Just bring that down and we'll take it out to the porch."

Sean handed the basket down to Chris, who then held the ladder stable while Sean made his descent.

"This is my great-great grandmother's Bible," said Barbara as she lovingly opened the front cover. "I don't know why my parents saved some of this stuff, but I'm glad they hung on to the Bible."

Back on the front porch, Sean began turning the pages of the Bible while Chris maintained an easy conversation with the family matron. There were some notations recorded in the pages, but nothing that referred to Alvah Dunning or his long-lost shipment from out west.

Once he finished with the large volume, Sean began flipping through the many old documents that filled the rest of the basket. It was jammed with a myriad of old postcards, letters, newspaper clippings, and other family-related documents. Some of the newspapers crumbled into dust when handled, so Sean tried his best to avoid coming in contact with those pages.

Chris was still chatting with Barbara when out of the corner of his eye, he caught a glimpse of Mike picking up his third slice of banana bread. He smiled to himself watching the loaf slowly vanishing.

"Now here's something you might want to check out," said Sean as he held up an old certificate. "This is a certificate for 200 shares of the Century Motor Vehicle Company, issued on June 2, 1901."

"You mean it might be worth a lot of money if I could sell it today?" asked Barbara.

"Uh, no. The company actually collapsed and went bankrupt about two years after those shares were purchased," Sean said.

"Then what good is it?" asked Barbara in a disappointed voice.

"Well, it was an interesting company that was founded in the city of Syracuse, and it produced some of the first electric and steam-powered cars," explained Sean. "The stock certificate itself might be worth a few dollars to a dealer."

Barbara just looked at him with a pout on her face. "A 'few dollars' doesn't do me much good."

Continuing to paw through the basket contents, Sean pulled out more postcards, some from a trip to Niagara Falls in the 1930s. He also came upon a program from President Calvin Coolidge's inauguration in March of 1925 along with a number of envelopes with cancellation marks over the early postage stamps.

"You're right, there isn't too much in here I've found that will help us out," said Sean as he moved another pile of papers to the side. "But some

THE DUTCHMAN'S GOLD

of the old stuff is interesting, especially if you have any younger relatives who collect stamps. There are some really old ones in here."

Chris was about to help Barbara by carrying the tray with the banana bread back into the house when Mike interrupted. "Hold on, young man, I'll just take one more piece," helping himself to his fourth slice.

"Mike!" exclaimed Barbara. "You're going to get sick."

"I didn't have breakfast this morning," complained the old veteran as he bit into the next slice.

Sean, who had been holding a short stack of papers in his left hand while sifting with his right, suddenly froze as if he'd seen a ghost. Chris noticed the expression on his face and recognized the meaning instantly.

"Find something?" he asked, leaning in Sean's direction.

Sean didn't answer, but instead sat completely still, staring at the yellowed form.

"Sean, what's up?"

"This is it," Sean said quietly, his eyes moving closer to the page as he inspected the faded print. "This is what we came for."

Barbara and Chris both jumped from their seats and crowded behind Sean's chair. Mike meanwhile remained rooted in place as he finished the last of his banana bread.

Receipt for package, shipped by Sender, Martha Sykes, from Syracuse, NY, to Recipient Michael Sykes, Jr., Raquette Lake, NY, shipment date November 6, 1913. Accepted for shipment by Freight Division, Syracuse Northern Railroad, forwarding to Raquette Lake Railway no later than November 9, 1913. One container only.

"So that was it," said Barbara solemnly. "This is our proof that there really was a case filled with gold, and it got stolen by the railroad."

"I'm sorry to dispute you, Barbara, but this doesn't prove or disprove any part of that story," remarked Chris.

"But, but, it's all there on the receipt," cried Barbara.

"First of all, there is nothing to prove that the case was loaded with gold," countered Chris. "Even if witnesses saw the contents previously, someone could have switched it for a pile of worthless rocks before it was shipped."

164

"Secondly," continued Chris, you have no proof that someone from the train actually took the case. Really, it could have been anyone."

"It's just not fair," repeated Barbara, shaking her head over and over again. "Someone ended up with all that money while my grandfather never got to purchase his house. That's what the gold was supposed to buy, you know."

"Would you mind if we took this railroad receipt document and made a copy of it?" asked Chris. "I could mail it back to you in a special cardboard envelope so it wouldn't be damaged."

"That's OK, honey, you can just take it," offered Barbara. "I don't need it back. It not like we could use it anymore to demand the case back. It's over one hundred years old, so I'm sure that whoever made off with it is long-since dead."

Once Sean completed his scan of the documents in the basket, they replaced it in the attic for Barbara and then prepared to leave for Syracuse.

"We will call you if we find anything, OK?" said Chris to Barbara. "We promise."

"I know you will," said Barbara with sincerity in her voice. "I really feel like I can trust you, and I appreciate all the information you've given me. I feel like I know a lot more about my own family since you visited."

"We appreciate your trust," said Chris.

"There's just one more thing I'd like to say . . ." Barbara said in a hesitating voice.

The two boys waited for her to proceed as she looked at them appealingly.

"When I think of all the people who died trying to get this case of gold or move it somewhere—Alvah Dunning, Luther Sykes, Martha Sykes, all of them. Please, boys, please be careful."

"We will, Barbara, we will," promised Sean as he took her hand in his. "We promise. It will be fine."

Before leaving, the two men also tried to say their goodbyes to Mike, who was the only living World War II veteran they knew. However, he had already gone back into the kitchen for another slice of banana bread.

The Dutchman's Gold

* * * * * *

The drive back to North Syracuse was uneventful, and Sean tried to make conversation as they motored along the New York State Thruway.

"Well, that was a nice trip, and we were able to locate the actual receipt that Martha Sykes received when she sent the package."

Silence.

"And that proves, if nothing else, that the crate was actually shipped up to Raquette Lake to her grandson's address, although it doesn't appear as though it ever made it there," continued Sean.

"Uh huh."

"Anyway, Barbara sure was a nice lady, and a genuine descendent of Alvah Dunning, no less. I'm really glad we got to meet her."

Once again, Sean's observations were met with a cathedral silence.

"OK, buddy, what's up? I know you too well to believe that you're just not talking. Something's going on inside that head of yours and I want to know what it is."

Without saying a word, Chris suddenly veered his Jeep off the Thruway and into a "Text Stop" made for drivers who want to make phone calls or send texts without risking an accident. He pulled into a parking space and immediately buried his head in his hands, rubbing his face as though lost in deep thought.

"What is it? What is it? What is it?" Chris said over and over again.

"What is what?" asked Sean, looking with concern at his friend. "What's bugging you?"

"That package, the one Martha Sykes shipped on November 6, 1913, and was to be delivered on the ninth; something is just bothering me about that date. November 9, 1913. *What the hell is it?*"

Sean quickly pulled out his smartphone and googled the date, November 9, 1913.

"Well, let's see; Thelma Hulbert, the famous English painter was born in the town of Bath on that day," suggested Sean.

"No," replied Chris.

"On November 1 of that year, the Notre Dame Fighting Irish beat the Army Cadets in football that day by a score of thirty-five to thirteen by using the forward pass, which had almost never been seen in the past," added Sean.

"No," said Chris again, still lost in thought.

"There were a lot of ships lost on November 9, too," noticed Sean. "Evidently there was a massive storm over the Great Lakes and parts of the northeast United States. But that's probably not it, either."

Chris suddenly lifted his head from his hands and looked at Sean, this time with a noticeably brighter expression.

"What was that?" he asked.

"On November 9, 1913, the worst part of the storm called 'The White Hurricane' struck the Great Lakes with winds topping eighty miles per hour and waves exceeding thirty-five feet in height. At least nineteen ships were sunk during the storm and two hundred and fifty people were killed. Six of those ships were never found. It must have been a pretty huge storm."

Chris sat silently for another moment, putting dates and events together in his mind, turning the story over and over again as he mentally worked the puzzle. He then quietly turned to Sean and made a request.

"Could you do me a favor, old buddy?"

"Sure, whatcha need?" asked Sean.

"The shipment from Martha Sykes was supposed to be delivered to her grandson, Michael Sykes Jr., on November 9, 1913. Could you please google 'The Great Train Wreck of 1913' for me and tell me the date it happened?"

Sean quickly opened a browser window on his phone and tapped in the information. His response came back in a nanosecond. He looked at it momentarily before addressing Chris with the information that appeared on his screen.

"You must be a Svengali," said Sean with wonder in his voice.

"Why, what was the date?" asked Chris.

"November 9, 1913."

CHAPTER EIGHTEEN

Catching a Train

June 4, 2020

CHRIS DROVE MOST OF THE WAY BACK TO NORTH SYRACUSE IN TOTAL silence, joined by Sean who was likewise muted. They both considered the implications of the coincidence: a locked case had been shipped from Syracuse to Raquette Lake on a train. Assuming that the transfer had been made as it should have, and the case was transferred from the Syracuse Northern Line to the Raquette Lake Railway, then it would have been onboard the railroad the precise day that the cars jumped the track and tumbled down the hill. That created a mountain of possibilities.

They were only five minutes from Chris's house when he reopened the conversation.

"I've been going over this in my head time after time, and I keep getting the same mental picture."

"You're talking about the case of gold shipment and the train going off the track, I assume," said Sean.

"Correct," stated Chris, still weighing out the possibilities. "There always is the chance that someone from the salvage crews who pulled the train cars out of the wreckage absconded with it. I mean, there must have been a lot of packages and materials thrown around, including cargo, mail, and stuff like that."

"True, but it doesn't sound as though that's what you're thinking, is it?"

CATCHING A TRAIN

"I'm not sure what I'm thinking," confessed Chris. "But I do know that we can't guess on this one. I'd like to find an expert, and quickly. I'd like to find someone who is both a train person as well as a historian who knows the area around where the accident occurred."

Sean glanced at his watch. "It's almost 5:00 PM, so I doubt we're going to find anyone in their office this afternoon. How about we make this 'call number one' for tomorrow morning?"

"Sounds good to me. I also have to check to find out in which county the wreck took place. It's either Hamilton or just west of there."

Once again, Sean tapped some characters into his cell phone and located the results.

"If the wreck took place along the shoreline of Fourth Lake between Old Forge and Inlet, that would place it in Herkimer County. Actually, it's all Herkimer County until almost the point where Route 28 enters Inlet, and then it crosses over into Hamilton County."

"I am hereby officially changing your name to Mr. Google," quipped Chris. "Anyway, thanks. I'll call someone at the Historical Association first thing in the morning."

"I'll be over at 8:00 AM tomorrow," said Sean. "Does that work for you?"

"Sure, I'll even provide breakfast," replied Chris. "And by the way, do you own any shovels?"

"I think so. Why?"

"Do me a favor and throw one in the trunk before you come over. It might save us the cost of buying one," suggested Chris.

"Are you thinking of burying something?" asked Sean.

"Nope. Just the opposite."

* * * * * *

Chris spent a quiet evening at home putting together his thoughts and looking at some maps of the Fulton Chain of Lakes. Around 7:30 PM, Kristi came over with a takeout dinner from a Syracuse Italian restaurant. It had been a few weeks since they'd been able to get together, so they

169

spent time catching up on current news and then snuggled up together on the couch for dinner and a movie.

Kristi was just as interested in learning about the contents of the trunk as Chris.

"If this Dunning guy really did ship a trunk full of gold from the Superstition Mountains to his sister in New York, he must have had some source for it out there. Maybe I was wrong about my initial prognosis about there not being gold in those mountains," she said.

"Well, we know there are some places in the region where gold had been discovered in the past," said Chris. "It's just not plentiful, and possibly not in the exact spot where we're looking."

"I've got the day off tomorrow since they are closing my building to blow out all the ventilation ducts. Do you two want company when you go to check out the path of the railway? It sounds like fun," she said.

"I'm not sure that digging in the mud for hours is my idea of a good time, and that's only if we get some good returns from the metal detector," replied Chris. "But sure, I'd love to have you along for company. Besides, you're much better-looking than Sean."

"Gee, thanks," giggled Kristi. "If that's the best you can do for a compliment, maybe I'll just stay at home and watch old episodes of *Seinfeld*!"

* * * * * *

When Sean arrived the following morning, he found Chris and Kristi in the backyard of the house testing out Sean's Troy Shadow X5 metal detector.

"Hey, did I give you permission to use that?" he called out jokingly as he approached the pair.

"Did I give you permission to leave it in my shed since last summer?" countered Chris. "The batteries were dead and starting to leak into the control box, so lucky for you that I did some maintenance for you."

"Thanks," replied Sean. "I guess I did forget to take it home with me. How's it working?"

"It appears to be good enough for our purposes, although there may be a fair amount of scrap iron where we're headed."

"No worries, I can adjust the sensitivity and other settings to account for the junk metals. I can even switch the search loops if we need it," said Sean.

"We tried burying a quarter down about nine inches, and it still picked it up pretty clearly," said Chris. "And what we're looking for today would be hundreds, if not thousands of times larger."

"And certainly much denser, depending on the quantity of gold that we're talking," added Kristi. "But how about that law you two told me about a couple years ago . . . remember? If you find any gold or silver in New York State, it immediately becomes property of the state? You're not allowed to keep it?"

"It all depends," replied Chris. "Are we talking about New York State laws or Tex Durham laws?"

"Yeah, that's right," sighed Kristi. "You told me about him."

The trio then headed into the house and Chris tossed a bag of bagels on the kitchen table.

"I've got cream cheese, peanut butter, or orange marmalade. Take your pick," he announced.

"Yummy. Now that's what I call gourmet dining," said Sean.

At 9:00 AM, Chris picked up his cell phone and dialed the number for the Herkimer County Historical Office. After reaching the attendant, he explained his needs and then quickly grabbed a pencil and notepad to write down a number. He thanked the person on the other end of the line and then hung up, noting that the entire call had taken less than a minute.

"Well, that was certainly productive," he noted as he looked at his own handwriting. "The woman at the Historical Office said not only is there an expert on the Great Train Wreck of 1913 who is associated with the office, but he's in the process of writing an article on it now. She gave me his phone number."

"What's his name?" asked Sean.

"Don't ask me to say it," replied Chris.

"Really, what's his name?"

"Ed S-z-c-z-e-p-a-n-s-k-i," said Chris, spelling out the name rather than saying it out loud. "Please don't ask me to try to pronounce it."

THE DUTCHMAN'S GOLD

"Just call him 'Ski' for short," suggested Kristi.

Chris dialed in the number given to him by the Historical Office and then waited for the other end to pick up. A voice responded on the third ring.

"Hello, is this Ed?" Chris asked.

"It is. Who is this, please?"

"Ed, this is Chris Carey. I'm with a couple other folks who are really interested in the Great Train Wreck of 1913, and we'd like to go out and see the site. Are you ever out there?"

"I'm out there quite often, especially this month," replied the train fanatic. "I'm trying to finish up some research and also get some more photos for an article I'm writing."

"Is there any chance we could bribe you into meeting us out there sometime early today?" asked Chris. "We're on a limited schedule, but we'd love to get an expert's view on the site and how the accident unfolded."

"Sure, I could meet you at the site," volunteered Ed. "It's 9:05 AM right now, so how about 10:30?"

"It's going to take me longer than that to get there, so how about noon, or a little before?"

"That will work for me," replied Ed. "As a matter of fact, I may already be there, so look for a white Ford F150 truck as you go by the historic sign marker. I'll be somewhere in the vicinity."

"Fantastic. I can't thank you enough," said Chris." We'll find you somehow."

With little time to spare and 106 miles of road to cover, the trio gulped the rest of their breakfasts and piled into Chris's Jeep. They tossed the shovels and metal detector into the rear compartment before hitting the road. Chris followed the Thruway initially and then used the smaller Routes 12 and 28 to pare some mileage off the trip. Stopping only once for coffee, they arrived slightly before 11:45 AM. The railroad enthusiast's truck was already parked by the side of the road.

Chris initially honked his horn twice before they saw their man through the trees. He was up on a rise, above the road, and taking pictures along the stretch of greenery.

Catching a Train

"Ed?" Sean called out to the man with the camera.

"Yes, that would be me," he replied. "You must be Chris."

"Actually, my friend here is Chris. I'm Sean, and this lovely lady with us is Kristi."

"Well, it's nice to meet all of you," replied Ed.

"I would have addressed you by your last name, but I wasn't about to attempt it," admitted Chris.

"No, unless you are Polish by birth, I'd leave it alone," he chuckled. "'Ed' will do just fine, thanks."

"So you're writing an article for a magazine," said Kristi excitedly. "That's really wonderful! Are you a writer by trade?"

"Heck no, I'm a retired construction worker," said Ed. "But I love railroads and I've done some writing for our local paper in the past, so I thought it would be a good challenge."

Ed looked much more like a construction worker than a writer. Not only was he an inch taller than Chris, but he also had broad shoulders and huge, work-hardened hands that seemed made for handling tools. He also possessed a bit of a beer belly that seemed to go with the total package. Chris guessed his weight at around 320 pounds.

"So what's your interest in the wreck?" asked Ed as he shook hands with each member of the group. "A lot of folks stop by and read the sign along the road,* but not many are interested enough to track down the full history."

"We just love traveling around chasing down history," said Chris, not wanting to disclose the full reason for their visit. "We were looking around the battleground at Saratoga last week, and yesterday we stopped by to visit Adirondack French Louie's grave in Speculator. After those stops, this sounded like a fun side trip, so here we are."

"Well, I'd be happy to show you around, as long as you're not writers trying to scoop me out of a story."

"No, not at all," Chris assured him. "We'd just like to poke around and see how the accident unfolded."

---

*The NY Department of Transportation erected a sign by the side of Route 28 announcing that "Here on November 9, 1913, a train struck a log, derailed, and went over the cliff killing three of its crew."

The Dutchman's Gold

"Fair enough," agreed Ed. "You're standing almost at the point where it all happened."

"Y'know, one thing that puzzles me looking around here is that I don't see any 'cliff' like the one they talked about online," said Sean. "There's an incline here, but certainly nothing that I'd call a cliff for the engine to roll off."

"You have to understand, the place has been graded several times over the last century," explained Ed. "This has been converted into more of a pedestrian and bike trail, now that it's part of the Old Forge-to-Inlet recreational pathway. People use this route every day for biking and hiking and jogging, so they put in a path that parallels the highway for quite a way. They also leveled out some of the incline that used to edge the old tracks, so it's a lot flatter than it used to be."

"Could you show us where the train cars came to rest after they derailed?" asked Chris.

"Sure, you're almost standing on top of the spot," replied the construction man. They have actual pictures of the wreck down at the Historical Society building down in Herkimer. I think I even have one or two of them saved to my cell phone, although I didn't take the clearest possible photos of the article. But you can still get a feel for the position of the cars and where they landed."

As Ed spoke, he turned on his phone and quickly scrolled through his photo collection.

"There we go," he cried triumphantly as he located the photos he desired. "Take a look; I've got a few of them on here."

Chris took the phone from him and immediately used his fingers to expand the view on the screen. As he zoomed in on the side of the first cargo cars, Sean slipped in behind him and shared the view of the photographs.

As much as Chris wanted to jump for joy, he managed to preserve a serious expression. The very first picture on Ed's phone confirmed everything that he hoped to find: a large sliding door was pulled all the way back, exposing the entire cargo bay of the car. In addition to shredded parts of the car wall itself, at least some of the freight had been jettisoned out of the opening as the car tumbled down the steep incline. In other

CATCHING A TRAIN

words, anything from inside could now be anywhere outside. Including being ground into the mud and water at the bottom of the cliff.

After scrolling through the follow-on sequence of photographs, Chris passed the phone to Sean who also examined the shots.

"Let me ask you something, and you may have to make a guess on this," Chris said as he prefaced his question. "Based on the photographs you've seen, including those on your phone, do you think the cars rolled over at least once on the way down the cliff?"

Ed gave Chris an appraising stare before speaking.

"Now that's a tough question to answer," he said, weighing his response. "If the cargo car you see in front came uncoupled, it's very possible it may have rolled once. I think you can see all the debris it left behind, as though it was throwing its cargo from the inside. And there certainly is damage to the car from top to bottom. But I think we'd be guessing more than anything."

"Yeah, I think so, too," said Chris.

"Why do I get the feeling that you're after more than just a basic story here?" asked Ed in a suspicious tone. "What difference does it make how the cars tumbled down the cliff? Are you looking for something specific that you're not telling me?"

"No, of course not," said Chris, smiling to disarm the man. "But I do like to try to figure out how things happened, and you've got to admit that this was one strange wreck. It's tragic that three men lost their lives here."

"You can say that again," agreed Ed. "It's a good thing there weren't more passengers onboard or it could have been much worse of a catastrophe."

"Well, we're going to take a hike and see what the rest of this trail looks like as we head toward Inlet," said Chris. "We should be back by 2:00 or 2:30 this afternoon. We'll see you then."

"I doubt that," countered Ed. "I've got to be gone by around 1:00. I'm helping a friend put a deck onto his house, so I'm gone for the rest of the day."

"Well, then, it's been nice meeting you, and thanks for the tour," said Chris. Sean and Kristi also said their goodbyes as the three turned and headed up to the path that led through the woods. Chris looked backward one last time to see Ed returning to his photo activity on the site.

They had walked about one hundred yards before Kristi looked at Chris with a curious expression on her face.

"OK, what's going on?" she asked him. "I know we're not going on a pleasure hike here, so why are we walking along this trail to nowhere?"

"Forty-five minutes," Chris said simply. "That's all we need to kill before Construction Dude goes away for the day. Then we can go back and do anything we want."

"You mean so we can set up the metal detector and start searching the ground?" asked Sean.

"Precisely," replied Chris. "I don't want that guy seeing us searching around the site of his precious crash, especially since we're probably breaking the law by doing so."

"Breaking the law? How are we breaking the law?" cried Kristi. "What's illegal about using a metal detector in the middle of nowhere, like this?"

"Because officially, we are inside a state park, no matter where we are inside the Adirondack 'Blue Line,' which means we are on state land and restricted. Additionally, there is a pair of laws, one of which replaced the other and they both restrict us from looking for 'antiquities,'" explained Chris. "First, the 1906 Antiquities Act says that we're not allowed to dig for or keep anything of historical interest that is over one hundred years old. Then that law was replaced about seventy years ago that changed the timeframe to items more than fifty years old. Either way, if the train crashed in 1913, we're stuck on the wrong side of the law."

"But wait a minute," protested Kristi. "Since when are rocks of 'historical interest,' assuming that the only thing in the case was gold or gold ore? I just don't get it."

"Nice try," said Chris, "but I don't think your argument would hold water in front of a judge."

"So we're just going to give up on it?" Kristi asked incredulously.

"Did I ever say that?" replied Chris.

Kristi continued to stare at her boyfriend while Sean broke into a smile.

CATCHING A TRAIN

"Let me guess," he asked through a grin. "Nighttime dig?"

"You got it," replied Chris. "I don't care about the value of the gold, or anything else about this train wreck story. But we do care about what is inside the case, assuming it's here. Is it low- or medium-grade ore? Or did Alvah Dunning really find the treasure of a lifetime somewhere in the Superstition Mountains?"

"Why would anyone ship a trunk full of low-grade ore across the country?" asked Sean. "That doesn't make sense."

"That's what I'm hoping to find out as well," agreed Chris.

The three walked down the path for about twenty minutes, enjoying each other's company and the bright sunshine of the early June day.

"Just about perfect," noted Sean as he looked up into the bright blue sky overhead.

"Except for the two thousand blackflies that keep trying to land in my hair," said Kristi, swatting the pesky little bugs away from her face.

"If you think it's bad now, just come here in early May," said Chris. "It's five times worse than this, easily."

In another five minutes, they made their timed about-face and returned to the site of the train wreck. As Ed had told them earlier, he had left with his truck and the site was now deserted.

Chris opened up the back of the Jeep and Sean removed the case containing the metal detector, assembling the device with the search loop and settings set to detect precious metals. As he worked, his mind was already thinking of alibis to pass along to any law enforcement personnel or likeminded concerned citizens who might stop by to protest their exploration.

"Hey, there's nothing wrong with looking, as long as we're not actually digging for anything, right?" asked Sean innocently.

"Right," said Chris. "After all, we all want to know if there are any parts of the train car still buried beneath the soil. We like trains."

Sean began sweeping the lower side of the hill on the northeast side of the search area, slowly combing the machine back and forth over the terrain. His headset allowed him to better hear both the louder as well as the quieter signals returned from the substrate beneath the electronic loop.

177

"Oh my God, there's a lot of iron down there," said Sean, frowning at the earth beneath his feet. "I'm getting almost continuous signals no matter where I sweep."

"Time to turn the sensitivity up?" asked Chris.

"Definitely," agreed Sean, making adjustments to the dials on his control box.

Within five minutes, Sean came to a halt, moving the detector in smaller circles and arcing movements.

"Hmm, I want to come back to this later," he said. He removed rolls of bright orange and then yellow tape from his pocket. He tore off a piece of the yellow tape and pushed it down into the grass.

"Something interesting?" asked Kristi.

"Yes, probably something small and silver, like a coin. But nothing big."

"What are the two colors of tape for?" asked Chris.

"Yellow means small or not as valuable a metal. Orange means bigger or better," summarized Sean, already continuing with his sweeps.

Sean had covered about forty feet of the site when he suddenly stopped and went into the same slow, detailed search mode. He walked the loop back and forth at least thirty times, listening and moving and then listening again.

"If we have time later, I want to check this one out, too," he said as he deposited a much larger length of the yellow tape on the ground, hiding it as much as possible in the tall grass.

"Large chunk of something," guessed Chris.

"Yeah, probably iron once again, but it still looks interesting."

"*Put the detector down in the grass now,*" Kristi said suddenly, in a loud, commanding voice.

Without turning the machine off, Sean lay the machine down in the tall weeds before turning around to face his friends. In the distance, about a quarter mile away, he could see a State Police car speeding along the highway in their direction.

"And look up there," Kristi said, pointing into a nearby maple tree. "There's an Eastern Crimson-Headed Warbler landing in its nest."

The police car cruised by the three would-be birders, on its way to other business.

"An Eastern Crimson-Headed Warbler?" repeated Chris, laughing at the made-up name. "Now that's about the funniest thing I've heard all day."

"Hey, it worked," replied Kristi, who was amused at her own creation.

Sean continued on his search, which was now about 60 percent complete. He stopped on a couple other occasions to deposit more tape in the grass, noting his suspicions about the identity of the buried object, usually being a coin or other small piece of metal.

"So far it's not looking good for anything major, is it?" asked Chris, following along the swath carved out on the hillside by the detector.

Sean shrugged his shoulders in a noncommittal gesture as he continued to listen through the headset.

"We have no idea if the case was even on this train," he said as he continued to work. "We have no idea if it got stolen by the original salvage team. We have no idea if it got tossed from the train. We have no idea if this is exactly where the freight car carrying the case landed. We have no idea . . . well, you know what I'm saying," he said, looking over his shoulder at Chris.

"Yes. Lots of variables," answered Chris.

The afternoon light began to dwindle slightly as more and more of their primary search area disappeared, all with very minor results. The detector turned up a series of minor objects, some of which were probably silver while others were "interesting" but more likely iron or other non-precious metal. They were now approaching 90 percent completion of their main search area.

Sean had descended down the slope one more time and was about to form the "U" in his pattern to begin the next search line when a loud humming broke the silence in his headset. He turned the volume down along with the sensitivity control and then turned them both down again.

"Wow," came the monosyllabic remark from Sean's lips.

"Wow?" repeated Chris. "We like 'wows.'"

Then more sweeps, followed by wider sweeps, and even more control adjustments on the sensitivity and frequency. He repeated the same sweeps over the same area and then shut the machine off.

Looking back to the highway, he proceeded back to the Jeep followed by Chris and Krista. There, he replaced the search loop on the detector

THE DUTCHMAN'S GOLD

with yet another coil before returning to the patch of ground he'd just searched. A smile appeared on his face as he continued to adjust the control and sweep even more arcs over the soil.

"Wow," he repeated once again, this time in an even more enthusiastic voice. "Whatever this is, it isn't small, and it isn't made out of iron."

"Precious metal?" asked Chris.

"Pretty sure," said Sean.

"Large?" asked Chris, again in one word.

"Very sure," replied Sean.

"Do you want to finish scanning the rest of the ground now?" asked Chris, looking at the remaining patch of grass and dirt still unswept.

"Do you really think we need to?" replied Sean, already turning the metal detector off. "I know what I'm listening to, and I've only heard a sound like that once before," he said.

"Let me guess; it was buried in the ground next to a fireplace on the shore of West Canada Lake," ventured Chris.*

"Correct. Now let's get out of here until it gets a lot darker."

Once the car was repacked with the detector, they all piled back in to start the trek back to Syracuse. "Kristi, once we drop you off at your car, we'll turn back around and try to make it all the way back here tonight for some fun and frolic."

"Why go all the way back just to drop me off," she said dejectedly. "Why can't I just stay and help out?"

"Because three people are easier to see than two people," stated Chris in a firm tone. "Plus, there's no need for any more of us to get arrested tonight than absolutely necessary."

"But I haven't been arrested in ages," she pouted. "This just isn't fair."

Chris just steered the car around a curve and rolled his eyeballs.

* * * * * *

It was after 8:00 PM before the Jeep rolled back into Chris's driveway. All three filed through the front door of the house, with Sean bringing

---

*This is where Chris and Sean discovered the long-lost Gordon Treasure in *Adirondack Trail of Gold* (North Country Books, 2012).

up the rear while carrying the two pizza boxes. Kristi was still petitioning to accompany the two on their return trip to Fourth Lake, but clearly not making any progress with her resolute boyfriend.

"I spent the whole day watching you guys wave your magic wand over that field. The least I should get out of it is to see you find the prize."

"I already told you," countered Chris, "I don't want to have you get arrested with the two of us, should anyone find us. It's just a dumb idea."

"Aaaaaarrrgggghhhh!" screamed Kristi. "It's like talking to a wall."

"At least it's a wall that cares enough to not let you get busted."

"Let's stop arguing and have some pizza," suggested Sean. "I don't know about you two, but I could eat both of these pies by myself."

"Did you know that gold makes up only .004 parts per million of the entire Earth's crust?" said Kristi.

"Fascinating," replied Chris. "Now let's dig into the pizza."

"At least let me come and sit in the car."

"*No!*"

Sean, meanwhile, had deposited the boxes onto the coffee table in front of the television and was already getting out some paper plates.

"Anyway, what are you going to do with the gold if you find it?" asked Kristi. "Are you going to turn it over to the state like the laws say?"

"We'll worry about that if we find it," replied Chris, still not sure of how to handle that with Tex. He knew the businessman funding their work would certainly not want anything turned over to the State of New York.

Sean filled in the missing answer for both of them.

"I think Tex would say, 'over my dead body,' or words to that effect."

"That's if he ever hears about it," added Chris. "Last time I checked the map, the town of Inlet wasn't in the state of Arizona."

The three talked for a while as they devoured their pizza, all the while keeping an eye on the clock.

"Do you have any idea when you'd like to get to work up there?" asked Sean.

"Not too early, but not too late, either," said Chris as he considered the matter. "We want it to be pitch dark, to cover up our movement. We also want most of the road traffic to be gone, so that we'll see a pair of head-lights a half mile away and will have time to duck out of sight if needed."

THE DUTCHMAN'S GOLD

"We won't start too early," said Sean, looking at the clock on the rear brick wall. "Even if we left now, we wouldn't make it up there before almost 10:30. It'll be plenty dark by then."

As Sean was speaking, his cell phone chimed a tone signifying that he had an incoming call.

"That would be my folks or Maggie," he guessed as he pulled the phone off his belt holder. Then, looking at the screen, he added, "It's neither."

"Sean here," he said after pressing the "Accept" button.

"Hello, Sean, this is Dr. Stanton Turner calling from the State Museum in Albany," came the voice from the device.

"Hello, Dr. Turner. You're working kind of late tonight, aren't you?"

"Goes with the territory," the voice continued. "I've been at a conference all day long today but I still had to come back here tonight to move some new materials into our climate-controlled storeroom. So here I am. By the way, is Chris with you right now?"

"He is," replied Sean.

"Why don't you put this on speakerphone so we can all chat at the same time?" asked Dr. Turner.

Sean pressed a button on his screen and then leaned the phone up against a magazine holder on the table.

"OK, can you hear me now?" he asked.

"Perfectly," answered Turner. "Hi, Chris."

"Hi, Dr. Turner. Thanks for calling us back so soon, and so late in the day. Did you have a chance to look at the photographs of the bracelet?"

"I did, and thank you for sending them to me," said Dr. Turner. "It's really a lovely piece. Where did you get it?"

"It's really not ours, and we 'found' it inside another museum," explained Chris. "But it has never been on display, and they have no idea what it is. I found it while going through a box of personal belongings from a hermit who lived in the Adirondack Mountains in the 1800s."

"Hmm, well, that makes no sense at all," said Dr. Turner. "The age of the piece agrees with the time period you mentioned, but its origin is definitely Native American, and from somewhere in the Southwest."

182

"Yeah, that lines up with this story," concurred Chris. "The guy's name was Alvah Dunning, and he supposedly spent one of his later years traveling out west to get away from civilization. He ended up returning the very next year, and this is something that evidently came back with him."

"Alvah Dunning . . . I know that name," said Turner thoughtfully. "He was somewhere up around Raquette Lake; a moose hunter, if I'm not mistaken."

"You know your state history," remarked Chris. "I'm really impressed."

"Anyway, the appearance of the stones and the work of the silver indicates to me that it's from one of a few tribes, probably Navajo, Hopi, or Zuni. They really have a lot of carryover from one to the next and even use the same mythological figures in many cases," explained the expert.

"How about Apache or Pima?" asked Chris.

"Probably not Apache," replied Dr. Turner. "My experience with their stuff has been that they didn't use turquoise nearly as much. A lot of silver, and also a fair amount of carved obsidian when they could find it. But not nearly as much turquois as the other tribes I just mentioned."

"And the Pima?" added Chris.

"Now you're getting pretty specific," remarked the doctor. "That's not a big population and never really was. As I recall, they lived along the Salt River in Arizona."

"That's near the Superstition Mountains, which is the area where Dunning lived for that year of his life."

"That would match up," said Dr. Turner. "I can't really say whether I've ever seen any jewelry from that tribe, so I'd just be guessing to say that the person who made that particular piece came from that tribe. But if he was in contact with them, it may be a good guess."

"I agree," said Chris, "although I don't know how much contact he actually had with the peoples."

"It wouldn't have been an easy bunch to befriend," said Dr. Turner. "They were a pretty primitive culture who spoke a Uto-Aztecan language. They were descended from a clan called the Hohokam, who disappeared from central Arizona about six hundred years ago."

"Now I'm even more impressed," remarked Chris. "You really know your Native American history, too."

"Not as well as you think," admitted Dr. Turner. "This time I'm reading off a screen. I'm pretty good with the origins of tribes here in New York State, but I get a little fuzzy when you move across the country."

"Well, thanks anyway, Doctor. You really have answered our questions, and I don't want to hold you up anymore," said Chris.

"No problem at all, boys. I'm always interested in looking at old relics from the past. Thanks for the opportunity."

After pressing the "Disconnect" button, Sean glanced over at Chris and noted, "Well, that really didn't tell us much, did it?"

"No, really just a confirmation that it is an older piece from the area around Arizona, without getting too specific. It's just one more piece of the puzzle that fits in."

"Speaking of the puzzle, shouldn't we be pushing off soon?" asked Sean, looking once again at the clock.

"Very true," agreed Chris. Then, turning to Kristi, he asked, "How would you like to take the rest of the pizza home with you?"

"The only slices left are from the double-anchovy pie, so no thanks," she replied with a scorn.

After walking Kristi out to her car, Chris and Sean were ready to depart. They decided to swap out the driving duties as Chris had already driven over four hours earlier in the day. Sean slid into the driver's side and adjusted the seat forward.

They had also refreshed the inventory of tools in the back of the vehicle, adding some smaller digging devices, a brush, and some mesh strainers for removing dirt from around different-sized nuggets. They also threw in a large, heavyweight canvas duffel bag that was left over from Sean's youth camp days. Chris completed the packing by adding a headlamp and a pair of powerful flashlights along with a large package of extra batteries.

"We really can't tell what we're going to find," said Chris as they pulled out onto the main road leading away from the A-frame house. "If we go by the assumption that the buried object is the original case that belonged to Dunning and then to his sister, it's been buried there for over a hundred years. It's also an area that gets pretty wet at times, so anything that was wood would have completely rotted away by now, leaving just the contents in the ground."

"Yup, I agree," said Sean.

"If the suitcase was some kind of metal, we might have the same dilemma," said Chris. "It probably would have rusted away to nothing by now."

"How about if it was made out of aluminum," suggested Sean. "It might still be intact."

"I don't know if they made aluminum cases at the start of the twentieth century," said Chris. "We'd have to call Doctor Google to look that one up."

"At your service," smiled Sean, humored by the nickname.

"You do know," Sean continued, "aluminum has been around longer than most people realize. Not only did the Wright brothers use it in the motor of their early airplane, but I think I read once about a Greek emperor receiving aluminum as a present shortly after the birth of Christ. It's been around a long time."

"I still don't think that's what we're going to find when we get back up to the wreck site," predicted Chris.

"Well, we'll know soon enough," said Sean. "We'll be on-site in just about two hours."

The two fell silent for a few minutes as they turned onto the Thruway to begin the high-speed portion of their journey. With little else to do, Chris decided that it might be a good idea to check in with Tracey. He texted her first to confirm that she was still awake and then selected her number on his phone directory.

"Hey, Sean, how ya doing, honey?" Tracey's melodic voice spilled from the phone.

Chris shot an appraising stare at his friend before speaking up. "Uh, actually, this is Chris. Your 'honey' is driving the car."

A peal of laughter came through the phone. "Oh, come on," she pleaded. "You know you're both 'honey' to me."

"Oh, sure, you say that *now*," said Chris, his voice full of sarcasm.

"No, really, you are!" she repeated, still giggling.

"Anyway, the two of us are just heading up to work on something that you helped us find," Chris said, crediting Tracey with tracking down the Simms family. "And both of us really want to thank you for all the ancestry work you've been doing. It was amazing that you found that Jacob Weiser was the grandfather of Tex Durham. I didn't tell you this last time we spoke, but that explains a lot."

"Cool," said Tracey. "I didn't think anything of it when I came across it in the database, but I found the same name in two different places, so I think it's right."

"I have no doubt about it," replied Chris. "Thanks again."

"Do you have anything else for me to work on right now?" asked Tracey.

"If you have time, see if you can track down any references to Jacob Weiser and what happened to him in his later years," said Chris. "This is probably going to be tough because many of the references question whether anyone by that name even existed. Some people speculate that Jacob Waltz and Jacob Weiser were actually one and the same."

"I can look into that for you," said Tracey. "Anything else?"

"No, although I think Sean here wants to come back down and take you out to Burger King again."

"Burger King? He treated me to a great dinner at my favorite bistro, and then he treated me to a couple CDs I wanted from a music store on the way back to campus. That's a far cry from Burger King."

Chris shot another piercing glance across the front seat at Sean, who cringed at Tracey's response.

"OK, just give us a call if you find anything on Jacob Weiser. And thanks again for all your hard work."

Once they hung up, Chris turned his level stare back in Sean's direction and waited for him to explain. Nothing followed.

"OK there, Romeo. Did Maggie help you pick out which CDs you were going to buy for our research assistant?"

"Oh my God, no," said Sean with a philosophical grin. "That's all I'd need is Maggie hearing about that."

"I bet," said Chris, looking out the windshield at the darkness of the highway.

CATCHING A TRAIN

"Actually, I haven't been seeing too much of her lately," added Sean. "She's gotten pretty heavily into her courses, and living away at school now . . . it's not like Albany is that far away, but we've really gone separate ways these past few months. It's not like we even missed each other when I went out to Arizona a few weeks ago.

"Hey, it happens," said Chris, not sure of how much his friend wanted to talk.

Both men had always enjoyed a comfortable relationship with one another, having been best friends since early in grade school. They shared many of the same interests and had double-dated at times during their later years. There was very little that they could not discuss between them, secure in their knowledge that everything remained strictly private between them.

"Are you thinking of asking Tracey to see you more often?" asked Chris.

"I don't know," said Sean. "I have to admit that I've thought about it since seeing her on Monday. But I think she might be seeing someone already—plus she lives in Philadelphia, which is five hours away."

"Yeah. But she is really nice, and what a looker!"

"Yes, she is good looking," added Sean.

CHAPTER NINETEEN

Alvah's Gift

June 5, 2020

IT WAS 11:40 PM WHEN THE SIGN ANNOUNCING THE SITE OF THE Great Train Wreck came into view along the southbound lane of Route 28. Sean drove the Jeep about one hundred yards beyond the sign and then made a U-turn before pulling the car onto the southbound shoulder of the road. It was very dark outside, and no other cars were on the road. They were completely alone in the pitch-black Adirondack night.

Sean made sure to stop the SUV about fifty yards before the historic sign in order to avoid any suspicion of passing cars, law enforcement, or otherwise. To the world, they looked like a typical tired driver who had pulled their car off the road for a nap or to spend the night.

The two agreed that they would hide the metal detector somewhere in the woods nearby while they worked to uncover the buried object. In case they were discovered, the last thing they needed in their vehicle was a metal detector, the trusted tool of any treasure hunter in the world. Besides, Sean had already used tape and marked the ground from where the loud signal had emanated. There should be no need for the metal detector other than to confirm that they had uncovered all of the metals buried in that spot.

After hiding the metal detector behind a row of trees, they approached the part of the clearing where Sean had detected the large buried mass. They were both relieved to see that the vegetation was tall enough that, if needed, they could both quickly fall to the ground and be completely concealed by the growth.

"Here's the plan," said Chris, evaluating the situation. "You're going to take the first digging shift, wearing the headlamp for lighting. I'm going to be standing as close to the road as I can get while still keeping the tall weeds around me, in case I need to duck for cover in a hurry. I'm not going to be using any light at all because I want to keep a sharp eye out for any cars approaching, even those a half mile away. If anything appears, no matter what the distance, I'm going to yell and you're going to kill your lamp. *Immediately*. Then we'll both disappear into the grass until the car is gone and I give the all clear."

"Sounds good," agreed Sean.

"Let me know as soon as you get tired and we'll switch places," promised Chris. "But you've got to keep your eyes on the road all the time. That light has got to be turned off before any driver comes into view of our area. Got it?"

"Got it," replied Sean.

"OK, let's go find the tape," said Chris.

They both walked together into the weeds, scanning their two flashlights back and forth while keeping one eye focused on the highway. The night was so dark that it seemed to swallow up the beams of their lights.

"You wouldn't believe what I was thinking on the drive home from here this afternoon," said Sean as he looked for the markers."

"What?" asked Chris.

"Wouldn't it be just our luck if one of those 'Adopt-a-Highway' clean-up groups came through here after our visit this afternoon," said Sean. "You know, those folks who walk around with the garbage bags and pick up all the loose trash and litter along the sides of the roads? And they came by here and picked up all our tape markers and put them in tidy little bags and took them away."

"You have a very twisted imagination, you know that?"

"I've got to be slightly twisted," replied Sean. "I'm here, aren't I?"

It wasn't long before they found the tape they'd placed at the spot of the promising metal detector sounding. The two managed to take their respective stations in the pitch black; Chris near the roadside while Sean prepared to commence digging at the marking tape. He had used the tape to outline the borders of the strong signal, so he had a rough plan to follow before even inserting the shovel in the ground. He activated the headlamp and made his first foray into the packed soil.

"Good Lord, this stuff is dense," Sean cried out, using his weight to step on the upper shoulder of the spade to penetrate the earth. "And there are a lot of weeds and other roots here, too. This might take longer than we expected."

"That's OK," Chris called out. "We have no time deadline tonight other than to be out of here before dawn."

"We might need it," replied Sean, struggling mightily with the first few shovelfuls.

It took a while, but the digging gradually became easier once Sean made it past the top layer of soil with all the roots. He started with a small surface area of about two square feet and gradually expanded the hole. He eventually cleared the topsoil off a patch of ground that was about two feet by three feet.

"Almost enough room to plant strawberries," he quipped.

About ten minutes into the digging, Sean was interrupted by a yell from Chris.

"OK, get ready to turn off your lamp and duck down," Chris hollered.

Sean looked up the highway to the south and saw the reflected light of a car getting ready to come into sight. It was well over a half mile away.

"Got it," called Sean as he shut down the light on his headband.

It took the car a seemingly long period of time to approach and pass. By coincidence, another vehicle then appeared going from north to south, so they had to wait for both to pass by before returning to work.

"I have to tell you," said Sean as he switched the lamp back on, "not only am I sweating from digging for the past ten minutes or so, but I think every mosquito in Herkimer County just joined me when I dived into the grass."

"You want some bug dope?" asked Chris. "I put some on before we started working."

"Sure," replied Sean. "In the meantime, I think I've already lost five pounds of blood. They've drained me."

About ten minutes later, Sean called for relief in the shoveling detail, and the two switched places.

"Now remember," advised Chris, "don't take your eyes off the road. I'll do the digging, your only job is the lookout."

Chris resumed the digging and quickly removed several additional yards of soil from the excavation. The entire hole was now about eighteen inches deep with no sign of uncovering anything other than more dirt.

"What do you think of the idea of getting the detector back over here and seeing what we've got for a signal?" asked Chris. "We're getting pretty deep. I'd almost expect to see something by now, but when I dig the shovel in as far as it will go, all I feel is more dirt."

"We could do that," agreed Sean. "You take over the watchman duties again while I go get the machine."

Chris returned to his sentry position while Sean found his way back into the trees and returned with the lightweight detector. He approached the digging site once again, this time with the headphones from the unit placed over the strap of his headlamp.

"I kind of feel like something out of *The Terminator*," he exclaimed, referencing the bionic figures in the action movie.

"You look like one, too," joked Chris.

With the machine turned on, Sean had to immediately adjust the set in order to keep the phones on his head. The signal was booming through his headset so that Chris could hear it from twenty feet away.

"Don't bother telling me," said Chris. "I can hear it from over here."

"Pretty amazing," agreed Sean as he removed the headset and hiked back to re-hide the detector. "We don't have to guess on this one, although I still don't know how deep it is. They probably pushed a lot of dirt around when they regraded that hill."

As Sean prepared to return to the guard position, another set of lights appeared in the distance. The two men were next to each other when they decided to dive again, this time closer to the road. The vehicle, a truck with an attached camper, soon rolled past and up the highway.

THE DUTCHMAN'S GOLD

"This is starting to become a little comical," said Sean.

"It will be funny until we get caught by the wrong people," returned Chris.

Chris once again took the shovel and recommenced his digging. For the first ten minutes, he maintained a steady pace and focused on evenly removing layers of dirt across the entire dimensions of the hole. It was now about thirty inches deep, with clean, even walls and a semi-level floor. Not wanting to test the pit again with the detector, he decided to make a single straight-down hole into the base of the excavation. His new probe had taken him about another twelve inches down when his shovel hit something solid. It felt like he was hitting the side of a metal garbage can that had seen better days.

"I got something," he called out to Sean.

"You want me to come over there and have a look with you?" called Sean from his watch post.

"No, you've got to stay there and look out. I'll try to get through this next layer and then use another flashlight to see what we've got."

"What's it look like?"

"It looks reddish, like something that rusted out. But I can't see much of it yet. I'm going to go back to the car and get the brush."

Chris climbed out of the pit and headed back to the Jeep. He was almost there when Sean gave voice once again.

"Down!" he called out, seeing yet more headlights approaching along the highway from the south.

This time it was two vehicles, one closely following the other as they snaked their way north to some Adirondack campsite or adventure. Chris simply knelt behind the Jeep until the two were out of sight.

Returning to the hole with the brush and small digging trowel, Chris was able to selectively remove dirt and flaking metal pieces from the bottom of the hole. The more dirt he cleared, the more of the rusted metallic material came into view. It was like peeling up layers of wet cardboard, except the decayed metal repeatedly fractured into large flat pieces of rust before then breaking into even smaller flakes.

It was a painstaking process that was not without risk. One of the things Chris had forgotten to pack in the car was a pair of work gloves, and he was afraid of "missing" with the trowel and getting a cut from the old, oxidized metal. He finally decided to return to the larger spade for digging, which wouldn't allow him the same degree of selectivity, but would cut through the rusted material with much greater ease.

While Chris toiled in the large rectangular hole, which was now almost three feet deep, Sean maintained his vigil on the roadway, looking for any distant changes in illumination that might signal the approach of an oncoming vehicle. There had been nothing in close to fifteen minutes, and Sean's mind began to wander. He glanced over at the excavation site and noticed that the headlamp worn by Chris was much closer to the ground than before, with Chris squatting down in the now-deep pit.

"It looks like we're digging a grave out here," quipped Sean, trying to make conversation.

Chris said nothing.

Sean noticed that the sounds of digging had ceased within the site. In fact, all noises had quieted entirely except for the musical chips of the crickets and the distant hoot of an owl. Silence permeated the darkness and hung over the grass like a wet blanket.

"Are you OK over there?" asked Sean, turning his head once again toward his partner's location.

Chris did not reply, instead climbing from out of the hole and brushing the dirt off his muddied jeans. He then approached Sean, still with the headlamp on so that Sean could not see the expression on his face.

"Think Tex would be interested in this?" asked Chris, extending a hand toward his partner.

Sean looked down at Chris's hand and gasped. In his palm was a piece of solid gold that was probably too big to be described as a "nugget." About two inches long and almost as wide, it appeared to be in its native state, as it was once removed from the ground.

"Oh . . . my . . . God," said Sean, spinning out his words with lengthy pauses in between.

"And there's a lot more where that came from," added Chris, his hand moving up and down as if he was mentally weighing the piece. "It feels like it weighs eight or ten ounces."

THE DUTCHMAN'S GOLD

"And look how clean it is!" exclaimed Sean, amazed at the purity of the sample. "It doesn't look like there's any quartz or other impurities mixed in anywhere. I didn't know that kind of deposit existed."

"Oh, yes, it runs the gamut," replied Chris. "I saw a photo once of a guy in Australia holding up a brick-sized chunk once that weighed in at sixty pounds. It was solid gold, without anything mixed in. He found it with a metal detector around 1980. So it does exist."

Sean continued to look between the nugget in Chris's hand and the gaping hole in the clearing. "Mind if I have a look?"

"I don't mind a bit," said Chris as he elbowed his friend. "But one of us *has* to keep an eye on the highway. We can't forget for a minute, or we can end up in big trouble with the law."

"Gotcha," replied Sean, turning around to resume his watch. "But let me know when you're ready to switch. This is getting very interesting."

Before returning to the dig site, Chris walked back to the Jeep and tossed two of the sieves into the duffel bag, and he also grabbed the brush. He carried these over to the hole and deposited them on the surface before stepping back into the hole.

Over the next twenty minutes, Sean could hear the alternating sounds of digging and scraping mixed with the clanging of rocks being shifted around inside the brass-ringed sieves. Only once during that time did Sean have to sound the alarm about approaching vehicles on the lonely highway.

"Good grief!" Chris hollered. "I just found two chunks the size of racquetballs! This is incredible."

"Is there more?"

"Yeah, I think quite a bit more," replied Chris, his voice somewhat muted from below. "I'm going to keep pulling up shovelfuls of dirt and straining them, at least until the obvious stuff comes up. Then we can check with the detector to make sure we've got it all."

"How much do you think we've got already?"

Chris lifted the duffel bag and made a thoughtful tug or two at its bulk. "Perhaps six or eight pounds, with more still coming."

Five minutes later, the two men traded places. Sean assumed the task of digging and extracting the gold while Chris took over the lookout duties.

194

"I can't believe this," Sean cried out a few minutes later. "I don't know whether to dig down or out. Either way, I'm pulling up more and more nuggets. Crazy."

"How big?"

"None as big as the two you found before, but some are pretty good-sized," replied Sean.

"OK, change that," Sean called out about three minutes later. "Here's one the size of a baseball! It must weigh four pounds all by itself!"

The two switched positions twice more over the next hour as they expanded the pit and worked to remove every piece of the gleaming metal they could see. It was a dark and messy job, made all the more difficult by the need to keep one person aside as a guard. Chris silently thanked himself for remembering to bring the headlamp, since digging and operating the sieve was already a two-handed process.

It was after 3:30 AM by the time they had cleared all the gold from the pit and were comfortable with the completeness of their work. Sean retrieved the metal detector from the trees and confirmed that there was nothing more than a few pea-sized chunks remaining, which they cleaned and tossed into the duffel bag with the rest of the haul.

Chris estimated the load to be somewhere between twenty and twenty-five pounds as he slung it into the trunk, burying it beneath the other equipment.

"Well, at least we can both work side by side to shovel the dirt back into the hole," said Sean. "I feel like I've already moved a dump truck full tonight."

"Sorry, buddy, but I don't think that's such a smart idea," replied Chris. "I think we still want to keep a watch set while we work. Any sheriff or trooper that pulls past here and sees us digging in the middle of nowhere at 3:30 AM is going to at least want to inspect our car. That just won't work."

"I hate it when you make sense," sighed Sean, grabbing a shovel and returning to the edge of the excavation.

Working quickly and taking turns, the pair was able to refill the hole and cover it with transplanted vegetation in about twenty minutes. As a final touch Chris dragged a couple large branches from beneath a dead tree over the closed pit, further camouflaging its existence.

"Not a bad bit of work," said Sean, inspecting the flat patch of ground. "You'd hardly know that anything happened here."

"What happened here?" asked Chris. "I don't know what you're talking about."

"Me neither," added Sean, playing along. "Forget I said anything."

It was after 4:00 AM by the time Chris pulled the Jeep back onto the road and started the drive back to Syracuse. They were both exhausted from the extremely long day as well as from their exertions over the past four hours. Nevertheless, they both seemed to find the energy to hold a conversation, if for no other reason than to keep Chris awake behind the wheel.

"I'm glad we were able to locate that on our first attempt," said Sean. "It was buried pretty deep considering we got such a strong signal from the detector."

"Well, you've got to admit, the target was pretty damn huge," remarked Chris. "It's not like we were searching for a silver dollar or a brass button."

"Speaking of silver dollars, do you want to go back and try to find those other little pings we got around that site?"

"You've got to be kidding me," said Chris, fixing him with a wide stare. "We're done, at least for now. You're welcome to return whenever you want and play 'find the missing dime.' I don't want to look at a shovel at least until we get back to Arizona."

"I'll second that," agreed Sean. "So what comes next?"

"Next, we go back to my place and bring the duffel with all the goodies inside where we can keep an eye on them until tomorrow morning," said Chris. "Then we rent a bank safe deposit box big enough to hold it all, just to keep it safe until we decide what to do with it."

"Good idea," murmured Sean.

"All except for two medium-sized pieces, which I have plans for."

"Ooh, do I detect another devious plan?" asked Sean.

"I think so," said Chris, "but I'm too tired to think it all the way through right now."

ALVAH'S GIFT

"Could you give me the *Reader's Digest* condensed version?" suggested Sean.

"OK, here's my thinking," began Chris. "First of all, we already know that Alvah Dunning found a pile of gold in the Superstitions, whether by accident or not. We know because we already found the case he shipped to his sister in Syracuse, plus the small nugget I found with his personal belongings in the museum at Blue Mountain Lake."

"OK, go ahead," prompted Sean.

"First, I think I'm going to pull a 'bait-and-switch' with the nuggets," said Chris. "I'm going to email a photo of a much larger piece of gold to Max and let him have Tex think that's the one we found in the museum. Actually, I'm going to tell him that we found two in the museum, and then bring him one of them. Except it will really be one from the train wreck site."

"Why, I'm surprised at you," remarked Sean with fake indignation. "That's just dishonest."

"When you stop to think about it, they all passed through Dunning's hands, and they all probably came from the same spot," argued Chris. "So what's the difference?"

"I'm just ribbing you, pay no attention," added Sean.

"The other nugget I'm going to hold back to use as a diversion once we get back out to the mountains."

"Fair enough," said Sean. "I guess I'll see it when the time is right."

* * * * * *

Rather than take the time to drive back to Little Falls and sleep in his own bed, Sean instead passed out on the sofa in Chris's living room. They slept until almost noon, which still gave them less than six hours of shut-eye before rising to start the new day.

While they ate some breakfast, Chris tapped out another email update to Max, which described their attempts to track down Alvah Dunning's descendants to try to find anything about his time out west. He avoided any mention of the train wreck site, instead only sharing the "enhanced" nugget from Adirondack Experience Museum in Blue Mountain Lake.

Max – please pass along to Mr. Durham that our first three days here have been more productive than we could have hoped. The subject of our investigation here has been Alvah Dunning, an Adirondack hermit who spent a year in the Superstition Mountains from 1899–1900. We are now positive that he not only lived in the area around Weaver's Needle, but that he located the Lost Dutchman Gold Mine (or came into contact with someone who did). We believe this because we found a nugget hidden with some old coins and the rest of his belongings in the storage of the Adirondack Experience Museum. We also found a rather cryptic map of the area along with a piece of jewelry that is most certainly of local origin. We are visiting an expert at our State Museum today to verify that. We're planning on flying back to Phoenix on Sunday and getting back into the field on Monday morning.

More to follow,
Chris & Sean

Sean looked over Chris's shoulder before he hit the "Send" button and noticed the size of the swapped-out nugget.

"Why are you sending Max a photo of a bigger nugget than the one that was really in the museum?" he asked. "Any nugget would suggest that Alvah found gold in the Superstition Mountains. It doesn't seem like size should make a difference."

"What you keep forgetting, my friend, is that we're dealing with Texans here," explained Chris. "To Texans, bigger is better every time."

"OK, I'll buy that theory, too."

"You're getting to be a real pushover," remarked Chris.

Chris was powering down the laptop when Sean's cell phone rang. Sean glanced at the screen and then hit the "Accept" button to take the call, which he immediately placed on speakerphone.

"Hey, Tracey, how ya doing?" Sean asked, trying to sound both friendly and businesslike at the same time.

"OK, but . . . were you just trying to call me?" Tracey asked in a hesitant voice.

"Call you? No, why?" asked Sean.

"Well, after we spoke last night, I got a call that had no one on it. It was right after we spoke, so I thought maybe it was you but you'd lost reception up in the Adirondacks."

"No, it wasn't us," said Chris, adding his voice to the conversation. "Is that the only time it's happened?"

"No, it happened again this morning, just about ten minutes ago," noted Tracey. "I've never had calls like that before, so I was just wondering if it was you."

Sean and Chris exchanged a pair of silent, alarmed glances before replying.

"It's probably nothing," said Chris, "but please let us know if anything else comes up that is out of the ordinary."

"OK, I'll do that. There's nothing else to tell you about this morning anyway, so I'll be in touch," said Tracey as she hung up her phone.

A pregnant pause hung in the air between the two men before Chris voiced his opinion.

"Well, assuming that is Tex or one of his henchmen, I doubt he's up to any trouble," he said, referring to the anonymous caller on Tracey's phone. "My guess is that he somehow got either her phone or her computer's IP address when she was running Durham's family tree investigation."

"I agree that he wouldn't hurt anyone, *probably*," agreed Sean. "But Good Lord, he sure does have long tentacles. He seems to want to control everything."

"It's one of the reasons why he always wins," said Chris.

* * * * * *

Before leaving Chris's home, the two transferred the collection of nuggets into a backpack, which looked less suspicious than the larger duffel bag they'd used at the wreck site. They placed the tiny, grain-sized bits from the wreck site inside a plastic bag to keep them together, while the larger chunks rode solo. The only two nuggets Chris withheld from the lot were a pair of relatively round pieces, both with rougher exteriors than many of the other portions. One of these bits was around twenty-five grams, the other around sixty, making the aggregate total worth upward of $5,400.

The banking services manager asked them to fill out some paperwork while she brought over samples of box sizes for them to inspect.

"Would you two like to try placing your goods inside these boxes to see which one works the best?" she asked.

"No," they both immediately replied in unison.

"I'm sure this middle one will work just fine," added Chris as he pointed to a moderate-sized strongbox.

Once inside the private room, Chris and Sean emptied the contents of the backpack into the box, wincing at the sounds of the rounder pieces as they rolled around the bottom of the metal box. Chris tried holding the box perfectly level as he returned to the vault with the banker, but still some of the nuggets ricocheted loudly around the container.

"My, what on earth do you have inside there?" the services manager said with an inquiring expression.

"It's my jewelry," replied Sean quickly. "I'm a rap singer, so I've got a lot of big chains and stuff."

She gave Sean a doubtful glance before setting the matter aside and replacing the safety box back into its locking slot on the shelf.

"You don't look like a rapper, but that's OK," she said as she led them from the vault.

Next on their agenda for the afternoon was to ship the turquoise bracelet back to Debbie at the Adirondack Experience Museum in Blue Mountain Lake. They stopped by a UPS shipping store where they had it wrapped in bubblepack and snugly packed in a small, specially designed box for small objects. Chris selected for it to be sent Certified Mail delivery with a significant bit of insurance on the package.

"I'm going to call Debbie later this afternoon anyway," Chris explained to Sean. "I want to discuss a couple things with her, and ask her for another favor."

"I think she'll be OK with anything you ask of her," replied Sean. "You seem to be her favorite son."

"We go way back," Chris said.

"Sure. You've been stealing her stuff for years," Sean quipped.

Now finished with returning the jewelry to the museum, Chris drove them back to his house in North Syracuse.

"OK, time to wrap up the afternoon work hours by taking care of some administrative details," said Chris.

The two hopped out of the Jeep and approached the front of Chris's house. They noticed a flat FedEx envelope tucked inside the outer door of the A-frame.

"No way," said Chris as he tore open the express package and pulled out the contents. "Airline tickets for Sunday. Already!"

"We just sent the email to Max about three hours ago," exclaimed Sean. "How is that possible?"

"The moss does not grow beneath Tex's feet," sighed Chris. "He has ways of getting things done in a hurry."

"As Tracey has found out . . ." said Sean, his voice trailing off.

Once inside the house, Chris asked Sean for a favor while he prepared to call Debbie at the museum.

"Would you please set up my scanner and make a digital copy of the map I copied at the Adirondack Museum?" he asked.

"Which map?"

"The one I've got in the manila folder on the table. It's the one that Alvah Dunning drew that resembles the area around Weaver's Needle."

"Sure. Whatcha going to do with it?" asked Sean.

"I'm going to forward it to Max so he can show Mr. Durham some of the clues we've uncovered back here in New York. We want Tex to feel like he's getting some bang for his buck by sending us here."

"You're really going to give Tex a copy of Dunning's map?" gasped Sean. "What happens if the gold we found actually comes from that location?"

"I know, but two factors come into play here," explained Chris. "First of all, this is his project, and he did pay for it. But secondly, I never said he was going to get the truth, the whole truth, and nothing but the truth from that map."

"Huh," grunted Sean.

"Once the map is scanned onto my laptop, I'm counting on you to use your imagination where the 'X' mark is moved to," said Chris with a grin. "I know you've got an active imagination."

"Yes, I do," said Sean. "And say no more. I've got this."

While Sean went about the task of setting up Chris's old flatbed scanner and connecting it to his laptop, Chris placed a call to Debbie at the museum. He was pleased that she was still in her office so late in the afternoon.

"Of course, I'm still here," the curator groaned over her seventh cup of coffee for the day. "Every tourist who has ever camped in the Adirondacks has stopped by my office today with an old photograph of their favorite backwoods lean-to. I'm about ready to hang a 'Do Not Disturb' sign on my door."

"That doesn't sound like you, but I can understand your frustrations," Chris said, commiserating with her.

"Now what can I do for you?" she continued. "Or shouldn't I ask?"

"Well, now that you *have* asked, I just thought I'd tell you that I already shipped the bracelet you lent me back to you this afternoon," said Chris. "My contact in the State Museum said that it looked like it was from one of three or four tribes living in the northern area of Arizona, perhaps Navajo, Hopi, or Zuni. But he really couldn't get much more specific than that because there was a big overlap in styles and workmanship."

"OK, that's still something," said Debbie. "I'll make sure to enter that into our database."

"There is one other thing that I'd like to ask of you," said Chris. "And I think you'll like this because you don't have to do anything for me. It's just a little favor involving the tiniest little white lie."

"OK," said Debbie in wary tone. "What are we lying about?"

"You remember the gold nugget we found in one of Alvah's boxes of personal things?"

"Of course I do. It's a nice piece of gold; nine and a half grams, as I recall," said Debbie.

"Exactly," replied Chris. "Except the photo I'm sending to our boss in Dallas is of a much larger nugget, probably around seventy grams."

There was an extended silence on the phone, followed by a prolonged sigh.

"I don't know your reason for doing that, and maybe I don't want to know," she said. "But just don't put a caption with the larger nugget saying that it's part of our collection, OK?"

"Of course I won't," chided Chris. "You know I only do things with the purest of intentions."

"Somehow I don't put 'pure' and 'Chris Carey' into the same category," said Debbie. "But thanks for getting back to me on the bracelet and getting it shipped back to us. I knew I could count on you."

His business with the museum complete, Chris walked around to the other side of the table to have a peek at Sean's work. He had already scanned Dunning's hand-drawn map of the area surrounding Weaver's Needle into an electronic file on the laptop, and was manipulating the image onscreen.

Sean was an expert in the use of Photoshop and most other image-editing applications. He had already cleaned up any stray markings on the map that had come from folding, and wear and tear, and was now working the image itself. Chris was impressed that his friend appeared to be editing the map purely from memory, as he had already replaced the original copy back into the file folder.

"This is the version of the map that we're sending back to Max?" asked Chris.

"Yup, that it is," replied Sean, his attention focused solely on the screen before him.

Chris had to smile as Sean deftly moved the "X" mark from the extreme eastern side of the map over to an area between the other two search teams' territories. He even matched the background shade of yellow behind the "X" so the map had no visible discolorations around the notations. It was a truly professional job.

"Now that's odd," said Chris as he bent closer to the screen. "There are a couple of smaller 'X's on the map that I didn't see before, along with two arrows pointing down from the north into the canyon around the Needle. I don't know how I missed them the first time I looked at this thing, but I guess I did."

The Dutchman's Gold

"No, you didn't," admitted Sean, still totally absorbed in his work. "They just weren't there the last time you saw the map."

Chris's grin spread wider across his face.

"Yeah, I guess that could be, too," he replied. "You know, you always say that I'm a devious person, but you're pretty good at it yourself."

"I aim to please," said Sean. "And you did tell me to use my imagination."

"You ought to write 'the treasure is buried here' beneath one of those arrows," joked Chris.

"If Dunning knew how to write, that would have been a nice touch," agreed Sean.

With the revised map complete, Sean made another copy of the electronic file that hid all traces of his electronic wizardry. Chris then opened a new email to Max to provide one final briefing for the day.

Max,

We've wrapped up what we can do here and are ready to fly back on Sunday. We got the airline tickets. Thanks. We're attaching a couple of items to this email. The first is a photo of one of the nuggets that we found while visiting the museum. Dunning no doubt found these in Arizona, as there is no gold here in the Adirondacks other than the smallest amounts of tracer gold. Also, we've attached a copy of the map that came from the same Adirondack Museum. It's raised a few questions, so maybe you can take a look at it and see if you can make sense of it.

See you next week,
Chris & Sean

The final action that Chris took before completing his packing the next morning was to look up the chemical formula of pyrite, otherwise known as "Fool's Gold." He then typed in "FeS_2: Pyrite" in bold letters and printed the label on his inkjet printer. Next, he cut out the label and enclosed it, along with the two nuggets, in a large piece of tinfoil.

"What's that for?" asked Sean, watching the handiwork from Chris's side.

"I think we can safely assume that my carry-on bag is going to get inspected with these little gems inside," explained Chris. "This way, if I've got them labeled as 'Fools Gold,' it won't be a big deal."

"You're pretty smart . . . and even more devious," grinned Sean.

"I've had a lot of practice," replied Chris. "I have a master's degree in deviousness."

CHAPTER TWENTY

Busted

June 7, 2020

IT WAS THEIR THIRD FLIGHT OUT TO PHOENIX IN THE PAST MONTH, and Chris and Sean were both getting used to the commute. True to his prediction, the TSA guard working the X-ray machine pulled Chris's bag aside to investigate the solid masses of gold.

"What are these for?" asked the uniformed sentry, picking up the larger piece and turning it over in his hand.

"Pyrite," replied Chris. "It's called 'Fool's Gold,' and it's a present for my niece. Looks pretty cool, doesn't it?"

"Wow," said the guard, looking at the rock one last time. "You could have fooled me. This thing looks like pure gold. I must be the 'Fool.'"

Moving to the gate, they found that they had early boarding privileges, as the tickets once again were first class. This appeared to be Tex Durham's only mode of transportation. The only difference this time was the initial leg stopped over in Charlotte, North Carolina, where they had a layover of over two hours.

Neither of the two had had time for lunch, so they decided on an early dinner at a fast-food bar-b-que joint in the terminal. Chris always found it fascinating the items that diners would order deep-fried, including pickles that had been subject to being submersed in oil and fried to a crisp.

"If I lived down here, I'm sure my arteries would be about ninety percent blocked by now," observed Chris as he bit into a pulled-pork sandwich topped with coleslaw.

"Yeah, but at least you'd die with a smile on your face," said Sean. "The only times I've seen Tracey eat, she restricts herself to things growing along the roadside. No thanks. I'll take a good burger any day of the week."

"What do you think they'd say if you ordered a beef on weck* down here?" asked Chris.

"About the same thing they'd say if you ordered a deep-fried pickle in Syracuse," replied Sean.

The final flight touched down in Phoenix slightly after 7:00 PM. They both headed to the luggage carousel before leaving the terminal. As they waited for their bags, Sean elbowed Chris with a knowing wink in his eye. He then opened his carry-on bag and signaled Chris to look inside.

Chris stooped over and peered into the leather case, immediately spotting their electronic spy-device detector.

"As long as Durham's giving us another rental vehicle here, we might as well do a quick scan to see what surprises he's got in store for us this time," remarked Sean.

"Good thinking," agreed Chris. "Until we can find anything in there and neutralize it, let's keep our comments on other topics."

Using the information provided with their plane tickets, they were able to pass through the rental car booth and into the lot within a matter of minutes. Sean gave a low whistle when he saw the vehicle sitting in the marked parking space.

"Wow—that's a 2020 Range Rover. With all the goodies," gushed Sean. "That's about an $85,000 ride."

"Probably more with all those goodies you're talking about," added Chris.

After depositing their bags in the front seat, Chris put his finger to his lips to signal "silence" to his partner. They then drove the vehicle to

---

*"Beef on weck" is a popular sandwich most commonly seen in Buffalo, New York. It is a roast beef sandwich, served on the rare side, with horseradish on a kummelweck roll.

the parking lot of a nearby hotel where they climbed out and activated the bug detector.

This time it was in the back seat on the passenger side, affixed to one of the luxury-feature display screens for watching movies and other videos. Chris lifted the electronic device from the metal support rack and examined it closely. He then replaced it in its original hiding spot and motioned for Sean to follow him out of the SUV. When they had moved about fifty feet away from the Range Rover, Chris quietly expressed his thoughts.

"That's not only a listening device and transmitter but a GPS as well. Anywhere we go, Durham will know about it before we shift into Park," he confided. "I don't believe our last vehicle had one of those."

Sean had very little to say, just shaking his head and remarking "Wow."

"Well, if nothing else, we do have the ace up our sleeve in that we know he's listening to us, but he doesn't know that we know he is," said Chris.

"And for what?" asked Sean. "What did we ever do to him to make him suspicious enough to want to track our movements?"

Chris shrugged and returned a philosophical expression. "Maybe that's just the way he is. In any case, let's not destroy it this time. Let's just leave it alone and keep our conversations on neutral topics."

"Sounds like a plan," said Sean.

After a relatively silent ride back to the hotel, the two men found themselves less than surprised to learn that they were checking back into the same two sixth-floor hotel rooms they'd occupied before.

"I wonder if the 'pre-bugged' rooms cost more," wondered Sean as they stepped away from the reception desk.

"I doubt that's a standard option in luxury hotels," replied Chris.

Instead of immediately returning to the field the next morning, the two had a meeting scheduled with Max in the same office as their original "kick-off" gathering. To both Chris and Sean, it meant one more night in air-conditioned comfort and a soft bed before returning to the rough environs of the mountains. They agreed to go out for a last expense-report-paid dinner prior to hitting the trail the following afternoon.

The restaurant of choice that night was the Arrogant Butcher, which was another moderate-length walk from their hotel that gave them the chance to stretch their legs out after a day of sitting in cars and planes.

The restaurant specialized in comfort food and a smattering of "small plates" featuring a lot of local ingredients. Sean picked out the Crab-Stuffed Chicken while Chris settled on the Butcher's Meatloaf, served with Potato Puree and French green beans. They agreed to wash it down with a pitcher of Four Peaks Scottish ale.

"I'm not really sure I'm ready to revert back to MREs after this," admitted Sean. "Eating on an expense account is just too easy on the taste buds."

"As I've told you before, don't get too used to it," advised Chris, taking another bite of his herbed whipped potatoes. "I'm not sure about you, but personally I can't think of too many more excuses for us to make trips out to conduct research."

"Neither can I, but let's wait to hear what Max has to say in our meeting tomorrow."

"Agreed," said Chris. "Maybe he'll tell us that Tex said we've already earned our quarter million and we can just go home."

"Not likely," moaned Sean. "Ugh, stuck in the hellhole until mid-July. Not sure I can take all that."

"For three thousand dollars a day, my guess is that you can tolerate the heat for another six weeks."

* * * * * *

It was Chris's style to show up for meetings with clients at least fifteen minutes early, and this Monday morning was no exception. The two men had no trouble finding their way back to the reception desk where they'd reported a few weeks earlier and received their mandatory security badges. They knew the drill now and pressed the elevator button to take them to the twelfth floor. Max was already waiting for them outside the leased conference room.

"Hey there, boys, it's good to have you back," Max greeted them as they stepped into the hallway. "How was your flight?"

The Dutchman's Gold

"Real good," said Chris, exchanging handshakes with the tall foreman. "It's good to be back. We can't wait to see how our discoveries from New York fit in with the hunting out here."

"I know that Mr. Durham is mighty interested in your New York connections, too. He flew in here this morning just to see you two," said Max.

"He did?" said Chris with a surprised expression on this face.

"Yup. All the way from Dallas. He doesn't normally do stuff like that, so you two should be pretty proud of your work back there."

Chris and Sean were both thinking similar thoughts. Should they be pleased or worried about Durham's surprise visit to welcome them back? It turned out, they wouldn't have long to wait.

Max held the conference room door open to let Chris and Sean into the room, and there he was. Tex Durham was sitting at the head of the conference table, staring at the three men entering the room with an impartial stare. Like the poker-faced card player bidding a bluff, he was impossible to read.

"Good morning, Mr. Durham," all three of the men said simultaneously.

"Good morning, men, come inside and pull up a seat," said the billionaire. "Help yourself to a cup of coffee, if you've a mind to." A coffeemaker had been placed on a side table with cups and accoutrements for their convenience. All three helped themselves to the caffeine bar before taking their seats.

Mr. Durham made no small talk before commencing his business.

"Boys, before we get going on our briefing this morning, I have a few remarks to make, and I want you to listen carefully."

Then, turning to Max, he addressed him individually. "What I have to say for the first few minutes is for the benefit of these two boys only. You can stay if you want to, or you can leave and come back in a few."

"I have to use the bathroom anyway," said Max as he stood up. "I'll be right back in." He then left the room and closed the door.

Durham waited until he had departed before turning his attention back to the other two.

"Boys, I didn't get where I am today by being stupid. I've gotten ahead in life by always knowing what is going on, who I can trust and who I can't," he said with ruthless candor.

"We'd like you to think that you can trust us," said Sean, expressing both their sentiments.

"Then why are you having some twenty-one-year-old college girl making inquiries into my family background? Did you feel like that is part of what you're being paid to find?"

"No, sir," stammered Chris, stunned at the abruptness of the accusation. "But to be quite honest about it, we were both shocked to learn that you and Shane were father-and-son, and we didn't know why that was kept a secret. We just wanted to make sure we weren't stepping on anyone's toes when we got ourselves into this project."

Tex reached out and pressed a button on a remote control panel on the table, which energized the room's video projection system. A photograph of Chris using his cell phone to take pictures in Durham's office instantly appeared on the screen.

"Yes, as you can see, I knew that you were interested in our family tree as soon as I saw you taking these photographs," he said. "And if you must know, the reason I don't advertise the fact that my son is working for me is by his request, not mine. As your female college associate already found out, Shane and I haven't always gotten along famously, so we're not as close as some might expect. But that's our business, and not yours. Do you understand?"

"Yes, sir," they both answered simultaneously. There was really nothing else they could say. They both felt busted and terribly exposed.

Durham fixed them both with a level stare for about five seconds, allowing the silence to stretch out in an ominous period of stillness.

"Alright then, now that we understand one another," he concluded.

"Yes, sir."

"OK, that being said, I've been following your reports to Max, and it sounds as though you've made some great discoveries a long way from Arizona," he said. His voice had reverted back to a much friendlier and paternal tone.

"We have, but it all started out right here at the museum in Apache Junction, the Lost Dutchman Museum," said Chris. "That's where we discovered the link to Alvah Dunning, the hermit who transplanted himself to the Superstition Mountains for a year," explained Chris.

"I read about him online," said Durham. "He looks like an interesting character, a real woodsman and individualist. But everything I read said that he went to the Dakotas for that year. Nothing was mentioned about this part of the country."

"The references are wrong," said Chris definitively. "I know we're changing history, but we have proof that Alvah Dunning was here, in Arizona and in the Superstition Mountains."

As Chris spoke, Max reentered the room and reclaimed his seat.

"Final answer?" said Durham, quoting the game show response.

"Final answer," replied Chris. As he spoke, he reached into his pocket and grabbed the smaller of the two nuggets they'd carried back from New York and dropped it on the table in front of the businessman. Allowing it to stop rattling on the surface, he looked at Durham and repeated, "Final answer."

Surprised as he was, Tex Durham had not mastered the art of negotiation by wearing his emotions on his sleeve. He looked at the large nugget with rather detached interest before expressing his enthusiasm with the find. Only then did he allow a smile to cross his face and address the two.

"Now that's a pretty nice-looking poker chip," he remarked. "Remind me again where this came from."

"We found a number of 'items of interest' at the museum located in Blue Mountain Lake," explained Chris. "A couple of those items were gold nuggets that they didn't even know they had. They were in a storage room with Dunning's possessions, although the other one was less than half the size of this one. We turned that one over to the museum, just to establish good faith. But this one we thought we'd bring out to show you as evidence that Dunning probably discovered the gold mine, or knew someone who did."

Chris was convinced that he sold the story in a believable manner and then fell silent to allow Durham time to respond.

Durham picked up the large nugget and turned it over in his hands repeatedly before passing it on to Max, who made a similar examination. The chunk of gold was then placed back in front of Durham, who ignored it as he continued his questioning.

"Max also forwarded me a copy of the map you found amongst this hermit's belongings."

As he spoke, Durham pressed another button on the remote causing the map to display on the large screen. Both Chris and Sean smiled to themselves seeing the altered image with the revised positions of the "X" marks, as well as Sean's newly added arrows on the northern part of the map.

"And this is Dunning's drawing of the area around Weaver's Needle?" asked Durham.

"We can't be sure, but it sure as heck looks like it, doesn't it?" replied Sean. "As a matter of fact, I'm surprised he came as close as it appears. For being an uneducated man who couldn't read or write, he sure drew a pretty good rendition of a topographic map of the area."

"I agree with you," said Max. "I already showed this to the boys out in the field, and both teams were pretty interested in going back and trying to locate any pits or potential signs in any of these spots."

"This one 'X' looks bigger than the others," noted Tex. "And doesn't it look like the arrows are pointing almost directly at it? Or maybe between that and the smaller 'X' to the right of it? That would actually be to the north, wouldn't it?"

"Maybe it has something to do with the tunnel that some people have supposedly seen in the early days," said Max excitedly. "I've heard that when you find the tunnel, you're at the mine."

Chris and Sean allowed the conversation to proceed between the two Texans while they sat quietly, adding infrequent feedback to the mix.

"Boys, what's your take on the markings on this map?" asked Durham, looking directly at Chris and Sean.

"We went as far as downloading some satellite imagery of the canyon walls around the Needle," said Chris. "Then we attempted to overlay the markings from Dunning's map over the top to see if there were any geologic abnormalities or signs of an old mine. But so far we've come up empty."

THE DUTCHMAN'S GOLD

Even as he spoke, Chris wondered whether his made-up story sounded good to the others seated at the table. Only Sean recognized the fictional account of the maps, while Tex and Max nodded their heads in appreciation.

"We'll take a further look at these sometime this week," added Durham. "I was also interested in some of the artifacts you found tying this Alvah Dunning guy into the local Indians in the area. That's even more proof that he was in our neck of the woods in the last days of the 1800s."

"Yes, it is," agreed Chris. "And that's significant because that means that this chunk of gold probably came from *our* mine." He said the word "our" as though it belonged to Durham and his group.

Durham leaned forward and picked up the large nugget and looked at it with appreciation. "I hope you boys don't mind if I take this back to Dallas and add it to the display in my office, do you?"

"Of course not, sir," replied Chris. "It's your money funding this project, so you have the rights to everything that comes out of it."

"One other thing we have to discuss," said the Texan. "I have checks for both of you for your first month's work. I'm surprised that neither of you has asked me about it so far."

Chris and Sean looked at each other before Chris spoke up for them both.

"To tell you the truth, you've done such a good job of paying for everything we've needed that we haven't even thought about getting a paycheck."

"I do my best, boys, I do my best to keep my employees happy. It's always kept me out of trouble somehow," said Durham.

"Well, it works for us," replied Sean.

"How do you want to receive this, in a check or wired into your checking accounts?"

"Into our accounts," they both responded simultaneously.

"As long as it's all there in good old-fashioned American greenbacks, right boys?"

"Yes, sir," they responded.

"Tex, it's Tex," cried Durham, suddenly returning to a first-name basis. "We're all in this together, boys. Now let's get back into the mountains and find the mother lode."

BUSTED

* * * * * *

Chris and Sean had already arranged to meet Alex at the trailhead the following morning to pick up their provisions for the week and load up Sammy for the hike in. They decided to use part of the afternoon to take an extended walk and find lunch somewhere along the way. There was a lot to discuss, and they were both very unsure of what to think about the events of their meeting with Durham.

"What makes me uncomfortable is that I don't know how much he knows," said Chris as they strolled along the crowded city street. "I can't figure out how he learned that Tracey had done a background check on him. He'd have no way of knowing that, at least that I can come up with."

"Even if he knew that someone, *anyone,* had looked into his family tree, how could he possibly have associated us with Tracey?" asked Sean. "Unless there are additional bugs and GPS tracers hidden that we don't know about. Like in my car back home. But how could he have bugged that?"

"You know what I never considered?" said Chris, thinking out loud. "There is an option on our cell phones that allows others to track our locations. And I never thought about turning that off because it's never mattered to us before. But as long as we're at it, let's both do that now."

They both entered their cell phone settings and de-activated all Privacy Options, including the ability to track their locations.

"I don't know if that will help, but it's a possibility," said Chris.

"Did you notice that Mr. Durham never mentioned the listening devices in our rental car and our hotel rooms?" asked Sean.

"Yeah, I noticed," said Chris.

"Is it possible that he thinks we haven't found them?"

"Well, since we destroyed the one in the last rental, I doubt it," surmised Chris.

"Yes, but there is one mounted in our new vehicle, so he obviously thinks we may be blind to some of his tricks," said Sean.

"That thought crossed my mind as well," replied Chris. "Maybe we just leave them where they are and keep our lips sealed while we're in earshot of any of them."

The Dutchman's Gold

"This whole thing has been rather bizarre from the start," said Sean. "Sometimes I don't know whether we're working for Mr. Durham or against him."

"As long as he signs our final paycheck, I guess it doesn't matter," signed Chris.

The two men then returned to their bugged rooms for a good night's sleep.

CHAPTER TWENTY-ONE

Return to the Hellhole

June 9, 2020

MONDAY MORNING WAS ONE OF THE FEW OVERCAST DAYS THEY'D EXPErienced as the two men drove their fully bugged luxury SUV across the flatlands in the direction of the Peralta Canyon Trail. Before climbing into the shiny new vehicle, Chris gave Sean the "all silent" signal to remind him of their self-imposed gag order.

Sean was the man behind the wheel this morning, and he gazed with wonder at all the navigation and messaging features that displayed automatically once he turned the engine on.

"I love these wheels, man," he said. "Mr. Durham sure does have a way with picking things."

"I know," said Chris, making certain that his voice was loud enough to register on the listening device in the back seat. "Tex is a great man to work for. I sure do hope we can come through for him and find the location of the mine. It would be wonderful to wander into a buried tunnel entrance leading to a few million dollars in high-quality ore."

"I'm right there with you, buddy," agreed Sean as he pulled out of the hotel parking lot. Meanwhile, Chris made eye contact and rolled his eyeballs at their faked enthusiasm.

They passed the next twenty minutes of the ride by discussing their plans for searching their next assigned areas of the map, prioritizing the order of the quadrats and other topics that they'd already decided days before. They both embellished their descriptions of their toils over the past few weeks, including how much rock and soil they had moved while attempting to discover the source of gold in their zone. Both men couldn't help but smile as their pretended conversation progressed through its paces.

They arrived at the Peralta Canyon Trail parking lot right on time, and were not surprised to see Alex sitting in his truck waiting for them. He always seemed to be on time, with the same satisfied, patient smile on his face.

"Hey man, Sammy's been waiting for you," said Alex in his ever-friendly tone. "He told me he liked going out on the trail with you two. He said you treat him real good."

"Sammy's a good old fellow. We like him, too," said Sean as he walked around the back of the trailer and patted the burro on the side of the face.

"See, he remembers you from last week," said Alex.

"He'd better," replied Sean. "He ate half of my dinner one night last time."

Alex gave the two men a guided tour of the saddlebags as he loaded up the animal. The contents included six gallons of water, six meals ready to eat (MREs), food for the burro, the two Glock handguns, and various other smaller items. Other items, such as their tent and sleeping gear, clothing, and other personal gear were divided between their two backpacks.

"Thanks for showing us good spots for hiding our prospecting gear in the canyon," said Chris to the guide. "It makes things so much easier to have that stuff already back in the mountains rather than carrying it in and out every time."

"Yes, that would not be very smart," agreed Alex. "Once you get used to the tricks, it's a lot easier to work back here."

Once everything was ready, the two wasted no time in hitting the trail. They wanted to clear the biggest part of the uphill before the heat began to crank up for the day. Although it was only about 2.2 miles up to the Saddle, the heat and extremely dry air resulted in very arid conditions that could dehydrate a body in very little time.

They were about two-thirds of the way up the incline when Sean heard the sounds of hooves approaching from the rear. He turned around in time to see three riders and a fourth horse with only saddlebags overtaking them quickly from behind. It was Jake, Shane, and Hoss on their way into the canyon for an extended stay on the western walls opposite the Needle. They slowed down as they approached the duo.

"Well, well, what do we have here?" asked Jake in a condescending tone. "Looks like a couple of New York City boys coming into the mountains to play."

"Jake," Chris said to the lead man, not willing to play their game. "Yeah, we're heading in for the rest of the week. We found some stuff that might pay off in our search areas."

"You both ought to climb on the back of that little burro of yours," Jake continued with a sneer. "You're both small enough so he could probably carry both of you."

"Thanks. We'll remember that," replied Chris.

"CRAP, LOOK AT THAT SNAKE," shouted Hoss, pointing to the ground near Sean's feet in feigned horror.

Sean, not ready for the group's play tactics, jumped before realizing it was all in humor. The three men from Team 2 broke out in laughter, slumped in their saddles. Chris and Sean were having none of it, but said nothing as the three giants had their laugh.

"Come on, boys," said Jake as he led the other two on horseback past Chris and Sean. "These two ain't even worth playin' with." And then they were gone.

"Jeez, did you see the guy in the middle?" asked Sean.

"Yeah, that was Hoss," recalled Chris.

"How tall was he?"

"Someone said six foot ten, but I don't recall for sure," replied Chris.

"Well, he looks even taller than that," said Sean. "And huge, too. I'm surprised they found a horse that could carry him."

"His horse looked pretty big, too."

By early afternoon, they had made it into their search area and retrieved their hidden tools. It was hard getting themselves to commence the backbreaking job of climbing up and down the canyon walls, searching, digging, and then starting the process over innumerable times as they slowly crossed off the search quadrats on their map. They took advantage of every puddle of standing water and trickle of stream to allow Sammy

THE DUTCHMAN'S GOLD

to quench his thirst in the arid desert sun. It being a four-day week in the field, they took advantage of their supply line and called Alex to stop by with more water and food for the burro on Thursday.

"So far, no one's bothered us for having a fire at night or camping wherever we wanted," observed Sean at their evening meal late that week. "I wonder why we seem to get away with things without getting a visit from the local ranger?"

"Our boss is buddy-buddy with the Commissioner of Parks," replied Chris in a tired tone. "I wouldn't be surprised if he's on the payroll, too."

"Think so?"

"We got our pistol permits in this state in less than a week," said Chris. "It's supposed to take over two months. Our applications couldn't have even been entered into the system yet. And you think they're going to bother us over a campfire?"

"Good point," agreed Sean. "I keep forgetting who we work for."

* * * * * *

Two more weeks of drudgery passed without incident. It was the same routine, day after day, hour after hour. The boredom became almost unbearable as the two became intimately familiar with every mile of canyon wall and rock, every change in hue of the massive spire that was Weaver's Needle.

"I thought Durham said he had information that would provide us with a guide to the mine," complained Sean. "The only insider information I've seen is what we found ourselves inside his office. And he even knew that we found it."

"I think he may have been talking about the changes mapped out after the earthquake, but that certainly hasn't amounted to a hill of beans, has it?"

"You know, changing the topic, it is rather bizarre what Barbara Simms told us about the curse of the case with the gold, isn't it?" asked Sean.

"Yeah, especially the last two, with Luther and Martha Sykes both dying within a day after viewing the contents of the suitcase," said Chris.

RETURN TO THE HELLHOLE

"Yeah, really," agreed Sean. "I mean, any sane person would know it's all just a really incredible coincidence, but still it's bizarre."

Sean waited for Chris's response, but none came. Instead, Chris turned toward Sean with a wide-eyed stare. Sean wasn't sure what to make of it, so he just watched his friend as his eyes bulged farther from the front of his face, his forehead and cheeks quickly turning a reddish hue. Within a second, his eyelids began to flutter, and the whites of his eyes appeared as his eyeballs rolled up in his head.

"Chris! CHRIS!" called Sean, watching saliva suddenly appear out of the corner of his mouth. Seeing his body begin to stiffen and topple to one side, he dived to catch him before he toppled to the ground.

"CHRIS!"

"Yeah, what's up?" asked Chris, a huge smile breaking across his face as he returned to his normal expression. "I do a pretty good zombie impersonation when I want to, don't I?"

"You sonofabitch!" cried Sean, taking a slug at Chris's arm. "You almost gave me a heart attack."

"Well, considering that's what probably killed the other people in 'the curse,' I'd say I got out of it rather lightly."

"Don't ever do that to me again, you hear me?" demanded Sean.

"OK, no more joking around," promised Chris.

The two men had almost completed searching yet another transect grid line on the search assignment when they happened upon a shelf of rock situated near the top of the canyon wall. Behind the shelf was an inset into the rock with an overhanging roof. It wasn't enough to label as a cave, but it was enough to protect one from the elements in a storm. Chris broke out a portable flashlight to investigate the inside of the space, which showed definite signs of previous mining activity. A pile of discarded rock had been moved to one side, while the floor held markings indicative of a pickax working the ground.

Sean was about to investigate some of the rocks in the heap when they both heard the sound; a hissing, rattling pitch that emanated no more than ten feet from their boots.

Chris was the first to spot the reptile, coiled in a small area between a larger boulder and a couple small pieces of ore. Its head and tail were both elevated around the rest of the body, poised to strike at anything that came within reach. Sean quickly opened his pack and withdrew his pistol and the magazine, which he'd kept separate for the duration of the trip.

"It's a good thing you've got that in your pack rather than loaded on Sammy," said Chris, looking at their friendly companion two hundred feet below. "But do you think we really need it?"

"I don't feel like picking that thing up by its tail and moving it outside, do you?" asked Sean as he loaded a round into the chamber and then pushed the magazine into the bottom of the weapon.

"No, but if you've got to fire that thing, just don't get us killed by a ricochet, OK?"

"I'll do my best," replied Sean as he lined up his shot. "But just to be safe, why don't you step outside while I do my best Wyatt Earp imitation."

Sean waited for Chris to move beyond the rock shelf and step out of sight while he moved as close as he dared to the venomous reptile. Then he pulled the trigger. A loud *CRACK* boomed from the rock enclosure that pulsed from the rear surface of the miniature cave and echoed out into the canyon. Chris wondered whether the men on the other two teams could hear the roar.

"Crap!" yelled Sean from inside the depression.

"You OK?" called Chris.

"Yeah, but I didn't hit him," replied Sean. "And he doesn't look happy."

BOOM! A second shot was fired. *BOOM, BOOM, BOOM*; three additional crescendos followed the initial blasts. Finally one last shot before Chris heard his friend celebrate inside the rock wall.

"Well, it's about time," cried Sean, looking down at the snake, which now sported a mostly detached head. Even in its deformed state, the tail still vibrated weakly, producing a faint but audible rattling sound.

Chris returned to the ledge to find his partner standing over the deceased serpent.

"Just be careful, buddy," he advised. "I've read of people being bitten by snakes that already appeared dead."

"I'm not going anywhere near that thing," said Sean. Using the metal end of his spade, he flipped the snake over and then tossed it to the other side of the space.

As they prepared to look around the interior walls of the depression, their satellite phone rang indicating an incoming call. Chris looked at the screen before pressing the "Accept" button.

"Hey, Team 3 here," he spoke, using their team number for lack of a better greeting.

"Hey y'all, it's Max here. Y'all OK over there?"

"Yeah, everything's fine. Why?"

"We just heard a whole bunch of shooting come from across the canyon and were wondering what was up," said Max. "It sounded like you were taking on the entire Apache nation."

"No, we're not fighting anyone over here. We just had a nice little rattler that was homesteading the same place we wanted to dig," explained Chris. "So Sean here took his head off with a well-placed shot. That's all."

"A 'well-placed shot,'" repeated Max. "Sounded more like five or six shots from over here."

"Yeah, it probably was," admitted Chris. "Sean here hadn't fired much before, and you gotta admit, a snake is a pretty small target to hit."

A quick silence was followed by yet another remark from Max. "He took six shots to kill a snake? You're kidding, right?"

"Nope."

"Well, OK then," concluded Max. "Just wanted to check up on you."

As Chris hung up the phone, Sean added his thoughts to the conversation. "I bet they're having a pretty good laugh about that," he said ruefully.

"Who cares," added Chris. "Just remember to take the magazine out of the pistol and remove the round in the chamber. And put the safety back on, too. Those things give me the willies."

Not seeing any additional reptiles in the cave, they resumed their inspection of the place, moving rock when they needed to do so. This was not on their mapped list of assigned search areas, so they didn't expect to find much of anything. Yet when they illuminated the left side of the depression, the flashlight beam reflected off the edge of a dull metallic surface that was mostly buried in rocky, dusty debris.

Sean scampered over to the partially hidden object and used the toe of his boot to lift it out of the rocky soil, in the event that something

THE DUTCHMAN'S GOLD

slithery was hiding beneath it. He then bent over and lifted it into the light to examine the piece. It was a round plate, perhaps ten inches in diameter, with a one-inch outer rim that was slightly elevated above the rest of the surface. It was simple in its design and obviously very old, and it had been left unmolested for a very long time.

"Looks like an old dinner plate," observed Chris, touching the outer rim of the piece. "My guess is tin. Either that or pewter."

"Pewter is mostly tin, isn't it?" asked Sean.

"About ninety percent," replied Chris. "If I'm not mistaken, there's about ten percent lead mixed into pewter as well, although this was made back in the days before they worried about eating off lead."

"And in good shape, too," added Sean. "I don't see any rust at all."

"If it's tin, there won't be any rust," said Chris. "You need iron in the presence of air and water for rust to occur."

"I knew that," replied Sean.

After inspecting the upper surface of the antique plate, Sean flipped it over to determine whether there were any markings on the back. Often, the crests or other patterns stamped onto the back of a plate could provide a clue to the name of the company that produced the piece. This then could give an indication as to its age and origin.

Using the light of the sun to illuminate the underside of the piece, the two men observed a pair of markings that had been stamped into the metal. One was a crest-like imprint with a shield and illegible characters surrounding the outside. The other was a winged character that was also non-descript for lack of visible detail. However, it was the third marking on the bottom side of the plate that drew their attention.

On the opposite side of the round bottom surface were two letters that had been scratched rather crudely into the soft metal. They appeared to be carved into the tin using a sharp-pointed object, such as a nail or a knife point. The characters weren't neat, nor were they straight or aligned. However, there could be no disputing the distinctiveness of the letters engraved in the metal such a long time ago.

They read simply, "JW."

CHAPTER TWENTY-TWO

Which JW?

June 25, 2020

CHRIS AND SEAN BOTH STOOD TRANSFIXED AT THE ENGRAVING BEFORE them. The implications were both immediate and significant, and struck them with the force of a loaded semi-tractor trailer.

"JW! You don't suppose that could be Jacob Waltz?" asked Sean in a wavering voice. "That this could be something he left behind while he was prospecting over a hundred years ago."

"It looks old enough to be over a hundred years old," replied Chris in a reverential tone. "But you know, 'JW' could also stand for Jacob Weiser."

"Oh my God, you're right," replied Sean. "They'd have the same initials, assuming that Weiser was actually a real person."

"According to Tracey, Jacob Weiser was not only a real person but the ancestor of our employer," countered Chris. "And I'm not really sure how you'd ever tell the difference between which man owned this, Waltz or Weiser, assuming that it was one or the other. Without handwriting samples of each to compare it to, it's impossible."

"But the exciting part is that if it *was* one of them, they were standing right where we are today, which means that we may be closing in on the location of the mine," said Sean excitedly.

"Very much so," agree Chris. "We need to mark the precise location of this pit on the map in order to report it out to Max and Mr. Durham. We could use a little goodwill between him and us right now."

"I agree," said Sean. "I imagine he's going to want to add this plate to his display cabinet back in Dallas. Let's give Max a call and let him know what we've found."

"I don't think we want to do that," replied Chris thoughtfully. "Let's wait until we get back to Phoenix tomorrow and call him using our regular cell phones."

"Why?" asked Sean with a puzzled expression.

"The chance of being hacked on our cell phones is super low, just because of the number of standard cell phones in use," replied Chris. "But satellite phones are still rather rare, and they can be hacked because the 'bad guys' have broken through many of the encryption algorithms. I've read that the crypto key for intercepting and reading most satellite phones can be had in very little time by a skilled hacker. And we don't want *anyone* to know what we just found. There'd be hundreds of mad dog prospectors up here in no time."

"OK, I see your point," agreed Sean. "We'll wait until we're back in town tomorrow."

"Hey, before we leave this humble abode, lend me your flashlight for a second, OK?" asked Chris.

Sean passed him his high-powered light, which Chris used to slowly sweep the bottom floor of the small cave. He was looking for additional artifacts, such as more dishes, cups, and other personal items. But what he saw was far more interesting.

Getting down on his knees, Chris bent over close to the soil and used the beam to illuminate a very small patch of dirt. This he moved slowly, from left to right and top to bottom in the small square of ground in front of him, as though he were looking for ants emerging from the ground. He then sat back on his haunches and smiled.

"See anything?" asked Sean, watching from the side.

"You tell me," replied Chris as he handed the torch back to Sean. "But you've got to look pretty closely or you'll miss it."

Sean took the light from Chris and knelt on the rocky ground in the same position. He turned on the beam and mimicked Chris's movements, once again with an eye on the ground following the light. It took him a few seconds to see the flakes of metallic gold and another minute to process the sight in his mind.

"Oh, wow," he murmured in awe. "That's a pretty sight. Where do you think it comes from?"

"Beats me," said Chris. "If you look around this place, you'll see that there aren't any rocks here that appear to be gold-bearing ore. My guess is that JW found some source of tracer gold in other locations and then carried it here. When he moved it to another location, the gold left trace flakes behind in the soil. That's about all I can say."

"Do we spend the time and collect what we see here?" asked Sean. "It doesn't look like enough to bother with."

"Normally I'd say 'no,'" agreed Chris. "But we want to be able to show this to Max and maybe even to Tex, so let's spend the time and pick up what we can."

The two spent the next twenty minutes on the ground, both with a pair of tweezers and their own lights as they hunted through the dusty earth collecting flakes that collectively weighed almost nothing. It was painstaking work, but they finally gathered every flake they could find and placed them all into a tiny glass vial filled with water.

"I like how the water magnifies the size of the gold flakes inside," said Sean. "I wonder how much this amount would sell for?"

"Not enough to buy the bottle of Coke from our rooms' convenience bar," replied Chris.

"Spoilsport."

The following day was Friday, so Chris and Sean made their weekly rendezvous with Alex to return Sammy to his stable for the weekend. They also passed him their handguns, not wanting to maintain custody of the weapons while staying back in their downtown hotel.

Rather than drive straight back to the hotel, Chris pulled into a shopping plaza on the outskirts of town and parked outside a small supermarket.

"Brown bagging it tonight instead of going out for dinner?" asked Sean.

"Not at all," replied Chris. "Not as long as Tex Durham's expense account is picking up the tabs. I just want to make an old-fashioned phone call from a phone booth, and then snag one item from our local neighborhood grocery store."

Sean followed Chris to a phone booth outside the store where Chris picked up the phone and used his phone card to call Tracey in Philadelphia. She answered on the first ring.

"Hey, it's Chris," he said, knowing that she would not recognize the incoming phone number on her smartphone.

"Hey! I almost didn't answer since I thought it would be a telemarketer," said the cheerful voice on the other end. "What are you two up to?"

"We just came out of the mountains, and we wanted to warn you about doing any more online investigating of Tex Durham. We found out last week that it was probably him who was checking up on you. He somehow found out that you were looking up his family tree, and he also found out that you were working with us."

"Oh, wonderful," Tracey replied.

"Yeah, sorry about that," said Chris. "But at least you don't have to worry about it being dangerous, and I doubt you've had any more callbacks, have you?"

"No, I haven't," replied Tracey. "But just to let you know, I've found a little more on this Weiser guy, although I still can't determine what eventually happened to him."

"What else did you find?"

"I've got database hits that found two of his offspring, both in the area in and around Texas, although both of those petered out pretty quickly, so I'm not sure how much good they are to you. One of those appears to be Tex Durham's father, but you already knew that from my last report."

"Yes, you gave us that a few weeks ago," said Chris.

"By the way, aren't you afraid that anyone is listening on this call?" asked Tracey.

"Not unless he's bugged every telephone in the state of Arizona," said Chris. "We're calling from a pay phone outside Phoenix."

"Oh, OK, in that case . . ." Tracey giggled. "Anything else I can get for you?"

"Now that you mention it, yes," said Chris. "I'm going to text you a photograph off of the bottom of a metal plate that we found out here. I'm going to focus on a couple small insignias that are stamped into the metal. I'd like you to take it to an antiques dealer who specializes in that kind of thing, if you can find one around Philly."

"I bet I can," replied Tracey. "What am I looking for?"

"Anything they can tell us about the plate, mainly how old it might be and where it was produced, whether in the United States or another country."

"OK, I can do that."

"You're the best," Chris said. "And I'll tell you what. I've got to run into this store for a minute to pick up something quick. I'll put Sean on the phone, I'm sure he wants to say hello."

Without waiting to hear her response or see the expression on Sean's face, he handed him the phone and entered the grocery store.

Sean was still talking on the phone when Chris reappeared from the store entrance. In his hand he held only a box of tinfoil. Sean turned the opposite direction to better shield his last words to their assistant before signing off the call.

"OK, Romeo, you ready?" Chris asked his partner.

"Very funny," Sean said sarcastically. "Just because I get a little friendly with another female, you turn it into a full-blown romance."

"I never said that, did I?" chuckled Chris as they unlocked the Jeep for the ride back to the hotel.

"But you were thinking it," replied Sean. "Don't try to deny it."

"How's Maggie doing?"

"Stop!"

*　*　*　*　*　*

Returning to downtown Phoenix, the two men found themselves berthed again in "their" rooms; the same two as they'd occupied on all their former stays. It was no longer a surprise, and the two listening devices were still concealed in the same hiding spots as before. They had become old friends over the past month.

Once they'd checked in, both Chris and Sean filed into Chris's room, where Chris tore several sheets of tinfoil from the box and, one by one, placed them against the bottom of the pewter plate.

"Making rubbings of the insignias?" asked Sean.

"Yeah. I don't imagine we'll hold on to this for very long," replied Chris as he massaged the plate bottom through the foil. Then, removing the foil and holding it up for inspection, he nodded approvingly and commented, "Not bad."

After making the first rubbing, Chris sat back and stared at the bottom side of the plate for some time, lost in thought.

"Thinking about keeping that thing for yourself?" asked Sean as he observed his friend.

"Me? No, of course not," replied Chris. "But something about this plate is bothering me and I can't figure out why."

"Like what?"

"I can't figure out what it is, but I feel like I've seen these crests that are stamped into the bottom somewhere before."

"How could that be possible?" asked Sean. "Unless you have a matching set of antique pewter-ware plates back in Syracuse."

"I don't know . . ." said Chris, his voice trailing off as he continued to examine the piece.

Chris then repeated the process to make two more foil rubbings before taking a series of pictures using his cell phone. He photographed some close-ups of the engravings, the initials carved in by the owner, and then some images of the entire plate, nicks and all. Next, he forwarded a few of the best photographs to Tracey via text message.

"Here you go," he texted onto the bottom of the screen. "See what you can find out and get back to us as soon as you have anything."

Next, Chris picked up the hotel's complimentary pen and notepad from the credenza and scrawled a note, which he showed to Sean without making a sound. It said:

Let's call Max from the room telephone and tell him about the plate. It will be fun to see how fast we hear from Tex.

Which JW?

Sean nodded while smiling at the idea. Meanwhile, Chris dialed the number from his phone's directory. The phone rang six times before going to Max's message recorder.

"Hey Max, this is Chris here," said Chris to the recorder. "We're back in Phoenix, and we have something to show you. We found an old antique tin plate in a cave way up on our side of the canyon. It's got the initials 'JW' carved into the back, so we think it might be from either Jacob Waltz or Jacob Weiser. You gotta see this thing; it's old and it looks like it's from someplace outside the United States. We're going to have it appraised by an expert as soon as we can. Oh, and one other thing. Inside the same little mini-cave where we found the plate, we also found a few flakes of gold, which we brought out as well. I don't think it came from that location; it looks like someone maybe brought it there and then carried it away to somewhere else. But tough to say for sure. Give me a call to discuss, and I'll tell you where we found it. Thanks. Talk then."

After hanging up the phone, Chris then hand-signaled for Sean to follow him out the door. Only when they were in the hallway, headed for the elevators did Chris gleefully exclaim, "I bet Durham calls us within the next fifteen minutes."

In exactly twelve minutes, Chris's cell phone chimed proclaiming an incoming call. However, it wasn't Durham but Max calling to return the original message.

"Hey, y'all, Max here," he called out in full volume over Chris's headset. "That's pretty exciting what you told me about. Mr. Durham's pretty hyped up about it, too."

"Ah, so you called him?"

"No, he called me," replied Max. "News like that travels pretty fast."

Chris smiled to himself, knowing that Tex couldn't have possibly found out about the discovery without the benefit of the transmitting device. One of his full-time sleuths must have recognized the importance of the phone message Chris left for Max and immediately contacted him with the news.

"Yes, it was pretty exciting to come across that thing, especially in such an out-of-the-way spot that wasn't even on our map of search locations,"

Chris said. "What do you want us to do with it? We could always lock it up in our room safe."

"No, that's OK," replied Max. "Mr. Durham is down in Tucson tomorrow for a meeting anyway. He said he was going to have his driver bring him up here to meet with you to take a look at this."

"Saturday morning?"

"Yup. It's all the same to Tex. He works seven days a week," said Max. "The guy is working even when he's out on his ranch."

"Where is his ranch?" asked Chris.

"Just drive anywhere into the northern part of central Texas and you'll probably be on his ranch," quipped Max. "He needs his helicopter just to go from one side of it to the other."

"That's impressive."

"Yup. Anyway, I'll call you once he lets me know what time tomorrow, but expect sometime around 9:00 AM."

"Will do," replied Chris. "Talk to you then."

The following morning, Chris and Sean left their room in time for a full breakfast at Butterfield's Pancake House, where they both ordered the Apple Baby Pancakes with all the fixings.

"Makes you feel almost human again," said Sean as he dug into his heaped plate.

"Yeah, except this is more like an apple pie than any breakfast food," remarked Chris as he sampled his first bites. "I'm going to have to run an extra three or four miles today just to burn this stuff off."

They arrived at the office building at the same time as Max, who rode the elevator to the twelfth floor with the two. Chris's watch had just turned to 8:45 AM when they opened the door to the conference room. He was not surprised to find that Tex Durham was already there. He stood up as soon as he saw the men and threw out a bear grip–like handshake to match his huge smile.

"Well, howdy, boys!" he called out in a bullhorn voice. "It's good to see you again. It seems like every time we get together you're bringing me some nice presents."

Chris lifted the paper-wrapped pewter plate from a brown paper bag and laid it on the table.

Which JW?

"Yes, I guess you could say we got a bit lucky on this one," replied Chris. "We just happened to see this little overhang from down below, and decided it might be worth our while to climb up and investigate. We never would have noticed it if the sun hadn't hit it just the right way. But it did, so here we are."

"No one who makes as many discoveries as you two does it by pure luck," said Tex, his face returning to a more serious expression. "That's why I hired you two. You use your brains to think things through and see other sides of the puzzle that most people don't consider. I like that. It takes all kinds of people to make a team work, and you two are my brains on this project."

As he spoke, Max shifted uncomfortably in his seat. Sean observed him out of a corner of his eye and noted the negative body language.

"So let's see this plate you boys found up in the mountains," said Durham. "I heard Max say that it's got some impressive initials carved onto the back."

"Yes, sir, it does," replied Chris as he removed the wrapping from the antique and passed it across the table. "We're not sure who 'JW' was, but anything is possible."

"It could very well be Jacob Weiser," said Durham as he examined the scrawled letters on the back of the plate. "This could be the first thing I've ever held in my hands that belonged to my granddaddy." As he spoke, his words sounded slightly choked by emotion.

"It could be, yes," replied Sean. "But it could also be Jacob Waltz, who worked with him. Or anyone else who shared the same initials."

"If it's all the same to you, I'd like to just think that this is my grand-dad's, and leave all the guessing to someone else," said the billionaire.

"Yes, sir," Chris said.

"Just to let you know, we took pictures and foil rubbings of the insignias on the back of the plate. We're having a friend take these to a couple experts on antique pewter and tinware to see if they can determine the origin. I'm thinking they maybe came from a craftsman or manufacturer in Germany sometime in the 1800s."

"Good idea," said Durham. "You'll let me know what they say?"

"Of course," said Chris. Then, uncomfortably, he brought up a subject he wasn't sure about introducing. "You know, sir, there is something you might want to consider with that plate."

"And what might that be?" replied the businessman, a posed smile still on his face.

"If that plate really did belong to Jacob Weiser, or Jacob Waltz, or *anyone* who was prospecting in those mountains during the last century, it really belongs in a museum exhibit where people could see and appreciate it as a historical artifact of the period."

"Thank you for the suggestion, boys," said Durham, maintaining the same frozen smile. "I'll keep that in my head for consideration."

Chris decided to drop the line of conversation and address a different topic. He reached into his right pocket and withdrew a small vial, which he placed on the table. "Here's another little present from us, although it probably isn't worth more than a few cents."

Durham lifted the vial and peered at the gold flakes at the bottom of the fluid. After completing his examination of the contents, he passed the container to Max.

"You're right, it's probably not worth anything. But where there's smoke, there's fire," said Durham optimistically. "I agree with your thoughts that it was probably from some larger pieces of gold that someone carried in there, and then moved away. There's no other explanation for a few flakes being in that spot, especially since none of the other rocks in the cave were gold-bearing ore. At least that's what I'm hearing from you. Max here will check out the site and do a full search from floor to ceiling."

"Max will . . . what?" asked Chris, surprised at the assignment.

Max interrupted from his side of the table to provide an explanation. "Mr. Durham has suggested that we rotate our search areas, in order to perhaps find things that the other teams have missed. So we're moving the two teams from our side of the canyon over to yours, and you're going to shift your search area to the northwest side of Weaver's Needle. We're hoping to increase our coverage and also our efficiency with that plan. Do you have any questions?"

Chris was too stunned to issue even a one-word response. Sean was able to get out a "No, we're fine with that," before resuming his silence.

Which JW?

"Good, good, now that that's all settled," said Durham, his hands both hitting the conference room table simultaneously, "I think we can all look forward to some good news real soon."

"We hope so, too, sir," mumbled Chris.

"Boys, I hope you realize that I have a rather personal interest in this whole gold mine hunt, and it's got a lot more to do than just the value of the gold, if we do find it."

Chris and Sean both sat silently and waited for Durham to continue.

"It's not something that I normally tell people, but I know your friend back in Philadelphia already tracked this down when you had her looking into my personal family tree." As he spoke, he shot a piercing glance at Chris and Sean. "But as you know, Jacob Weiser was my father's father, and he was a very good man. He lived a good life as a hard-working man. A righteous man. Until the day he was murdered by the Indians. Murdered in cold blood, for doing nothing but putting a shovel in the ground."

"I'm sorry, sir," said Chris.

"'Sorry' ain't never going to bring a corpse back to life," said Durham, his voice rising in volume and emotion.

"There was no reason for killing him except for the goddam Apaches' love of killing white men. If it was up to me, I'd kill every goddam redskin I could get my hands on. And their women and children. I'd get them off the earth permanently and piss on their graves."

Chris and Sean were stunned into silence. More than Durham's use of slurs against Native Americans, his full, vitriolic hatred of anyone of Native American descent was on full display.

"I know you think I'm probably being cruel, but that was my grandpa they murdered," shouted Durham. "MY GRANDPA!"

"That was a long time ago," remarked Chris.

"Well, one thing I know is that the gold mine is still out there somewhere. And not one cent of it is going to go to no Indians. We're going to find it, and we're going to clean it out until there isn't so much as a snotball-sized piece of gold in it. Any questions, boys?"

"No, sir," they both answered in unison.

"OK then," replied Durham. "Max here will give you new maps with your revised assignments on them. Good luck in your search, and keep

THE DUTCHMAN'S GOLD

up the good work." The Texan was already striding toward the door as he said his last words.

The door to the conference room slammed shut leaving Chris, Sean, and Max alone in the silence. It was a moment before anyone spoke.

"I take it that Mr. Durham doesn't have a very high opinion of Native Americans," Chris said quietly to Max.

"Probably not," Max replied. "Do you?"

"People are people," stated Chris, with Sean nodding his approval.

Max gave an appraising stare at the two before continuing on with his words. As he prepared to speak, he unfolded a large map that was on the table and slid it in front of the two men.

"Assuming that you two will be out in the field this week, this is the area where you'll be searching."

Chris and Sean looked over the topographic features and observed the overall terrain of the area, which appeared to be very rough. It also comprised a much larger area than their previous search sectors. It contained a great many "points of interest" highlighted in yellow marker, none of which had been previously explored by anyone on the teams.

Chris looked up suddenly and caught Max's attention.

"Could I ask you an honest question?" he said, eyeballing the foreman across the table.

"Shoot," replied Max.

"Now that we've found some pretty good clues indicating we might be within spitting distance of the mine, it's pretty frustrating being pulled off and sent to some distant part of the canyon," said Chris.

"Is there a question in there somewhere?" asked Max, his expression turning stone-like.

"There is," replied Chris, his stare meeting that of the foreman's. "Does everyone have the same 'incentive bonus' in their pay if they are the ones to actually find the lost mine?"

"I don't know, but I wouldn't get your blood to boiling if they do. We're only swapping out search areas because we're much better suited to the rough kind of searching than you," said Max, his face concealing a menacing scowl that was just below the surface. "So if you don't like our

236

WHICH JW?

arrangement, you can always back out now. I'm sure Mr. Durham will be happy to pay you for the time that you've spent here."

"That's OK," said Chris. "I'm still in. I just want to know where we stand."

All three of the men stood simultaneously, as if on cue. Max started to turn toward the door before Chris summoned him back.

"Max," he called out.

"Yes," Max replied.

Chris stuck out his extended arm to offer a handshake. "We're still all on the same team. We'll do as you ask."

Max returned the handshake with Chris and then Sean. "Just see that you do."

CHAPTER TWENTY-THREE

Starting Over

June 29, 2020

MONDAY MORNING BROUGHT SOME STARK REALITIES TO THE TWO MEN as they started their weekly trek back into the circular canyon. Among those were the realizations that they were definitely the "odd men out" of the three search parties. Also hitting home was the related fact that they would probably never be permitted to claim any share of the "incentive pay," which had been staked at 2 percent of the value of any gold in excess of $5 million.

"In case you were wondering, it would have taken only 174 pounds of gold bullion to reach the five-million-dollar mark, assuming a an eighteen-hundred-dollars-an-ounce price tag," announced Sean, who had done the computing on his cell phone calculator.

"That's nice," said Chris as he took the lead on the upward path to Fremont Saddle. "Do you have any other fun facts to amaze and entertain us?"

"As a matter of fact, I do," said Sean. "In order to accumulate two hundred and forty pounds of gold, you'd need to fill a block that was slightly over seven inches on each side."

"That's all?"

"Yup. Gold is heavy stuff."

"It's hard to believe that a cube that's only seven inches on each side weighs more than my entire body," observed Chris.

238

STARTING OVER

"That's what my body felt like after eating those apple-stuffed pancakes on Saturday morning."

"So if Tex says we're so good at finding things, how come we've been booted out of our area after making some promising finds?" wondered Chris out loud. "If you ask my opinion, Tex Durham just wants to make sure that his son and buddies get all the incentives while we're left with our base paychecks."

"Think so?" asked Sean.

"I'm not one hundred percent certain, but maybe ninety-nine percent," said Chris.

"Close enough."

By the time they descended into the bottom of the canyon to start their trek north, the other two search teams had established themselves high on the rock walls where they themselves had been the week before. Although they appeared as small as ants in the distance, they were clearly visible as they approached the promising outcroppings near the top of the cirque.

Chris and Sean also discovered another disadvantage to their new territory. It took a lot longer to circumnavigate the rocky ground surrounding Weaver's Needle, as they needed to do to move north and west through the desert heights.

"We'll do whatever you ask us to do," whined Sean in a high, squeaky voice as he mimicked Chris's promise to Max on Saturday.

It was getting into the later part of the afternoon before they reached their destination. Fortunately, it had rained recently, and Sammy found a small stream of runoff water that fed a pool, from which he drank his fill. He appeared to be getting quite used to their routines, and both men addressed him from time to time as though he were human.

Even though they had already spent a long day hiking into their assigned area and were fatigued from the heat, they managed to find and search two of the areas highlighted on their new map.

"What a surprise, only dirt and rocks," noted Sean. "This place is just like all the others. Dirt and rocks."

"What's the number on this one?" asked Chris.

"6B," replied Sean after referring to the topographic overlay map.

The Dutchman's Gold

"I don't know how they're doing up in our old spot," said Chris. "But I'm glad we emptied out every flake of gold we could see, as little as it was. I wouldn't want to waste a single speck on that crew."

"I'm in complete agreement with you there," said Sean.

Later, as they sat in front of a small fire eating their evening meal, Sean began to chuckle to himself.

"Penny for your thoughts," said Chris.

"Oh, it's really nothing. But I do have an idea that I think would be pretty funny," commented Sean.

"Is it sneaky, nasty, and aimed at getting back at our buddies on the other wall of the canyon?" asked Chris.

"It is."

"Then I'll give you a lot more than that penny for your thoughts. I'll buy the first two rounds of beers when we get out of here this week," offered Chris.

"Well, try this one on for size," began Sean. "We know our hotel rooms are bugged. But we don't know if Tex knows that we know they're bugged. Are you following me so far?"

"Gotcha," confirmed Chris.

"OK, so we go back to the hotel at the end of the week and call someone . . . your mother. My mother. Your great-aunt Matilda."

"I don't have a great-aunt Matilda," said Chris.

"Yes, but Durham doesn't know that. Anyway, we use our hotel phone to tell them that we've found the location of the Lost Dutchman Gold Mine. We'll give them the coordinates of our current site, good old 6B. Let's let Tex and Sons think that we've found the hen that lays the golden egg."

Chris considered the plot for a few moments before he began to smile himself.

"You know, it really wouldn't accomplish anything, but it would be pretty damn funny," he said with a twinkle in his eye. "Then we could hang out down here and see who showed up."

"That's the idea," replied Sean. "It would serve them right."

After agreeing on the prank, they sat back and enjoyed the arrival of the cooler evening. The northwest end of the canyon circling Weaver's

STARTING OVER

Needle was even quieter and more desolate than their previous location, and they could hear every bird and creature's call for miles around. Fully outfitted with all their needs, they were able to enjoy the full extent of the wilderness without a care in the world besides that of their supposed "teammates" at the other end of the loop.

* * * * * *

Another week of the daily, dusty slog. Their schedule marched on in a monotonous, unending procession of heat-filled days that had them wishing they were already at the end of their verbal contract. They had completed the exploration of exactly six of their assigned locations in the new area, with twelve still remaining. They both realized that whatever initial enthusiasm they held for the job had long-since vanished like the evening sun dipping over the canyon walls. Between the heat, the dehydrated food packs, their teammates, and their troublesome employer, they were ready to call it quits at the drop of a hat.

Only two weeks left to go.

After turning over their faithful burro and handguns to Alex, they headed back to Phoenix for one of their last stays in the luxury hotel. Unsure of the wisdom of Sean's scheme, they decided to go ahead with it anyway. They decided there was nothing illegal about relaying a totally fictional account of an event to a friend from the privacy of your own hotel room. After all, wasn't the only illegal activity of the moment in the listening device hidden in their living spaces?

The two men decided to wait until sometime after midday on Sunday to initiate the stunt, which would discourage any of the other teams from voyaging into the mountains at night time just to arrive before any others. It ended up being almost 5:00 PM by the time they actually dialed the number. Chris had already called Kristi back in New York ahead of time, using his cell phone from a park about a block away from the hotel.

"You want me to *what?*" cried Kristi, surprised at the nature of the call. "It sounds to me like this Tex dude is bad enough as it is without getting him ticked off with some hair-brained scheme like this."

The Dutchman's Gold

After assuring her that the call made sense, and they weren't putting themselves in harm's way, Kristi finally agreed to take the call. She asked Chris to call the house phone in her apartment building in order to preserve the sanctity of her cell number.

The call came in like clockwork. At exactly 5:00 PM on Sunday afternoon, Chris lifted the phone off the hook in his hotel room and dialed the number in Kristi's apartment. Sean looked on from behind as the phone on the other end rang.

"Hello, honey?" said Chris in greeting.

"Hey! I didn't expect to hear from you today!" came Kristi's cheerful voice through the earpiece. Sean rolled his eyes at her remark, since they had just agreed on this call ten minutes earlier.

"It's going well. No, it's going really, *really* well," said Chris, almost beside himself with cheer.

"Oh my God," said Kristi, now injecting a hushed tone into her word. "You sound like you found something."

"We can't say for sure, but there is a possibility that we may have found it. The mother lode," said Chris in a crescendo tone. "We found a spot where everything lines up. The location. The clues. The landmarks. *Everything!*"

"When will you know?" asked Kristi.

"Soon enough," replied Chris. "Probably tomorrow morning. And you wouldn't believe the irony in the whole thing. The only reason we found what we found was because the foreman moved us out of our last area. They thought we'd found the mine in our original search zone, so they bumped us out and took it for themselves. So we might end up splitting millions of dollars in incentive pay just for ending up in the right place at the right time."

"How far are you from your original location?" asked Kristi.

"As the crow flies, only about a mile and a half, but longer on foot," replied Chris.

"Is it easy to find? You'd think that other prospectors would have visited there long ago," remarked Kristi.

"Yeah, we thought the same thing," agreed Chris. "So it looks like 6B is going to make us both multi-millionaires."

STARTING OVER

"6B? What's that?" asked Kristi, playing her role perfectly.

"6B is the numbering on the map that corresponds to the place where we think the mine was hidden. It's just a number, sorry for the confusion," added Chris.

"No worries," said Kristi. "But good luck, sweetheart. I hope you find the mine tomorrow and it's everything you ever dreamed it to be!"

"Thanks, and me, too," replied Chris. "If this comes through like we think it will, we could buy any house we wanted, you could go back to school for your PhD—heck, neither of us would have to work again."

"OK, honey, do what you've got to do and give me a call. I can't wait to hear."

"Will do . . . goodnight!"

After hanging up the phone, Chris motioned for Sean to follow him from the room. They proceeded to a quiet bar across the street for a relaxing Sunday dinner.

"Well, all things considered, I'd say that went pretty well," noted Chris. As he spoke, he dialed the number of his girlfriend's cell phone.

"You goofball!" Kristi exclaimed as she answered her phone. "That's probably the silliest thing I've done since we flooded the girls' bathroom in high school."

"Yes, but I think it worked," said Chris.

"And what's that about me going back to school for a PhD? Are you out of your mind?" she cried. "That's the last thing on earth I want and you know it."

"Shh . . . it was all an act. None of the extra stuff matters. And you pulled off your part perfectly. I'm proud of you," exclaimed Chris.

"You'd better be," said Kristi. "Because this is going to cost you dearly when you get back home."

"Promises, promises," replied Chris with an even wider smile.

* * * * * *

Monday morning was no different than any other start to the workweek, although both men anticipated the antics they'd see on arriving at the site of search area 6B.

THE DUTCHMAN'S GOLD

"I bet they'll have both teams in there with 'shovels, rakes and implements of destruction,'" said Sean, quoting Arlo Guthrie Jr.'s "Alice's Restaurant" ballad.

"Thinking this all the way through, I bet they won't be all that pleased when they find out that we've sent them onto a red herring," said Chris.

"Not our fault or our problem," answered Sean. "They chose to illegally eavesdrop, so it's all on them."

As they made their descent into the canyon and commenced their long hike around the Needle, they both noticed that their old search area, up near the cave where they'd discovered the tin plate, was devoid of activity.

"Doesn't look like much going on up there today," observed Sean.

"Nope. I bet they've moved on to greener pastures."

They passed one of their designated rest stops where Sammy could once again gulp water until fully sated. Chris, meanwhile, removed his pack and rummaged through the contents looking for his pocket knife.

"Bummer," he exclaimed as he pulled out a pen-shaped device.

"What's that?" asked Chris.

"That's the mini-recorder I bought in the spy store our first weekend here," said Sean. "I stuck it in my pack to move it into the hotel safe, but I forgot to take it out in the room. So I've got to carry it with me the whole week."

"I'd better watch what I say," quipped Chris as Sean shoved the device into a front pocket.

As they rounded a geological rock formation in the base of the canyon, a bustle of activity suddenly came into view. At least seven horses were tied to a sugar berry tree, their owners nowhere in sight. Chris and Sean both looked up the steep incline to the area that was noted as "Location 6B" on their map. The location was absolutely teeming with active bodies.

"Geez, I hope they don't find anything," observed Sean. "You and I spent two hours combing that pit on Friday. It would be pretty darn embarrassing if they showed up today and pulled out a half ton of gold."

"Yes, it would," agreed Chris. "But we both know that's not going to happen."

"What now?" asked Sean.

"I don't know about you, but I think we ought to go up and join the party," suggested Chris.

It was a steep and moderately long climb up to the cave opening where they'd spent time the previous week. As they approached, the other men from Teams 1 and 2 took notice of their presence, although none gave greeting. It was a rather awkward moment, and the two men felt quite out of place.

Chris decided to make his remark to Max, who was standing below the outer lip of the cave observing the activity.

"Hey, we're surprised to see you here. I thought you wanted to work the southern end of the canyon while we came over here to the north?"

"Changed our minds," said Max, without making eye contact. "Tex found some new material in his collection of old manuscripts, so he called me and asked me to get the other two teams up here working inside this cave. So that's what we're doing here."

"Ah, I see," said Chris, allowing the sarcasm to appear in his speech. "So I suppose we should just go somewhere else today, and then maybe come back after you've made sure that there's nothing here. Or maybe you'd like us to just go sit in the corner with our dunce caps on. Because that's exactly what this is starting to feel like."

Sean winced as he listened to his friend's strongly worded remarks to the foreman, wondering what his response would be.

Max stood there for a moment totally transfixed, the anger showing on his face. He was about to reply when voices were heard from above.

"OK, all clear," came the report. It sounded to Chris like Shane's voice, but he wasn't familiar enough with the other men to know for sure.

"OK," called Max, "Hoss and Big Jim, let's bring 'em up!"

With that, the two big men began heaving in on the lines that were tied off to a thin but solid rock post. With synchronized motions, they both heaved away until a pair of arms appeared over the outer lip of the cave entrance. Jake and Shane soon appeared as they swung legs over the upper edge of the cave drop-off.

Shane headed immediately for his canteen, while Jake directed his eyes narrowly at Chris, who was standing nearby.

"What are *you* doin' here?" he asked with a vicious snarl from the back of his throat, as a dog would growl when threatened.

"Just doing what Mr. Durham asked us to do," replied Chris, no longer with the sarcasm. "He said he switched our search areas because he wanted his best people in position to look up yonder on that set of walls. His best people . . . I guess that would be you." As he spoke, he motioned toward the entire northern end of the canyon.

Jake wasn't in a good mood, and didn't know what to make of Chris's friendly attitude. He didn't appreciate hearing that from a "college boy."

"Chris here says that he feels like he ought to go sit in a corner with his stupid hat on. Him and his friend," said Max. "I guess he don't like us looking in his hole in the ground."

"I never said any such thing, Max. I was only kidding around when I said we'd been moved. It's all good. We'll search wherever we're told to search. We said the same thing to Mr. Durham on Saturday."

"Is that so?" asked Jake as he approached Chris, menacing in all regards. His six-foot-seven frame looked even bigger since he was standing slightly uphill from Chris's position. Sean, at five foot ten, felt positively dwarfed. "Well, I think you ought to go down into that cave right now and have a look around, seein' as how you're the one who thought it was filled with gold. As a matter of fact, I'll help you get there."

"We were both planning on conducting an in-depth search tomorrow morning," said Chris. "We're not going down there today. We're trying to follow the search plan that Mr. Durham gave us."

"Well, I've been running the show for Tex's projects for almost four years now, and I'll goddam let you know when you're searchin' and when you're standin' around doing whatever you college frat boys do," sneered Jake, his face now up close to Chris's and looking down at him. "And right now, you're goin' down in that pit and you're gonna search every inch of it on your hands and knees until I tell you to come out. Unless you want to try to make me change my mind."

Every sentence and every word of Jake's rant was louder than the previous line, and the other members of Jake's and Max's teams were now circling them to see what Chris and Sean would do about it.

There wasn't much they could do. They were miles away from any help, and they probably wouldn't have received assistance from anyone in Tex's employment if they had been able to make contact. It was an ugly scene, and Big Jim, Hoss, and the rest seemed to be enjoying the bullying. Even Max was wearing a smile as he watched Jake imposing his will on the two.

Chris decided to try to save face by volunteering to cede to Jake's forced demand.

"OK, we'll tie a line to the top and search this pit today," Chris offered. "We'll do the work we were supposed to do today sometime tomorrow instead."

As Chris spoke, he started removing a length of climbing rope from his backpack. The rope was his own stock, high-tech Yale Cordage 7/16-inch climbing line that he used when exploring caves back east. It was a woven, 24-strand double-braided line that would withstand a heavy fall, if needed, and boasted a 5,600-pound breaking strength. Chris trusted it with his life.

"What do you need that piece of shit for?" interrupted Jake. "We've already got two real ropes going down into the pit. Now you two get over that wall and we'll lower you down. Now *move it before I make you move!*"

With the rest of the huge crew watching, Chris and Sean both stepped over the lip of the cave and took hold of the old-style hemp ropes used by the other teams. Chris could feel the fibers of the line cutting into his hands, as they had not been afforded the time to put on their gloves.

The two both began their descents to the floor of the cave-like pit, which was about ten feet below the entrance. The floor was a rocky mixture of large and small stones that completely covered the surface floor from one side of the depression to the other.

Neither Chris nor Sean was surprised when, halfway down their drop, they heard a loud "Oops" from up above, followed by a freefall to the bottom of the pit. They had both been dropped at the same time, part of a coordinated movement from Jake and his friends up above.

The Dutchman's Gold

"Aww, shoot, I sure am sorry that happened," called Jake from above. "We must have lost our grip on the ropes. You two college boys OK down there?"

Even though they had only fallen about five feet of the total ten-foot drop, the rocky floor made a stable landing almost impossible. Both Chris and Sean were glad they had been wearing their backpacks, as they both went over backward on impact with the ground. Sean groaned as his left ankle twisted on the first rock that contacted the flat of his foot. Chris, meanwhile, made a more balanced landing, but his right elbow smashed against a sharp-edged boulder. He came to rest on his side, massaging his right arm with his other hand.

From above, the sounds of laughter could be heard for several minutes, although the volume diminished as the crowd moved away from the opening of the cave. The two ropes suddenly vanished entirely as they were pulled up out of the opening.

"You two boys have a good time exploring down there," Jake called from above. "And don't call us if you need anything."

Then they were gone.

It took several minutes for Chris and Sean to both return to a seated position.

"How is your ankle?" asked Chris, still rubbing his sore elbow.

"It's probably OK," said Sean as he rotated his foot in small circles, exercising the joint and tendons. "It felt really bad when it hit, but it's feeling better as I move it around."

"I'd like to ice this elbow, but obviously that's not very possible right now," added Chris.

"Not unless we hang around here for six or seven months," said Sean.

By now, all sounds had ceased from above, as the two other crews had obviously abandoned the area. The fact that they may have left two injured men to struggle or die on the mountain didn't appear to enter their thinking.

"Do you think you can free-climb the wall of this thing to get out, or do you want me to scale it myself and then throw you a line?" asked Chris.

Sean cast an appraising stare at the front wall of the pit, noting its uneven surface with a bounty of handholds and footings.

248

STARTING OVER

"It actually looks pretty simple," said Sean as he evaluated the surface. "I'm only afraid that if I do lose my footing, I might jam my ankle even further. So I guess I'd gladly accept a line if you don't mind making the first ascent."

Chris also glanced at the ten feet of rock leading up to the cave opening and agreed with his friend.

"You're right, it doesn't look like much of a challenge," said Chris. "It hardly qualifies as an 'ascent.'"

"Just be careful of where you put your hands," warned Sean. "You never know where you'll find one of our favorite rattling reptiles."

"Gotcha," replied Chris as he stood upright and took his first handhold on the red brick-like surface.

Considering that he had just been dumped down a pit and taken a nasty fall, it took him a surprisingly short amount of time to reach the top. With both arms over the upper ledge, he threw his right leg up and over the lip before pulling the rest of his body over the threshold.

"How's the view up there?" asked Sean from below, appreciating his friend's agility and climbing acumen. "I take it we're all alone in our end of the canyon?"

"We're all alone in our end of the canyon," repeated Chris. "You feel like coming up now, or do you plan on staying down there for a couple days?"

"Ha ha, you're pretty funny," called Sean in a sarcastic tone. "If you don't mind, would you please tie a fixed line to something solid up there, in case I can't bear much weight on this foot?"

"Sure," said Chris as he secured his climbing line to the rock column in front of the ledge. "And then, once you make it up here, we've got to talk."

"Yeah, agreed," noted Sean. Using Chris's line, he was able to make it to the top in short order. He swung both his legs over the ledge and came to rest in a seated position, looking at Chris.

"Well, that was a whole lot of fun," said Sean, still rotating his foot to test the joint. "Somehow I take it we're not the most popular kids on the block."

"Yes, but I never would have guessed this kind of behavior," replied Chris.

The two men walked over to a low, flat rock about fifty feet away that made a convenient seat. They sat down there to rest and collect their thoughts.

"That was outright dangerous. Stupid. Boneheaded. Ignorant. Have I missed anything?" asked Chris.

"No. So what do you want to do now?"

"First, let's make sure that we have everything still in one piece," said Chris. Then, looking down the slope at their burro, he added, "At least Sammy's still here."

"I wonder if their horses were pushing him around, too," mused Sean.

Chris next checked his backpack and was able to account for all his belongings. However, his luck ran out when he inventoried the contents of his pockets.

"Too bad I had our satellite phone in my back pocket," he said as he sadly withdrew the crushed remains of the device. The frame of the phone was bent, with a puncture mark intruding through the keyboard into the electronics of the interior. Additionally, the screen was smashed into a thousand small shards of glass, which he shook off into the dirt.

"I hope we don't need to make any emergency phone calls this week," said Sean.

"Or receive any," added Chris.

Sean performed a similar check of his belongings and found only two problems.

"My canteen looks like someone fired a grenade into the side," he observed, noting the large dent on one of the surfaces. "I must have landed on it when I fell backward onto the rock down there. It's probably a good thing, or that dent might have been in my back instead."

Then, standing up again, Sean looked slightly dismayed as he felt his pockets checking for his small personal items.

"Lose your keys?" asked Chris.

"No, but my recorder's gone."

"Your recorder?"

"Yeah, you know, that pen recorder I accidently had in my pack," explained Sean. "I moved it into my front pocket for safe keeping, but now it's gone." He quickly looked through his backpack to confirm it wasn't stowed inside. "Nope, it's gone."

"Maybe it fell out when you got jarred in the pit," suggested Chris.

"Maybe. I want to make another trip down there anyway," replied Sean.

"So do I," said Chris. "I noticed something really curious down there that I just want to check out."

"Like what?" queried Sean, a curious expression on his face.

"I noticed something when I hit the ground down there. It didn't feel natural."

"I noticed the same thing," exclaimed Sean with a wide-eyed stare. "Describe what you mean. I want to see if it's the same thing I felt."

"I could swear that the moment I hit the floor of the pit, something moved," said Chris. "I don't know whether it was more of a vertical 'bounce' or a lateral thrusting, but I could swear I felt some reactive motion from the bottom."

"The rock on the bottom of that place was different, too."

"I noticed that as well," said Chris. In the other cave-like depressions, the bottom was rough and gritty, with jagged surfaces that all seemed to be part of the actual cave floor. But this one was filled with rounder stones that didn't seem to match the geological strata of the cave itself."

"My God, you're starting to sound like your girlfriend now."

"We could probably use a good geologist here right now," said Chris.

"Anyway, my vote is that we take a timeout for lunch now and then head back down into the cave and check things out," suggested Sean.

"I agree, but I say we head down there a bit slower this time."

"Agreed," said Sean.

Before eating a quick lunch of granola bars and peanut butter, Chris trotted down the hill to set up Sammy with his grain bag. The burro appeared quite happy and was still chewing on some desert grass that was growing by the side of the trail. He took care of the animal and was back up the hill within a matter of minutes.

"Y'know what?" he asked Chris as he returned to the stone bench to grab his lunch bars.

"You want me to guess?" quipped Sean.

THE DUTCHMAN'S GOLD

"Now I really wish I still had our satellite phone in one piece. I had an epiphany on the way back up that hill just now."

"An epiphany? Wow, sounds painful," said Sean, still joking.

"Please stop," said Chris. "I thought you were hurt. So act it."

"Sorry. So what's this brainstorm you had?"

"Do you remember how I said that the markings on the bottom of that pewter plate looked so familiar? The manufacturer's crests stamped into the bottom surface?"

"Of course," replied Sean. "Did it just come back to you?"

"Yes," replied Chris. "While I was going through Alvah Dunning's personal belongings at the Adirondack Experience Museum, I came across an old drinking vessel that look like it was made of either tin or pewter. It had a pair of insignias on the bottom that remind me of the ones we saw on the bottom of the pewter plate."

"Hmm, interesting," said Sean.

"If our phone was working right now, I'd call Debbie in Blue Mountain Lake and ask her to send me a photograph of that mug."

"We can do that next weekend," said Sean. "Right now, I'd like to go back down into the cave and look around again."

"Lead the way, my friend."

After checking the holding power of the rope on the rock column, they prepared to make the descent back into the cave. They decided that Chris would go first, as Sean was still watching his twisted ankle. Once Chris reached the bottom, Sean let himself down the wall until they were both at the bottom.

Even though it was still the middle of the afternoon, with plenty of daylight, they both turned on their flashlights to better illuminate the floor of the cave. Unlike some of the other "locations of interest," this one more closely fit the description of an actual cave, except that it ended ten feet below the surface with no other outlet. It was an unusually shaped spot with some signs that it had been explored at an earlier date in time.

"Hey, that looks like your recorder," remarked Chris as he directed his beam at a spot between two of the larger stones on the floor. The device was shiny and had a single red light glowing on its side.

"It is. Thanks," said Sean as he bent to pick it up. He then examined the device closely before letting out an audible "hmmm."

"What's up?" asked Chris.

"Well, I know this was turned off inside my pocket, but it's on now. The motion of it falling from my pocket when I tumbled over backward must have pushed the 'on' switch into the powered-on position."

"Too bad. That means your batteries are probably a bit run down," said Chris.

"No, they wouldn't be," replied Sean. "It uses almost no power unless it's actively listening and recording sound."

"If it fell out of your pocket when we hit the ground, then it would have recorded everything that Jake and his crew said, and it also would have recorded our attempts to climb out of the cave," proposed Chris.

"OK, that combined took about five to ten minutes. This thing's been recording for over a half hour," said Sean.

"It's a dumb electronic device. Maybe it just never shut itself off."

"Maybe," said Sean as he turned the switch setting to "Play Audio."

The recorder began playback of the debacle in the cave starting at the precise moment when Sean hit the rocky floor, which proved his theory that it was activated by the movement of the device being torn from his pants pocket. Unfortunately, it wasn't activated to record the conversations and events leading up to them being dropped into the cave, but it caught everything that followed.

The two men listened as it played back their recovery from the fall, and their ensuing climb back to the top of the ledge. It also caught Jake saying, "Aww, shoot, I sure am sorry that happened," followed by, "We must have lost our grip on the ropes. You two college boys OK down there?"

"Not much we can do with this," said Sean ruefully. "Nobody would be interested in listening to Jake taunting us."

"I agree."

The device continued its playback of Chris and Sean climbing from the pit. Sean turned the volume up to maximum in order to hear the sounds of the escape.

"Well, that was exciting," said Chris. "Sounds like a made-for-television movie."

"Shh!" hissed Sean as he held his hand for silence.

Chris didn't respond. He just paused in place, listening along with Sean to the seemingly silent recorder.

"Do you hear that?" asked Sean, his voice barely higher than a whisper.

"No. Hear what?" said Chris, lowering his volume to match Sean's.

Sean answered with only a hand signal, indicating that he wanted Chris's ear next to the recorder with his own.

Together, the two huddled next to the device as it broadcast a puzzling sound. Emanating from the speaker of the miniature recorder were muddled voices, which sounded as though they were coming from far off. They were too faint to be understood, yet they did not sound like they were of the English language.

Chris looked at Sean, semi-puzzled and made the only suggestion that made sense.

"That must have been recorded in the spy store we visited in Scottsdale. There's no other way there could be anything already recorded on that thing."

"No, that's impossible," said Sean. "I put a brand-new memory card in it last weekend, and it hasn't been turned on since then.

"Are you sure it was a new card?"

"Yes. I unwrapped it from its plastic cover myself and installed it into the recorder. There's no way these voices were on this device before an hour ago," promised Sean.

"And we can tell they're not from Jake, Shane, Hoss, or those other guys?"

"No way. Listen to the voices."

Only about two or three of the recorded lines were sufficiently audible to make out the words, but they certainly were not in English.

"Any other theories?" asked Sean as he looked as his friend.

I don't know," Chris replied. "Do you believe in ghosts?"

CHAPTER TWENTY-FOUR

Do You Believe in Ghosts?

June 29, 2020

STANDING AT THE BOTTOM OF THE PIT, CHRIS AND SEAN BOTH LOOKED to repeat their experience of earlier that afternoon. They currently felt nothing resembling the semblance of movement beneath their feet, which puzzled them both.

"Look at it this way," proposed Sean. "When we both fell to the ground at the same time, it created the impact of close to four hundred pounds being dropped from five feet up. That might be hard to re-create from where we stand now."

"True, but we can do our best to simulate the impact," said Chris. "We need to create a genuinely flat patch of ground in here where we're not afraid to land with force. Then we need to find the highest spot inside this cave from which to jump."

They both agreed that the boulder on the far right side of the ground area would give them an extra two feet of height, and it was big enough so they could both climb on top for a simultaneous launch. It was the flat landing zone that gave them trouble.

"OK, let's scoop as much of that dirt and pebble material into the middle of the floor surface. The closer we can land to the middle of the cave floor, the better," advised Chris.

They spent the next fifteen minutes using their hands and feet to push the dirt around the cave bottom until they had leveled off a sufficient landing area. Chris tested it with a couple up-and-down hops before giving it his stamp of approval.

"OK, I say we go for it," urged Sean. "Everyone on top of the launch pad."

"On the count of three," prompted Chris. "One, two ... THREE!"

They both launched themselves as high in the air as possible, attaining a height of over three feet including the two-foot step-up from the boulder. They landed with a crash, both stamping the earth as hard as possible. Sean winced and hopped on one foot, favoring his left leg.

"Maybe that wasn't such a good idea," he said.

"Maybe not," agreed Chris. "But did you feel that?"

"Yeah, I did," replied Sean. "There's a definite shake in there. What the heck do you think could be the cause of it?"

"Beats the heck out of me, but this is where I think we get busy with our hands."

"Huh?" replied Sean, surprised at the response.

"I believe that we have a fake floor to this cave that is buried beneath a foot or two of well-placed stone," explained Chris. "So my plan is to start moving the stones on the left side of the pit over to the right side until we can at least see what we're dealing with."

"OK, assuming that you're right," said Sean, "you think we'll have enough space to pile up all this rock on one side of the cave without it tumbling back on us?"

Chris just shrugged his shoulders and smiled back at him.

"Or worse yet, we stack so much weight on one side of the floor that whatever is holding up the pile simply gives way?"

"In that case, we take the express elevator down to the bottom floor," said Chris.

"Personally, I vote for Plan B."

"What's Plan B?"

"A cold beer and a plate full of steamed shrimp with cocktail sauce," said Sean. "But I doubt you'd vote for that."

"Maybe some other time," said Chris. "Now come on and give me a hand with this."

The two men spent the next ninety minutes lifting heavy rocks from one side of the cave and carrying them over to the other side, where they stacked them up as tightly as possible to the cave wall. It was an extremely slow, arduous, and strenuous activity that tapped their strength as almost nothing had before. The combination of the bending and lifting, when added to the heat of the summer Arizona desert, was almost unbearable, and they slowed to a snail's pace.

At 5:00 PM, Sean turned to Chris with an exhausted look and announced, "I've had it. I'm done for the day."

"It looks like closing time anyway," said Chris, looking at his watch. "Let's head down and see how Sammy's doing."

The two men climbed back out of the cave and then went down the hill with their packs and rejoined with the burro, who seemed genuinely happy for the company.

"You know, I never thought I'd see the day when I'd become better friends with a burro than with my girlfriend," remarked Sean.

"I'm not sure I want to respond to that one," grinned Chris. "There are too many good answers, and none of them are nice!"

After unloading a gallon water jug and some food packs from one of their cargo bags, Sean observed that "those guys could have done a lot more damage than they actually did," referring to Jake and the others. "If they really wanted to mess with us, they could have taken a knife to our water bottles."

"Eh, I don't think they wanted to risk killing us," Chris thought out loud. "They just wanted to mess with our minds."

"Never mind. Being dropped into a cave is not my idea of a good time."

"Yes, but it sure had a silver lining," replied Chris. "Anything we find at the bottom of that hellhole up there will be because of them."

"Probably just some more rattlesnakes," mumbled Sean.

The two men set up their camp directly beneath the mouth of the cave. Sammy stayed nearby and nuzzled Sean's back as they sat near the fire, which helped warm the night air. Even though the temperature had been as high as 100 degrees during the day, it sunk into the low 60s at night, which felt even colder by comparison. They talked through their evening meal, and then into the sunset later on.

The Dutchman's Gold

"You don't suppose those guys are coming back here tomorrow?" asked Sean, wondering about the following day.

"No, I'm pretty sure we've seen the last of them, and them of us," replied Chris with an air of certainty in his voice. "They're sure that there's nothing in that pit, and I'm guessing that they know we're the ones who set them up to searching it."

"I guess that whole thing about claiming we thought we'd found the mine wasn't such a good idea, was it?" asked Sean. "I probably should have thought it through a little better before stirring up a hornet's nest like that."

"It's OK. We couldn't have guessed they'd have that reaction," said Chris. "And besides, we're college boys. We're supposed to be trouble-makers."

* * * * * *

The excitement of a potential discovery had the two men up early the following morning, although they both dreaded the extreme exertion they foresaw in the day. After a quick breakfast and a "tending-to-Sammy" session, they headed up the mountainside toward the now-familiar cave. Their fixed line for descending into the hole was still in place from the previous day.

"Ready to get to work?" asked Chris as he performed a series of stretching exercises.

"Let's do it."

After descending back down the drop-off, they both donned pairs of heavy leather work gloves and prepared to recommence the job of moving several tons of rock. They both found that the combination of a good night's rest and the cooler morning temperatures permitted them to perform more efficiently in their arduous task.

Bend. Lift. Move. Stack. Return and do again.

Over and over again, with large rocks weighing between thirty to sixty pounds. Twice they encountered small boulders weighing in at close to one hundred pounds that required a combined effort. Before long, the entire floor of the cave began to take on a sloped appearance as the material piled up on one side of the cave, but vanished from the other. Even with the air temperature still in the high 60s, Sean noticed they were both sweating.

"I'm ready for a break already," panted Sean after forty-five minutes of the strenuous activity.

"I'll join you," agreed Chris as he wiped off his forehead with a bandana.

"Think we're making progress?" asked Sean.

"Yeah, lots of it," said Chris as he motioned to one side with his head. "I think I see something through the rocks about another foot deeper. I can't be sure of what it is, but it looks like a thick beam."

The two men both drained half of their canteens before Chris directed his flashlight beam into a crevice in the rocks.

"See what I mean?" he asked excitedly. "I can't be sure of what it is or how it's put together, but that is *not* a rock down there.

The discovery of a bottom layer of wood reinvigorated the two, and they both resumed their task with increased vigor. Beginning with the spot where they first saw the wood beam through the stones, they began a systematic removal of debris, expanding the clearing until it finally spanned a rectangular pattern of about four feet by three feet. Through the opening, a lattice of wide, thick beams appeared, which supported the massive layer of rocks above.

"This is insane," remarked Sean. "I can't imagine the sheer amount of labor spent building this thing. And these rocks don't even look like they came from this cave."

"I don't think they did, either," said Chris. "And Lord knows where these beams came from, although they look like they were once part of the framework of another mining operation somewhere."

"You mean they were all carried here from somewhere outside, and then up this mountainside to this location?" asked Sean incredulously. "That must have taken an amazing amount of manpower. I don't know how long these things are, but I'm pretty sure they are eight by eight inches and must weigh a ton."

"Yeah, but you put six or eight bodies on each one and they can be moved."

THE DUTCHMAN'S GOLD

"I don't know," said Sean as he scratched his head.

"Did you know that the stones that make up Stonehenge over in England weigh about twenty-five tons apiece and were transported over twenty miles to their final location?" asked Chris to back up his point. "They built that sometime between four and five thousand years ago, so they probably didn't use heavy construction equipment for that job, either."

"OK, I get your point," conceded Sean.

"Anyway, now that we can see what's down there, let's poke both our lights through one of the openings and look around," suggested Chris.

Sean quickly retrieved his own flashlight from his pack and joined Chris by the largest opening in the beams. The abyss below their feet was inky black and seemed to wholly swallow the feeble light from their small bulbs.

"Let's try adding the two headlamps to this and see if we can see any more," suggested Sean.

"We don't have them with us," replied Chris. "They're down with Sammy and the rest of our supplies."

"No worries, I'm on my way," said Sean, already climbing the rope to reach the surface.

"Hey, as long as you're going down there, remember to bring the other hardhat up with you," called Chris. "And bring along the extra climbing line and my Jumar ascenders*, too."

Chris had long been a fan of exploring caves in upstate New York and other locations around the country. He was well versed in climbing techniques and equipment. Sean often joined him in his explorations of the "wilderness beneath the surface."

Sean returned in about ten minutes with a satchel containing the hardhat, rope, and equipment.

"OK, I changed out the batteries in the headlamps, so if we can't see anything down there now, we're in trouble," said Sean as he rejoined Chris at the bottom of the pit.

---

*Jumar ascenders are a device, often used by spelunkers while exploring caves, that provide assistance to climbing a fixed line when free climbing is too difficult.

The two men combined the strength of the four lights into a single, powerful search beam that illuminated the lower hollow into an entirely visible space. What they saw took their breath away.

"It's another cave, bigger than the one we're in now," whispered Sean in awe.

"No, it's simply a continuation of the cave we're already standing in," observed Chris, noting a garment hanging on the rock wall, along with other signs of human activity.

"Think this whole place was carved out by human hands?" asked Sean.

"No, I think the cave is natural, but it's obviously been worked and expanded by humans. Possibly over a very long period of time."

"I'm amazed that this whole platform of rock can be held up by a grid of eight-by-eight-inch beams," said Sean. "It doesn't seem possible."

"An overlapping grid of beams that size could probably support a lot more weight than what you see here," replied Chris. "I guess we'll see how it's supported once we get down there."

The two men were still excitedly viewing the large abyss below when they heard the sound. It was a rapid, high-pitched rattling sound that originated from below, somewhere inside the depth of the newly discovered part of the cave.

"Oh, lovely. One of my favorite creatures," moaned Sean.

Within a few moments, a second rattling sound joined the first, an ominous forecast of what was in store for them if they proceeded into the depths below.

"Do you really feel like going down there?" asked Sean, dreading the response from his partner.

Chris turned around and looked at Sean with a surprised expression. "You're kidding, right?" he asked in shock. "We've come all this way, spent seven weeks living in a frying pan, eaten by bugs, chased, and finally dropped into a cave, and you want to give up because of a reptile? I'm surprised at you!"

"Most reptiles I've met can't kill you with a single bite," complained Sean.

THE DUTCHMAN'S GOLD

"That's what snakebite kits are for," said Chris as he held up his first aid kit. "Now, I'll go first, just to prove that it's safe, and you follow whenever you're ready."

Chris took the second climbing line and tied it securely to one of the heavy wooden beams. He then dropped the other end into the opening, noting that it took a second to hit the bottom.

"That's got to be close to twenty feet to the floor," he noted.

Chris attached one of the headlamps to his hardhat and placed it on his head. He then tucked the flashlight and pair of Jumar ascenders into his pockets and maneuvered his body into one of the square openings between the wooden beams. He then started his slide down the rope. Up above, Sean noticed that the pair of rattlesnakes had both gone silent, and he could hear the sounds of Chris's gloved hands as they slid down the line.

"OK, whenever you're ready, buddy," called Chris from below. "It's a straight drop, about eighteen feet with a clean floor. No problems, just drop straight down."

Without responding, Sean followed suit and began his descent, landing next to his partner on the lower cave floor.

"The eagle has landed," said Sean, borrowing Neil Armstrong's quote from the surface of the moon.

"That's one small step for Sean, one giant leap for our checking accounts," quipped Chris as he followed Sean's lead.

"I've got to admit, I don't like this," warned Sean. "I'd feel much more comfortable if I knew where those two snakes were hiding."

"I've got to admit, that has me kind of puzzled," said Chris. "There's no light and no food down here, so what the heck are they living on?"

"Rats, maybe?" postulated Sean.

They discussed the possibilities as they scanned the cave walls, working in a clockwise pattern from left to right. The darkness was almost impenetrable beyond the beam of the light, so viewing the entire chamber at one time was impossible.

They had completed about three-quarters of their inspection when Chris suddenly noticed an interesting feature in the cave.

"Tunnel," he said, pointing his flashlight and headlamp toward a low, oval opening in the rear wall.

262

"Oh my God," gasped Sean, who further illuminated the opening with his headlamp. "It's so dark in here I almost didn't see that at all. I wonder how far it goes."

"Beats me, but let's see how much we can see before either of us climbs through there," said Chris as he moved closer to the opening.

"Keep your eyes peeled for low slithery things," advised Sean. "We know there are at least two of them down here."

Slowly, in tandem, the two men approached the hole leading through the rock. Because it was about five feet wide by only four feet high, they both had to assume extreme crouched positions and "duck walk" forward into the opening.

"It looks like it goes for a distance, but I don't see a snake in sight," said Sean thankfully.

"True, but do you notice anything else?" asked Chris. His eyes were partially closed, and he had his hands extended to his sides.

"Air?" asked Sean in a hesitating voice.

"Wind. I feel a faint but definite flow of air, which means that this thing is connected to another opening somewhere not too far away."

"There's all kinds of rumors about a tunnel leading to the Lost Dutchman Mine," said Sean excitedly.

"Yes, I know," said Chris. "Along with the other seven hundred clues in the book."

"I'm just saying . . ." replied Sean.

"Anyway, since I don't see any rabid-looking serpents in there, I'm going in," said Chris as he prepared to pass through the tunnel entrance.

"Just be careful. And try to stay within earshot of me if you can," advised Sean.

"Don't worry, I'm not planning on doing anything stupid."

Sean then watched in amusement as Chris squatted even closer to the ground and began wriggling his way into the opening.

"I ought to take a video of this and send it back to Kristi," said Sean gleefully.

"Go ahead," replied Chris. "She knows I won a limbo contest back when I was in high school."

It took him all of about a minute to squeeze his tall limber frame through the orifice and into the wider passageway on the other side.

From there, the route opened up significantly, but not enough to allow him to stand upright to his full height.

As Sean stood transfixed at the sight of his friend's body disappearing into the length of cave on the other side, he heard the sound that once again made his blood freeze. One, then two sets of rattles suddenly sounded their angry tones from somewhere in Chris's vicinity. But from his distant position, he could do nothing to help, and he knew Chris was not carrying his weapon. Wherever the venomous reptiles lay, they had Chris at their mercy. Sean silently prayed that he could avoid their strikes and return through the tunnel entrance without injury.

Suddenly, the two sets of rattles sounded their deathly knell, but right in front of Sean's bent knees. He was almost inside the tunnel opening, and for all he knew, the snakes could be within three feet of his boots. They sounded that close, making Sean recoil and start backing rapidly.

Just as suddenly, Chris's wide-eyed, smiling face popped into view and exclaimed, "Hey . . . *watch out for the rattlesnake!*"

With that, he held up two carved sticks, one in each hand, and each with two sets of rattles tied to the ends with a leather strap. He quickly shook the pair of sticks, which produced the rattling sounds they had heard only moments ago.

It took Sean all of a second to view the noisemakers and determine their significance.

"You mean . . . th . . . th . . . that's what we were hearing?" he asked, stammering slightly.

"That's what we were hearing," repeated Chris with a grin. "These are our two rattlesnakes."

"But I don't understand," said Sean, still somewhat confused. "Who, or what was using those to impersonate a snake? And whoever it was, are they still in here with us?"

"Good questions," said Chris as he wriggled his was back through the opening. "But I do know one piece of equipment I want to have with us. Excuse me for a minute."

Chris then used his Jumar ascenders to climb the rope to the chamber above, where he grabbed his backpack and tossed it to Sean below.

Do You Believe in Ghosts?

"Whatcha need?" asked Sean. "That first aid kit?"

"Hardly," said Chris as he slid down the rope one more time. He then opened the pack and pulled out the Glock handgun, which he loaded with his full magazine.

"Should I bring mine, too?" asked Sean. He noticed that Chris had brought both of the pistols down from the upper level.

"It wouldn't hurt," said Chris. "And no, I'm not worried about whoever was trying to scare us with the rattlesnake sounds. But I am concerned about what else is over there."

"What's that?" asked Sean as he loaded his own weapon.

"Come with me and see for yourself. It's pretty spectacular."

Sean found that he didn't need to duck down nearly as far as Chris, due to his compact stature and shorter legs. Still, he had to waddle at least eight to ten feet in order to clear the low entrance to the tunnel. Once through, he was able to stand to his full height, keeping an eye out to avoid hitting his head on some of the lower overhead projections.

"I like the rattle-maker sticks," remarked Sean. "Who do you think was using them?"

"I think whoever it was probably wanted to ensure that it scared off any unwanted visitors," surmised Chris.

"The carvings on the handle and the leather strapping almost look Native American to me," noted Sean. "Do you suppose there are still any Natives up here in the mountains?" asked Sean.

"I don't know if they are Native Americans or not," said Chris, "but whoever it is chews Wrigley's Spearmint gum."

"How do you know that?" asked Sean.

"There's a wrapper of a fifteen-pack lying on the ground over there," replied Chris, pointing to the discarded paper.

"Hmm . . . that could be anyone's," observed Sean.

"True."

"So is that what you thought was 'so spectacular,' a chewing gum wrapper?" asked Sean sarcastically.

"No, what I thought was spectacular was the massive vein of gold that's right around the next corner. I've never seen or heard of anything quite like it."

Sean froze in place, not sure whether to believe his friend. He decided to give him a chance.

"What vein of gold?"

Chris backed up and gleefully beckoned him around a corner in the cave, where he pointed to a large, irregularly shaped infusion of sparkling metal in the host rock. It was between five and six feet high and over a foot wide and completely filled with the precious metal that had almost no imperfections or infusions. It was solid gold, with chunks falling from the sides that were as big as cue balls.

Chris already had the benefit of witnessing the quarry of wealth for several minutes and was slightly more subdued than his partner. Sean, however, was dumbstruck.

"Do you think this is it?" asked Sean. "I mean, Jacob Waltz's mine?"

"I do," replied Chris, still talking in a hushed tone. "And I also think that we're not alone in here, which is why I asked you to bring along your 'friend.'" As he said the word "friend," he patted the Glock that was holstered on his waist.

Sean's words to Chris turned into a whisper as he tried to keep their conversation as private as possible.

"Are you expecting to get attacked in here?"

"I doubt it," replied Chris. "It depends on who is mining this vein. But I can tell by looking at it that it's been picked on for some time now. Just look along here; you can tell there's signs of a geology pick or small ax all up and down the crevice. Someone has been in here, probably recently, and I'm sure they want to protect their investment."

"Who?"

"I really couldn't say," said Chris. "To tell you the truth, if they're local Native Americans, I say 'good!' Let them have it. They really could use it, especially since so many of them are so poor and our government has screwed them around so many times already."

"Who are the other possibilities?" asked Sean.

"It could be anyone, including a criminal element that I don't care to think about," said Chris.

"Yeah, but that possibility doesn't make sense to me," said Sean. "If they really are criminals, or outlaws, or even off-the-grid American prospectors trying to get rich quick, they would have cleaned this place out as soon as they found it. But that's not what's going on here."

"I'm thinking the same thing," concurred Chris.

"So what do you want to do about it?"

"Nothing right now. It's almost 5:00 PM," said Chris. "Let's gather our stuff and head down to camp. We can discuss it later and try to make sense of it all."

"Don't you think we ought to at least cover up our tracks above, maybe toss a few of those rocks back over the openings in the beams?" asked Sean.

"It's 5:00 PM, the sun's going down in a few hours, and we're in one of the most remote places in the country. Who's going to bother it?"

"Yeah, I hadn't really thought of it that way," Sean conceded. "Let's go."

Before they exited the tunnel cave, Chris picked out a fist-sized nugget along with a smaller piece and put them in his pocket. "I think we're entitled to a few samples, anyway."

"I promise I won't tell anyone," said Sean as he picked up a nice-sized piece for himself.

Considering that they had just solved a mystery that had its origins in the 1890s and had developed continuously over the past 130 years, the two felt very little elation as they prepared their evening meals and set up their small tent. The word "contentment" probably described their emotions more accurately, and they still weren't sure what to do about informing their employer, the morally bankrupt Tex Durham.

"You realize how much gold might be in that vein, I hope," mused Sean. "That thing is probably almost as tall as I am, and maybe fifteen inches wide in spots."

"We also can't tell how deep into the rock it runs," added Chris. "The vein might even grow wider as it runs away from the surface and into the earth."

"We're looking at thousands of Troy ounces as a minimum," stated Sean.

"I think we're looking at potentially thousands of pounds," said Chris.

Sean quickly turned on his private cell phone and accessed the calculator function. Tapping in a quick series of numbers, he turned to Chris with his report.

THE DUTCHMAN'S GOLD

"So if we go with a value of eighteen hundred dollars per ounce, and we accept a total weight of two thousand pounds, we're talking a net value of 57.6 million dollars."

"So our take would be two percent of everything over five million dollars, right?" asked Chris, trying to recall the details of Durham's original proposal.

Sean tapped in a new line of numbers and arrived at the final bottom line.

"If those are the numbers, then our bonus would come to 1,052,000 dollars!" he announced.

"That's not a bad payday for a two-month gig," Chris agreed.

After finishing their meals, the two sat side by side on the ground and watched the evening sky fade into darkness. It passed through a beautiful crimson red en route to a diminishing hue of dark purple. All the sunsets had been beautiful in their desert environment, and they wondered how they compared to those in the Adirondack Mountains back home.

"Anyway, that's a lot of money, although not enough to make us really rich," said Sean. "It's not like each of us could retire on half of 1,052,000 dollars."

"I wouldn't want to anyway," said Chris thoughtfully. "I won't be ready to sit back and take it easy for a long, long time. And besides, I'd still like to see who is picking at that gold up there, and for what," said Chris.

"I do know what you mean," said Sean.

Chris then continued to speak. "We both know that Durham won't share his finds with anyone, besides the two percent he'll give to the finder, assuming that he lives up to his end of the bargain. And with his hatred that he expressed for the Native American population, they'd never see Dollar One from it, either. He'd rape and pillage the ground for everything he could get until that vein was completely empty. Part of me believes that he's doing this purely out of spite, to make sure that no one else finds the gold and benefits from it. Personally, I'd rather see the original indigenous people of this land get to benefit from the natural resources that once belonged to them."

"That is because you are both honorable men," sounded a low, deep voice from directly behind the two.

At the sound of the voice, both Chris and Sean swung so quickly on the ground that Sean actually toppled over backward. Chris, astonished at the appearance, jumped up to his knees before the visitor put up his right hand and calmly said:

"Please, my friends, remain seated. I am very sorry if I startled you. That was not my intention."

The man was obviously a Native American. He was dressed in mostly native garb, with leather pants and a matching blouse-type shirt that was adorned with feathers and claws that Chris guessed to be from either a brown or a black bear. He wore a headband that was red and black with several feathers protruding from the top. His feet were clad in low moccasins that looked to be more designed for comfort than desert travel.

"We never heard you approach," said Chris, unsure of how to address this apparition from nowhere. "Have you been here long?"

"I have been with you since you arrived, although I have not made myself visible to you," the man said. "I observe many visitors to our lands, but choose to become known to few."

"We're honored to have you with us," said Chris in a sincere tone. "Would you like to join us at our fire?" As he spoke, he slid aside to make room between himself and Sean.

The Native American slowly sat between the two and placed his hands toward the fire, bringing them apart and then together again, as though gathering energy from the flames. Neither Chris nor Sean understood his movements, so they simply watched him for a moment in silence.

"My name is Chris, and my friend here is Sean," said Chris, who still wasn't sure how to address the newcomer or even whether it was considered proper. For perhaps the first time in his adult life, Chris felt completely socially uneasy with a situation. Sean was equally unsure of what to say.

"My name is Charging Bull, of the Pima Tribe," said the man solemnly. "My people have lived in the mountains and along the plains and rivers of this region for over three hundred generations. It is the land of my father, and my father's father."

"Both of us are from the other side of the country, in New York," said Sean, trying to enter the conversation. "It's a very long distance from here, over twenty-four hundred miles."

The man smiled and turned to Sean. "Yes, I know. I attended a white man's school outside of Phoenix. I know of your home, and most of the United States as well, although I have never traveled there."

"If I may ask, why have you chosen to honor us with your visit?" asked Chris.

"You chose to visit me first," replied Charging Bull. "I was behind you when you entered our sacred domain today. You are one of very few white men who have ever been to that place on the mountain."

"Do you mean inside the cave, where we saw the vein of gold in the rock?" asked Chris.

"That is the place," said Charging Bull as he stared straight ahead into the fire.

"We found it purely by accident," admitted Chris. "We were thrown into the cave by some very bad men who are supposed to be working with us. We only became suspicious of a false floor when we felt it move when we landed."

"I saw the other men, and I agree they are not honorable," said Charging Bull. "I have seen some of them before, and they are enemies of my people. If I could have helped you earlier today, I would have done so."

"Did you build that floor to hide the vein of gold from people like us?" asked Chris.

"That was the work of my father's father," said the old warrior. "The cave holds not only the gold you speak of but also a holy pool of water that is on a lower level. Our people worship in that place, and it is of great significance to our way of life."

"But you are mining the gold? Or at least someone is," continued Chris.

Charging Bull smiled before answering. "Obsession with gold and other forms of wealth is only a white man's game. Our ancestors cared little for the riches brought by its presence. Even their jewelry was made of silver, not gold, because of its sturdiness and durability. Our enemies, the Apaches, felt the same way and did not use the gold for their own purposes. They killed outsiders who tried to take it, but only because they were angered that those invaders would take *anything* without asking."

Do You Believe in Ghosts?

"The person who paid us to come here was the grandson of one of those killed by early Apaches, or by someone else in these mountains," said Chris. "That's why he has such a deep hatred of the Native American people, regardless of their origin. He is a ruthless man who holds a grudge like no one I've ever met, and he will do anything to get what he wants."

"Including gold that he does not need and may never use?" asked Charging Bull. "Including killing anyone who gets in his way?"

"We wouldn't put anything past him," said Sean. "We know he doesn't trust us, even though we tried to help him as much as we could before we discovered his true intentions."

"The gold that is inside the bottom of the cave, is that your people who are mining it?" asked Chris.

"It is my people, and has always been my people," said Charging Bull. "There are stories passed down from our ancestors about a man, once, who found the cave and began to take some gold away with him. But the Apaches found him and killed him in a very bloody way that scared away others from coming here. Once my father's father built the false wooden floor, no one has visited since."

"But most of the gold is still in the rock down there," noted Chris. "If your people are poor and could benefit from having more food and clothing, why not mine the gold from the vein and sell it? Obviously you know of its value."

"My people have taken the gold from the earth and used it when needed," Charging Bull replied. "But we use it only when needed, and we take only as much as we need. We believe that wealth is more in your heart and soul than in your wallet. We teach our children to live in harmony with the land. The same would be true with hunting to obtain food for my family. If I needed to feed five people for a day, would I hunt an elk?"

"Those are very wise words," said Chris. "Many of our people would be much better if they followed these words themselves."

"There is another reason why we could not take large amounts of gold from the cave and sell it all at once," said Charging Bull. "If we carried a

THE DUTCHMAN'S GOLD

sack full of gold into town to sell for cash, it would attract much attention. People would follow us up into the mountains and would give us no peace. They would not rest until they discovered our holy places. They would steal our gold and pollute our waters. We would have nothing left. This is why we bring only a small amount with us whenever we need to trade it for cash."

"It seems like even a small nugget weighing a few ounces would draw a prospector's attention," said Sean.

"That is true," agreed Charging Bull. "That is why we bring in only fine particles and gold dust from the rock, not a big piece such as the ones you took from the cave today."

Chris reached into his pocket and removed the two nuggets he'd taken from the cave, and then he offered them to Charging Bull.

"Yes, we did take a few pieces from the vein inside the cave," he said. "But they really belong to your people, so you may take them back and return them to the cave. I am sorry; I did not know they were being used to provide goods for your people."

The man once again held up his hand signifying that he did not wish to take the ingots from Chris.

"That is OK," said Charging Bull. "Please let this be a peace offering between us, that we shall live together without conflict."

"We don't need a gift to live together peacefully," said Chris. "We do not wish to take what isn't ours. So please . . ."

Still, the visitor refused to take back the chunks of gold, so Chris decided to change the subject.

"We've been working back here for many weeks now, and we've never seen anyone else besides a few hikers passing through. Do many of your people live back here? And where are they? We never see any of them."

"Yes, some of our people live here," said Charging Bull. "Others live north, near the Salt River. Our ancestors of many generations ago came from there and were called the 'River People.' You would seldom see any of those people, as they live in harmony with the earth and are seldom seen."

He then took notice of the small fire before him and spoke again.

"You share some of the same values as my people," he said as he waved his hands again at the flames. "Most white men would start a fire using large logs from many trees and send flames high into the sky. Your fire uses only what it needs to stay alive. Yet you can still receive warmth and cook your food. It is all you need and all you take. This is good."

"Many people take more than they can use, all to create an illusion of wealth," said Chris.

"Wealth means nothing if your heart is not in the right place," replied Charging Bull. "If not, much of one's life can be an illusion."

Chris cleared his throat and then began to address the topic of the gold mine.

"I know you must be somewhat worried about us finding the mine today," he said. "But I want you to know that Sean and I would never tell anyone about the gold or its location. If you use that to provide for your people, then you shall have it without interference from us. We will only be here for one more week before our stay here is over. We will tell the people we work for nothing about your cave, or your mine, or even about meeting you here. Our lips are sealed. On that you have our solemn word."

Sean nodded enthusiastically to signify his approval of Chris's words.

"Thank you for your promise and your commitment to my people," Charging Bull said in a wavering voice. "There are not many men in today's world who would walk away from such things without regret. You are truly honorable men."

"I do have to ask you, though," said Chris, trying to lighten the mood. "When we were in the cave near the gold vein, we saw several things that belonged to your people. What surprised me was the Wrigley's gum wrapper on the ground."

The man turned toward Chris with a smile appearing on his face and gave a single, one-word reply.

"Kids."

"I do have one more question, if you don't mind," asked Chris.

"I do not mind," replied Charging Bull.

"Over a hundred years ago, there was another white man from our side of the country who visited these mountains. He came and stayed for one year before returning home. He was well known as a hunter and marksman and lived amongst the native people out here. They gave him the name 'Ghost Hawk.' We know this because we found jewelry that is of local origin with his belongings. We also found a drawing of him that was done by a Native American artist named Soaring Spirit. Are you familiar with either of those men?"

Charging Bull's face took on a thoughtful expression as he recalled the lore of early days. "I have heard much of the times of Soaring Spirit, as he was a bright light among our people. His art recorded much of the history of our day and our people, and he will always be remembered. This other man you speak of, 'Ghost Hawk,' I have also heard his stories passed down. He was a very quiet man who lived alone and did not seek out company. We lived in peace with him, and even the Apaches feared his rifle. But I know nothing else about him."

"Do you know where he lived?"

"I'm sorry," replied Charging Bull. "That was never passed down with the stories."

"That's OK," said Chris. "Thank you for what you have told us."

With that, the man stood and held his hands toward the fire one final time.

"Thank you for being our friends. I leave you now, so please go in peace."

Chris and Sean listened to the words while still staring into the fire, mesmerized by the appearance and genuine character of this modern-day member of the Pima tribe. It was a day they would both long remember.

Simultaneously, both men stood to wish Charging Bull farewell. However, when they turned to say their goodbyes, there was nothing there. Only the earth and the mountain rising behind. Their new friend had somehow vanished without a sound, just as he had appeared.

"Talk about illusions," murmured Chris.

CHAPTER TWENTY-FIVE

Party at the Ranch
July 4, 2020

FOLLOWING THEIR EXIT FROM THE MOUNTAINS THAT WEEK, CHRIS and Sean immediately called their families to ensure that no one had been attempting to reach them on their broken satellite phone. Chris also noticed that Debbie had texted him a pair of photographs she made of the pewter mug contained in Alvah Dunning's box of possessions. One of the photos showed a clear image of two crests stamped into the metal on the bottom of the vessel. They were an exact match of the two imprints on the bottom of the plate found by Chris and Sean on the side of the mountain.

Chris flipped through to the second photograph of the text and read Debbie's note explaining the image. It said:

There was a third marking below the handle of the cup, although I didn't know whether it was important to you or not. So I'm sending you the photo anyway.

Chris scrolled down to view the second photograph, and what he saw made him catch his breath.

There, scrawled in the metal, were the initials "JW."

Turning to show Sean, he summarized what they had both suspected since Chris initially raised the possibility. "It looks like this

THE DUTCHMAN'S GOLD

confirms that Alvah did bring this cup home from the Superstition Mountains," he said.

"That was pretty good that you remembered the cup from your visit to Blue Mountain Lake," said Sean. "I never would have recalled two little stamps from just a brief look."

"Well, if we ever needed one more piece of proof about where Dunning took his one-year sabbatical, this is it," concluded Chris.

Chris's next move was to call Tex Durham's office to explain to his secretary their lack of ability to communicate with the outside world. He was pleasantly surprised to find that his regular cell phone was operational from their remote location, which he chalked up to their position high on the mountain ridge. He neglected to pass along the story of how the satellite phone was destroyed, but he did request that she find a way to get them a replacement for their final week on the job.

The secretary put Chris on hold, and he was surprised when Tex himself picked up the phone at the end of the pause.

"What is this I hear about you mashing up one of my expensive satellite phone gizmos?" he asked in a voice that expressed fake anger.

"Sorry, Mr. Durham. I took a fall last Monday and landed directly on top of it. I'm afraid it's dialed its last numbers," explained Chris.

"Well, that's no matter, as long as you're OK," said Durham. "How exactly was it that you fell that hard?"

"We were descending to the bottom of a pit on the north side of the canyon, and I lost my grip on a rope," replied Chris, applying a slight twist of the truth.

"And I take it you didn't find anything down there?"

"Not a thing," replied Chris. "Just like all the other spots, we searched it on our hands and knees but didn't come up with a single speck."

Sean was listening to Chris's accounting nearby and grinned at his friend's take on the story.

"Well, I'll tell you what I want the two of you to do," said Durham. "I'm planning on throwing a big shindig here for the Fourth of July. I've even hired a fireworks company to come out and set up a real nice display out here, just like you'd see in most cities back home. And we'll be roasting a pig and have lots of good drink, and I've even hired a band

PARTY AT THE RANCH

to come out and entertain us. I'd like you to come by the ranch and join us. I'll have a replacement phone for you there, so you'll kill two birds with one stone."

"It sounds wonderful," said Chris. "We'd love to join you, but that's over one thousand miles from Phoenix, isn't it? We'd be on the road for at least two days each way."

"Heck, you think I'd do that to you?" replied the Texan. "Just get yourselves to the private terminal at the Scottsdale airport by 7:30 AM on the morning of the Fourth. There will be a private jet waiting for you. Just tell the people at security that you're guests of Mr. Durham."

"Wow, thank you," said Chris, surprised at the extravagance of the offer. "We'll be there."

"Good. I'll have my secretary send you the details before tomorrow."

* * * * * *

Sean took the wheel for the drive back to the Phoenix hotel, which left Chris free to call Tracey in Philadelphia. Before making the call, he checked to see if the listening device was still installed in the SUV, which it was.

"Don't worry," said Chris to his friend in a cryptic manner. "We'll keep it nice and clean for our customers." Then he dialed Tracey's number.

"Hey, in case you couldn't reach us this week, our satellite phone was broken," Chris explained.

"Yes, I tried once or twice," said Tracey. "I was getting worried about you two, maybe getting eaten by a bear or mountain lion."

"Not me," joked Chris. "I'd be too tough to eat. I probably wouldn't taste too good, either."

Tracey giggled in the background listening to Chris's commentary. "Anyway, I found an expert on tin- and pewterware right here in the Philly area, and I visited him at a show he was doing in the Philadelphia Convention Center. I got some good stuff from him. I think you'll be proud of me."

"Cool. Tell me what you got," prompted Chris.

"Well, the two insignias on the back of the plate are early crests from a company called ARS Roders. They're a German manufacturer that got started all the way back in 1789, in a town called Soltau, which is in the

THE DUTCHMAN'S GOLD

district of Heidekreis, Germany. Don't ask me where that is, but that's where they come from."

"Good work, Tracey," said Chris. "We were hoping they were of German origin, since Jacob Waltz supposedly came over to the States from Germany, perhaps in the 1840s. We also have a cup we found in the Adirondack Museum that matches these same insignias."

"The plate definitely was from Germany," confirmed Tracey.

"And we also now know that not only was the drinking vessel up in the Adirondack Experience Museum also from Germany but also part of the same set because they found the same initials stamped on the side," said Chris. "Which is even more proof to us that Alvah Dunning either met Jacob Waltz or found some of his belongings somewhere in the mountains. How else could he have ended up with a cup from Germany?"

"I don't know," replied Tracey. "How?"

"It doesn't matter," replied Chris. "But how about I'll pass the phone to Sean now. He's been dying to talk to you all week."

Sean gave his friend a very dirty look as he took the phone. They talked about little things from their visit together until the SUV arrived back at their hotel.

* * * * * *

Once back in the pub inside the hotel lobby, Chris and Sean discussed their results from the previous week.

"Do you think that anyone will know that we did little or no actual work after Monday this week?" wondered Sean.

"How would anyone know?" asked Chris. "And what would the point have been anyway? We both knew where the mine was by then, so why bother spending ten hours a day shimmying up and down countless slopes for nothing?"

"I still think you did a great job making up notes for the final fourteen sites we supposedly checked out," smiled Sean. "Some of those were pretty detailed accountings."

"I'm a business consultant. I'm good at making up accountings," replied Chris.

278

PARTY AT THE RANCH

* * * * * *

True to Max's promise, Chris and Sean were met at the airport gate in Scottsdale by a tall, lanky man in a pilot's outfit who led them down the boarding ramp and onto a sleek, Embraer Phenom 100 private jet.

"Nice looking aircraft," noted Sean as he peeked out the ramp window at the attractive swept tapered nose and the red, gray, and black designs on the exterior.

"Yeah, it's beautiful, if you have a spare 4.5 million dollars lying around, not to mention the costs for fuel, maintenance, and flight crews," agreed the pilot. "Then again, Mr. Durham doesn't have to worry about small details like that."

Traveling at almost 450 knots, they covered the distance to Dallas in little more than two hours, where they were met by another chauffeur-driven limo who drove the pair into the Texas countryside. It wasn't long before the large wooden gates of the Durham ranch appeared on the horizon.

Chris and Sean were both amazed at the size of Tex Durham's ranch. From the time they passed through the entry gates and onto the private lane, it seemed like several miles before the homestead came into view. The house itself wasn't enormous, nor was it ostentatious in its design or architecture. It was, however, surrounded by a number of outbuildings, in addition to an outdoor pool, horse corrals, and guest buildings. The huge parking lot in front of the house provided space for at least thirty vehicles, and was already filled to capacity when they arrived. The limo driver dropped them off at an attendant's booth at the head of the lot.

Rather than enter through the front door of the billionaire's house, they walked around the side to where a large crowd of friends were congregating on an oversized patio. At least two dozen oversized tables were positioned around a makeshift dance floor that had been laid down over the top of the concrete-and-stone surface. A quartet of musicians were playing a variety of country songs while a few dancers braved the scanty turnout on the dance floor to perform the two-step.

THE DUTCHMAN'S GOLD

One of the tables on the far side of the patio was occupied by the six men of Tex's other two teams. Their table was situated next to the bar that Tex had arranged for the guests. Based on the number of empty beer bottles already scattered across their table, Chris and Sean guessed that they had already been present an hour or two. They also weren't surprised that none of them so much as turned around to acknowledge their arrival.

"Looks like we're not going to get voted as the 'Most Popular' members at the party either," remarked Sean.

"Good. I always prefer to remain anonymous," said Chris.

Tex Durham had been entertaining a group of local politicians at a table near the pool, but broke apart to come address the two men.

"I believe I have something that you need," he said, holding a new satellite phone in his extended palm. "And this time, try to keep it in one piece."

"We'll do that," smiled Chris.

"So do you boys have anything more to tell me about, now that you're down to your final week on the job?" asked Durham. "I know you both like pokin' around the books and museums, so I thought maybe you'd come up with some more information we could use after you've headed back east."

"As a matter of fact, we have found some more about that Alvah Dunning fellow we were telling you about, the one who had that chunk of gold with his belongings back in the museum back home," said Chris.

"Yes, I remember," said Durham. "I have that nugget in my display case, right alongside the plate from my grandfather."

Chris noticed how the Texan had neatly adopted the only version of the story that linked himself to the antique pewter plate.

"Well, the cup in Blue Mountain Lake had the exact same manufacturer's crests stamped into the bottom as the plate, but the cup was found in New York State with the rest of Dunning's possessions," explained Chris. "Not only that, but the cup also had the same initials carved into the side: 'JW.'"

"Any chance of you getting that cup for my collection?" asked Durham. "After all, it did belong to my grandfather."

"I'm afraid you'll have to fight that battle with the museum," replied Chris. "It's part of their property since it was received by a local donor, and I doubt they'd want to part with it. But I could ask for you."

"I'd be obliged," said the billionaire.

"Anyway, we also found out that both the plate and the cup were produced by a company called ARS Roders, which is located in Northern Germany, said Chris. And the fact that the mug ended up with Alvah Dunning is even more proof that he met Jacob Waltz or Jacob Weiser at some point in time."

"These are all good connections and things to know," said Durham. "But I sure wish we could connect the dots that lead to the mine."

"We still have another week," remarked Sean. "We'll do our best to overturn every stone until we find whatever can be found."

"Maybe I can help sweeten the pot a little," proposed Durham. "I'll tell you what I'm going to do. Since this is your last week on the job, I'm going to let you keep ten percent of anything you round up out there, OK?"

"That's very generous of you, sir, but there's no reason to do that," replied Chris.

"That's right, sir," added Sean. "We're going to get through every last site marked on our search map, and if there's anything out there, we're going to find it."

"I hope so, boys. And remember, we agreed when we started that anything you find in this here state belongs to me. You know I'm going to hold you to that, right?" asked Durham.

"Haven't we been forthcoming with all our finds so far?" asked Chris.

"Of course you have, boys, and I thank you for it," said Durham.

"Are you calling off the entire search after the end of this week?" asked Sean.

"No, I'm keeping the other two teams on through the end of September," replied Durham. "We've got a few more ideas we want to check out still. But I know you've both got your own businesses to tend to back home, so we're going to let you go home after this week and keep the rest of the boys on the job."

THE DUTCHMAN'S GOLD

"It's been fun," said Chris as both of them rose to shake hands with their employer. As they did, they noticed he seemed to maneuver his left hand into his right before gripping either of their hands. They quickly learned the reason for his prestidigitations. After the wealthy tycoon walked away, they both found that they were left holding a "challenge coin"* from Tex's company.

Sean turned the coin over in his hand and observed the seal of "Southern Corp United" engraved over the outline of Texas on the front. On the back was a likeness of Tex himself, with the famous "Don't Tread on Me" motto wrapped around the portrait. Both men also noticed the words ".999 Gold—One Ounce" stamped around the outline border.

"I do believe we've each just received an eighteen-hundred-dollar bonus," said Chris as he held up the coin.

"Better than a sharp stick in the eye," replied Sean.

* * * * * *

Rather than hang around the ranch for another five hours until the fireworks display, the two men excused themselves to head back to the airport a couple hours early. Durham altered the arrangements for the same limo and jet in order to return the two back to Scottsdale by 8:00 PM that evening.

After landing at the small airport in Scottsdale, the two men reclaimed their SUV from the parking lot and commenced their drive back to Phoenix. On the way back to the hotel, Chris unexpectedly steered the Range Rover into a "big box" hardware store and pulled into a parking space.

"What's up?" asked Sean with a puzzled expression.

Chris winked at his friend and replied, "My pair of work gloves is shot. I need a new pair." He winked again at the end of his line, signaling Sean that he didn't want to explain inside the bugged SUV.

Once they got inside the store, Chris shared his thinking with Sean.

---

*A challenge coin is a commemorative piece that is made to honor a person or other entity with symbols, crests, and other artwork. Initially used by the military, they have become a common expression of gratitude between a military or corporate leader and the recipient.

"I want to pick up a rock hammer as well as a chisel. We need some plastic bags and a roll of masking tape as well," he explained.

"For what?"

"I don't want to leave them all empty-handed," replied Chris. "We're going to take the smaller of the two nuggets I grabbed from the cave last week and smash it into smithereens."

"How big is a smithereen?" asked Sean.

"Just big enough to attract an entire team of buffoons to a remote trickle of water on the side of a mountain."

"Aha, I believe I see your intentions," remarked Sean. "Pretty sneaky idea. But last time we tried something sneaky, we paid a rather heavy price."

"All I'm planning on doing is depositing small bits of gold up and down the bottom few hundred feet of any tiny flow of water," said Chris. "The rest we can drop into a vial and claim that we'd already picked it from the substrate. I'm bringing a gold pan with us this week to help with the ruse."

"What's the purpose?" asked Sean.

"Let's call it 'establishing good will' before leaving the job."

"Good will is a good thing," replied Sean. "But only in limited quantities."

After picking up their supplies, they drove back to the hotel where Chris silently retrieved the smaller of the two nuggets he'd taken from the mine from the safe in his hotel room. They then took the elevator to the rooftop patio deck, which was devoid of people in the early evening hours.

Chris placed the gold nugget on a heavy rock slab in the patio and positioned the rock, hammer, and the chisel. "Do you want to take the first swings or should I?" he asked.

"I think I'd enjoy creating the first smithereens," replied Sean, taking the pair of tools from his friend.

Sean's first swings immediately broke the piece into a number of smaller chunks, which he was able to further reduce into finer and finer bits. It took a surprisingly short amount of time before there was nothing of the mass larger than particles half the size of a pea. Chris used a piece of paper and the small brush from his shaving kit to lift all but a few flakes into a series of four small vials. He then held the containers up in the air for them to admire.

"Pretty stuff, isn't it?" asked Chris. "And lots of pieces, which is a good thing for us, especially since we want to seed a few hundred feet of the mountain."

"Too bad we're giving it away," replied Sean.

"Eh, easy come, easy go," sighed Chris. "Consider it like a 'get-out-of-jail-free' card."

The two used the masking tape to clean up any residual flakes and then headed back to Chris's room, where they locked up the vials. They then immediately departed to catch a late dinner in town.

"You know, once we head back to New York, we have a *huge* piece of unfinished business to take care of," said Sean as they walked along the crowded sidewalks of the city.

Chris thought for a moment before turning his head toward his friend. "You mean the gold from the train wreck?"

"Precisely," replied Sean. "I've been thinking all afternoon about Tex Durham's words to us. You know, he said that 'anything we find in this state belongs to him.'"

"Ha, now that's funny," said Chris, laughing out loud. "I think he screwed himself out of some cash on that one, didn't he?"

"My thoughts exactly," agreed Sean. "But have you given any thought as to what should become of it?"

"Yes, I have," said Chris. "I'm going to take my entire share of it, convert it into cash and bet it all on one spin of the Roulette wheel."

"Come on, be serious," said Sean.

"OK, seriously? If we report it publicly, the entire cache becomes the property of New York State. Figuring that the weight of the gold is around twenty pounds, that means we're handing over about 416,000 dollars to our favorite governor, who will probably use it to buy a few extra limousines that they don't need. Bad idea."

"So what's the alternative?" asked Sean.

"Well, as long as we're about to rewrite the history of Alvah Dunning's last years, how about we donate the entire haul to the museum at Blue Mountain Lake and let Debbie have a field day with the publicity?"

"Great idea," replied Sean, nodding enthusiastically.

"My only recommendation is that we ask Debbie to call it an 'anonymous donation' so she doesn't broadcast our names all over the country," added Chris. "I don't want Durham's blood pressure to go crazy when he finds out that we uncovered twenty pounds of gold without sharing the loot."

"You really think he's not going to figure that one out by himself?" asked Sean.

"Not for a moment," replied Chris. "I'm just hoping that if I say that to myself enough times, maybe I'll start to believe it."

Chapter Twenty-Six

The Final Week

July 6, 2020

CHRIS AND SEAN DROVE OUT TO THE TRAILHEAD ON MONDAY MORNing with mixed emotions. They had hiked and sweated and cursed at the elements almost constantly over the past two months, seldom enjoying their time during the heat of the summer days. Yet the utter beauty and solitude of their surroundings, coupled with the absence of traffic, phone calls, and emails was a welcome respite from their normal overscheduled lives back home. They both loved and hated their employment conditions at the same time, although their incompatibility with the other team members tipped the scale to the negative.

Arriving on time, they stopped to pick up their supplies from Alex, who helped them load the bundles into Sammy's assortment of saddlebags for the final time.

"You two boys want anything special this week, since it's your last time into the mountains?" asked the friendly guide. "Anything special to drink maybe, to help you celebrate your final trip?"

"No thanks, Alex," replied Sean. "I think we'll just take our normal reload on Wednesday, if you're going to be back around the north side of the canyon. If you can't make it on Wednesday, just call and let us know."

"You got it, my friend," replied Alex with a smile. "You know, you two are different than the guys on the other two teams. Those hombres can drink up a storm. I usually carry in three or four bottles of whisky every

The Final Week

week for them, in addition to their food and water. But you two never ask for any booze."

"No, there really isn't any need for booze back in those mountains," said Chris, returning the smile. "But we appreciate every jug of water and package of food you've brought us just as much. You've been a real help and a genuine friend."

Alex looked as though he was about to break into tears.

"You have a safe time and I'll see you on Wednesday, OK?" he asked the two.

"Of course," replied Sean, touched by the display of sentimentality.

"I'm going to miss you two after you're gone."

After saying their farewells, Chris and Sean headed up the trail to Fremont Saddle one last time before returning to their amended search area. They both knew it would be a slow and rather lazy week, as they had nothing left to uncover in the desolate desert wilderness. They spent their days lounging around the remaining search zones in whatever shade they could find, keep one eye out for anything that slithered sideways across the sand.

Both men passed some time by trying to remember their most urgent tasks to tackle once they returned to their offices, but neither was able to recall their slate of "to do" items. At one point, Sean pulled out a harmonica that Maggie had given to him as a present. However, his attempts at coaxing a tune from its comb were so feeble that he quickly gave up. At one point, they even resorted to betting on the outcome of a fight-to-the-death between a large black scorpion and a solitary spider wasp. Sean won with his bet on the wasp, and Chris agreed to pay the wager of one beer at the end of the week.

Some of the monotony was abated with Alex's midweek visit on Wednesday afternoon, when he stopped off with several gallon jugs of water and another two nights' meals. Chris and Sean were both overjoyed when the guide removed a large tinfoil-wrapped parcel that was still partially frozen, having been packed in a specially insulated case of dry ice.

"Just for you two, I picked up some flat iron steaks," announced the guide. "You two have been my favorite people here this summer, so I wanted to do something special for you."

"Thank you so much," both men said together. "And tell Mr. Durham that we appreciate it as well."

"This is not from Mr. Durham," Alex said. "I bought this myself for you, because I wanted a good way to thank you for being my friends."

Chris and Sean knew that Alex could little afford to purchase steaks on his salary, but there was little they could do but graciously accept the offerings and thank him for his generosity.

"You two are so different from the others who work for Mr. Durham," he said. "You look me up if you ever come out here again, OK?"

* * * * * *

The following morning was Thursday, and both men agreed it was time to play their final card on Tex's band of hooligans. It had rained two nights earlier, and a small flow of runoff was still dribbling down the remains of a nearly dry culvert. It originated in one of the pits identified as a "site of interest" on their search map, which made it all the more attractive.

"Not much more than what drains out of a urinal," observed Chris as he looked down at the nearly stagnant drip of water passing through the pebbles.

"Eww . . . now that's just gross," replied Sean.

"But it's actually just about perfect for our purposes," noted Chris. "Let's get busy seeding this sucker with flakes from our sample of smithereens."

Chris passed one of the vials to Sean and kept one for himself. He held the other two in reserve in order to pass two vials to Max once they reconnected on the final day of their venture.

"Don't drop any more than a flake or two every few feet," instructed Chris as he began the process of seeding the lower portion of the gulch.

Sean meanwhile headed upward to the higher elevations of the tiny ravine. They both agreed to drop the larger bits into some of the deeper pools where the volume of water was much greater. By conserving their small supply, they were able to meet in the middle with gold particles to spare. Together, they had seeded over two hundred feet of the runoff.

THE FINAL WEEK

After bumping into each other halfway down the slope, they found themselves wondering about what to do with the remaining chips of gold inside their two "seeding vials."

"I have a great idea," said Sean excitedly. "Let's go all the way back to the top of this gulch, where it leaves that pit up there, and casually spread the remaining bits up there. It will make it look like the gold is being drawn out of the rock at the base of the hole in the ground up there."

Chris considered the proposal for a minute before giving it his seal of approval.

"It sounds like a reasonable idea," he said. "And besides, we're out of here tomorrow anyway, so what harm could it do? We're going to give them these other two vials of gold anyway just to whet their appetites."

As they climbed the slope, they suddenly encountered a large rattle-snake that curled its body around several juvenile snakes, each less than a foot in length. The mother carefully herded its brood beneath a large boulder with a wide access gap that permitted easy entry to the space beneath. While she rattled her tail, she completed the job of hiding her young until there was nothing left to see.

Chris smiled as he opened one of the still-filled vials and selected three or four large crumbs of gold and dropped them near the crack beneath the snake rock.

"I can't resist," admitted Chris in a sinister tone. "I want to see Jake reach down and try to pick up these little gems."

"That's pretty bad," said Sean. "Don't you feel just a little bit guilty, baiting them like that?"

"About as guilty as they felt dropping us into a rock-filled cave," replied Chris.

"Me too. I feel so sneaky and devious," said Sean. "And the sad part is, I'm loving it."

"Same here," replied Chris, "except I'm feeling no guilt whatsoever."

* * * * * *

The two men completed seeding the gulch by 11:00 AM, after which they rested for a short while and then consumed their lunch. Sean made

THE DUTCHMAN'S GOLD

the call to Max just a few minutes before noon. Max answered his satellite phone on the third ring.

"Kinney here," he simply stated as he addressed the caller.

"Max, it's Sean, over here on the north canyon wall," he said nonchalantly.

"Yeah Sean, whatcha got?"

"Gold, believe it or not," replied Sean. "We're in a bit of a mostly dry runoff here below site 8C, and we're picking up a lot of small nuggets, some in water and some in dry dirt. Some aren't much more than flakes while others are about the size of a kidney bean. We've already filled one of the ten-cc vials, and starting a second. There's quite a bit of it up and down the gulch as far as we can see. You want us to just keep picking up whatever we can see?"

There was a pause in the background as Max unfolded and consulted one of the many maps to view the location of site 8C.

"That's real good news, Sean," said Max over the speakerphone. "Good work. I'm going to call Mr. Durham and see what he wants us to do, but I'm sure at least one of our teams will be over to help you sometime this afternoon."

"Roger that," replied Sean. "You want us to keep picking until then?"

"Yes, go ahead," said Max. "Grab as much as you can, and we'll be there to help out soon."

"Thanks, and out," said Sean, trying to sound official.

"How was that?" asked Sean, looking at his friend.

"Perfect, maestro," replied Chris, following suit. "Unless I miss my guess, the whole lot of them will arrive within two to three hours, and they'll dismiss us immediately."

"Cool! Are you suggesting we get our last day off for free?"

"That's just my guess," surmised Chris. "Max and his cohorts will probably want any bonus for themselves, and they'll think they've found the jackpot once we turn over the pittance we have here. They'll probably let us go, and then start collecting the little bits and pieces from here to the top. If they find everything, it should come to about three ounces."

"Too bad. They could make more by working at Burger King for a week," noted Sean.

The Final Week

"Probably not," replied Chris. "And anyway, that's their problem, not ours."

True to Chris's prognostication, the other two teams showed up on cue at 2:30 PM. They came in single file, on horseback led by Max and followed by the others on their steeds. By design, Chris stood about fifty feet from the bottom of the canyon floor, panning dish in hand accompanied by Sean observing by his side. They had carefully selected three or four larger bits of gold to position in the pan as they swirled the water around in a circular pattern. Neither of the men were genuinely familiar with the nuances of panning for gold, but they just assumed that their new audience of observers would be solely interested in those bits that were visible to the naked eye.

Max led the way as the column of men, now on foot, proceeded in single file up the slope to their standing position.

"You got all our attention with your call," said Max. "Let's see what you've got."

"I know we're not very skilled at this," admitted Chris, "but we've only been going since about 10:00 this morning, and look what we've got already."

Chris held out the two remaining filled vials of gold bits and flakes, inducing a series of "ooohs" from the assemblage.

Max took the vials from Chris and held them up to the sunlight as he inspected the shiny contents. "That's some nice dust," he observed, rotating the vials from side to side to judge their mass. "That's maybe a couple ounces you got in there."

"Yeah, that's my guess, too, maybe a little less," said Chris. "But we've only been going for an hour or two. It seems to be even better the farther we go uphill."

As Chris spoke, the others gathered round and viewed the vials from close in. Even Jake seemed impressed and offered no negative opinions on the find.

"Anyway, I spoke to Mr. Durham on the way over here, and he agreed with my opinion that you two can just call it a week. You've got a long flight back to New York tomorrow, so just feel free to make your way back to the lot whenever you're ready. Al will be there to collect your burro and the Glocks. I think he might even have the tickets for your flights."

"That sounds great," agreed Chris. "But will we ever find out whether this leads up to the Lost Dutchman Gold Mine?" As he spoke, he motioned up the hill toward the pit situated far above. "This is the most gold we've seen since we got out here."

"Of course," said Max. "Thanks for everything you've done, and we'll be sure to keep you updated if we find anything big."

Chris and Sean were shocked that not only Max shook their hands but each of the other five men did as well. None of them said anything to the departing party members, but the very fact that they were willing to shake hands was a major surprise.

As Chris and Sean were preparing to commence their trek from the canyon back to the parking area, they overheard Max and Jake assigning the men to various sections of the slope. Each was tasked with locating and picking every bit of gold that was visible in the gulch. Max had taken the panning dish from Sean and was preparing to start sifting the sediments from the bottom of the runoff.

"Wow, that was the performance of a lifetime," said Sean, complimenting his friend once they were out of earshot.

"Yeah, almost worthy of an Oscar," Chris responded, looking back at his friend.

"Aren't Oscar awards cast out of gold?" asked Sean out of curiosity.

"I don't know," replied Chris. "This is the first one I've ever won."

Chapter Twenty-Seven

Coming Home
July 10, 2020

TRUE TO MAX'S WORD, NOT ONLY HAD DURHAM EXPRESS-SHIPPED AIRplane tickets to Alex, but he even had them bumped up a day for a Friday departure. The words "First Class" appeared prominently on the boarding passes, consistent with all their other flights.

Chris and Sean got to the airport over an hour before the scheduled boarding time. Neither wanted to risk getting hung up in the security and X-ray scanning lines, so they left plenty of time to spare. After hitting a Starbucks store in the terminal, they both found seats at their gate and shared a leftover newspaper to kill the spare time.

Chris was halfway through the "International Business" section when his phone rang. He glanced at the screen and was surprised to see Tex Durham's personal number displayed. He answered the call immediately.

"Yes, sir," he said.

"Hey, how you boys doing this morning? I expect you're probably at the airport by now."

"Yes, sir," replied Chris as he put down his paper. "Our flight goes out in a little less than an hour."

"Well, I just wanted to say thanks before you left this part of the country," said the tycoon. "And Max called and told me about the few ounces you boys found in the gulch yesterday. It wasn't much, but it's more than everyone on the team combined has pulled in so far, so it's a good start."

The Dutchman's Gold

"Yes, sir, we know that there was more of the stuff farther up the slope, but Max said they'd take over and finish the picking."

"That they did," acknowledged Durham. "They came up with about two to three ounces of pure gold pieces, although they had to call it quits a lot earlier then they'd wanted."

"Why's that?" asked Chris. "We know there was more up there for the taking."

"That's true, and they are going to head back there within a day or so," said Durham. "But they had to get Jake out of there and to a doctor in a hurry. Seems he got into a slight tussle with a rattlesnake, and Jake came in second."

"Oh no!" exclaimed Chris.

"Yeah, the thing nailed him on his right hand. It sounded like the thing's fangs went right through the flesh between his thumb and forefinger."

"I hope he'll be OK," said Chris, feigning his best concerned voice.

"I think so," replied the billionaire. "He's a tough kid; he'll be just fine.

"Well, please do us a favor, sir, and make sure you tell Jake that we're awfully sorry that happened. And also tell him that if he's ever in our part of the country that he should be sure to look us up."

"I'll do that," promised Durham. "Now you two have a safe flight, and your final paycheck will be in your accounts before your wheels touch down in New York."

"Thank you, sir," said Chris. "It was a pleasure doing business with you."

Chris hung up the phone and turned to Sean, who had been listening to every word.

"Another fine acting bit on your part," said Sean with a smile. "You're getting pretty good at it."

"It comes with the territory," replied Chris.

"Did I hear correctly that it was Jake who got nailed by the rattle-snake?"

"You did," confirmed Chris. "And what a shame; they had to get him out of the mountains to see a doctor immediately. You know, you really have to watch yourself back there. Anything can happen."

Coming Home

"Yes, it couldn't have happened to a nicer guy," added Sean.

The two friends were still smirking when a movement in Chris's peripheral vision attracted his attention from behind his seat. From his initial vantage point, he saw only the fabric of a suit or sports coat that appeared to be draped directly on his left shoulder.

Turning in his seat, he looked up to see an astonishing sight. There, in plain view and standing behind the pair, was Charging Bull, dressed in tan slacks and a light plaid sports coat. He was also wearing a fashionable tie that matched the outfit, which was so discordant with his apparel of their last meeting.

"Oh my God," said Chris, lost for anything else to say. "You're the last person in the world I'd expect to see here."

"I wanted very much to speak to you once more before you left us," said the man in his deep voice. "I know you are leaving and not returning, and I also know that you have kept your word about remaining silent about your visit to the cave. You have proven what I have thought about you, proven that it was true. You are men of honor, and I am glad to have known you."

"The same is true for us," said Sean. "We're very glad that we met you, although I wish we'd had the chance to meet many more of your people."

"Maybe someday, if you return and the time is right, we can arrange that," said Charging Bull.

"I never would have recognized you in those clothes," continued Sean. "That's a far cry from your leather garb of last week."

"When moving through the white man's world, it is best to dress like a white man."

"I think I liked the leather pants and jacket more," said Chris, expressing his preference for the authentic Native American clothing.

"Then that is how you should remember me. Goodbye, my friends."

Chris and Sean were both distracted for a moment by an announcement about a gate change in the terminal, but it turned out to be a different flight. Their diversion lasted less than a second, after which they turned back to say their goodbyes to Charging Bull.

He was gone.

The two men rose and scanned the terminal in all directions. Even though there were very few people moving through the gate area and surrounding hallways, Charging Bull was nowhere to be seen. He had disappeared like a ghost.

"Where . . . where . . . where did he go?" stammered Sean. "He couldn't just vanish into thin air?"

"He couldn't, but he did," stated Chris, who was just as puzzled.

"Coming to think of it, only ticketed passengers can get into this part of the airport," said Sean, shaking his head in wonder. "How could he even have made it past security to visit us? That's impossible."

"Also, assuming that he had some kind of a pass to get through security, how could he have known where to find us in this airport?" said Chris. "It's one of the largest in the country! There are four main terminals with something like one hundred gates. Unless Durham gave him the gate number, and we both know that didn't happen."

"Another thing," added Sean. "We weren't even supposed to fly out until tomorrow morning. He couldn't have known we were leaving today. We only found that out ourselves less than twenty-four hours ago."

"Are you sure we didn't get a few peyote buttons mixed in with last night's dinner?" asked Chris, referring to the hallucinogenic cacti known for its psychoactive properties.

"Not unless Jake or Max spiked the beef stew."

* * * * * *

The same day that Chris and Sean arrived back in Syracuse, Chris placed a call to Barbara Simms in Canastota, to tell her about finding the gold from the train wreck. Sean listened as he stood next to his friend making the call.

"Oh my God, you found it?" she cried. Sean could hear her excited voice from several feet away.

"Yes, we did, and it was the paper receipt that we found in your house that led to the discovery," Chris replied. "That let us know that the case was onboard a train of the Raquette Lake Railway when it crashed, which killed three members of the crew. We figured that the case may have been thrown from the freight car and buried in the mud below the tracks. So from there, it became a simple search-and-retrieve project."

"It's funny that I never heard anything about finding the gold on the news," remarked Barbara.

"No, and you won't, either," said Chris. "If we announce that we found it, the whole thing has to get turned over to the state. It's the law."

"That's pretty greedy of them," commented Barbara. "Especially since it used to belong to my grandmother and grandfather."

"Well, we have an idea in mind for the gold, but I first wanted to contact you and ask if you wanted it, since it is actually yours, or your ancestors'. I wouldn't consider offering it to anyone else if you wanted it."

"Son, I'd rather that you stayed as far away from me as possible with that stuff," pleaded the elderly woman. "When I think of all the family members who died because of that curse, it just terrifies me. And now you're telling me that another three men died in a crash on the train that was carrying the case? I want nothing to do with it. And I'd feel more comfortable if you didn't handle it either."

After assuring Barbara that they would be careful, Chris's next call went to the Adirondack Experience Museum, where he arranged an appointment with Debbie Santori for the following Monday afternoon.

Monday morning, Kristi drove up from her apartment near Ithaca to keep the two company on their excursion up into the Adirondacks. Following an early lunch, the three piled into Chris's Jeep and headed off down the Thruway.

"Did you get to the bank vault this morning?" asked Sean.

"Yup, I cleaned it out," replied Chris. "The entire load is in the back."

"Cleaned what out of the vault?" asked Kristi.

"You'll see," replied Chris in a mysterious voice.

Kristi turned to look at Sean, who was sitting in the back seat wearing a smile. "I hate when he does that," she said.

They arrived at the museum on the side of the hill about ten minutes before their scheduled 3:00 PM meeting. Chris and Sean stopped at the reception desk in the lobby while Kristi wandered into the bookstore.

THE DUTCHMAN'S GOLD

Debbie appeared within a few minutes and led them all into her office in the museum's administration section.

"OK, now what's so important that you had to see me today, within days after flying home from two months in the desert?" she asked with fake impatience. "This had better be good."

"It is," murmured Sean. "You'll like it."

Debbie turned her gaze toward Chris, who teasingly remained silent for a few moments.

"Come on, come on, don't keep me in suspense," she cried. "The last two times you've been up here have resulted in a couple of our most popular exhibits. So what have you got for me?"

Chris bent down to the floor and heaved a heavy, reinforced backpack onto the desk. Alongside the backpack he placed a manila envelope containing some old yellowed papers.

"Do you feel like rewriting some history today?" he asked the curator.

"That depends on which history you're talking about," replied Debbie.

"Actually, there are two accepted pieces of Adirondack folklore that are about to receive a facelift," said Chris.

The next thirty minutes were spent outlining Alvah Dunning's life, including his place of birth and his various homesteads as he moved from lake to lake throughout his life. They then moved on to the time when he abandoned the Adirondacks entirely and moved across the country.

"The commonly accepted story is that he took a northern route on the railroads and ended up settling in the areas between North and South Dakota," explained Chris.

"And you have evidence to prove otherwise?" asked Debbie.

"Well, yes, we do have some proof, but you have the rest right here in your museum," replied Chris as he opened up the manila folder. "First of all, the turquoise bracelet that I sent back to you a couple months ago was obtained from a Native American artist, probably in the central part of Arizona and probably from the Pima tribe. We also found a sketch of Dunning in a museum near the Superstition Mountains down there that had been drawn by a famous Pima artist of that era. That alone should establish his location in Arizona, not in the Dakotas."

298

"How would he have made it all the way down to Arizona?" asked Debbie.

"We have no idea where he intended to go," replied Chris. "It could have been by total accident. He couldn't read, so maybe he ended up on the wrong train."

"Hmm, that's possible," agreed Debbie. "So what else do you have?"

Chris proceeded to display the shipping document that Dunning was given when he sent the case full of gold from Phoenix across to his sister in Syracuse.

"How do you like that?" Debbie wondered out loud. "I know some Adirondack biographers who are going to be interested in this."

"Not only that, but you remember the photographs of the drinking cup you sent me with the initials and insignias carved into the bottom and sides?"

"Of course," said Debbie. "I sent you some photos of those as you asked me to do."

"Well, not only did Alvah Dunning carry that mug back from Arizona, but it is connected with some of the main figures linked to the Lost Dutchman Gold Mine," said Chris.

"I've heard of that," exclaimed Debbie. "That's really famous out there. They have their own museum and everything."

"Yes, they do," concurred Chris. "It's kind of a tourist trap, but if you want to know anything about the mine or the prospectors of that day, that's where you go."

Debbie looked across her desk with a curious expression on her face, her eyes shifting back and forth between the two men and the filled backpack.

"This is all interesting stuff," she said. "But I also know that you wouldn't expect to open a new exhibit to announce that Alvah Dunning took a wrong turn in Kansas City or wherever he was when he turned south. So what is it that you really wanted to show me?"

Chris looked at Sean and said, "Why don't you do the honors?"

Sean began recounting the story of how Alvah Dunning must have come in contact with one of the miners and obtained a large quantity of gold, which was shipped back to his sister in Syracuse, as per the form in the manila folder.

"OK, where did it go from there?" Debbie asked.

"It remained in the custody of his sister, Martha Sykes, for over thirteen years. Martha was terrified of the case and believed that it was cursed, since several people who had handled it died of mysterious causes, including her husband Luther several years earlier."

"Go on," Debbie said. "This is getting interesting."

"Finally, Martha Sykes decided to ship the case of gold to her grandson to help him pay for a house," explained Sean. "But the shipment never made it to Raquette Lake as planned. She shipped it a few days before November 9, 1913, which might ring a bell to you."

Debbie thought for a moment, trying to recall the date in Adirondack history before giving up the effort. "No, I'm sorry, but my recall of 1913 isn't what it should be," she admitted.

"But you do know about the Great Train Wreck of 1913, right?" Sean asked.

"Of course!" she exclaimed. "That was down below Inlet; the train jumped the track and rolled down a cliff."

"Taking the case with Alvah Dunning's gold with it," concluded Sean.

"Oh my God! How did you piece that one together?"

"We got lucky finding a few clues with a living descendant of Martha Sykes who still lives here in the state," said Sean. As he spoke, he pulled the receipt for the transferred case from the folder. "This is a form that the granddaughter of Martha Sykes still had in her attic. From this, we were able to determine that the shipment of gold was on the train on the day of the derailment. And since it never made it to Raquette Lake, and it was never found at the scene, we guessed that it had been thrown out of the freight car and buried in the water and mud at the bottom of the cliff."

"Wow, that's quite a story," said Debbie. "Are you going to try to prove it by hunting for the gold? By this time, over a hundred years later, that might be harder than finding a needle in the haystack."

"Here's your needle," said Sean, patting the backpack.

Debbie's eyes grew wider as she turned her attention to the canvas backpack sitting before her on the desk.

"Oh no, you haven't done it again, have you?" she asked in a whisper.

"Sorry, but I'm afraid we have," said Chris, rejoining the conversation.

"But . . . but how?"

"We worked with a volunteer from the Herkimer County Historical Society who walked us through the site of the crash and put us almost right on top of the spot where the freight car landed. From there it became a simple matter of using a metal detector to mark the spots, then returning in the dark of night to try our luck with the shovels," explained Chris. "I'll grant you we did get lucky, and the gold was right where we thought it would be."

"So what's the plan then?" asked Debbie. "What's going to become of it?"

"Well, as you probably know, the State of New York owns all gold and silver found within its borders. But if a *museum* received it as a historical donation and used it as part of an exhibit that was linked to both Alvah Dunning *and* the Great Train Wreck of 1913, I know we could get an exemption from the state to keep and display the exhibit."

"You really think so?" asked Debbie.

"If not by conventional methods, I'll ask my dad to have his law firm work it out directly with the governor's office," Chris replied. "My father has a lot of friends in high places."

"If you don't mind me asking, just how much gold is in there?"

"About twenty-two pounds, four ounces," replied Chris. "That works out to about 356 ounces, which at eighteen hundred dollars an ounce comes out to almost 640,000 dollars. So I think you might want to lock it up. Perhaps even right now."

"I'll put it into our high-value safe immediately," she replied. Then, after looking thoughtfully at the folder on her desk, she asked if she could keep the original papers that tracked the shipment of the case of gold from one location to the next around the country. "All this will make a great supporting story for the new exhibit."

THE DUTCHMAN'S GOLD

"They are yours," said Chris. "We brought them here for that very purpose."

Debbie looked at the two men as though seeing them for the first time.

"You know, you two have done more to increase the popularity of this museum than anyone else in its history. I'll get a team to start working on this right away, but I can't imagine how much this is going to do for our organization."

"The 'two of them'? What about me?" asked Kristi.

"I'm sorry, but I don't believe we've met. Who are you?" asked Debbie.

"Never mind," replied Kristi, shooting a look at Chris.

* * * * * *

The next several weeks flew by in a blur of activity as both Chris and Sean worked long hours to make up for the lost time in the Superstition Mountains. Chris took Kristi away for a long weekend in Newport, Rhode Island, to make up for the time spent away. Sean tried reaching Maggie to ask her if she wanted to visit the Jersey shore for part of a week, but she never returned his calls.

Over Labor Day weekend, Chris's father, Chris Carey Sr., drove up from his law firm in Washington, D.C., to spend a week at the family's hilltop residence near Utica. It was a rare occasion when both his parents were in residence at the same time, so Chris decided to spend a few days living at the rural mansion. He could still get work done while spending time with the entire family.

On Saturday afternoon, Theresa and Chris Sr. decided to host one of their famous bar-b-que lunch parties on the back deck. They had invited the entire extended family, along with the local friends of both parents. Chris Sr. also asked a number of his local attorney acquaintances to join him at the event.

Chris was standing just outside the back door of the house, talking to his mother, when he noticed that Sean had arrived. He had come through the house and was about to emerge through the rear door onto the patio.

Theresa, who was always the consummate host, wanted Sean's girlfriend to meet Denny, Chris's grandfather. She turned to him and began the introduction:

"Denny, you know Sean, of course, but I don't know if you've ever met Sean's girlfriend, Ma—" Instead of finishing the word "Maggie," Theresa's voice halted in mid-sentence as Tracey came out the door following Sean, holding his hand.

Sean was trying not to laugh as he overheard the gaffe. "Denny, I'd like you to meet my girlfriend, Tracey." Tracey looked positively stunning, her long, brownish-blond hair sweeping across the top of an off-the-shoulder red sun dress.

"My goodness, young lady, you'd better watch yourself with this one," said Denny, the elderly patriarch of the family. "You can't trust these young bucks these days."

Chris meanwhile almost choked on the last bite of his hotdog.

"I didn't know you were up here in New York," he said to the recent college graduate. "I assume Sean here isn't still paying you for research."

"No, hardly," she smiled, her bright blue eyes lighting up the entire patio. "Sean had promised me that he'd take me to Niagara Falls, so we did that last weekend. Then we spent the last several days visiting some of the vineyards on the Finger Lakes Wine Trail. It's been such a great time, and we stayed in some of the cutest bed and breakfasts down around some of those lakes. I never knew Sean was such an expert on wines."

"I never knew that either," said Chris, smiling at his friend. Sean intentionally avoided Chris's gaze. "Sounds like you two had a really wonderful time."

As the group chatted, Chris Sr. wandered over and cast a glance at his son, indicating that he wanted a word. Chris broke apart from the group in order to be alone with his dad.

"Hi, son—it's been a long time since you and I have had a chance to talk," he said as he patted Chris's shoulder.

"I know," nodded Chris. "Well, we were gone almost all of June, July, and into August, so it's been busy."

"Well, it sounds as though you had a productive summer," said the father. "I'm on the distribution list for emails and notices from the museum up in Blue Mountain Lake, and I see they've got their new exhibit almost ready. And your mom told me about your part in digging up the gold that had been lost in the Great Train Wreck incident. But I also noticed that your name isn't mentioned on the museum's website description of that event. Why not?"

"It's a long story, Dad. But basically, the guy who hired us to help look for the Lost Dutchman Gold Mine is not the type of person you'd label as a kind, benevolent soul," explained Chris. "If he knew that we located the shipment of gold that Alvah Dunning sent back to his sister from the gold mine in Arizona, you can bet that he'd be all over it, trying to claim it for himself."

"Yes, as you know, I looked into some of his business dealings, and I have about the same opinion on the guy as you. He's somehow managed to acquire just about everything he's ever set out to own."

"He owns half of Texas, for crying out loud," exclaimed Chris. "And yes, he has a funny way of always getting what he wants, regardless of how he gets it."

"Good move then, keeping it anonymous," agreed Chris Sr.

"It probably doesn't matter; he'll find out anyway," said Chris.

"So am I correct in assuming that you gave all of the gold from Dunning's shipment to the museum?"

"That's correct," replied Chris. "Every speck of it. I wasn't about to turn over a single gram to the state government."

"So what about the Lost Dutchman Gold Mine that you were paid to help find?" asked Chris Sr. "It's a fascinating story, although a lot of people don't believe it ever existed, but I'm sure you know that already."

"Yes, Dad," replied Chris, not returning his father's stare.

"'Yes, Dad' what?" repeated Chris Sr., turning the question back around on his son.

"It is a fascinating story," said Chris.

"And you didn't find the mine, did you? In two months of searching?"

"It's a fascinating story," repeated Chris, a vague smile creeping onto his face.

"That's nice," said his father, still staring directly into his son's eyes.

"You know, the world of sniffing out treasures is a complicated and risky business," continued Chris Sr. "Almost no one walks away with the big prize, and certainly not on a consistent basis. The failure rate is probably about ninety-five percent, if not higher."

"I agree," said Chris. "It takes intuition, hard work, good people, and a lot of luck."

"But when you went after the Gordon Treasure in Lake Champlain, you scored a direct hit on your first try. Speaking in baseball terms, you were one-for-one."

"True," replied Chris.

"Then, a couple years later, you not only discovered that the priceless 1804 silver dollars existed, but you found three thousand of them buried in a spot that was frequented by tens of thousands of people each year."

"Uh huh," mumbled Chris, not sure where this was leading.

"That raised your record to two-for-two."

"OK, I agree."

"All I'm trying to establish is that you've had a track record that is probably unmatched in this crazy hobby of yours, if that's what you call it."

"Neither Sean nor I are really 'treasure hunters,' Dad," said Chris. "We've always been interested in these things purely from a historical perspective."

"True, but somehow you've succeeded in finding things of great value that others have missed for centuries. This doesn't sound like it's purely due to luck."

"Well, as I told you, I'm afraid we failed this time."

"I don't believe that for a second," said the father. "First of all, you found a pile of gold at the site of the train wreck that no one else ever knew existed."

"True again," admitted Chris. "But we had documentation that no one else ever saw."

"It doesn't matter. You found it. That makes three-for-three."

THE DUTCHMAN'S GOLD

"Yes, if you don't count the search for the Lost Dutchman," Chris argued.

Chris's father then reached into his pocket and pulled out a large object, which his hand only partially concealed.

"By the way, earlier this morning your mother asked me to put a letter on your desk in your room inside the house here. I saw something interesting as I was dropping it off. I didn't know you'd taken up lifting weights?"

"Lifting weights?" Chris asked. "Sorry, but I don't understand."

"Yes, maybe doing some hand-strengthening exercises with a four or five-pound weight," said his father. As he spoke, he exposed the larger nugget that Chris had removed from the Lost Dutchman Gold Mine and flipped it up in the air, catching it again neatly in the same hand. The piece was extremely large to be referred to as a "nugget," being fairly round and almost two inches in diameter.

"Ah yes, that's a piece of lead that I got from a plumbing outfit in Syracuse," said Chris, not really expecting his father to believe it. "I thought it would be kind of cool if I spray-painted it gold. It looks real, doesn't it?"

"I'll ask you the same question over again: You didn't find the mine, did you?"

Chris sighed and looked at his father before answering the question indirectly.

"Let me ask you a question," he began. "Let's say that someone paid you to look for something that had been lost for over a century. Hundreds, if not thousands, of people had spent their lives looking for the same thing but had failed. But let's say that you got really lucky and bumped into this thing by accident. But then you found out that someone else has been using this thing to feed their families. And if you took it away to sell, for no other reason than for profit, those other people would have to go hungry and go without clothing and medicine and other life essentials. Would you be able to look them in the eye and still walk away with that thing?"

Chris Sr. was silent for a moment as he imagined the scenario described by his son.

"By any chance, would these other people using this thing be Native American?" he asked.

"Yes," replied Chris.

"I figured as much," said Chris Sr.

"So please excuse us if we don't end up on television this time. Not only that, but we won't be invited to the state capital, or to the governor's mansion, or even to our own press conference. You're holding one of the only remnants of a discovery that will remain a secret as long as Sean and I are alive to protect it."

Chris's father's eyes watered up as he put his arm around his son.

"Congratulations, son," he said. "You've just gone five-for-four."

Somewhere, in the vast open spaces of the Arizona desert, Charging Bull would have agreed.

About the Author

Larry Weill has led a career that is as diverse and interesting as the subjects in his books. An avid outdoorsman, he has hiked and climbed extensively throughout the Adirondacks and the Northeast since his days as a wilderness park ranger. He has also worked as a financial planner, a technical writer, a trainer, and a career naval officer.

A self-avowed "people watcher," Weill has an interesting knack for observing and describing in people their many amusing habits and traits. He is the author of *Excuse Me, Sir . . . Your Socks Are on Fire* (North Country Books), his original book about his days as a wilderness park ranger in the West Canada Lakes Wilderness of New York State. His later books—*Pardon Me, Sir . . . There's a Moose in Your Tent*, *Forgive Me, Ma'am . . . Bears Don't Wear Blue*, and *Thanks Anyway, Sir . . . But I'll Sleep in the Tree*—have entertained a new generation of Adirondack enthusiasts and generated a renewed interest in the concept of wilderness camping in New York's largest state park. Weill's last two novels, *Adirondack Trail of Gold* and *In Marcy's Shadow*, were his first ventures into the genre of historical fiction and have also captivated the audience of Adirondack readers. He has since further diversified his writings to include travel guides on the Adirondacks and the Erie Canal, as well as completing a book of memoirs on the Vietnam War, titled *Super Slick*, with coauthor and Vietnam War vet Tom Feigel.

Weill still lives in Rochester, New York, with his wife Patty. They vacation and hike in the Adirondacks annually.